T0192969

THE DEAL

ALSO BY ADAM GITTLIN

The Men Downstairs
The Deal: About Face

THE DEAL

A Novel

ADAM GITTLIN

Oceanview Publishing

LONGBOAT KEY, FLORIDA

ISBN 978-1-933515-13-7 (hc)
ISBN 978-1-60809-106-5 (pb)

Published in the United States by Oceanview Publishing,
Longboat Key, Florida
www.oceanviewpub.com

2 4 6 8 10 9 7 5 3 1

PRINTED IN THE UNITED STATES OF AMERICA

For Theo

ACKNOWLEDGMENTS

I would like to offer special thanks to Pat and Bob Gussin, Susan Greger, and everyone at Oceanview Publishing for all your hard work and support. I'm honored to be part of your family.

Most men never have a true mentor; I've been fortunate enough to have two. Thank you to my father and most trusted friend, Bruce Gittlin—whose comprehension of the commercial real estate industry is limitless—and Howard Tenenbaum for teaching me the real estate game at different stages of my career. Thanks also to Gary Rosen, Andrea Soloway and all the professionals who shape New York City's commercial real estate market every day.

I wish to thank my sister Gail, as well as my close friends Dr. Jason Auerbach, Dr. Laurence Schimmel, and Michael Tuckman, for continuing to review my work and provide feedback. Your suggestions remain an integral part of my process. I also wish to thank Susan Hayes, George Foster, Victoria Preminger, and Brian Goldman. Your contributions to *The Deal* are both significant and appreciated.

I want to extend a warm thank you to Rosemary, Fraser, and David Seitel, as well as Uncle H. You have all been a terrific support system for my writing endeavors and an important source of insight not just for my projects, but in my life. Thank you for accepting me as one of you own. I wish also to extend a special thank you to Joann Weber—my toughest critic; an inspiration to all who knew her.

Lastly, I wish to thank my mother, Ethel Gittlin, who embodies the creative spirit. If it wasn't for your love of story, and your desire since my college days to pass 'killer reads' my way, I wouldn't be sitting here.

THE DEAL

CHAPTER 1

I can't tell you where I am.

Not if I want to stay alive.

Right now the sun is smiling on me, a silky rainbow of marine life is swimming through the clearest water I have ever seen, and there is fine, soft sand between my toes. I have left behind everything and everyone I love. I have been forced to flee my luxurious, thriving existence because of a string of choices, some made by me, but most by others. And while I struggle to grasp the breadth of all that's just happened, I still can't deny the constant fire in my gut that makes me crawl once I can no longer walk. Some call it sheer determination. Others call it flat out greed. Me, I'm not sure what I make of it. I've never had a reason to question any of it until now.

I'm drinking again. I have a drink in my left hand right now. Sapphire and tonic, three olives. One for each of the weeks that has passed since it all happened, since my world started spinning so furiously that it reached tornado proportions. I believe so much more in my life, myself now. I understand so much more about my life and myself now. Or do I? I have gained a lot and I have lost perhaps even more. Now I'm simply waiting for the dust in my mind to settle so I can figure out how to go on. Like I said, I can't tell you where I am. But I could sure use the therapy of telling you how I got here.

CHAPTER 2

It was a picture perfect early summer day. I left my Park Avenue penthouse at six A.M., as I had every morning for the previous four years, and headed for the elevator. As I exited the building, sunlight slammed me in the face. There were no clouds to conceal its strength.

I nodded good morning to Clarence, my cordial, top-shelf, yet somewhat nosy, white-gloved doorman.

"Enjoy your party, Mr. Gray?"

"I did Clarence," I replied. "I did."

"Yes, Doorman Parker believes there is probably the tape to prove it."

Clarence, a guy approaching forty who had been my doorman for the past four years, vicariously lived through my life. The party he referred to was my thirtieth birthday gathering a few nights earlier at Soho's classic French bistro, Balthazar. An intimate party I threw for myself for about sixty of my closest friends. One of the other two doormen, Damon, must have told him about the twenty-two-year-old Elite Modeling Agency '10' who ended up spending the night.

While others would have still been recovering from both the amount and combination of substances I had put in my body over that weekend, I was not. In fact, quite the contrary, I felt outstanding. My intense, highly charged industry, lifestyle, and upbringing had seasoned me for this type of living, if living is what you'd call it.

My cordovan leather briefcase, bulging with documents and architectural drawings, was in my left hand. As I walked my morning line, up Park Avenue then through a still groggy Grand Central Station, my mind happily revisited my birthday party—the perfect downtown space filled with the ideal combination of friends, players, women, and clients. The energy in the air that night was just right. There were many intense conversations going on. Some would lead to business, others would lead to sex. There were bellinis, martinis, three-tier platters of shellfish, and steak frites. Just the right undertones of illicit behavior surrounded me. It had been a full-throttle evening of want as opposed to need, a flawless night of covert moneymaking and scandalous overindulgence.

As I walked, I gave the same "Good Morning" to the same people I do each day. Looking back on it now, this was the last day I actually meant it. In one of my recent nightmares I have even walked my morning line, at six A.M. on Tuesday, June 7, 2004, only to find my jaw locked when I tried to speak. On sight of me some of the regulars fled, others laughed or gently turned away. Annie the croissant lady, terrified, began to sob. I still don't know which of the two of us she was afraid for. Like I said, the dust is just beginning to settle.

At 6:12 A.M., after showing my proper photo identification, I entered the Chrysler Center, home of Platinum Commercial Building and Land. PCBL is one of the most unique and important real estate companies in the world. Its only business is commercial real estate brokerage and the company deals only with property in New York City. PCBL represents women and men, old individuals, and the affairs of some of the great young business minds of today. All clients have one thing in common. They either own commercial real estate in Manhattan or they need some.

My name is Jonah Gray. I am the youngest member of the most successful team at PCBL. I graduated from NYU's Stern School of Business in 1998, two years immediately following the completion of my undergraduate business work at Penn. I am an only child. My mother died when I was five from breast cancer. My father Stan, on the other hand, has been the driving force in my life since the time of my earliest memories and my reason for getting into real estate. He owns five office buildings in the Park Avenue South submarket of the city, totaling around 1.6 million square feet, to go along with various other business interests both domestic and overseas. The five properties, today worth around one hundred million dollars each, were left to him by my grandfather, the type of man who also left him some Swiss bank accounts.

Grandpa was the beginning of my family's real estate, as well as societal lineage. Pop carried on that tradition, only in what one might call a slightly more intense fashion. Some over the years have referred to him as brilliant, others have peppered their descriptions with words such as "tyrant" and "rogue." I've heard him called both famous and infamous, both cowardly and brave. One thing is definitely for sure. To sit down with my father and hammer out a deal meant you were in for the ride of your life. To understand my father, envision someone in a bear suit scaring the shit out of you at night in the woods. Now imagine that individual taking off the suit, only to reveal that he truly is, in fact, the black bear you had feared all along. A black bear that is foaming at the mouth.

From an early age my father, Pop as I always referred to him, made it clear that we live in a tough world, and an even tougher city. A place where you need to bend the rules at times, even skirt them, in order stay on top. From the time I started school, my father told me never to cheat, unless I was absolutely sure that the teacher wasn't looking. When I would ask about the other kids seeing me, he would tell me that was the easy part. He'd say, "You find the 'problem' at recess and you punch him square in the nose, as hard as you can, to make him keep his mouth shut. If the teacher sees you and punishes you, that's even better. You've let the little rat know that you'll do whatever it takes to keep him quiet. And you've also most likely found yourself a grunt, someone willing to fall into place behind you. What's important is that you look out for yourself and get what you need. Always. At all costs."

I have been around the business of buildings my whole life. I grew up listening to my father as he explained how deals got made and as he gasped for air when deals were lost. I always knew real estate would be my game, I just never knew in what capacity. Until, that is, my sophomore year in Philly. That was when I discovered publications like the *Wall Street Journal* and *Fortune* and it all started to come together in my mind. The largest organizations in the world need ridiculously large blocks of office space. And many of these companies are headquartered in New York City, my stomping ground.

Let me tell you how the business of buildings works.

Call it Commercial Real Estate 101.

Commercial real estate in New York City is angry, wise, green with both cash and envy, and arrogant. It is lawyers, accountants, architects, and interior designers. It is tricky, direct, relentless, and powerful. It is CEOs, families, partners, and analysts.

Commercial real estate in New York City is elusive, misleading, empowering, and humbling. It is pretenders, artists, women, and men. It is creative, tangible, sheltering, and versatile. It is players, gamblers, winners, and losers.

Commercial real estate in New York City is invigorating, lavish, challenging, and cold. It is engineers, moguls, insiders, and outsiders. It is honor, reflexes, hunches, and facts. It is conspirators, visionaries, monsters, and saints.

Usually a company's largest expense, commercial real estate is *per square foot*. There is a base rental number, which is a certain dollar amount *per square foot* of the said leased space per year, to be paid from tenant to landlord. Before we go any further, if you don't know the difference between "Landlord" and "Tenant" you might want to go ask someone. Above that, there are other expenses to be paid *per square foot* on top of the base rental. These expenses include, but are not limited to, electricity, the tenant's proportionate share of the property taxes, and monies for the buildings' operating expenses and staff, for example, engineers and porters—those individuals manning the actual, physical property each day and night. As a landlord, this aggregate number is your rent. As a tenant, this aggregate number is also your rent.

I am a commercial real estate broker, broker defined in the dictionary as "One who acts as an agent for others, as in negotiating contracts, purchases, or sales in return for a fee or commission." As a broker, do I care what the final rental terms are of the negotiated lease? Yes, but no. Yes if I'm representing the landlord, I want it to be high. And yes if I'm representing the tenant, I want it to be low. High and low against what? The market conditions, which tend to follow the general economy. But no, I don't care two years down the road because either way I get paid. Nicely.

A wise man once explained to me what "benchmarking" is. Not the generic, bullshit definition that anyone can regurgitate of setting a standard or raising the bar, but the real definition, to know your competition in excruciating detail. This is what leads to the ultimate ability for decision making. In the New York City commercial real estate world, all it takes is the drop of a dime to go from chasing your competition to leading it, and vice versa. Knowledge —understanding the business as well as the people — is the undeniable edge.

My expertise, as well as the rest of my team's expertise, is in the brokerage of large blocks of office space for lease. Not the brokerage of property sales. But that's not to say we haven't had a hand in the sale of some large properties, because we have. It's just not what we have become known for. Yet representing a buyer as opposed to a seller is the same thing as representing a tenant to a landlord. The simple fact is that taking all of the necessary elements of the deal right in front of you, everything from the tenant roster and lease lengths to the market conditions to the amount of usable versus nonusable space in the property, what's known as the "Loss Factor," to the building's occupancy level, is how you generate the purchase price for a building. Like everything else, on a *per square foot* basis. Of course it's a bit more complicated, but not really. If you stick to the basics, you'll never lose your way. Like if you were to find yourself on a deserted island with no gym. Push-ups and sit-ups would keep you in terrific shape. It's not brain surgery. What separates the men from the boys is those with a creative genius, those who always stay a brush stroke ahead in painting the big picture. That's something my father told me once, just another piece of his advice that pops from my memory like an ice cube from a tray.

CHAPTER 3

This world, so I thought, was all I wanted. Not love, knowledge, or peace but power and money. Lots of it. "Hate a nickel," my father once said to me, "because it isn't a dime." He also said, as I got older, there would be no better education for me than going out on my own for a while before just waltzing into Gray Properties, the family business. So when I graduated number one in my class from Stern, armed with an MBA in international business, I immediately met with Tommy Wingate.

Tommy was the guy who handled all of the leasing in my father's properties, meaning he negotiated deals with all incoming tenants on my father's behalf, and he had done so for twenty years. Tommy was sharp, rational, and mild mannered. He was the perfect complement for my father. They made a killer "good cop, bad cop" tandem in a conference room. I had known Tommy for most of my life. Therefore I knew he was one of the hotshots at PCBL in a killer "dual-agency" situation, meaning he knew all sides of the business so well that he didn't just represent owners, he represented outside tenants shopping New York City for large blocks of office space as well. When it came to independent, triple-A tenants, Tommy represented the biggest and the best. He was responsible for closing at least two of the ten largest real estate deals in the city every year. Everyone in the business wanted a spot on Tommy's team. At the time we met he was forty-three with two young soldiers working for him. And he was looking for a third.

We met one day for lunch at Nello, a chic Madison Avenue Northern Italian haunt that serves up fifty-dollar plates of pasta and serious people watching. By the time I left, I had been offered the position, either because I was a longtime client's son or because I just showed that much promise. I like to think it was a little of both, but I'll never know for sure. Either way, it didn't take long for me to understand what it meant to be in my new universe.

For the first month all I was allowed to do was walk around New York City with a pad and a pen. I wasn't to speak on the phone or mention anything regarding real estate to any of Tommy's clients. Both were grounds for dismissal. My job for thirty days was to walk through commercial properties from dawn to dusk and get to know each one as though it was a person, each address simply a name. Since it was pre-9/11, it was a lot easier to freely roam buildings back then. So I was to take notes on everything from the current state of the lobby to the functionality of the elevators, the carpeting in all of the shared hallways, as well as the cleanliness of the shared-floor restrooms. I was to take notes on each particular property's tenant roster, climate control, security situation, loading dock capacity. I was to get to know everything about each building's personality, its tendencies and quirks. I wasn't allowed, for that month, to mention or even think about deals or money. I was to spend every waking second for those thirty days learning about my product. Most important, I was told to be diligent about my notes. Tommy took a copy of them each night to scour.

I made quick work of winning Tommy over. He loved the records I kept. He said they indicated to him that I inherently knew exactly what to be looking for, which made sense since I had grown up around the profession's complexities and jargon. My father had taught me well. Tommy would test me. He'd give me the building, and I'd tell him everything from the property's nickname, if it had one, to the year it was built. I would comment on renovations that were happening along with whom the owner was and who handled the leasing. Each night, between my lavish partying and a couple hours of sleep, I would study my notes until I knew each fact cold. Tommy seldom stumped me. I was determined, and he knew it.

Soon I was referred to as a full-fledged member of the team, and I was out drumming up business. Tommy had two younger associates, Jake Donald and Perry York. Each was three years my senior and had been with Tommy since they graduated from college, which if you took into account business school, made them both about five years ahead of me in terms of seniority. The original plan among the three was to never bring anyone else on board. Fortunately for me, their client roster and customers' demands became too great, and they were left with no choice. I was in the right place at the right time. Depending, that is, on how you look at it.

Jake was raised in northern New Jersey and attended Rutgers University. A bit on the heavy side, he was a whiz at drumming up business. Because of his love for the finer things from top-shelf drugs to courtside seats, passions we both shared, he was the ideal team member for keeping clients happy until all hours of the night. He loved Hugo Boss suits and a manicure, he lived for Sunday football in Central Park with his friends and dinner at The Old Homestead Steakhouse, a meatpacking district staple turning out colossal slabs of beef and lobsters the size of small children. We were very much alike and took to each other as people destined for certain friendship often do.

Perry was raised in the City. She was five foot six with lustrous, long brown hair and fairway green eyes. She had a terrific body, something that surprised me once I learned she had a two-year-old child. A stickler for detail, Perry was the team member who never left a stone unturned. She loved to get a deal done. She would extrapolate leases until late into the night. She checked and double-checked the work of the attorneys. She liked to play devil's advocate in discussions and force everyone to see all sides of a deal. She was delicate and smart, deliberate and cunning, with just the right dose of "bitch." In short she was great for the team. When it came to deal making, she was always prepared. Tommy loved her for this. As for me, I probably would have tried to sleep with her so it was a good thing she was married. From day one I admired Perry, and we, too, became the best of friends. Perhaps it was because we were so different, not just in our lifestyles but in our approach for getting results. Maybe I helped Perry feel young again. At the time she was only twenty-six so I know that seems silly, but she had been married for three years and had a child. A boy named Max. As she put it, she had jumped into adulthood "overnight."

I was a perfect complement for the group. As I learned a little while after joining them, Tommy had already started to fade into the background of the team's day-to-day happenings, something, frankly, he had earned. He was successful on a level beyond most forty-three-year-old men. He could afford to play puppet master and have strong, well-armed foot soldiers who worked to further both his name as well as his bank account. He had personally trained Perry and Jake while raising a family and positioning himself politically within the industry and firm. He was owed a time to handpick his clients and close the deals. He taught Perry and Jake everything they knew. They were two of the best in the business. Their work situation seemed enviable but they would both tell you, just as I am, the timing of my arrival couldn't have been better.

Their own success was beginning to suffocate them. More deals were streaming in than there was time for. They needed new blood. Once they accepted that I was more than competent, and as hungry as they were, we were one happy family. This just made us stronger. We enjoyed the long hours we spent together whether at Il Mulino for dinner with clients, or the Rainbow Room for lunch to discuss strategy, it didn't matter. We had an expense account larger than most Americans' salaries. The money was mind-blowing.

My first monster deal came six months into my second year. It was a client I found, a prominent financial institution. Jake and Perry both helped me put the deal together. Two hundred thousand square feet in a mid-town property. The rent averaged $55.00 per square foot over a fifteen-year lease. As far as how a commission works, it's simple. You take the average yearly rate for the term of the lease, which is usually somewhere between three and fifteen years, and multiply this by a percentage for each year of the lease.

For a long-term lease this percentage usually begins around 5 percent for the first couple of years and works its way down — you get the idea. Once the aggregate number has been devised by adding up the fees taken for each year, 40 percent goes to PCBL and our team splits the rest. Anyway, for the aforementioned deal, taking into account that according to the lease the yearly rent accumulated by 3 percent annually, the average yearly rent was around thirteen million dollars. To be precise, PCBL's commission was $5,651,479.00 with our team getting a $3,390,088.38 share. Tommy got the largest cut of any deal we made. For this one he and I split 60 percent of our team's share, since it was my client. Jake and Perry each got 20 percent. One deal and I walked away with a little over 1.1 million dollars. Now granted, not every deal made is of this size, but just like that I was wealthy. Not wealthy because my family was wealthy, but wealthy because I was wealthy. I had more money by far than any of my friends, guys who were doing pretty fucking well. In year two I made almost $2.3 million. I gambled in Monte Carlo for vacation and had a VIP table at any club in Manhattan. Life was good. My thirst for success was insatiable.

Like I said, I was terribly wealthy. I understand now I was far from rich.

CHAPTER 4

By 6:20 A.M. I had settled into my office, a mix of a sophistication and technological advancement. PCBL is not one for being stingy so our headquarters are state of the art. All of the molding, as well as the doors and furniture, are mahogany. There is a lot of glass and the floors are lined with plush, hunter green carpeting. The walls are a light shade of cream and are accented with black-and-white stills of the Manhattan skyline as seen through the lenses of award-winning photographers. Color in the space is primarily supplied through fresh, strategically placed eclectic floral arrangements that are changed out every third day. It is the kind of space that could be confused for a prestigious law firm.

The office is completely wireless, aside from the actual telephone on each desk being plugged into the wall. Everything is heat sensor activated from the light switches to the climate control; rooms actually adjust their temperature based on occupancy. Flat-panel monitors are the norm, and each office is furnished with a desktop as well as a compatible laptop, God forbid someone should be caught without access to the e-world.

"Awesome party, man."

Jake, always in early like myself, had walked into my office. He'd been in D.C. the previous day, and we hadn't yet recapped. I was sitting at my desk looking at my morning schedule. I looked up.

"You think?"

"Don't be an idiot. You know it was tremendous."

He sat down in one of the chairs facing my desk. He started flipping a quarter in his hand as he spoke to me. Jake always had a quarter with him. When he was fifteen on some ski trip in Vermont, he got separated from his group or something. I don't really know the details, but he insists having a quarter to make a phone call saved his life. Anyway, now he always has one with him.

"And I must say kudos on having Carolyn invite Alan Lansing. How the fuck did you know he'd be in town?"

Carolyn is my assistant and she's second to none. She's a native New Yorker, a hard worker, and a woman who, as much as she hates to admit it, always wanted more. She'll tell you she's content as she goes about her business, but there's a reason she plays every New York State Lottery under the sun whether it's daily, weekly, one of those scratch offs, whatever. As for Alan Lansing, he's the CEO of ARAMAX Pharmaceutical, and a potential client. He splits his time between Los Angeles and New York.

"I have my sources."

"You fucking devil. Hey, how about that girl who showed up with Brian? I've seen her in all these ads lately. What's her name? Ellen . . . Eileen . . ."

"Elena."

"Eeellleennnnaa," he repeated, letting the name roll from his tongue slowly. "Definitely Scandinavian or Czech. Is he fucking her?"

"Uh-uh."

"Why not?"

"You'd have to ask him."

"How are you so sure?"

"Because after the party she spent the night at my place."

We both laughed. Jake grabbed his love handles.

"Maybe if I lost some of this weight I could have some sort of a sex life too. I mean face it, I may not have your body, but I definitely have a better personality than you."

"Let me guess, all the girls want to be your best friend."

"Fuck you. Hey, let's talk LANG and SKILES."

Just like that, as was the case most mornings, we went through each of the deals we were working on together. At 6:45 A.M. we called down to the deli for coffee and bagels. It was a normal morning. Normal, that is, until 7:10 A.M. when the phone rang. This was the phone call that would eventually turn my life upside down.

I hit the speaker button.

"Jonah Gray."

"Jonah, Andreu."

"Andreu?" I probed further.

"Wow. I guess it has been a long time."

Then the voice hit me.

"Andreu!" I exclaimed. "Andreu fucking Zhamovsky, you ghost! How the hell are you?"

"I'm well, Jonah. I'm well."

"What's it been, two, three years?"

"Something like that."

Andreu Zhamovsky, son of Alexander and Galina Zhamovsky. Back in the days of Communist Russia, Alexander was a key player in the country's natural reserves ministry. "Post-enlightenment," as I like to call it, he was awarded the largest ownership interest in, and control of, Prevkos, which today is one of the world's most vital natural gas corporations. As I tell you this, Prevkos sits somewhere around number two hundred on the list of the world's five hundred largest companies. The organization controls over 50 percent of the country's gas reserves and produces about 90 percent of all Russian gas. The firm's primary exploration fields are located in the Nadym-Pur-Taz region of western Siberia. It is the largest vertically integrated natural gas company in all of Russia, engaged in everything from geological exploration to natural gas production and transportation. Prevkos is one of the most influential corporations traded on the Russia Trading System, Russia's equivalent of our big board, the New York Stock Exchange, and, subsidiaries included, it employs over three hundred thousand people. Needless to say, the Zhamovsky family is one loaded clan.

During the 1970s, amid growing talks and realization of one day privatizing business, many potentially well-to-do Russian businessmen were sent all over the world for classified, politically motivated seminars. The simple goal of these seminars was well-defined: to learn what it takes to stand alone in industry without government intervention or direction. One of these secret seminars was held in New York City. My father, considered an expert in Western business practices, was a speaker at that seminar. That's where my father and the Zhamovskys first met.

My father and the Zhamovskys kept in touch over the years, becoming close friends. Every summer, even after my mother died, they would meet my father and me in the south of France for a vacation. That is how Andreu, only six weeks my junior, and I became friends. We would write letters a couple of times a year, and as we got older we'd phone each other from time to time. When my father and I were traveling in Europe or Asia, Andreu and I would do our best to get together. But as the years went on, we started to lose touch. Not because we wanted to, but because each of us became so focused on the respective directions of our lives. Lives which were literally continents apart.

I never really got all the details, but Alexander Zhamovsky tragically died in 1998. From what I understand he was mugged and murdered late one night in a Russian subway station, a mode of transportation I always found odd for him considering his wealth. Anyway, Andreu has been key in running Prevkos ever since.

"How's life in Siberia?"

"Oh Jonah, you owe it to yourself to get to Russia. Our country is truly beginning to thrive again. It's such an exciting time."

"No doubt that fares well for Prevkos —"

"I can't complain. We've worked hard at positioning ourselves for the future."

"Listen to you, you sound so serious," I said. "It's a bit frightening."

"I am serious, Jonah. I have to be. If you don't mind my asking, when did you become so easily frightened? You wouldn't last one second in the Russian business world."

"That's a little more like it."

"Seriously though, Jonah, it's not like I'm the only one who's been taking things seriously."

"Meaning?"

"Meaning I've been following your career. You've been putting together some pretty incredible deals."

"And how would you know that?"

"Come on, you think Americans are the only ones on the Internet?"

"Point taken."

"I've printed out all of the articles about your business conquests. And I must say, it looks like you are in a prime position to make a run at surpassing the real-estate legacy of your father. Which I must add would be no simple feat."

This comment resonated with me. Love him or hate him, my father was a real-estate beast. I couldn't help but feel complimented by the comparison.

"Easy there, Stalker," I shot back. "Why the fuck you so interested anyway? I make tollbooth change compared to you."

"It's not about the money, Jonah. I keep up with you because it helps me feel connected. It's like e-mailing without actually having to e-mail."

I didn't quite get the analogy. Still don't.

"How's your mother these days?" I asked.

"She's terrific. Thanks for asking. Tell you what, I know it's last minute, but why don't you clear your schedule and we can talk over dinner."

"Dinner?"

"I'm in New York, Jonah."

I quietly motioned to Jake to close the door. Then I sat down.

"What are you talking about? You're here?"

"I got into town last night."

"Business, I take it."

"As a matter of fact it is business. I came here to talk with you."

"About what?"

"Let's for now just say that my firm is looking to branch out in some new directions that concern your industry. It's not that I desire to be so vague, but I'm not comfortable discussing the matter over phone lines so early in the process."

"Fair enough."

"I hate to impose, but I promise that it will be worth your while."

I leaned forward and glanced at my Outlook schedule: Drinks with M. Tate were slated for that evening.

"I know you're a busy man," he continued, "but how often do I get to—"

I cut him off. A guy of Andreu Zhamovsky's stature and influence is the type of individual you do your best not to disappoint.

"Don't be silly. I'm looking at my schedule right now. I'm fine for tonight."

"Excellent. That's just great. I don't want you to have to go to any trouble so I'll pick the place and call you back this afternoon."

"That's fine. I'm actually going to be out of the office all afternoon so just leave word with my assistant, Carolyn. I'll tell her to expect your call."

A few seconds later I hit the speaker button again and he was gone. Jake and I blankly stared at one another.

"What the fuck was that?" he asked.

"I have no idea. Is Carolyn in yet?"

Carolyn was often in extra early — something I rewarded her generously for at the end of each year. She did this for me because she knew it helped me to organize my day.

"I think I just saw her walk by, toward her desk."

I hit speaker and dialed Carolyn's extension.

"Good morning, Jonah."

"Good morning, sunshine. I need you to call Tate's office for me. I need you to let him know that I can't meet him this evening. And when you can, check Perry's, Jake's, and Tommy's schedules for me. I need them all to be free and clear first thing tomorrow morning."

"I already see that Perry has an eight o'clock breakfast with Jerry Winkler."

"Reschedule it. I have a feeling we're going to need a closed-door session."

CHAPTER 5

At 8:15 P.M. I walked into Sushi Samba on Park South, between 20th and 21st. The place was a bit passé, but I figured I'd give my foreign friend a break. Anyway, the joint was packed.

"May I help you this evening?"

"Jonah Gray. There's going to be two of us tonight. Has —"

The hostess cut me off.

"Of course, Mr. Gray. The rest of your party is having a drink at the back bar."

My eyes made their way past the centrally located sushi bar all the way to a small gathering at the back of the room. The wet bar unfortunately consisted of only five stools with thirty-five young hotshots looking to get a drink. Andreu was waving to me. He was sitting on the first stool in what seemed to be the exact farthest point away from me in the entire restaurant.

The space was colorful. Shades of orange and red were the cornerstone of the décor, a dance of Far Eastern and South American culture. Waiters floated around with ice blue, pink, and crystal clear drinks on trays, which became tiny prisms as the room's light energetically raced through them. Wooden planks with colorful pieces of fresh fish were scattered throughout. A wide, thin chandelier of smoked glass bubbles covered the ceiling.

I carved a path through the crowd. When I almost reached the bar, Andreu stood up. Someone unaware of my approach stood in my way.

"Please, excuse my friend here — Excuse him, please."

Andreu immediately began shooing the guy aside.

"Please, don't you know who this is?" he said.

All of a sudden, all eyes were on me.

"You'll have to excuse my friend," I said jokingly to the small crowd. "He's from out of town."

"I may be from out of town," he continued in his Russian accent, "but you must not be as famous as I've been told. It doesn't seem like anyone recognizes you."

"Then they must not read the business section very often."

We laughed. Then, we hugged.

"You look great," Andreu said. "What are you drinking?"

We had the bartender's attention, so I ordered straight away.

"Sapphire and tonic. Three olives."

"Still with the gin, I see."

"How about you, little girl? What are you going with, Kir Royale? Like some little topless model running around St. Tropez?"

Andreu looked good. He was, as always, clad in European fashion. He wore a navy Versace suit with a lime green ETRO shirt, no tie. His skin was tanned. His brown hair was getting long, yet he wore it sort of messy a la Hugh Grant.

"Fuck you, my friend. Bourbon tonight, a man's drink."

Andreu took a long swallow of the rust-colored liquid that filled his glass.

"Really, though, it's good to see you," he continued.

"It's nice to see you too. You seem . . . content."

"I am content, Jonah. Things have been great."

"I imagine they have. From the looks of you, all day is spent lying in the sun."

"I was just in Antalya."

Antalya is a Turkish oceanside resort town.

"I'm allowed holiday, aren't I?" Andreu asked innocently.

The bartender placed my cocktail in front of me. I picked it up and we clinked glasses.

"Anyway, sounds like you're working hard enough for both of us. You've become a superstar."

"You get fired by your board of directors or something? You looking to land a job as my publicist?"

"You've always known what you want, Jonah. I have always admired that."

"Seriously, do you owe me money or something? Or did you really just come all this way to kiss my ass?"

He started laughing.

"I remember you saying it to me, man."

My expression became serious. This comment confused me.

"You remember me saying what?"

"It was the summer between your two years of business school when you and your father met us in Antibes. It was a few years before my father died. We were sitting by the pool at the Hotel Du Cap, overlooking the Mediterannean. You had just been talking to some gorgeous blond girl in a white bikini. When she excused herself you took a sip of your Domaines Ott and closed your eyes, putting your face right in the sun's rays."

"The detail here is a bit eerie, my friend," I said jokingly. "Have you been noticing me from afar or some shit like that?"

"Shut up, won't you? Anyway, that was when you said to me the strangest thing. You go, eyes still closed as you faced the sky, 'I need to get back to school!' "

"I said that?"

"You said that. And I remember thinking to myself, 'How the fuck can this guy be thinking about school at a time like this?' So, I asked you. I said, 'Why the fuck would you want to be back in school right now?' "

"Yeah? What'd I say?"

"That the sooner you could get back to school, the closer you would be to taking New York City as your own."

I thought for a moment.

"Yeah, that sounds about right. I definitely could have said that."

"I know you, Jonah. I know that even though you come from

cash you had dreams you wanted to fulfill on your own. How does that feel?"

"You must need something from me. Is that why you're in Manhattan?"

"You're damn right. I do need something from you. I promise you, you're going to love me for it!"

We were seated in the corner of the dining room at the most secluded table available. Immediately, the waiter approached us and we ordered another round of drinks. As I glanced around, I noticed what a varied bunch we were amongst. At the sushi bar was a fifty-something Italian looking guy with slicked-back hair and way too many rings on his thick fingers. He was wearing jeans, a white button-down, and some type of black leather vest. With him was a physically gifted black woman, who must have been almost six feet tall, sporting a shaved head. She too was in jeans, and a lavender button-down shirt open to her navel as her large chest basically jumped out of her bra. Two tables down from us was a group of four—two couples. The two girls were playing games under the table while the two guys were doing the same. I pointed.

"New York City in the summer. I love it." Andreu exclaimed.

"How's your mother? Still at it with the art?"

"Every day. And your father? Still scaring the shit out of everyone?"

"Every day."

We laughed again.

"She still as interested in the company as she used to be?"

"Nah. Once my father died she went from art and Prevkos to just art."

"How about you? Tell me about the natural gas business."

"Ahhh, Jonah, all we have done over the years is grow and grow. We are as big as we have ever been. Not to mention the . . . how do Americans say . . . perks for running a company so vital to our country's success. I'm Mr. Worldwide. More access to people and places than Putin!"

"I do my own reading from time to time about you and Prevkos.

You seemed, I don't know, so casual about everything when you took over for your father. I never doubted your intelligence but you were so young for such a huge role that I can't help saying I was concerned. I'm happy to realize that I didn't need to be. Your father would be pleased with the job you've done."

Andreu appreciatively tipped his near-empty glass, and then the waiter appeared with our fresh drinks. He told us the specials. We, in turn, told him we needed a few more minutes to decide.

"Who you dating, these days? Or should I ask first how many there are?" Andreu went on.

"Please, as if you're not the future poster boy for bigamy."

Andreu clutched a fistful of the shirt covering his chest and hunched forward over the table.

"Ouch, right into my heart. Please, stop twisting."

"Being serious here for a moment, Andreu. What really brings you to New York?"

Andreu took a sip of his drink.

"Were you surprised to hear from me this morning?"

"You might say that."

"I'm here because Prevkos has decided to expand their business."

"How so?"

"We've been having serious internal discussions over the last six months or so, and we want to get involved here in the United States."

"In the natural gas business."

"Not exactly."

"Then I'm not sure I follow you."

At that moment the waiter appeared.

"Are you ready to order?"

"Sure," Andreu said.

We quickly grabbed the menus and scanned.

Andreu continued, "I'll start with a spicy tuna roll and a green salad. Then I'll go with the filet mignon cooked rare. Tell me about the sauce it comes in. Spicy?"

"Quite. It's a Brazilian —"

"Good then, that'll be fine. The spicier the better."

The waiter was without pen and paper, as all good New York City waiters are.

"And for you, sir?"

"I'll start with the blue-corn crusted calamari, followed by the Arctic Char in the tomato salsa."

"Very good, gentlemen."

The waiter walked away.

"Like I was saying, I'm not following you."

"Real estate, Jonah. We are looking to get involved in buildings."

"Excuse me?"

I looked at Andreu as if he were kidding.

"What do you mean get involved with buildings?"

"What the fuck do you think I mean? We want to buy some buildings. An entire portfolio perhaps."

"Oh, an entire portfolio perhaps? Listen to you. Andreu, you guys don't know the first thing about real estate in this city."

"But you do. And we understand good business. It's no secret what has happened to the real estate market over the last couple of years, especially since 9/11. We feel there are definitely valuable opportunities out there and we want to invest in something solid. Something we truly feel will grow in value over the course of the next generation."

"Very nice. Capitalize on my country's misery."

"Don't be a dickhead," Andreu said, acknowledging my twisting of his words. "It's part of our diversification and risk disbursement strategy for the future. There are too many growing threats in both the physical and economical climates surrounding the world's natural gas environment for us not to get involved with other industries. It's a simple situation of trying to throw off some risk."

I took a long sip of my drink, finishing it.

"How long have you and your firm been thinking about this?"

"We have been discussing it off and on for years. At this point we are one of the largest companies in the world. We have liquid reserves coming out of our asses. With what has happened to the economic climate, and the fact that the commercial real estate market here is on the rebound, the timing just seems right. We happen to be in a perfect position to ride this wave."

"Why me?"

"Because I trust you. More importantly, because you're the best."

I got the attention of the waiter.

"Yes?"

"We need another round."

"And two shots of the strongest vodka you pussy Americans drink," Andreu added.

"Shots?" I asked.

"You look like you could use one."

"Andreu, what are you looking to do? I mean, do you want to go in with partners, do you want Class A property as opposed to Class B—"

"No partners, Jonah. Just Prevkos. And as far as what to buy, that's why I've come to you on behalf of our entire board."

"How much are you looking to part with?"

"Half a billion to get our feet wet. If all goes as planned, we build from there."

I was stunned. I couldn't say a fucking word. Andreu leaned forward.

"Looks like I finally got your attention."

"You want me to shop for New York City buildings with a half billion dollars of your shareholders' money?"

"Now we're getting somewhere."

"This is crazy."

"Too much for you to handle?"

"Not even close," I retorted. "I just don't think you fully understand what you're getting into here."

"Oh yeah? Why's that?"

"New York City commercial real estate is tricky. Most of the properties are owned by enormous corporations or major families who don't just give up what's been theirs for almost a century. If it's not one of them, it is some real estate conglomerate that has probably gone public in the last few years."

"I don't give a fuck who owns what. I don't care if we have to get what we want from General Electric or fight the board of Vornado. I don't mind if I have to knock some old farts dick in the dirt — everything has a price. Everyone is always going to listen if they are being offered a premium."

The first clue that Andreu had actually been doing his homework.

"Did you just say Vornado?"

"Come on, Jonah. You didn't think I'd come to talk with you before doing my research?"

I was impressed. Vornado is one of the largest REITs, or Real Estate Investment Trusts, in the country. Within the last few years they had picked up a substantial amount of property in the city.

"I decided on you because you are very trusted within the industry, and your team is well respected. This is what my board needs. We need someone to go in with all the artillery possible. I know you have worked hard to get where you are, but this will take you to a whole new level. I'm giving you the opportunity to make the deal of a lifetime. If nothing else, think of the commission."

I already had been, since I heard the words "half a billion" dollars. The truth was this would most likely be one of the biggest deals I would close in my life, and we both knew it.

"I should mention, Jonah, that there is a catch."

"Isn't there always?"

"We need this deal to close within three weeks."

"Excuse me?"

"You heard me. Three weeks."

"Not possible," I said flatly.

"9/11, Jonah. By sun-up the next morning, American Express had a lease in place for a million square feet in New Jersey."

"Apples to oranges," I countered, testing him. "There is a significant difference between leasing space and buying it."

"It's all just business, Jonah. It's all just negotiated terms and money."

"Not possible," I said again.

"Why not?"

"Why not? Shit, Andreu, I could drop fifty reasons without pausing."

"Give me the most significant one."

"Due diligence. You have no idea how many different exercises there are for a potential buyer to perform the due diligence of a commercial property. Everything from roof inspection to systems evaluations to the property's code compliance history to zoning—there are more things that need to be checked than you can imagine. That's why a due diligence period is usually from ninety to a hundred and twenty days. It's basically a forensic process, and what I've just explained is only for a single building. It's a whole different paradigm for an entire portfolio, one that includes intense dissection and forecasting of inflation, interest, and vacancy rates as well as future construction costs. What you are asking us to complete in three weeks is unheard of."

"I understand that the due diligence, done correctly, takes a long time. But does it have to take that long — let's just say — in a perfect world?"

"Where are we going here, Andreu?"

"Please, old friend, humor me."

Our fresh drinks were placed on the table. I thought for a second, took a nice swallow of my cocktail, and thought for a second more.

"In a Utopian society, I guess not."

"Why not?"

"Like everything else, the timing issue could probably be cured with money."

"Explain."

"Simply put, these people are contractors and salaried employees. People with lives, families, other professional commitments. They are not the types of individuals who are on call twenty-four hours a day, seven days a week like surgeons. You have to remember, it is very hard to get people to really care about entities owned by others. At the end of the day, people only care about what's theirs."

"And money talks." Andreu followed along.

"Exactly. The inspection teams you are talking about retaining would have to be paid a serious premium for their time."

Andreu cracked a half smirk as he shifted his weight.

"Money is not an issue here, Jonah. We understand that we are creating some — um — trying circumstances, but we also understand that we are going to have to pay for creating such circumstances. All you have to do is get everything lined up."

Andreu picked up his shot then handed me mine before continuing. "Let me worry about supplying the necessary resources."

He held up his still full shot glass, and cocked his head as if he was looking for me to toast, validate his words. I wasn't ready.

"Attorneys."

"Attorneys?" Andreu mimicked.

"Absolutely. Not just with the actual transfer of title, but even to deal with the minutia of the language in the contracts between Prevkos and, let's say, the companies performing the inspections. These people don't begin to attack a building without the proper measures having been taken. Their rates, their protection against claims, there are all types of legal issues that can and will arise. I promise you, it will only make things that much tougher trying to negotiate these types of agreements with your counsel halfway around the globe."

"Of course. We'd have to grant you power of attorney."

"You're pretty quick to say that considering you're responsible for running one of the largest corporations in the world."

"No, I'm not, Jonah. Trust me, it's something our board has had extensive discussions about. We wouldn't pretend to be so arrogant as to think we could negotiate such contracts. We are very comfortable giving you power of attorney. To protect ourselves, we would do so in a way that gives you such power only for our real estate affairs and negotiations in New York City, and only for a limited period of time. In this case, the three weeks we are talking about. This way, no offense, you couldn't touch any other areas of our business outside this deal even if you wanted to."

"No offense taken. Andreu, what about government agencies, municipalities from both countries? I understand the desired timing is strictly an internal decision driven by perceived market conditions, but people are going to start asking a lot of questions pertaining to the need for such a fast transaction."

"Meaning?" countered Andreu, fully understanding where I was going.

"I'm just asking the questions I should be, Andreu."

"You think we massage our numbers, Jonah?" he went on, smiling.

"What I'm saying is that, as we both know, Russian firms are perceived to handle their internal finances differently than American firms. I just want to remind you that people will start asking questions about Prevkos. And they'll start asking fast."

"Which is precisely what I want. Our financials are impeccable. As a public company we're used to offering ourselves up for unequivocal scrutiny. The quicker the questions come, the faster the answers come. It will just make those involved that much more comfortable with us in terms of making a fast, clean transaction."

"I'll need to get a copy of your proof of citizenship and identity. In fact, I'll need it for whoever will have the authority to deliver decisions on behalf of your shareholders. It's strictly enforced company policy for international transactions. All board members or—"

"I represent the official voice of the board, Jonah. Always. And I have no problem giving you all of my papers."

"You're talking about a lot of cash here. Not just for whatever property you obtain, but for the due diligence alone involved in selecting the right purchase."

"The beauty of living in the age of wire transfers, my friend. I understand you would need to keep funds on hand. We set up an account over here and I supply you immediately with the funds you need to do your homework. Once we've settled on the target, we zap the money overseas and put it in escrow until it is time to, hopefully, pull the trigger."

"Cash held in escrow in the States would have to be with the bank of PCBL's choice, Andreu."

That meant Salton Lynear Bank, the preferred financial services provider of PCBL.

"Since we're talking about so much cash it is imperative I'm able to utilize my relationships. It's the only way to ensure moving cash through the unavoidable red tape as quickly as we'll need to."

"Of course. I understand that," Andreu responded.

"Who handles your banking?" I asked.

"We deal with Tenvix."

Tenvix International, headquartered in Moscow. I was familiar with the bank.

"I'll need to have access to them."

"Igor Larianov leads the team that handles all of our financial affairs," Andreu offered up. "He speaks English almost as well as I do. I'll put you directly in touch with him."

"It's a must. If we're making a play based on money, then I need the ability to manipulate and distribute money as I see fit. Meaning I need access to all important banking institutions helping us to make this happen. Plain and simple."

"I agree with you. Done."

Andreu leaned back in his chair.

"Admit it, Jonah. It's sounding more and more attainable by the second. And I imagine the concerns you just threw at me were your strongest ones. Am I right?"

He was right. There were other issues, and it was certain that others would come up along the way, but these were the two most glaring examples. It was all about having the necessary resources to make people move mountains. People only care about what's in their pocket. And what more could I really want than to get people to jump to make my deal with someone else's money? The more I thought about it — the challenge, the rush, the victory — the more

I clung to the obvious. I had nothing to lose. No deal, no payday. And I always made the deal.

"It couldn't just be me."

"What couldn't just be you?"

"The one granted power of attorney. It would need to be all four members of my team. We would all need the ability to maneuver independently of one another. We would each need the power to make important, quick, potentially deal-altering decisions."

"Except for authorizing wire, or for that matter any type of cash, transfers," he shot quickly back at me, like a dart. "All money trans-actions need your authorization. With regard to access to my com-pany and our lawyers and the ability to make decisions to further a potential deal — all four need it, all four got it."

Andreu just stared at me, waiting for more words. I didn't give him any.

"Admit it," he said. "Not bad."

At this point I smiled. It was starting to actually feel possible.

"No," I countered. "Not bad at all."

Andreu again raised his shot glass.

"Now will you drink this shot with me?"

I raised my glass as well and we threw them back. Another question jumped up and bit me.

"Why three weeks?"

"We'll get to that, Jonah. Can we just enjoy our cocktails?"

I gave him my answer — no — without using any words.

"I absolutely understand that what I am asking of you is no easy task. But we came to you for a reason, and there will be other incentives offered to your team that we'll get into. For now, I just have one more question."

Andreu took a sip of his drink without taking his eyes away from mine.

"You ready to make a truly obscene amount of money?"

CHAPTER 6

The four of us were in Tommy's office at 8:00 A.M. sharp Wednesday morning. Tommy was sitting behind his desk. Perry and Jake were sitting on a brown, leather couch against the opposite wall and I was in a matching armchair to the side of the room's central glass coffee table. Perry, in a charcoal, pinstriped Ralph Lauren pantsuit and dark-rimmed, porno-librarian glasses, as I liked to refer to them, was holding a pad and pen. Jake was sipping his latte and Tommy had his arms folded behind his head as he got settled. He exhaled, and then started in:

"Now—"

He was cutoff as the phone rang. He instinctively threw his arm forward and with his index finger and acute precision depressed a button that put him through to Candace, his secretary.

"Yes, Tommy?"

"I said no calls, Candace. Please!"

"Sor—"

Before she could even apologize, he had gotten rid of her. He resumed his position, and tried once again to relax and focus.

"Now Jonah, tell me what the fuck is going on here."

The floor was mine.

I used to love the spotlight.

I used to think it mattered.

"What's going on here, Tommy, is a mountain of cash dropped in our laps."

"Let's skip the drama, Curtis. Let's talk real estate. Let's talk facts."

Tommy liked to call me Curtis, referring to Curtis Martin, the workhorse, star running back of the New York Jets.

"I have been offered the opportunity — we have — to put together a deal that will be one of the most lucrative and interesting we ever get to close as a team."

Tommy's cash sensors kicked in.

"Who?"

"Andreu Zhamovsky. Prevkos."

"The natural gas character from Russia."

"That's right. He called me yesterday morning and told me he was in town. And that he wanted to meet for dinner."

"Refresh my memory."

"Our parents were friends. We met as kids and were sort of close, you know, like pen pal close, as we grew up. When we got older it got harder to keep in touch. Different worlds, literally. But we were a lot alike. In certain ways he was like the Russian version of me."

"You mean there are two of you?" Perry quipped.

"By the time I was in college, we spoke once every couple of years. But I would see him when I went on vacation with my father."

"What's their interest in us?"

"Today, Prevkos is one of the largest companies in the world. And apparently they are looking to expand into the commercial real estate arena. Here, in New York City."

"Why not in Russia? Or in Europe?" asked Tommy.

"Because for the long term they believe New York will give them the most value for their money—even more than London or Beijing. They see Manhattan's continuing recovery as something that works in their favor. Besides, it's perfect for Andreu."

"What is?" asked Jake.

"New York City. It's Andreu's kind of game. That alone adds value in his mind. He loves excitement. He loves everything about being here. He has since he was a kid."

"He wants to buy property here because he likes excitement?" Perry asked, doing the devil's advocate thing she does so well.

"Prevkos wants to buy property here because overseas real estate is part of their future diversification and risk-aversion strategy. They want to enter new industries and they've been doing their homework. They feel there are deals to be made, here and now, in New York City. Think about it. The economy worldwide is in a complete state of flux. Who is actually thriving? Those who have strategically placed themselves within their respective marketplace. Prevkos has never been as strong as they are today. They are prime for small, tactful diversification."

"How much do you actually know about them as a firm as opposed to as a family?" asked Tommy.

"My guess is that he probably stayed up all night doing his research online to all corners of the earth," remarked Perry.

She knew me so well.

"Greedy fuck," joked Jake.

Tommy just stared at me. He knew Perry was right.

"Prevkos is at its highest level, financially and influentially, in the history of the company. They have the money. And Andreu, who's been helping run the show since his dad died in ninety-nine, has complete control of the board."

All four were silent in thought. Then, I said, "If you were in their position, can you tell me you wouldn't look at the idea of purchasing property in Manhattan as an intriguing opportunity? Today — right now?"

No one said a word. Case closed.

"A foreign property investor can be tricky, Jonah." Tommy said.

"We discussed this. My understanding is that not only are their financials representative of their reputation, the banks associated with them are all for broadening their practices. They have an endless list of references, both the firm and Andreu personally. I already explained to him exactly what documentation we would need, to which he responded we would have everything we requested from the moment we accepted the assignment."

"Let's talk brokerage," Tommy continued.

"I pointed out we only work with signed brokerage agreements drawn up by our attorneys, which is non-negotiable. Andreu was fine with this."

"How about commissions?"

"I explained to him how our commission structure works, and that we start at six percent on the first five million of the purchase price."

The way the commission on a sale works is quite elementary. For the first five million dollars of the purchase price, the commission is 6 percent. On the portion between five and ten million, the commission is 4 percent. On the portion between ten and fifty million, 3 percent. If the price is higher still, on the portion between fifty and one hundred million the commission is two percent. Any portion that goes over a hundred million is calculated at 1 percent. The aggregate number, keeping in mind that this structure is subject to negotiation, is the price tag for the service.

"Now, like I said, they've been doing their homework. Andreu asked why I should automatically expect to start at six points when the average in a good market is usually somewhere between four and five and a half."

"And?" asked Jake.

"I told him because we were the best, which is why he came to us in the first place. So we took another shot, laughed a little more, and shook hands on my terms. A flat commission to be paid up front, in one lump sum, by Prevkos to us upon the completion of the transaction. I told him we would only accept the assignment if Prevkos would pay our commission and chase the seller down for the money themselves. Andreu asked why, and I said because this would allow us to focus on the deal. Andreu said no problem, they'd cover our cash."

A look of displeasure, one I had anticipated, glazed Tommy's face.

"Why would you negotiate the percentage without discussing it with me first?"

"Because I wanted him to know that our team's mutual trust and willingness to work together is of the utmost importance. That we're not nitpickers and we're all equally empowered. Which I thought was probably a good idea since they're looking to spend approximately half a billion dollars."

Silence. Their chins were dimpling the carpet.

"You heard me right. One half of a billion dollars, give or take. Which, when multiplied by our simple pricing scheme, comes out to a commission of roughly six point seven million dollars. Four million just for us."

Even Perry was able to loosen up for a split second.

"Holy shit!" she exclaimed through laughter.

"And that's just to get rolling," I added. "This goes well and, according to Andreu, their plan will likely be to keep acquiring."

"Jonah, if you're fucking with us — seriously — it would be sick to fuck with people to this degree." Jake continued.

Now you have to understand something. It's not like we were foreign to big money. We're all young to have amassed the seven-, in Tommy's position, eight-figure portfolios we have. But this was different. Historically it has taken us a number of solid, industry-leading deals a year to each clear a couple million. For Tommy and me, this three-week deal alone would be over $1.2 million each.

"This is all for real. I have laid it out to you guys exactly as it has been presented to me."

Tommy smiled.

"You look like you have something to say," I said.

"I'm thinking that this one time I'll let you slide on the commission negotiation."

We all let out subdued chuckles.

"And I'm also thinking that this all sounds too easy. I mean I understand that this fell into our lap because of the relationship here. But still, something sounds off. There must be a catch."

Tommy has never been one to miss anything about anything when it comes to real estate.

"There is, Captain. There is absolutely a catch."

Jake was disappointed.

"I knew this was horseshit. I knew —"

"Just shut the fuck up for another minute," I barked. "The catch is as good for us as it is bad. We have three weeks to close whatever deal it is we find for them, assuming it is acceptable. No questions asked."

"Why?" asked Perry.

"Because Prevkos has been promising their shareholders diversification in the wake of the ever-changing natural gas industry climate for too long. Andreu very clearly explained that his board feels they need to be able to show shareholders movement on this front by the end of the third quarter. This is the major motivation for doing any of this."

"Why the urgency for such a quick transition?" continued Tommy.

"Because they are thinking aggressively that the world's economic markets are going to turn around, coupled with the fact they want to show investors that they are being proactive offsetting some of the growing risk that comes with the natural gas industry. They want to show their shareholders they are looking to act responsibly. They want all their ducks in a row and this is the time-frame they have set for themselves, as overly ambitious as it may seem. Their goal is to capitalize on today's interest rates, which we all know are going to go up after this fall's presidential election, if not sooner, and have time to get their arms around their new venture before November. They don't just want ample time to learn about whatever buildings they buy. They want time to watch and understand the Manhattan real estate market and how their buildings function within that market so they can, should it matter, if need be react to whoever ends up as president."

Tommy ran his hands through his hair, pausing for a split second halfway through.

"Do they realize what they're asking?"

Perry jumped in.

"Let me guess. Yes, because they have done their homework."

I have always found Perry's dry attitude and simple, angry sexiness endearing. But she was being a bit more sarcastic and ungrateful than I felt was necessary. I looked her squarely in the face.

"Is there any particular reason you're being such a complete bitch this morning? Have I done something to offend you?"

"Did I say that you did? Trust me, Jonah, you'll know when you have offended me."

Tommy jumped in.

"Take it easy, guys."

"Perhaps it's the fact that I just dropped a fucking multimillion dollar pay day in your lap."

"Seriously guys, enough!"

Perry took a deep breath, looked at the ground for a second, than again at me.

"I am not being offensive on purpose, Jonah. And I apologize if it appears that I am. I just know that you sometimes love to forge ahead without stopping—

"— to look at all the puppies in the litter."

I knew her so well I was able to finish her sentences.

"Exactly." She conceded.

I addressed them once again as a group.

"I asked Andreu if he understood how difficult this could be, and he said he did. He told me he got it from a due diligence standpoint as well as the fact that such circumstances would ultimately affect his purchase price. When I explained that moving at the speed he needed would require Prevkos keeping the applicable funds for the transaction in escrow on this side of the ocean, with our financial institution of choice, again he said it was no problem. Then he proceeded to tell me that it was fine if we can't handle it. He has a few backups he feels are extremely qualified and will be more than willing to step up to the challenge."

"And what did you say?"

"That I needed to discuss it with you guys, but that we would probably be ready to accept the opportunity."

"Didn't you say the catch was also a plus for us?" asked Jake.

"Most definitely. Because they understand just how difficult it may be to do what they have asked of us, they have offered us a bonus for getting them what they want. They have offered us, assuming we close, a million American dollars worth of Prevkos stock, each, at the day's closing price, simply for the trouble of working under such trying time constraints. That's one million each, on top of our commission, in case you missed it the first time."

I stood up and walked over to the window. I was staring into midtown Manhattan as the sun's rays sliced their way through the morning clouds. Tommy and I were silent. We were both thinking. Perry and Jake were having a conversation. After a few seconds, I turned back around. I looked at Tommy, as did Perry and Jake.

"I must tell you guys straight up that I absolutely plan on accepting this assignment."

"We probably don't have much time to decide," added Tommy.

I looked at my watch, which, on this morning, was a steel Rolex Daytona with a mother-of-pearl face. The sunlight hitting it accented the swirls of pink and hazel weaving in and out of the number slots, which were each marked simply with a diamond. I'm a bit of a watch freak.

"They need to know by eleven o'clock A.M., our time."

Perry was still prodding.

"I'm just concerned about the rest of our clients, along with our pending deals. How do we just take three weeks away from all of our other obligations?"

"Perry, we're the best team in this fucking city. Would you actually even consider walking away from this because of the possibility of multitasking even more than we already do everyday?"

Of course not. Finally, she had no further arguments. Tommy was in, I could see it in his eyes. As for Jake I didn't even need to see his eyes. The thought of this much money had him sold from the beginning.

"Can anyone at this point see a single negative in trying to put this together?" he asked.

"We don't make the deal, we don't get paid, which is no different than any other deal we've ever had to close. It's that simple," I added.

"What do you say, guys?" asked Tommy. "Has Jonah ever led us astray?"

We unanimously voted to take on the project, and immediately we were in broker mode. Which meant moving at lightening speed.

"I'll let Andreu know and have Carolyn get the commission agreement specifics over to Waterman's office."

Ely Waterman is one of our attorneys.

"Once Ely has it, I already have the information for the attorney they'll be using. He'll be sending it directly to their counsel once he has our approval. Andreu will get me everything that we need from their end via e-mail and fax."

"Jake," Tommy jumped in, "I'll handle the Seven Eighty-nine Seventh Avenue closing this afternoon by myself. This way you can get started also."

"Not a problem, Tommy."

"Don't kid yourselves," Tommy went on, reminding us, "these three upcoming weeks are going to be a motherfucker. You're going to need every second you can get."

We all nodded.

"Now, any ideas for exactly how we should proceed since we have three weeks to come up with the perfect, half a billion dollar block of property for these people?"

"Absolutely!" said Perry, without hesitation.

I sat back down.

She continued, "We all have a very good idea as to the pulse of the market right now, and we all know exactly where the owners' minds tend to be. Not just owners as a whole, but many owners individually. Each of us takes the next twenty-four hours to come up with the ideal, feasible possibility that's out there. Something that with the right offer, and some solid massaging, is in your mind at least eighty-five percent viable. Something that combines the right piece of valuable space with the right ownership who, given the right circumstances, would be more than happy to sell."

Perry was sharp. She was right on.

"Given the time frame, it has to be at least eighty-five percent possible. Twenty-four hours. We compare what each of us has come up with."

"I'll handle what I can with all of your other deals," continued Tommy.

"Captain?" I asked, puzzled.

Tommy's basically semiretired. He's put a lot of hard years in, and has earned the right to just supervise us and collect cash accordingly. Every once in a while he's needed to push a deal past the finish line, but not so often anymore. The fact he was willing to get back in the trenches to help pick up the slack spoke volumes.

"I'm pretty clear on what stage each of your deals are at, and I'll handle as much as I can. Get me all appropriate contacts: opposing counsel and brokers, vendors, consultants, everyone. Then give me all of the current leases with the final term sheets."

A term sheet simply highlights the most important negotiated items in a lease. It's a nice tool for double-checking attorneys' work.

"Give me floor plans, financial analyses, whatever you think I may need. Any objections?"

There were none. How could there be?

CHAPTER 7

12:55 P.M.

Perry and I were in Au Bon Pain, on East 43rd Street, having lunch. She was sipping her lemonade through a straw as her eyes stared at something behind me. I was eating a tuna wrap.

"What's going on, Per?"

Without moving her head she brought her eyes back to mine.

"What are you staring at?"

She took her lips from the straw, leaving a bit of her lipstick on its tip.

"That little girl back there. Sitting with her mother."

I turned around. There was an adorable little blond girl, wearing a pink dress and a white bow in her hair, sitting at a small table with her mom. She was more interested in the chocolate chip cookie on the table than the sandwich her mother was trying to get her to eat. When I turned back around Perry had returned to her lemonade.

"Cute little kid," I said.

Perry was quiet. Her gaze had returned to the child. I was getting annoyed.

"Perry, seriously, do you want to talk about what's going on or do you want to stare at the little girl all afternoon?"

Perry became angry.

"Can you not be such a fucking dick? God, I can't take one moment to myself to look at a child without you feeling as though this means the big Prevkos deal doesn't mean shit to me?"

Then the sarcasm.

"Don't worry, Jonah. I promise not to let you down."

Like I said, Perry and I are close. Which at times like this means I unfortunately get to see a side of her that no one else in our professional lives even knows exists. The Perry that has so much trapped inside, so many personal demons she struggles with each day, just as we all do. They all just see organized, simple, intelligent, and conservative Perry. Even Tommy and Jake. Don't get me wrong, they're all close too. But for some reason Perry has always felt comfortable and I guess safe opening up more to me.

"I see an open table by the window. Maybe I'll just pick myself up and —"

The right corner of her mouth turned up ever so slightly.

"— you know, since I must be such a prick."

"Stop it, Jonah. I know, I'm sorry. I'm being a bit crazy."

I put my sandwich down and took a sip of iced tea. I leaned back comfortably, enjoying one of the only times I get to relax, even for just a few minutes, each day.

Perry continued, "It's just that, you know —"

"What?"

"I just wish I could go back and be five again. Like that cute girl over there. Even just for one day."

"Yeah? I don't think I would. Life at that age is entirely based on counting on everyone else for anything you want or need. Half the fun of getting older is you get to learn about all of the things you had been sheltered from. And, unfortunately, a lot of those things turn out to be some of the best parts of life."

We both chuckled.

"Seriously though, Jonah. When you're that young it is so much easier to be happy all the time."

She was looking at the girl again.

"During the summer, when we were kids, I remember Ryan and I used to take anything we could find in the fridge and make it into a popsicle."

Ryan is her younger sister who lives in Seattle.

"Orange juice, lemonade, grapefruit juice, you name it. We'd just pour it into a Dixie Cup and throw in toothpicks or plastic spoons or whatever we could find. There was nothing like going back to the freezer a couple hours later to get them. We were so excited. We'd just tear the cup off in one continuous swirl and there they were. We'd take them outside and race to eat them before they melted."

"Wow. Sounds great."

She looked at me with an expression that acknowledged the validity of my returned sarcasm. She had asked for it.

"No, really, especially the part about the toothpicks. It must have been crazy fun trying to hold those big, oblong popsicles on those wimpy little sticks. Let me guess — when you two were feeling really slick, you went for some iced tea. Maybe cranberry juice. And you even threw in a bit of vodka for good measure. Which, unfortunately, made them take a little longer to freeze."

Perry threw her napkin at me.

"You know what I'm saying, Jonah!"

"Yeah, I do," I conceded.

We sat for a moment in silence. I leaned forward over the table on my elbows.

"What's going on with you today, Perry?"

"What? Why do you say that?"

"Oh, I don't know. Maybe because you haven't made one mention of the deal we just had dropped in our laps. Potentially one of the biggest deals of our careers. Or maybe it's all this talk about popsicles and plastic spoons?"

She didn't respond. I leaned back again in my chair.

"I know you, Perry. You get excited by the challenge of a new deal no matter what size it is. You usually won't shut the fuck up about it for the first three days. Your strategizing, your constant brainstorming and thinking out loud — we usually have to throw you out of our offices. In walks the deal we've all talked about so many times and you don't say one thing about it. Not one thing."

Her eyes fell to her lap for a split second before she consciously raised them back up.

"I think he's doing it again."

She was referring to her gynecologist husband, Brian. A year and a half earlier, when she was pregnant with their kid, she found out the dirty bastard had been cheating on her. Not only is he a scumbag, but he's not the smartest guy either. She had a sense it was going on, but he really got busted when Perry's best friend walked into Peter Luger's only to find the moron all over one of his patients at a corner table, the two of them dripping adultery onto their shared porterhouse steaks. During his "coming clean" to Perry, he admitted going to the legendary New York Steakhouse because it was in Brooklyn, out of the way of their mainstream lives. I'm sorry, did someone forget to mention to this guy that if you put Peter Luger's in Dallas, it would still be the most popular restaurant in New York City?

"Who?" I said innocently.

She rolled her eyes.

"Per, what makes you say that?"

"I don't know. I just have this feeling. And it absolutely pisses me off."

"That you feel paranoid all the time?"

"No. Well, yeah, but I was thinking more along the lines of the fact that I ever allowed him to stay."

This was the only truly weak thing Perry could ever recall doing. Keeping Brian around. And it tormented her, knowing that she had to give up so much of her pride in order to at least give her child the chance of growing up with a father. She hated him for putting her in that position. She loathed him for playing the father-figure card as he groveled. Almost as much as she hated the fact her father-in-law, as she learned post-marriage, was a childhood friend of a certain figurehead of a family in the waste management business.

For a while it had seemed things had gotten back pretty close to normal. I was a bit surprised by all of this.

"Well, there must be something that would make you think so?"

"It's just the way he acts. It's — I don't know."

"Perry, do you have any concrete evidence about this?"

She thought for a second. Perhaps even looking for something she could reference as a stretch.

"Uh-uh. No."

"Then I really think you need to give him the benefit of the doubt here, at least for the time being. I mean after all, it was you who allowed him to remain in your life."

Yes, I was being a good friend. But equally important, I needed her to get past this for now. Quickly. There was work to be done.

"Am I wrong?"

"No. I know, I'm probably just acting crazy. But it's just this sense I have. I know when he's not acting like himself, when he's up to something."

"Perry, why make yourself nuts like this? You two have been through a lot in a short amount of time. I imagine you're not always exactly the same person he married either."

She looked at me sharply.

"Again, am I wrong?"

She grabbed her lemonade and took a long sip.

"I guess not. You may be right."

Manipulating her in a way I often used to with people, almost as a personal challenge, I could feel it. She was ready to talk business. Which brought me to my next challenge, the game at hand for approximately the next twenty-four hours. Until the next morning in Tommy's office, it was Perry, Jake, and I against one another in coming up with the perfect prospect. Why was I looking at it as a game? Because I knew Perry and Jake were also. We all love outdoing one another. We all appreciate the fact that it is this type of friendly, competitive behavior that always brings out our best. As much as we all love to impress Tommy, we love to impress one another.

"So, any ideas about who may fit the bill?"

"Absolutely."

"Let's hear it?"

"I don't think so, Jonah. I think it's best if we all stay on our own until tomorrow morning."

"Why? Let's get a jump on some strategy."

Perry laughed.

"Please, I know you Jonah. You probably worked on this last night, even though we hadn't talked about it, and already think you're the only one to have it figured out. So you think, I must add."

"So I think?"

"That's right, smart ass. It would be foolish of you to think that no matter what's on my mind, I'm not focused here. I knew who our top prospect in Manhattan was for this type of deal the moment you laid it all out on the table."

"Is that so?"

"Damn right. My mind may be doing some serious juggling right now, but that doesn't mean I'd let anything get in the way of a deal like this."

It was nice to know her killer instinct was intact no matter how torn up she was inside. I was sure Perry was dead serious when she implied she had thought of the perfect prospect.

CHAPTER 8

At 7:30 P.M. I met my father at Harry Cipriani, a tiny, East Side Venetian power spot in the Sherry Netherland Hotel, for a drink. I was meeting some friends on the Upper East Side for dinner a bit later, so figured I had some time to catch up with Pop. We sat at the bar amid the diamond-dripping, air-kissing clientele. He had already placed our order with Sonny. I had a Sapphire and tonic coming while he went with his usual Jameson on the rocks.

Our drinks were placed down in front of us. My father took one look at his, pointed his finger at it and called to the bartender.

"Sonny."

The barkeep swung his eyes back to us.

"Sonny, what the fuck is this? How about pouring me a little booze over this ice?"

Sonny picked up the drink.

"Of course, Mr. Gray. I'm terribly —"

"Get us some fried zucchini out here also. I haven't eaten a god-damn thing all day."

"Of course," Sonny cowered, "right away."

Pop returned his attention to me.

"Fucking crooked —"

Without asking he reached out and adjusted my necktie. I checked out the vintage Omega Seamaster on his wrist as he did.

"You ever going to let me try that watch on?"

Pop smirked. It was the only one from his collection I'd never touched. The truth is, after so many years of asking, it wasn't the watch I was interested in anymore. It was if he'd say yes. As usual, he changed directions.

"What did Andreu say when you accepted?"

"That he knew I would. He said he's been following my career and that my track record shows I'm up for the challenge."

"They've been looking to do something like this for a long time?"

"According to Andreu they've been shaping their new risk-management strategy for a while. Overseas real estate is just going to be one of the pieces."

"Sounds like they're looking to make a powerhouse of a deal, Jonah. You just make sure you do whatever it takes to get them what they want. And don't fuck this up. A company as big as Prevkos only gives you one bite of the apple, no matter who you are. Remember that."

"Please, Dad, the only reason we're even having this conversation is because of your relationship with Alexander and Galina."

"That's probably true. But what if you had turned out like Jerry Mandel's kid? All into heroin or crack or whatever it was that got him killed. What would this opportunity have meant then?"

"How do you know I haven't? You know — gotten into heroin?"

Pop just laughed.

"I don't care if you eat the shit for breakfast. Whatever it takes to keep your focus, your edge. You keep closing deals, that's what matters."

He took a long gulp of his whiskey.

"It's no different than when you were in high school. I knew you were smoking pot and into all kinds of shit, but I didn't bother you. You were kicking ass in the classroom. And that's what counted."

He scooped some salted almonds from a dish on the bar and flung a couple into his mouth.

"What have you come up with?"

I brought him up to speed not only with regard to what it was

Andreu wanted, but what our initial game plan was. My father, dapper as always, looked especially good that night. He was dressed in Brioni from head to toe, highlighting his navy pin-striped suit and white spread-collar dress shirt with a silver necktie that was perfectly knotted as always. Pop was ever a big believer in the perfect knot. Not the little shit four-in-hand knot that most guys' fathers teach them when they're eight, but a classy, almost regal Windsor knot. True, it takes a few more steps than the four-in-hand or even the semi-Windsor, but it's worth it. Pop truly felt it could make or break even the finest suits. The perfect Windsor knot: serious width and thickness, symmetrical, perfect center dimple, and just a touch brash.

"You look good, Pop. Almost like you're up to something."

More laughter.

"What does that mean? Can't a man look sharp?"

"It was you who once told me that looking sharp is one thing; looking ready to make a deal is another."

Pop flashed me an approving smile.

"You're finally fucking learning something. I'm meeting Joe Kelso for dinner."

"Who?" I asked.

"Cherry-Vail. He's the CEO."

"Now we're getting somewhere."

Cherry-Vail, one of the largest advertising companies in the country, was in the process of looking for a large block of office space in Manhattan. My dad had known a guy on the board of directors for years, so they had come to him directly to discuss a deal for a new Manhattan office. My father had a block of sixty-five thousand square feet coming up the following year. Cherry-Vail was looking to take that sixty-five and add it to another fifteen thousand contiguous feet he had available. In a situation like this it wasn't just about the eighty thousand square feet being leased in a recovering market. It was more than that. It was about the constant quest to add as much prestige as possible to the tenant roster.

"A little dog and pony show tonight," I continued.

"Kelso is the decision maker. He wants to meet in person to

discuss some of the specifics. I figure why not do so over Bellinis and the best Veal Milanese in the universe."

When it comes to the art of the deal, few possess the unshakable focus of my father. It is from him that I learned you have to be willing to go beyond the facts and figures of a term sheet, you have to be bigger than the amount reflected by your net worth, which for him is roughly between seven and eight hundred million dollars. Like anything in life, he taught me, you always need to remember that without the little parts the big parts don't work. You have to be willing to go the extra yard, not sometimes, but all the time, to get a deal done. A businessman in the game is only as good as his last deal, the same way an athlete still playing is only as good as his last season.

I often remember a conversation we had when I was in business school. I was involved in some mock trial based around a huge corporate scandal. I was an expert witness for the defense. I explained to him that our grades would be affected by the trial's outcome, and that it appeared we were going down in flames.

"I'm in a corner, Pop. I need this grade."

"Then what the fuck are you doing wasting your time calling me? Get out there and attack the situation head-on!"

"How, Pop? I told you, I've exhausted all of my options."

"Bullshit. Don't ever let me hear those words come through your lips again. That kind of a statement only comes from a soft, weak business mind. Options are infinite. Don't ever let anyone tell you otherwise. If the rules don't work, then you throw those fucking rules out the window."

"But Pop, when — why would —"

"If there's a trial going on, then there must be a jury. Am I right?"

"Of course."

"You find out who the poorest students are on that jury, the students on financial aid, and you float them a sizable incentive to ensure a certain outcome. Mission accomplished. Everyone gets something they need."

"Yeah, but what if —"

"Stop thinking so much, Jonah. You need to learn to react. You need to understand that the ability to pull the trigger, in any situation, is what separates the men from the boys."

I sat silently and processed the words.

"You must always stay on the offensive. You must always keep pushing forward at all costs. Are you hearing me?"

"Attack the situation. Go get what I need."

"Now we're getting somewhere."

His answer was to pay the jury off.

I did.

We won.

"Enough about this boring crap," Pop went on as he crunched on some more nuts, "Tell me what you've got for Andreu."

My father, the man who taught me to tell time in a meeting by glancing at the other guy's watch and never my own, also taught me that you never unveil the full picture until you have your facts 100 percent in order. Not 80 percent, not 99.9 percent — 100 percent. As with life, in business you have to own everything that comes out of your mouth. You have to be the words, regardless of whether those words are true or false, regardless of whom they may hurt. There can never be one shred of doubt. Every syllable that passes your lips, every thought, fact, must come out as if it were carved in stone someplace.

"I still have one or two questions that need answering before I've got it all lined up."

"He came to you because your team's the best. Because he has confidence in your ability to dazzle, as he should. At least tell me this — you going to dazzle him?"

"So far, Pop, my hunches have been right on."

"You didn't answer my question."

Frankly it wasn't just the Andreu Zhamovskys of the world who I had ever been concerned with dazzling.

"With all due respect, I may even dazzle you with this one."

His eyes started to wander over my shoulder, around the dining room.

"Yeah, well, I guess we'll see about that."

Then, as if he'd been tagged with an epiphany, he returned his vision to me.

"Actually, you came kind of close with that last deal. The Levingworth Building. Down on Water Street."

"Nothing like this, Pop. I mean it, nothing like this."

"You keep it up, one day I just may let you work for me."

I felt lucky, honored by this comment. I felt chosen, almost loved.

If only I'd had the clarity to be confused, and not awed, by such words.

"This is a huge opportunity, Jonah. Don't fuck it up. Remember, you see an opening, you pull the trigger. There's always time to clean up any leftover mess later. You just do whatever it takes to make Andreu happy and get this done."

At this moment I absolutely felt as if I had stumbled on to the perfect deal, an ideal, creative fit for Prevkos. Little did I know that what I had conjured up in my mind would prove to simply be the tip of the iceberg.

Release time.

Table for eight in the center of the dining room at davidburke and donatella. The space was subtly bold, crisp, sleek. It was white, warm, kissed with shades of red, and quietly flaunting flowers. To my left was my best friend since I was four years old, Tanqueray Luckman. In case you are wondering, yes, his parents are in fact alcoholics. And no, they are not into whiskey.

Everyone else at the table was friends of either L, what I've called him since we were kids, or me in college. The whole group together has been close since we all graduated and moved to the area. Across the round table from me were Lance and Michael, both married. The rest of us were single, something probably obvious to those who have witnessed our times out together on the town.

Dinner had been fantastic, and by eleven thirty-five we were all sitting around the table pretty hammered. L and I headed to the bathroom to pull a couple of lines. We crammed into the tiny unisex cell, and turned on the water to smother our sharp, deliberate snorts. L pulled out his vial and, on the marble around the sink, dumped a small, snowy pile. He broke the mound into two thick tracks then leaned over them.

"Just like our days at Helton," he muttered right before sending the turbo-charged powder towards his brain, "No one looking after us then, no one looking after us now."

The Helton School was the snobby, uptown private high school we attended. Since every kid there was more screwed up than the next one, it was basically just a day-care center for rich teenagers with both the means and desire to self-medicate, to slip their respective realities.

We took one step out of the bathroom and both stopped as our eyes scanned the dining room from afar. Everyone back at the table was ordering coffee or another cocktail, but the atmosphere had quickly gone somber. Before my mouth could even quiver, L had read my mind.

"Bar."

We made a right, climbed a two-step staircase and headed back toward the entrance. A long banquette that had sprouted candlelit tables for two lined the wall on the right, the length of the bar ran parallel on our left. Once we settled in at the end, where the long, smooth wooden plank and its base curled toward the wall and we could turn and see the whole spread, I noticed something else. Or, I should say, someone.

Elizabeth Heltman.

Elizabeth and I had dated a couple years earlier. As for the last time we had sex, that was this past New Year's Eve in Aspen when we randomly ended up at the same party.

"Two Sapphire and tonic," L ordered.

I took another glance at Elizabeth who was tall and slim with fantastic straight red hair that ended just past her shoulders. She didn't see me. Though sitting at the bar, she was engrossed in the conversation she was having on her cell and staring at her near-empty wine glass.

L continued with the story he had started telling me.

"I'm telling you, man, I wanted to wring the little stain's neck. You think I need this chump slinking in through my back door like we're in high school sneaking in through your kitchen at four A.M.? I mean who does he think he is, all five foot two of him, coming into my family's warehouse and demanding cash from me like that? Like we're trying to scam him or something? Shit, we've been the biggest distributors in the city for three generations."

Luckman Meat. That's the name of L's family business. They have been the largest meat distributor in New York City for the last, well, you know. They are loaded, which is a good thing, since I can't imagine L poor. His tastes and preferences in life simply wouldn't allow it.

"Such nerve," I continued, mocking him.

L grabbed the drinks from the bar and handed me one. As he did, I snuck another peek at Elizabeth who still didn't see me.

"Hey, don't come off acting like that shit should fly," L went on. "You if anyone knows how irritating it is when someone steps on your toes. Especially in your own backyard. To make things worse, he had this crazy rotweiller with him. Just walked right in with it."

"Dogs are only crazy because of the people caring for them," I commented.

"Anyway, the only way he could calm him down was to rub him on his dick."

I choked.

"What did you just say?"

"You heard me. The dog just turned over on his back and the guy—"

Unnecessary for this story maybe. But I often find in life you can gauge how close two people are by what they are willing to say to each other. I couldn't resist this example. It's amazing what comes out of his mouth.

"It's amazing what comes out of your mouth."

We each took a huge gulp from our drink.

"It's not like you to be so quiet about what deals you're closing," L said. Something going on?"

"You might say that."

"Let's hear it."

"Unfortunately, I can't tell you about it. Not yet anyway."

L hated when I did that. He always took it personally, like I was making it out to be that he wasn't important enough to hear about it.

"See, why do you pull that? What, you think I'm gonna start running around the restaurant screaming about your fucking business?"

I started laughing. Watching L get worked up was truly hilarious. The best part was how mad he got when you laughed at him for it.

"Seriously —" he went on.

"I'm sorry, Man. It's only fair to —"

"The team. I know, I've heard it all before."

L picked up his cocktail and took another long sip.

"At least tell me this —"

His smile returned.

"— Good shit?"

"Tremendous." I responded.

We clinked glasses.

L started another story, but because I was so fucked up he quickly lost me. My mind started twisting, working furiously, as I careened into thoughts of Andreu Zhamovsky and my team's assignment. I looked once more at Elizabeth and began to find myself a bit tense, an oddity for me. So I pulled out my leather cigar case from my inside pocket and removed a Monte Cristo #2, which where I come from is a delicacy.

Yes, I'm fully aware that New York City has become one large nonsmoking section. But since I knew both David Burke and Donatella from their past restaurant successes, and since the crowd had thinned a bit, I lit up anyway. L didn't flinch. It was a couple others, including Elizabeth, who did.

We stared at one another for a brief moment. Then, glint in her eye, she ended her phone call and started my way. Just as she almost reached me the front door opened to my left and some guy walked in. Elizabeth immediately disengaged. She turned toward the bar and put her glass down. Mr. Anonymous, his noticeably taller-than-average height and nice suit providing an interesting contrast with his fading hair line and weak chin, shot right toward her.

Just feet from us the two kissed hello. I smiled slightly, surprising myself, as I remembered our fun times together. Then I jumped back into my hang out time with L.

Imagine my astonishment when her mystery man turned my way and addressed me.

"Excuse me, but I don't think you're allowed to smoke that in here. That's why they have a limo parked out front. It's the smoking section."

Astounded and admittedly a bit impressed by the size of the guy's balls, I didn't answer. I just looked at him, then Elizabeth, who was more in anticipation of what I was about to say than any of us. I looked back at her guy.

"I'll tell you what," I responded, pointing to some vacant space behind me, "Since it's late and the place is clearing out, I'll stand all the way over here and—"

"They don't want you smoking in here," he interrupted. "Like I said, they have a limo out front. It's the smoking section. I know because I come here, like, all the time."

It was a draw for what bothered me more about the guy. The fact he had cut me off or the reality he was the prototype poser.

"Is that so?" I taunted. "You mean, like, all the time?"

L couldn't keep from laughing.

"I said the establishment doesn't—"

"If the establishment wants the cigar out, then someone who works for the establishment can tell me so."

"Honey, let's just—" Elizabeth tried to interject.

"Actually," he continued, "I'm telling you so."

Now I was pissed. Not just because this guy was killing my high but because Elizabeth's happiness had only seconds earlier mattered to me.

He took a step toward me. Enjoying the free fall of being both drunk and wired, and threatened just enough to want to teach this yutz a lesson, I drew a large mouthful of smoke and blew it toward him.

"And who the fuck are you?" I asked.

I actually used to look forward to moments like this. Instantly everything about me intensified. My posture, my vision, my purpose. I could feel everyone's eyes reaching out for me, grabbing at me as if they were hands. This mattered to me, it invigorated me. This type of attention helped remind me I was alive, it helped me feel like more than just another pawn on the chessboard of life. It made me feel like the mighty king that stands head and shoulders above all the other pieces.

Only now do I realize that's what everyone, everything is. Just pieces.

"Excuse me?"

"You can't hear or something?" I went on. "I asked who you are. Because if by chance you were actually someone, I'd maybe consider putting it out."

"Fuck you," he said as he took another step toward me.

"Sheldon!" Elizabeth tried again, this time reaching for him.

I looked past my adversary's left shoulder. Once he noticed my attention had shifted he turned to see why. My boys were now standing in the bar, and they were staring directly at him.

He turned back to me, squinted, and spoke in a quiet, direct tone.

"Who do you think you are?"

In my little episode of narcissistic immaturity the answer to the question was an easy one. You see, a restaurant like davidburke and donatella loves a presence like mine. They love having people see me there, some guy who's in articles for the deals he puts together. Some young hotshot who can eat wherever he wants but chooses to eat their salmon, tip their waiters, and drink their booze. Again, I didn't respond. I had become so jaded, lost, that I simply felt no need to explain myself. I understand now that had I been sober, standing there with L in some kind of out-of-body experience, I would have been embarrassed to even know me.

At that moment the manager, Luis, came over and immediately asked the other guy if perhaps he'd be more comfortable in another part of the restaurant. But at the same time the bartender let me know my ride home had arrived.

"Don't worry about it, Luis," I said. "My car's out front."

"Mr. Gray, I am sure it is no trouble at all for the gentleman. He —"

"Trouble for me?" a bewildered Sheldon blurted out.

I cut him off.

"Seriously, it's no bother. It's time for me to get out of here anyway."

I removed my wallet from my pant's pocket. I pulled out my Amex Centurion Card, the quintessential symbol of a true money-man, then handed it to Luis along with a fifty and my business card.

"I don't feel like waiting. Messenger the card to my office tomorrow."

"Of course, sir. Very good."

I turned to L —

"Tell everyone dinner's on me."

— and then back to Sheldon.

"You know, Shelly, I've got a little secret for you."

I moved my eyes to Elizabeth thinking that with one simple phrase I could ruin both their nights. Perhaps I could tell him about the time I met her parents. Or maybe he'd find it interesting, if he didn't already know, that she feels sexiest in nothing but black lace lingerie. Either way, it didn't matter. A little sharpening of the tongue was all it would take to satisfy me and make the two of them feel like shit.

"Oh yeah, asshole? And what's that?"

Elizabeth, behind him, was quietly pleading with bulging eyes. I couldn't help thinking how pretty she was when she smiled or that I had already hurt her in the past.

"The next round's on me. Have a good night."

I left the restaurant, jumped into the Town Car waiting for me, and headed home.

I always loved nights like this with my friends. Nights to let loose and rage a little bit in order to purge the excess energy I wasn't able to get rid of destroying opponents in the conference room — my version of the battlefield. My boys have always been very important to me. I had no idea this was to be my last night spent with any of them.

As I stumbled into my apartment I was greeted by my favorite little soul in the world, Neo. My six-pound, white, long-haired Chihuahua named after Keanu Reeves's all too cool character from *The Matrix* trilogy. Neo lives for going crazy as I come through the door. I threw my Purple Label suit jacket on the old-fashioned, freestanding coatrack in the front foyer, and immediately sprawled myself out on the hardwood floor so Neo could stand on my chest and lick my face. Something we both always looked forward to.

After more than a few swipes of Neo's sandpapery tongue across my skin, I stood up and carried my little partner into the kitchen. I placed him on the black marble countertop next to the sink as he began to shudder with excitement, tapping his two little front paws against the cold rock excitedly. Although late, as often was the case, it was Neo's dinner time.

I put Neo on the floor with his bowl of food, a combination of wet, canned dog food and some grilled chicken my maid prepared for him. I grabbed a Corona from the refrigerator and headed back out of the kitchen past the dining and living rooms, down the corridor past my guest bedroom, second bathroom, and study. When I got to my bedroom I stripped off my shirt and socks and went straight for the glass doors in the corner of the room, doors that led to my eight hundred square foot terrace overlooking Midtown's east side. On the deck table there was a glass ashtray from Tiffany, a gift from my grandmother that I imagined she would be ecstatic to know I used strictly for marijuana since I don't, and never have, smoked cigarettes. There was a half-smoked joint in the little glass bowl's mouth, and since I wasn't fucked-up enough already I reached for it and lit it with a book of matches from Ben Benson's.

I struck a match, and as I got past the inevitable nanosecond of having to smell sulfur, I took a long pull of the dense weed cigarette as I leaned back in one of the deck lounge chairs. I then exhaled as slowly as I had inhaled, immediately taking another serious puff before placing the joint back on the ashtray's edge and again grabbing my beer. I leaned back into position as Neo came charging outside and jumped right up on my lap. He was trying to climb up me in order to give me another kiss, so I leaned forward and met him halfway as he licked my nose. Then, since a slight midnight breeze had taken hold of the city that night, Neo curled himself up into a ball in my lap as he drifted into sleep, his tired eyes falling against his will within seconds. I didn't want to wake him, so I remained still for the next half hour as I enjoyed the rest of my beer and surveyed the glowing topography of the city, a vast mountain range of concrete, glass, and steel that had afforded me every aspect of my surroundings.

At one twenty, after a good game of challenging myself to properly identify numerous randomly selected properties from the horizon, I reentered my bedroom, placing a slumbering Neo underneath the blanket on my bed. I headed back down my main corridor all the way to the front foyer, where I retrieved my briefcase before heading to the study. Wearing nothing more than the suit pants I had been in all day, I settled in to the room, a warm, sophisticated study I had modeled after my father's. The walls, all comprised of dark, stained wood bookshelves lined with everything from classics to beach reads, surrounded me comfortably as I settled in to the oversized, dark leather chair behind my desk. My feet welcomed the plush, black carpet as I turned on my desktop computer and pulled all of my necessary documents from my briefcase. I turned on the desk lamp, which created just enough illumination for my workspace while simultaneously reminding me of what time it in fact was. The apartment was dead quiet, the only faint sounds coming from the streets down below just past the windows behind me. I began to work furiously.

CHAPTER 9

Thursday morning. Exactly forty-eight hours after Andreu Zhamovsky had become the focal point of our lives, we were in Tommy's office ready to each lay our brilliant idea on the table. As always each of us was secretly hoping to outshine the others. Tommy was behind his desk and the three of us were each in our usual spots around his office. Much like any family when in a common gathering place, we were no different. We had our set places, places that made us feel safe, places that reminded us we belonged no matter what. Like my buddy L's family growing up, each family member, all six of them, would take the same place around the dinner table every night. This never changed, because none of them were willing to let it. That's family.

All four of us were drinking our morning Starbucks. My night had run right into my morning, so even though I looked as sharp as I did every day, I hadn't yet had any downtime to wash the prior evening out of my system. For all I cared my Starbucks may as well have been another glass of Sapphire. It didn't matter. I was pumped. Even more so by the fact that I could tell they were too.

"Let's get to it straight away, guys," Tommy began. "I have a breakfast with Jon Robard in an hour."

"Thanks, Tommy," Jake said.

Jon Robard was the lead broker on the other side of a deal Jake had been putting together for six months. Jon was representing the owner of a class A building at 55th and Park. Jake was representing Chenowith Publishing that was seeking fifty thousand square feet. They were about to close on two full, contiguous floors, and the window of opportunity was closing for us to lock in our desired numbers. The deal couldn't be put off. Tommy was sitting in for Jake.

"Now he's all set with fifty-two dollars per square foot in years one, two, and three. Is that right? Or are they still trying to bump you up starting year three as opposed to four?" continued Tommy.

"We're airtight at fifty-two, year one through, and including, year three." Jake responded.

"Fine."

Tommy then ran his eyes over page sixteen of the lease once again, the page outlining the base rental prices for the space over the term of the lease. These numbers are given as an annual figure for each year of the term, that when divided by the number of square feet being rented gives you the rental cost per square foot.

"Fine," Tommy said again, as he quickly thumbed through the rest of the document. "Electric, the option to take the floor above in two thousand seven. Everything else seems in place."

Tommy put the lease, and Jake's deal, aside.

"Let's go. Perry, you start."

Perry was ready to go, I could see it in every aspect of her that morning. Her dark brown Armani pantsuit matched the crisp look in her eye. Her hair was shapely yet full and her make up was slight but just enough to give her that extra little oomph. She looked like she was about to stand up and litigate the biggest case of her life in front of a packed courtroom. She was excited. She was so Perry.

"Cantrol Petroleum," she began.

"Twelve sixty-eight Sixth Avenue," I added.

Tommy, a hint of fatherly advice injected into his upcoming remark, was concerned.

"Public corporation with a tough board. Be careful here, Perry."

"I spoke to their broker about a week ago, and the word is their financial situation is far worse than even The Street knows. They may have no choice but to alter their office space situation."

"Doug Welsh has been handling their real estate affairs for years. Why would he be opening up about this so easily?" asked Jake.

"Did I say broker? I meant to say new broker. Does the name Auerbach mean anything to any of you?"

James Auerbach is a hotshot broker on a top team at a rival firm. Not only is he a respected adversary, he is someone we often exchange sensitive information with. A relationship founded on the basis that he is, coincidentally, one of Perry's closest friends from college.

"You've got to be fucking kidding me," exclaimed Tommy.

"Kidding I am not, Captain."

"Why are they switching?"

"Because they are as arrogant as every other large fucking corporation out there who wants to blame every little thing on someone else. All of the sudden, while watching their stock price plunge, some old, crusty executive sat back and took notice of the monstrosity of a building they reside in. Then he realized they were laying off people and half of the entire property is empty and they are bleeding because of it. When he realized he was running out of people to point his finger at, he decided it was time to hold Doug Welsh accountable for the fact they were stuck with so much space. They hadn't planned well enough for a downturn in the economy. Between the fact that they're having a hard time recovering and the world's current oil situation."

"Why wouldn't you have mentioned this to us?"

"Because to tell you the truth it wasn't such a big deal when James told me, and, more importantly, it hadn't yet been locked up."

"And now? Is Auerbach's position locked up now?" asked Tommy.

"It is. I spoke with James yesterday afternoon and he confirmed his involvement with Cantrol. He has signed an exclusive agreement for his team to handle all of their Manhattan real estate affairs."

"Did the two of you discuss Cantrol's position as of today?" I asked.

"We did and it's no secret to them that the sales market is hot. The board would absolutely be willing to look at a possible sale of their world headquarters on Sixth Avenue."

"Refresh our memories regarding the specifics of the property."

"One million fifty thousand square feet. Built in 1974, the building is forty-five stories tall, each floor a touch more than twenty-three and a half thousand rentable square feet."

"Loss factor?" I asked.

"James says about thirty-two percent on a full floor. All building heating and cooling systems have been replaced within the last four years. The lobby and elevator cabs were all part of a thirty-five million dollar renovation completed last summer."

"How many elevators in the building?" continued Tommy.

"Twenty passenger and four freight."

"I haven't been in there for a while," Jake commented. "How much space does Cantrol actually occupy?"

"Around two hundred thousand square feet. The bottom nine floors, of which at least three basically sit empty."

"And the rest of the tenant roster?" Jake continued.

"Aside from what's vacant, fantastic. A couple of international banks and four law firms, all with decent-sized blocks. No one's lease comes up for at least four and a half years and this is one of the law firms that happens to be the smallest tenant in the property. They specialize in class-action litigation, not a bad niche in 2004. Needless to say, their practice is thriving."

Perry stood up and handed us each a package containing all of the information she had just revealed. Included were further specifics regarding the property as well as floor plans.

"All in, we're looking at a transaction in the half a billion dollar range, give or take in either direction. At my request, James has made it clear he will provide any documentation we request as required by our due diligence."

As always, Perry had set the bar quite high. She was perfectly prepared and had come up with a fantastic scenario. One property, which from a due diligence point of view would undoubtedly help logistically with regard to our time constraints.

"Any questions?"

"Fantastic, Perry. Just great," commented Tommy. "Sounds potentially nice and neat and it's a phenomenal property."

"A trophy building. High-profile, imposing, perfect for the Zhamovsky mindset." I added.

"Why thank you both very much," Perry said.

A sweet, confident yet appreciative smile slowly made its way across Perry's face, the same satisfied look she gets when she knows she has put forth a job well done.

"All right, Jake. Let's keep going," Tommy said.

Perry locked her eyes with mine, forcing me to give her even further approval. I felt sad, yet flattered at the same time. Sad that Perry was so focused on my attention toward her, but flattered for the very same reason. I gently nodded and mouthed "not bad," broadening her smile.

"What have you got?" Tommy continued.

Jake was pumped. He was even wearing a tiebar that morning, something he only puts on if it is time to sequester every single ounce of his most professional self. Something that reminds him of the power broker he had worked so hard to become.

"Slevin portfolio."

The Slevin clan. Two brothers in their sixties, Ray and Lawrence, each with a son, Jagger and Leo respectively. Don't ask. The word is that Ray Slevin is a diehard Stones fan. Anyway, the Slevin family owns seven properties along the Park Avenue South corridor, between 14th and 30th streets, right on the avenue. During the Internet boom running from the late nineties through the millennium, this was possibly the hottest submarket of New York City. Internet firms, advertising agencies both high-tech and standard, you name it; if it was a creative company and had to do with the evolving e-world we were living in, they only wanted to be headquartered on Park South. Rents went through the roof and occupancy rates skyrocketed accordingly. Today, different story. This is possibly the submarket that suffered the most in the wake of someone sticking a pin in the bloated stomach of our economy. Post 9/11 there was more sublease space available than direct space, meaning there was more space being offered by firms locked into leases who no longer needed it than there was being offered by landlords directly. That is how many firms along this corridor collapsed, which means I don't even need to tell you what happened to the rents. On the positive side, the Park South submarket has been recovering at a decent pace like the rest of the city.

Jagger and Leo Slevin are pricks. Period. Two loaded little brats born on third base who live with the attitude and arrogance of guys who hit a triple. They act as agents on the family's seven properties, meaning they are the brokers who negotiate all incoming deals on behalf of ownership. Talk about a nice setup. I have inside knowledge that their fathers pay them full commissions for these deals on top of huge salaries, even though they will one day own the buildings. Too bad they're such fucking morons.

Their fathers are actually decent guys, which makes it even sadder. This family has put a lot of cash in our pockets over the years and we've put a number of fantastic tenants in their properties. The Slevins have great respect for our team and, having just come through some tough years, things were again looking up for their holdings. I knew someone would bring them up, and perhaps I would have too if it wasn't for one thing.

"Sexy enough?" I asked.

"Correct me if I'm wrong here, but according to Jonah, flash and excitement is as important to this guy as the potential to prosper," added Tommy.

"I hear you guys, but just bear with me. Jonah, you said your Russky friend is a bit of an ego maniac. But I also heard you say that he's a smart businessman looking to expand into a realm completely new to him, leading the charge for one of the world's largest company's board of directors. I imagine the number one issue for them will be financial sensibility here, not just flash on its own. After all, there are going to be a number of people to answer to on their end."

So far neither Tommy nor I could discount Jake's comments. We continued to listen quietly.

"This isn't to say that I haven't taken the sexiness your guy craves into account. As I looked over the Slevin portfolio, comparing it to other potential transactions out there, it was the one that made the most sense to me for a couple of reasons. You mentioned that your boy controls the popular vote of his board. Therefore, I knew we needed an angle that would appeal to him on a personal level on top of the financial sensibility."

Jake paused, heightening our anticipation.

"And —" Perry finally said.

"And, what's the one aspect of Park South/Union Square that not only continues to thrive, but did so in the shit market we all just trudged through?"

I saw where Jake was going. I loved it.

"The nightlife," I said.

"You got it, killer. The nightlife. Out of the seven Slevin-owned properties, four have happening, high-end, glitzy restaurants as the retail tenants. One more has Stark, the hottest bar and lounge to open in months, written up in *New York Magazine* just last week. If Zhamovsky wants sexy, few things are sexier than being the number one VIP in some of the hottest restaurants and clubs in Manhattan."

"Great angle, Jake. I like it," Tommy said. "Very smart."

"Is there really such a thing as a 'sexy value' in real estate?" asked Perry, forcing us all to think a bit deeper.

"Look at this market we're in," I responded. "The winning property in any market will always have some type of allure. In a market mirroring a recovering economy, it is all about tremendous value, tremendous 'bang for your buck' for all buyers, even high-end."

"You really see 'sexy' and 'value' coexisting?" she further challenged me.

"Today, interests are seeking property with real value, coupled with that extra something that separates a certain property from all others in its class. To get people to buy in markets like this, there must be that added dimension. Perhaps something that caters to a certain unique use for the property, maybe a potentially niche, future location — something. Just look at what's happened over the last couple years in the Meatpacking District. Conversely, a market like the one we left behind pre-millennium change, the type of market we're trying to get to once again, has a different type of high-end buyer. The one willing to pay a premium for what he wants. You're just used to focusing on sexy in a topped-out market, Perry, but sexy is alive and well in each type of market. It's all about where you look for it."

"Amen," Tommy intervened. "Let's keep going. Numbers —"

Perry dropped her head back to the notes she was keeping. She hated coming up short in an intellectual confrontation.

"Park South's vacancy rate hovers around eleven percent. Deals are being done in the mid twenties per square foot," Jake started. "In an up market, Park South always performs. It simply always has. In a market on the upswing with money to spend, Park South is the perfect place to get situated for the, eventually, profitable future. How long that future lasts is an entirely different story."

"And not our worry." I shamelessly threw in.

"Total square footage for the seven properties?" Continued Tommy.

"One million five hundred seventy-five thousand ten rentable square feet. An average of two hundred twenty-five thousand square feet per property. I'm thinking we pay in the neighborhood of two hundred ninety-five dollars per square foot. Agreed?"

We all agreed.

"Four hundred sixty-four million six hundred twenty-seven thousand nine hundred fifty dollars. We get them a unique, niche type of portfolio that overnight makes them the premier landlord in one of Manhattan's most interesting submarkets. In doing so, we look like heroes coming in well under the half a billion they came here willing to spend. We need to inch up, we'll still most likely end up below our client's ceiling."

"How are the buildings physically?"

Jake stood up and handed us each a package.

"In this package you will find the specifics for each property. Square footage, structural history of the property including all renovations and the years they took place, building system specifics, building system upgrades, if any, etcetera."

Jake's prospect was definitely a solid one, but one nonetheless with an inherent, real obstacle we were all unfortunately aware of.

"Given the time constraints, who do we deal with?"

The Slevin family was in two different camps of thought. The older generation, who had held onto these properties so long they were basically mortgage free, were all for selling out one day. Ray and Lawrence were both at peace with the fact that their grandchildren's grandchildren would live like kings from the property value they had amassed. As for Jagger and Leo, a bit of a different story. Like I said, these two are complete pricks. And they have never had a problem letting everyone know that all family business decisions are to come through them, not their fathers. Nonetheless, it is hard not to see their side of the coin. As for their feelings toward the portfolio, simple. Ride out the market until an even more prosperous day, a day when the economic environment enables them to cash out much higher. After all, why should they have to throw in their chips when they are only in their thirties, sitting on a mortgage-free portfolio that still has the ability to turn a profit even in a down market?

"We deal with Jagger and Leo."

"I agree," Tommy said. "You tell me why."

Tommy Wingate. Always the teacher.

"Because the key to having your way with the Slevin boys is a simple one. Give them respect. At the end of the day, that's all these two poor schmucks are looking for. You cross them, you go to Ray and Lawrence first, they'll never trust you and they'll do everything possible to make life difficult even if it doesn't have to be. Today, all four love us. We go through the proper channels, even though the two jerkoffs are the harder sell, we stand a much better chance of pulling this off."

"Good thought. Now, how do we sell them?"

No brainer.

"No brainer," Jake continued, "we convince them on as long a recovery period for the economy as possible. We refer to things like the awful national employment reports that keep coming out each month. Fuck, we make them think we see oncoming plateaus or even regression. We make them think the years of reality from over extension and uncertainty that most likely lie ahead couldn't possibly be worth the chance of a few extra bucks."

Bingo. Convince them that getting out now may in the long run prove to be the wise, yet unobvious choice.

"Any thoughts?" asked Tommy.

"Definitely worth looking into," Perry said.

"I think it works," I added. "It can't hurt to have a number of different possibilities to work off of and discreetly play off one another."

"Yeah, we're not really dealing with much time here. The more worthy, viable deals we can work, the better," Tommy said. "All right, Curtis, you're up."

I could literally feel my facial skin surrender as my game face took over.

"I've had a couple of interesting conversations with Sam Archmont during the last few weeks."

Sam Archmont is one of my favorite clients. He's a top dog at one of the largest banks in the United States, Gallo Booth West, headquartered on the West Coast.

"How is he doing?" asked Tommy.

"He's the same fucked up lunatic he's always been. He's great. He sends his best to all three of you."

I met Sam Archmont through my father about five years ago. The two had been long-time friends. The guy was in his mid-sixties at the time but believe it or not, once we knew who the other one was, we kept running into each other at the gym where we both belonged. He's one of those Jack LaLanne types, old and leathery but fit as a fiddle. Turns out when he was young he did some time and became obsessed with working out while he was behind bars. So now, to prove his physical prowess, each year he does a different stunt at his birthday party. I know, like Jack LaLanne. That's why I used the analogy. Last year Sam ran across hot coals. Good thing the paramedics were standing by because the poor old bastard's bunions couldn't even thwart that kind of heat. I don't think the old fool took more than three steps before his inner child, who by the way sounded like a little girl, was screaming for dear mercy.

Anyway, about the third or fourth time I ran into him we got to talking. It turned out they were looking to upgrade their East Coast headquarters, and I scheduled a meeting between him, one of the integral players internally for handling their real estate affairs, and Tommy. To make a long story short, ten months later we moved them into 120,000 square feet of space averaging $52.00 per square foot over the course of a twelve-year lease. Just last year they exercised an option on their lease for another 30,000 square feet of space in the same property, which meant another commission for us. Sam Archmont has made me a lot of cash over the years. But this alone isn't the reason he's one of my favorite clients. Sam Archmont handles lending for the bank, as it relates to commercial real estate property. He's an amazing source of information for me. He's got his finger on the pulse of anything and everything when it comes to the landlords of New York City's office buildings. This is why he's always been my favorite client. Along with the fact he's probably the craziest guy in the world to go out on the town with.

"Anyway," I continued, "during one of our chats, Sam mentioned something to me about Lloyd Murdoch. And I found what he had to say interesting solely because of its market relevance."

Lloyd Murdoch is a fifty-something, second generation landlord in Manhattan. His family owns ten properties throughout the city, some that carry heavy financing. They are a definite player in the New York City commercial real estate market, and Lloyd is their leader.

"Once I spoke with Andreu Zhamovsky, I saw a whole new relevance to what I had been told."

"Which was?" Perry asked.

"That Four Ninety and Four Ninety-five Madison Avenue were about to become R.E.O. properties."

R.E.O properties. Otherwise known as "Real Estate Owned properties" or properties that have been taken back by a bank because the borrower has defaulted on his mortgage and the foreclosure auction didn't attract any bids. In this case, most likely because the properties were so heavily leveraged the debt service is worth more than the property.

All three perked up, as if a snake had bitten them in the ass.

"Four Ninety and Four Ninety-five!" exclaimed Jake. "Come on!"

Four Ninety and Four Ninety-five are two huge, gorgeous, mirror-image properties facing each other on Madison Avenue in the high Forties.

"I'm telling you," I went on, "I shit you not."

"I assume you checked back with Sam," Tommy said.

I handed them each yet another precisely organized package.

"Sam didn't just have peripheral knowledge here. Gallo was the actual lender. The buildings were officially taken back by the bank last Thursday."

"I've always heard Murdoch likes to toe the line," Tommy added.

The truth is that the element of the unknown is one of the things that made this so interesting. Lloyd Murdoch is someone none of us have really ever dealt with. Tommy knew him in passing from his early days in the business, but that was it.

"Why hasn't there been any press yet?" asked Jake, looking around. "Did any of you hear about any type of foreclosure auction?"

"That I'm not sure of yet. Sam wouldn't discuss anything more with me over the phone. But a car's picking me up here around three and I'm heading out east to his place."

His place is a 7,000-square-foot dream house on Ocean Drive in East Hampton, sitting right on the beach.

"He's getting married tonight on the beach behind his house. I told him it was urgent that I had this information, and he told me we could sit down beforehand."

"Another marriage?" said Perry, half jokingly. "Does this guy get married once a month?"

"The package I just handed you is all of the specifics about the buildings. But I imagine, or should I say hope, none of it is anything new for you."

I said that because not only are 490 and 495 Madison Avenue legendary buildings, but the four of us closed a one-hundred-thousand-square-foot deal in 490 just last year. A deal no one in the market ever thought we'd get done. Beautiful lobbies, high-speed elevators, top-tier tenants, these two buildings are the cream of the class A building crop. Each has 700,000 rentable square feet or twenty-six floors at just a shade under 27,000 rentable square feet each. They run along the avenue, taking up the full city block, prominently staring one another down, seemingly keeping the other in line. Each of us felt close to these two buildings. The 490 transaction was one of the most difficult we ever closed as a team.

Normally in that type of a deal situation we'd form a working-business relationship with ownership. Not the case with Murdoch. He's the definition of the secretive type. He left all areas of negotiating and finalizing the deal in the hands of his brokerage team. We never once dealt with him, something that made what I had proposed all the more intriguing.

"Did Sam give you any indication about what happened at all?" probed Perry.

"He didn't. But I think I know what may be going on. Larry Peterson —"

I handed them each yet another package, this one filled with articles.

"— I remember my father telling me about this guy, and a little game he played to save his ass in the early nineties."

"Watch the games, Jonah. None of us, especially you, can afford another Murray-Gate." Tommy warned.

Tommy took a look at the pile of reading material I just handed him.

"Do you ever sleep, Jonah?"

I turned to Perry and Jake.

"I assume there is no need to refresh your memories with regard to the commercial real estate collapse of the early nineties. Larry Peterson, a heavy Garmento landlord —"

Garmento being the lingo used to term anyone who works in the Garment District.

"— was simply drowning in his investments. Before he knew it, the market had dried up so severely that his buildings were all sitting half empty. Anyway, because of this he found all of his lenders breathing down his neck. So what did he do? He tactfully defaulted on his mortgage terms intentionally so the buildings would end up back in the banks' hands. But as we all know, banks hate being put in this situation for one simple reason. They are not in the business of buildings. So what did Larry Peterson do?"

Perry jumped in.

"He bought his property back all over again, this time at lower prices dictated by the 'at the time' current market conditions."

"That's exactly right," I replied. "And how did he do that? How was he able to get the buildings past foreclosure and back into the hands of his desired bank? Relationships. He had the bank help him keep it all quiet with the promise of buying the buildings back at current market values, numbers much lower than what he originally paid. He aligned himself with new partners, helped the institutions clear up existing tax liens, got the lenders whole again, swallowed his losses, and jumped right back in."

"So assuming that's the case," added Jake, "we'd be entering the arena looking to buy these two buildings right out from under Murdoch? Who's looking to simply, very under the radar, restructure and buy his own buildings back?"

"And why not?" I said.

"Devil's advocate —"

Perry looked at me with those smart, diligent eyes.

"— what's to say the bank would want to deal with us just coming in with some buyer they had never done business with before? I mean, here they are in a position to nicely and neatly hand the property back to its past owner, someone they as an institution have done business with; have a history with."

"I'll tell you what's to say, Perry. The fact that here we are coming in with cash and willing to respectfully engage in a bidding war, something we all know our competition most likely will not be able to take part in. Now I know that banks don't like dealing in buildings because it's not their business, but what banks are in the business of is making money. Not only are we, cash in hand, an appropriate, willing buyer, we come with the added bonus of not having just defaulted on a mortgage."

I paused, giving them all a chance to respond. No one did.

"Am I wrong?"

As the three of us spoke further, it occurred to me that even though we had each taken this situation as a chance to outdo one another, none of us had. Which in this case was a good thing. We had all won. Each potential deal was a solid, viable prospect.

The more we talked, the more obvious the plan became. We were going to pursue all three deals, each team member taking the point, or lead position, for the deal they had brought forward. The key to this approach working was a simple one. Under no circumstances at all, ever, was any prospect to find out about either of the others. People tend to be more giving and forthcoming when they think they are negotiating against themselves as opposed to multiple interests. For a moment, in deference to Perry, we mulled the idea of intentionally leaking all three deals to the media, hence lighting a small fire under each potential seller's ass. But we decided against it. We all agreed that in the end, hostility fostered from such a situation could have a potential seller holding things up at crunch time for any one of a million reasons. And we decided it made more sense to use our strong relationships and records, creating a comfortable environment that would have people doing what they could to help a potential deal come to fruition.

We left Tommy's office that morning running. We never looked back.

CHAPTER 10

I walked into Jake's office, or the room in PCBL Headquarters better known as the shrine to the New York Jets. Signed jerseys by the likes of Johnny "Lam" Jones and Joe Klecko were hanging on the wall, while shiny green and white helmets tagged with black squiggly lines were on display in glass cases. In the corner farthest away from Jake's desk were Joe Namath's shoulder pads and cleats from a play-off game along with a signed photograph by number twelve himself, a picture taken of he and Jake when they met in Atlanta at the 2000 Super Bowl. These three items were placed together in one larger glass case forming the room's feature piece. Not only was it on a pedestal, it had its own direct spotlight shooting down from above.

He was sitting behind his desk, leaning back in his chair with his Bruno Maglis up on his desk. He was talking on the phone by way of a wireless headset, throwing a mini Jets' football up in the air repeatedly. As I entered, with one motion Jake threw me the ball and leaned forward, placing his feet back on the floor and grabbing a pen. Without breaking stride in his conversation he quickly wrote something on a piece of paper and handed it to me. It read "Jagger Slevin." He motioned for me to shut the door, which I did before sitting down.

"I'm telling you, man, we're talking about a very interested par-ty," Jake continued into the tiny microphone in front of his mouth. "Someone who has done their research, and has decided they would like to, if nothing else, get a dialogue going. Maybe simply for informational purposes, possibly for reasons a bit more interesting should the opportunity present itself."

Jake is fun to watch in action. He's a real smooth character, but one armed with knowledge to the hilt. A dangerous combination. Especially for a moron like Jagger Slevin.

"Nope, nope, that's all I feel comfortable with telling you for now. Just meet me for lunch, I promise to let you in on a lot more."

One of the first things my father taught me in life, and one of the first things Tommy reminded me of in real estate, get them in person. For reasons too endless to count. For example, to see if their expressions actually match their words, to show them they're worth more than a phone call, to make sure your words are only falling on intended ears, etc.

"I can't do it on Tuesday," Jake went on. "I've got a closing that morning that may run through lunch. I would change a lunch date tomorrow, but the potential client is coming in from Boston. Just meet me. Cancel whatever the fuck it is you have and meet me. Trust me."

After a little more verbal wrestling, Jake finally landed his lunch meeting. He took off his headset and carelessly threw it on the desk.

"Done. One o'clock. Oak Room."

"Not bad. Only one problem now."

"What's that?"

"You have to actually sit there and have a meal with him."

"That I do. You think it's wrong if I start doing shots to deal with the pain?"

He turned to his computer screen to look at his e-mail.

"Shouldn't you be off trying to close some half-a-billion-dollar deal or something?"

"I should, smart ass," I began. "but I thought of something you should probably know, and I didn't want to forget to tell you."

"And what's that?"

"The garage deal Jagger and Leo have been trying to develop by Union Square."

"What about it?"

"It fell apart. I saw Goldman when I was out last night."

Brad Goldman is a broker from a rival firm.

"We were talking about the Union Square market when he said something about Bert and Ernie having trouble securing the financing terms they were looking for. Maybe a sore subject. You mentioned trying to get him for lunch, so I didn't want you getting off on the wrong foot."

"Good thought. Thanks."

"Don't sweat it," I said.

As I started to get up, Jake pulled his eyes from the screen and looked at me again.

"Hey—"

"What's up?"

"Let me ask you something," he went on, pulling a quarter from his pocket to flip. "What would you do to celebrate if we make this deal? You know, what would you indulge in as a little gift to yourself?"

Funny thing, up until this point I hadn't yet even asked myself that. Probably because I think, in my mind, the answer was such an obvious one. Jake began to answer his own question.

"I'm thinking maybe buy an interest, albeit a very small interest, in the Jets. Fuck, I'll take a half-point interest if they'll give it to me. Or con some actress into thinking I'm cool and sailing around the world with her. How 'bout you? What would you do?"

"I'd probably drink too much, sleep too little, use too many recreational drugs, sleep with as many hot women as possible, and work like a maniac."

"Well then, what's the point? I mean, isn't that your life now?"

"It sure is. Except out there, somewhere, are a lot of other brokers who claim they have brokered the most impressive deal this city has ever seen. I want us to end that debate once and for all."

That was the point.

CHAPTER 11

As the limo cruised east down the L.I.E. toward the Hamptons, I was riding in the back, solo. Even though the air-conditioning was blasting I had the sun-roof opened so I could watch as the clear sky, lightly painted with thin cirrus clouds, went speeding by. The TV, muted, was on CNN. Wolf Blitzer, at his usual studio post, was sharing a split screen with legendary GE Chairman Jack Welch. My suit jacket was off and there were papers spilling out of my briefcase all over the seat around me.

While I was speaking on my cell phone, my eyes couldn't help getting stuck on the site of the wet bar. Bottles of premium booze staring me in the face, I slowly tore my corneas away, forcing them instead to settle on the Diet Coke in the cup holder to my left.

"— and I've been in New York enough times to know that the Hamptons are about one thing, partying. Business, please!"

Andreu Zhamovsky's voice was blasting from my cell phone. He was busting my balls.

"Just admit it, Jonah, I promise not to hold it against you. You're jerking around when you should be working on my deal."

"You finished yet?" I asked. "Because if you're not, let me know when you are so we can get started."

Andreu was back in Russia, and had been for about twenty-four hours. He was speaking to me from his office in Moscow.

I quickly reached over and took the plastic bottle of soda, throwing down a healthy sip before replacing it. Then I spent the next hour explaining our plan. Using my words with the precision of a surgeon wielding his scalpel, I detailed everything from our approach, to all the players involved, to exposure levels within each of the three potential deals, to ballpark financial figures. Understanding that time constraints were playing a major role in every facet of what we were trying to achieve, Andreu was able to stay with me and see the reasoning for trying to position all three deals at the same time.

Through tinted glass, I watched Long Island whiz by as we continued our discussion.

"So, you will essentially be conducting each deal as if it is the only deal," Andreu said.

"Exactly. We set them all up and pick the one we like best. We come up with a solid, well-staged out for the two we decide to pass on. You know, to keep all relations as strong as possible."

"As if something unexpected has happened from our end."

"Perhaps."

"Won't the others be a bit pissed when they read about the deal that was, in fact, made?"

"Andreu, don't worry about that. Trust me, some element of that made deal will be the nucleus of the reason they're given for our backing out with them. What we tell them will perfectly explain why the deal we did works for us today, and why theirs didn't, thus leaving the door open to them with regard to any potential future business. Besides, we don't really have a fucking choice here. It's just too risky to pursue one deal exclusively."

"Whatever you say, Jonah. I trust you."

"Good. Because it's time for the next order of business."

"And what's that?"

I took another sip of my Diet Coke.

"Each prospect is going to want some good faith cash up front. Meaning they are going to want some money, as a gesture of good faith on our part, even above the initial deposit required while we do our due diligence. Pretty much just a guarantee from us that we are not wasting their time, since they will need to put their own time and resources into pursuing such a deal."

"This is normally how it works?" asked Andreu.

"It is."

"Then that's what we do. How much cash are we talking about?"

"Not much at all. Anywhere between fifty and a hundred thousand, depending on the landlord. Only thing that sucks is that we won't be able to retrieve the money from the two deals we pass on. But without it, we'll never get everyone to the table."

"We eat the good faith cash from the two deals we don't do?"

"There's no way around this if we're to do it right. We'll just work the loss into our final target numbers."

"You just tell me how much, and where to have the money wired."

"Good. I'll have all the information you need probably by the weekend, the end of the day tomorrow. Now —"

Andreu and I spoke for a few more minutes before hanging up. Everything was falling perfectly in place. Most important, Andreu Zhamovsky was doing what he had said he would. Trust us. Because of this trust, the team was already moving at a furious pace.

I glanced at the seat next to me, my eyes settling on my briefcase. Inside, between some files, was my cigar case. Made from dark leather, it's the perfect size for keeping close. Wide enough to hold three thick, stocky cigars side by side, but thin enough to fit perfectly into my suits' inside jacket pockets. I grabbed it and slid off the top, exposing the top portion of the three Monte Cristo #2s inside.

I turned my attention to the TV, deciding I would take a moment to check on some stock quotes from the ticker streaming across the bottom of the flat-panel screen. As my eyes fixated on the shiny rectangle, I raised the open cigar case. I stopped it within an inch of my nostrils, taking a couple of nice, long whiffs, savoring the aroma. My eyes never strayed from the tiny letters skating across the bottom of the screen.

My cell phone rang. Without moving the cigar case or my head,

I raised the mobile device with my free hand to where I could see the caller ID by simply moving my eyes. It was Perry. I dropped the leather case back into my briefcase, and hit send.

"What's up?"

"Apples."

"Apples," I mimicked.

"Special green ones James's wife loves. I'm on my way over to his office right now, so I figured I'd arm him with a little surprise for the missus for when he goes home this evening. Apparently she only likes to buy them from this one store, and I happened to be passing by, so —"

"Passing by," I cut her off. "Sounds more like looking to turn on that subtle little charm of yours right from the get go."

"Gee, you think," she said innocently, mocking me.

"How many blocks out of the way did you have to go? Seven?"

"Eleven."

We both laughed.

"It's nice to hear you laugh. Things are okay?"

Perry knew exactly what things I was referring to.

"Sure. Things are fine."

I hated interrupting her playful tone, but I guess I just needed to ask. Looking back now I'm curious which I was more concerned about at that moment. Her well-being or that of my deal.

"I'm telling you," she continued, "anyway I didn't call because I'm looking for your shoulder."

"Ah. Tell me, what part of my body is it that you're looking for?"

"Your unfortunately small, yet sometimes surprising brain. I need to talk elevators."

"What's up?"

"Twelve sixty-eight Sixth Avenue. They have a full elevator bank that hasn't been properly upgraded."

"Regarding what?"

"Motor."

"Four separate elevator banks total. Correct?"

"Correct."

"And the other three?"

"Perfect. Each has gone through a full restoration of all systems within the last three years."

"So then why the —"

"Let's just say ownership wasn't exactly expecting the last few years. Like a lot of city properties, they're strapped for funds. The final elevator bank is teetering on the brink of questionable stability, but they figured they had some time before having to deal with it."

"Are the elevators safe?"

"They are. But more importantly we're definitely talking amortizing the cost of the necessary refurbishing program across the purchase price. I don't care if it saves us a penny per square foot."

"Sounds like you're on top of it. Why the call?"

"Elevator consultant. I won't use Farkus again after last month's Lexington Avenue disaster, and I couldn't remember the name of the guy you used for the project at Five Ninety-five Madison. The guy from Dynamo —"

"Chambers. Sandy."

"Chambers, that's right."

"Ultracompetent. Corning still calls to thank me for finding him."

Greg Corning. Some twenty-nine-year-old asshole whose grandfather left him two mortgage-free properties. Our team handled all of his leasing. From day one the creep took a liking to me, so I always led the account. Truth is, in a perfect world I'd never even fart on a guy like this, let alone represent him. But in the imperfect world we do live in, back-scratching is simply part of the game. Because not only are his two buildings high rent, thus stuffing our pockets, but he knows a ton of people. And you never know what you may need down the line.

From anyone.

"You have his number with you?"

"I do."

I reached into my briefcase and pulled out my BlackBerry.

"Five-five-five-three-three-nine-three."

"Thanks."

I tossed the BlackBerry back into my briefcase and finished off my Diet Coke.

"You almost there?" Perry asked.

"Probably about another hour."

"You gonna stay for the wedding?"

"I don't know. I'll play it by ear depending on the time."

"Bash in the Hamptons, beautiful, exquisitely dressed women, open bar. I don't know, something tells me somehow you'll find the time to stick around at least for a little while."

"I may. But don't worry, Per. There are only so many tall, physically flawless model types I can sleep with in this lifetime."

"Oh, is that right hotshot?"

"It is."

"Well if you do stay tonight, do me one favor."

"Name it."

"I want you to look around the party tonight, and when you find the hottest girl there wearing the sexiest little dress, the one who starts to make your blood start rushing around inside your body, I want you to close your eyes. Are you with me?"

"I am," I said.

"Good. I want you to close your eyes. Then I want you to picture me in whatever she's wearing."

Ouch.

CHAPTER 12

As the limo rolled up to the front of Sam Archmont's beach palace, I was reminded of one of the true signs of real wealth which is beachfront property on so much land you can barely see your neighbors. The home was an architectural dance of glass and edges, a confident yet soothing structure that begged for the sea's breezes to rush through it. It was like the house from the Julia Roberts film *Sleeping with the Enemy*, only with a welcoming, positive energy.

I rang the doorbell. I could hear its faint, electronic chime ringing throughout the entire house. Within moments an older gentleman, dressed in a black suit and white gloves, opened the door. He invited me in, and I crossed the threshold into the massive front foyer. The walls were three stories high, stark white, with bold, abstract oil paintings hanging prominently. Each work of art was comprised of more intense, brilliant color than the one previous.

"Mr. Gray," the butler stated.

"I am."

"Mr. Archmont is expecting you. If you'll please follow me ."

Instead of continuing on into the belly of the mansion, we made a sharp left. We walked down a narrow hallway past what seemed like three hundred doors before the butler eventually came to a stop. He stood next to door number three hundred and one's entrance.

"Please have a seat in Mr. Archmont's study. He should only be a few minutes. Perhaps I can bring you something to drink?"

"Thank you, but I'm actually all set for now," I responded.

He nodded and left.

I continued on into Sam's study, placing my briefcase down next to the brown leather L-shaped couch. I stayed on my feet and slowly moved about the room. The office alone must have been a thousand square feet. Apparently, when Sam mentioned he was spending more and more time working at his beach house he wasn't kidding. The walls were adorned with yet more abstract artwork, except for the wall directly behind Sam's desk. That one was reserved for tons of framed photographs of all different sizes that seemed to be of family and friends. The kind of private wall, I realize now, that everyone should have in order to keep track of what's, at the end of the day, actually important.

A laptop was open on Sam's desk, turned on, showing an Excel spreadsheet, but I purposely avoided glancing at it for fear of appearing nosy should he enter the room. As I continued to absorb my surroundings, my eyes settled on a glass sculpture that was resting on its own pedestal in one of the corners. It was of a clear, large fish, exquisitely detailed, with a smaller fish of the exact same kind seemingly suspended in the center. The little fish inside was a brilliant combination of royal blue and yellow. Fascinated, I moved closer.

"Venetian."

Sam Archmont had quietly entered the room. He was wearing a white, terry-cloth robe, exposing more of his chest than I needed to see, and white slippers. His thinning gray hair was wet. He had a low-hanging, gold Star of David on a thick, gold chain around his neck.

"It's fantastic," I remarked.

"It's dick!" he snapped back. "This putz, Sy Feld was trying to screw me on a deal. Bastard ends up in Venice on holiday and figures he'll try to butter me up with some fucking blown glass."

I started laughing; Sam knocked a sip of Scotch from the lo-ball glass he was holding in his left hand.

"Fucking clown, but it does liven up the room," he continued. We shook hands.

"Please," he said, motioning for me to have a seat. "You look well, young man. You look good. Have you been in the gym?"

"I'm getting there as much as I can, which definitely isn't as much as it used to be."

"That's probably why I've been reading about you so much lately. You're spending all your time either in the office or on the town spinning your web. You're looking to close deals —"

Sam took a seat behind his desk.

"Just like your father."

"Thanks for having me out to the house, Sam. I know it's a big day for you, but as I explained earlier I'm in a bit of a time crunch."

"Please, Jonah, it stops being a big day after the third time around. By number six it's little more than a reason to throw a bash."

Sam hit a button on the telephone, which was on his desk.

"What can I bring you?" asked a sweet, Latin female voice coming through the speaker.

"Bring me another Dewar's on the rocks, Catalina. And a —"

Sam paused, waiting for me to place a drink order.

"Nothing for me, Sam. Thanks."

"What nothing? I'm spending possibly my last moments on this earth as a single man, and you won't share a drink with me?"

I leaned forward in order to ensure being heard.

"Sapphire and tonic would be great. Olives instead of lime."

Sam pushed the button once again, disconnecting the line.

"You ever heard such a perky, spicy voice? Catalina — the name means 'pure.' But to see her is to have thoughts that are anything but. I'm telling you, kid, what a great little piece of Spanish ass."

What a scumbag. Late sixties, about to marry a stripper one-third his age, talking about the help as if he were sitting in a high-school locker room.

"How about you, Jonah? You sleeping with everything you can get your dick near?"

"I've always loved your knack for subtlety, Sam."

"Who has time for subtle? I'm an old man."

"My dating life is quite healthy. Thanks for asking."

Sam threw back the absolute last sip of his tired drink, which was at this point melted ice lightly colored with just a remaining splash of Scotch.

"Stop being so fucking proper. Don't worry, you're not talking to your old man," he joked. "Anyway, let's get to it. What's all of this about? Why the urgency?"

"Lloyd Murdoch. I want you to expand on what you told me about his...situation."

"His properties on Madison."

"Exactly."

"You mind my asking why it's of such interest?"

"I may have a buyer, Sam. A real buyer."

"Can I ask who?"

"I can't say. I don't have their authorization at this point. But I will tell you this, they're willing participants looking to come to the table with cash."

Catalina appeared with our drinks. I stood up to receive mine and clinked cocktail glasses with Sam, who never got out of his seat.

"There has to be more. I mean—I know you. You wouldn't have taken a ride out here if it was that simple."

"I need to know the whole situation, Sam. I need to know how serious the bank is about finding the right owner."

"Meaning what?"

I got up and walked over to the open window. I watched a lone seagull slice through the cloudless sky.

"Tell me what happened. The bank has to have a vested interest in this situation if a foreclosure proceeding for such high-profile buildings could happen so quietly. It simply must. No two ways about it between keeping not only the interested parties quiet but silencing the people handling the proper filing from the city's side."

I turned again to Sam.

"Your bank, prior to Murdoch's foreclosure, struck a deal to get whole and help him get his buildings back. A deal most likely contingent on both parties' abilities to keep it all quiet."

Sam wasn't ready to speak. He sipped his drink and continued to listen.

"I mean," I continued, "I can see why he's possibly reassigning funds. One thirteen Eighth Avenue is going through a twenty-nine million dollar renovation. At Seven twelve Third, he just made something like six deals over the last two months that all require full build-outs."

A "full build-out" means the landlord has to construct the actual space for the incoming tenant on their own nickel, which can run anywhere from $45 to $75 *per square foot* in a typical situation. Let's just say, for example, that one of the six deals is for 25,000 square feet, and the landlord has agreed to a $50 build-out. That's $1,250,000.

"It's obvious," I continued, "that the well dried up faster than Mr. Murdoch ever anticipated. Something had to give."

"You're always dialed in, Jonah. I love that about you."

Sam paused. I could see him mentally separating what he should and should not reveal.

"You're definitely on the right track, kid. But you've understood for a long time that landlords often find themselves in the situation of reallocating funds."

"I didn't get to Seventeen Penn Plaza yet," I continued.

The baffled, surprised look that came across his face was priceless. 17 Penn Plaza, a landmark office building across the street from Madison Square Garden. Lloyd Murdoch is half owner of the property, a building with a sizable outstanding mortgage. But he's not the problem. The problem is the other 50 percent owner, Murdoch's partner Graham Levitt, a wannabe player with a drinking problem.

"Levitt, the drunk that he is, finally bottomed out. He can't even come up with the mortgage payments anymore, let alone any of the cash for the upcoming lobby and elevator renovation program. And apparently he hasn't been able to for almost six months. Murdoch's been covering for him, and in return Levitt had no choice but to give up a portion of his interest."

I took a sip of my drink.

"How am I doing?"

"I'll never understand how you do it for such a young guy."

Knowledge is king in real estate, that is how I did it. Once in my world I made sure to align myself with as many sources of information as possible. In this case, Kenny Danzis. He's the agent for the property, a guy a couple of years older than myself. Tommy and I saved a 50,000-square-foot tenant of ours from walking away from a deal in 17 Penn Plaza in the beginning of 2002, when the market was for shit. Now anytime I run into the guy, he sings like a bird about everything going on in the property. Doesn't hurt either that he handles his liquor like some little freshman girl from Omaha.

"You put all those things together, Sam, along with the other financial responsibilities from the properties I haven't even mentioned, and Mr. Murdoch's got one hell of a nut to cover."

I returned to my seat.

"There hasn't been any press, which means a top priority has been put on keeping this thing pretty damn low. Am I right?" I continued. "Which means, I would imagine, one thing."

Sam took a long, accepting sip of his Scotch.

"What's that?"

"He's planning on buying it back. He accepted his default in order to structure a more manageable deal."

Nothing.

"Tommy mentioned to me that this guy has always toed the line. Is Gallo helping him this time around? Is Gallo helping him pull a Larry Peterson?"

"How do you mean?"

"You know exactly how I mean. Did he borrow from someone else to pay off the debt service, then come to buy-back terms with you guys before he accepted the default?"

Finally, the long sigh.

"I don't know."

"Sam, don't —"

"Jonah, I don't know."

Sam had never lied to me. I could tell from his eyes that this time was no different.

"I haven't been involved with these properties at all. I can tell you that I believe you are correct about Mr. Murdoch's intentions. But as far as any prior deal is concerned, I just don't know."

"How do I find out?"

"My turn, first," he retorted. "Tell me more about this potential buyer. How solid are they?"

"Diamond. They are triple A quality, want to pay cash, and they want to move fast."

"Why?"

"Again, I'm not at liberty to say."

"I'm insulted. I thought this trust we had between us was a two-way street."

"Let's just say they are looking to take their firm to a safer, more risk-savvy level, one that requires some strategic acquisitions in the near term."

"Are they looking at any other buildings at this point?"

Stick to the plan, I reminded myself. We want everyone thinking they are only bidding against themselves. Stick to the plan, get what you need.

"Not yet. I thought we should see how we could do here first, considering Four Ninety and Four Ninety-five are a perfect fit for what they are looking to do."

I had hit my threshold of saying all that I wanted to. We both took a sip of our drinks. It was time to switch gears.

"I hope this hasn't been too much of a bother, Sam. I mean your wedding is going to be getting started soon."

"Please, Jonah, never a problem. I see so much of me in you. Have since the day we met."

"I appreciate that. And I definitely appreciate you accommodating the fact that I couldn't wait to deal with this."

I had buttered him up just right. It was time for the hook.

"Tell me, who can I get the inside scoop on all this from. You know, about what everyone's real intentions are here? I mean, I'd rather not waste any time here if there's no reason to."

"Of course not," Sam agreed. "Jack Merrill is handling the account. You know him?"

"I don't."

"Top guy—I've known him a long time. I'll give him a call and bring him up to speed on the interest from your end. If he indicates to me that he'd like to hear what you have to say, I'll have you call him directly. This way I can kill three birds with one stone for you. Find out if there's a deal to be made, brief him on the situation, and give him an immediate comfort level with you. Sound good?"

My father once told me that business, like life, is all about a consistent string of victories leading to that one glorious triumph.

"Sounds excellent. I take it Jack won't be here tonight?"

"He won't," Sam went on. "I do my best not to bring too many business relationships to my weddings. Too many stuffy types tend to make for a glum party, you know?"

"I do."

"How about you?" asked Sam, swallowing the remnants of his drink. "You going to stick around?"

"I'm not sure. Wouldn't I fall into the stuffy, business-relationship type you were just referring to?"

"I've seen the way you party and I've even stared, admittedly inappropriately, at the girls you date. The sight of any one of them naked for ten seconds would kill me. You're my kind of stuffy."

CHAPTER 13

When I reentered the front foyer I was surprised to see all of the activity. A waiter dressed in a tuxedo and white gloves approached me with a tray of filled champagne glasses.

"Monsieur."

I took a glass, and before my first sip had even slid down my throat there was another waiter trailing with a platter of mini-quiche. I waved him off, and downed the sweet liquid in my flute before the initial penguin could get away. I took another, replacing the spot on the tray of my fresh drink with the glass I had just polished off.

Beyond the front foyer I could see the crowd gathering. There were men and women of all ages. They all had one thing in common: money. Some were more casual than others, but everyone was draped in designer clothes be it a Canali tuxedo or a Valentino couture cocktail dress. The rear wall of the house, leading out to the terrace and beach, was glass from the floor to the two-story high ceiling. Everything seemed to be made of either white or pale gray marble, and the women all looked beautiful as the summer sun snuck away against the backdrop of a clear, aqua sky. The amalgamation of separate conversations bounced between the walls, running together creating one muffled, monotone sound.

Thinking of all the work that lay ahead, I turned toward the front where my limo waited. Inside the stretch there were a couple more drinks and a nice joint, both items that undoubtedly would have helped me get a little sleep. I readied myself for my first step. Only just as I did, in blew all the reason I needed to stay.

She stood about five and a half feet tall, wearing the sexiest pale blue, clinging, satin summer dress that stopped a few inches above her tanned knees. She had on strappy little matching Jimmy Choos, and her toenails were painted a shade of blue that perfectly mirrored her dress. Her eyes were a glowing, icy gray. They almost appeared transparent. I know because she made sure to look at me as she brushed by. Her straight, chin-length auburn hair showed off her chiseled facial features. Her figure could have made even a blind man fall to his knees. I watched from behind, dazzled, as she sauntered into the house.

As she made it outside, standing just beyond one of the sliding glass doors leading out back, she pulled her cell from her tiny gold purse and answered it. I followed her, making a quick stop at the bar before my approach. I offered her champagne without a word as she ended her call. She smiled appreciatively, placed her cell back in her purse, and took it from me.

"Jonah Gray."

"Well, Jonah Gray, don't you think it's a little early in this relationship for you to be trying to get me drunk?"

"Actually, all I really wanted to find out is if your name and voice are as pretty as the rest of you."

Ever so slightly, the corner of her mouth turned up.

"Very smooth there, Mr. Gray," she said. "Very smooth indeed. Although, what makes you so sure I'm your type?"

"I don't have a type," I conceded, truthfully. "Although I did have a phase once. It was in college. Brunettes who liked to wear their hair in a ponytail and looked great from behind running on a treadmill."

Giggling, she extended her hand.

"Angie Sheppard."

I took her hand, which I couldn't help noticing fit perfectly in mine.

"It's a pleasure to meet you, Angie."

Few things are as sexy as a woman with a perfectly stern yet feminine handshake.

"Are you a guest of the bride or the groom?" I asked.

"The groom. My family's beach house is the one right next door. You may have seen it on your way, depending on which direction you were coming. From the look of you, my guess is that you passed it."

"And why would you say that?"

"Because you're one hundred percent city boy. You were definitely driving east."

"White, three-story ultracontemporary, perched on its own hill about thirty feet above sea level. Set far back off the dunes, possibly the best view of the ocean imaginable."

Again, the smile. Perfect, cloud white teeth framed by glossy, enticing lips.

"How long have you known Sam?"

"About ten years, since he bought this house. I know the whole family."

A harp started to play George Michael's "Careless Whisper." We both laughed.

"Are you here alone tonight, Angie?"

"Actually, I am. My father got held up out west on business, so he and my mother were unable to get back in time. I'm representing the whole family."

"Whole family, meaning you're an only child," I mentioned. "So am I."

We paused and both immediately focused again on the ridiculous song. More laughter.

"Nothing like the classics," she quipped.

The setting for the party was definitely happening, yet far from standard. It was very Sam Archmont. Very in line with a financially loaded sixty-nine-year-old party machine marrying his sixth wife, a twenty-three-year-old dancer from Scores. The huge pool had been covered over with Plexiglas, acting as the dance floor, while the surrounding terrace was where the tables were placed. No assigned seating, just tables to casually sit at whenever you felt like eating. There was to be no set dinner, just trays of mouthwatering hors d'oeuvres to be passed throughout the entire evening. Very chic. The actual ceremony was to take place by the water.

We started to walk together as we talked, and I noticed a few people slow dancing over the turquoise water as the sun continued to lower. The sky was starting to melt into neon streaks of pink and orange.

"Care to dance? I think we still have a little bit of time before the ceremony."

"You don't stop with the charm, do you? Are you as good with your feet as you seem to be with your mouth?"

Now we were getting somewhere. We stepped on to the edge of the dance floor, and casually, gently pulled each other close around the waist with our left arms as we held our champagne glasses with our right. I could feel her tight lower back muscles underneath the soft material acting as her second skin. I was so close that I could see the tiny yellow speckles scattered within the color of her eyes. Her subtle, flowery smell was intoxicating.

"I never asked," she continued, "which side of the marriage are you here for? You better not say you know the bride through work."

"Very cute. Actually I'm here with Sam as well. I came out of the city for a quick business meeting earlier, and he asked me to stay for the party."

"You seem young to be riding out to Sam Archmont's Hamptons house for a private business meeting right before he gets married. Should I be impressed?"

"I don't know. That depends on what impresses you."

At that moment a waiter appeared carrying a tray of chilled vodka shots in assorted flavors.

"Interested?" I asked.

"I'm not sure."

I was. I took one straight up.

"Why not," she decided. "We're celebrating, aren't we? I'll have one of the vanilla."

We clinked our tiny glasses and drank the shots, immediately placing them back on the tray of the waiting penguin. By this time the harp player had moved into Billy Ocean's "Suddenly," and we were again dancing ever so slowly. It was at this time that I noticed a crowd gathering on the opposite side of the terrace. We once again cleaved our way through the sea of guests. As we approached, we looked at each other as the thick, unmistakable smell of marijuana became stronger with each step.

Like I said, not your run-of-the-mill wedding. A crowd had gathered around a table that had a hookah in its center, a hookah being a water pipe with the extraordinary capability of letting five different people smoke from it at the same time. The apparatus is quite simple. In the center is the main water chamber and bowl where the weed is actually lit. Around it, extending from the center like tentacles from an octopus, are five equidistant, thin rubber hoses each with a mouthpiece.

This was classic. In spot number one was an older man wearing an Armani tuxedo, balding and holding a Jack Daniels in his free hand. I would have never guessed his profession if it hadn't been for one of his buddies yelling, 'Hey, counselor! You learn to smoke that shit at Harvard?' In spot number two was a very distinguished looking woman, slender and tall wearing some of the finest jewelry I have ever seen to go along with her black evening dress. She appeared to be a socialite type, the kind who seemed like she ran a large philanthropic organization or sat on the board of one of the museums. In spot number three was Teddy, one of the waiters and the crowd favorite. In spot number four was the bride-to-be wearing, believe it or not, something that resembled a barely there wedding dress made mostly of Lycra. In spot number five was Timmy, the florist for the affair and a man gayer than a pastel rainbow.

Everyone got ready and another waiter, standing on a chair in order to reach the center chamber, lit the bowl perched atop. Through the brown glass we could see the small pile of pot flare up as smoke funneled into the five participants' lungs. Ms. Socialite, coughing, was the first to pull away.

"Who's up next?" asked the man whose job was to ignite the giant pot instrument.

"We are," Angie chimed in.

"We are?" I responded, surprised.

"Trust me, charm boy," she continued half jokingly, "I'm not half as innocent as you think."

The crowd, drawn to Angie's sexiness just as I was, started to clap and hoot, egging us on. Truth is I didn't need any coaxing. I had simply been trying to be a gentleman and, I must admit, I was genuinely shocked by her versatility. Something that, for better or worse, immediately reminded me of myself. We took our places, and within moments were drawing the delicious smoke for ourselves, our eyes teasingly glancing at each other the whole time.

Eventually it was time for the wedding. Rows of chairs were set up facing the water. An ornate chuppah, made from what seemed to be a million different types of flowers, stood where the sea and shore met. A bit loopy from probably the wildest cocktail hour anyone had ever seen, all of the guests boisterously took their seats against the mixed sounds of the settling waves and the purring breeze. What was left of a beautiful day was creating a magical night. Soon the harp from up by the pool was once again playing, only now it had been brought down to the sand along with someone playing the violin.

I briefly turned around and admired the rear view of Sam Archmont's house. Then my eyes started to again come forward, stopping at the sight of Angie's striking profile. I glanced down, unable to control my eyes, at the blue satin spaghetti strap lying across her perfectly contoured shoulder. I lifted my eyes. Angie had turned toward me. Busted. She loved it. Again, the lip curl.

At this moment a man wearing what seemed to be a tight, white tuxedo with gold trim began making his way down the aisle. He was very tall and very tan, stuck somewhere between bronze and orange as a result of all the time he had spent at the tanning salon. The odd thing was that not only was he wearing a tallis, he was carrying what appeared to be the *ketubah*, or Jewish marriage certificate.

"What is that?" I asked.

"That's Rabbi Frank. He's the hottest thing out East. He's been doing all the weddings."

A telling sign of the apocalypse. The "in" rabbi.

"That's a rabbi? The way this party's been going I figured he was the stripper."

Angie started laughing.

As we made our way deeper and deeper into the evening, Angie and I never left the other's side. A band showed up by the pool and we did some dancing, inching closer physically with each passing song. The pool was lit with bulbs underneath the glass, light shooting up into the night's darkness from below us. I ran into a few people here and there I knew from the industry, introducing her almost as if she were, in fact, my significant other. There was that kind of a comfort level going on. What I still can't decide on is whether everything was really happening as it seemed or if on some subconscious level I was seeing everything as I ideally wanted to. She was definitely hot, oozing with sexiness, reassuringly confident, the whole thing. But on the other hand, I was definitely fucked up.

After yet another chilled vodka shot on the dance floor, Angie put her mouth up to my ear so I could hear her over the music. As her warm words hit me I could sense that her lips were only a hair away from my skin.

"I need to excuse myself," she said.

"Of course."

She gracefully pressed her lips against the corner of mine as she softly put her hand on my cheek.

"Meet me in one of the upstairs bathrooms in five minutes. When you get to the top of the stairs just make a right and keep going. It will be the one farthest down."

I went over to the bar and ordered what must have been my hundred and fiftieth drink, a chilled shot of Grey Goose to go with all of the others. Then I sent off a member of Sam's staff to fetch my briefcase. I still had some last minute items to go over before the morning's team meeting and my instinct was to head for the limo. But my sense of reason found itself trying, unsuccessfully, to get past the image planted in my brain. The one of Angie walking away from me on the dance floor, the rippling water's reflection bouncing aimlessly off the shiny material covering her perfect body.

Within a minute the staff member returned with my briefcase, placing it at my feet. I immediately lifted it up, placed it on one of the bar stools, opened it and took out my cigar case. Even just a few minutes are enough for a couple satisfying puffs. Inside were three fresh Monte Cristo #2s. I pulled one out and rested the large, three-chamber leather carrier on the bar as I clipped and began lighting the thick, wide end. I began to savor the moment, eyes closed, when a guy abruptly rumbled up to the bar beside me. I reopened my eyes just as he picked up my cigar case, lifting it to his nose for a nice, long whiff.

"Pal . . . do you mind?" I started.

"Monte Cristo #2. Fantastic cigar."

The guy turned to me.

"John Robie. Sorry, I couldn't help myself once I smelled the aroma."

John Robie was tall and in shape. His necktie was folded and in his shirt chest pocket. His top two buttons were undone. He was drinking a Diet Coke and reeked of way too much aftershave. Beads of sweat dotted his hairline. Again, he took my case and passed it underneath his nose. After another second's thought I figured there was no harm done. The guy seemed on the level.

"Not a problem. You've got good taste."

Truth is he did. There's nothing better to smoke, that's legal, than a Monte Cristo #2. But I only had these last three. Carolyn had ordered more that hadn't arrived yet so I wasn't feeling all that generous.

"How much you spend on a box of these?" John asked.

"Too much," I responded. "But I'd pay even more."

John ordered another Diet Coke. But as the bartender was pouring it, all of a sudden John started to nervously survey his surroundings. Like he was looking for someone, or something.

"You all right, man?" I asked.

"Yeah . . . I'm . . . yeah . . ."

He was answering me, even though he wasn't really paying attention to me.

"My cell phone—" he continued.

His eyes finally settled on mine.

"I left my cell phone!"

Then, in a flash, John Robie went running toward the house weaving in and out of guests like some crazed lunatic. I looked at the bartender who was placing his fresh drink on the bar.

"You think he's coming back?"

I looked at the bar next to the glass of soda where my cigar case had been placed. It was gone along with John Robie. All that remained was the small leather cap that slid on top.

"He'd better be—" I started.

I looked at my watch. It was almost five minutes, almost time for my post-party encounter with Angie.

"— and it better be soon. I've got an appointment."

I wasn't happy, but the truth is that what was waiting for me upstairs smelled a hell of a lot nicer than even those cigars. So, realizing that Robie was pretty jittery, which meant he could have run off with the case and not even realized it, I prepared to let it go. A couple of minutes later, I again looked at my watch. Eight minutes. I took one last slow-motion puff of my cigar and started to put it out in the ash tray.

All of a sudden Robie reappeared.

"Hey, sorry, man. I almost stole these from you by accident."

"Don't sweat it. You find your phone?"

Like I gave a shit. As I looked at the case in his hand I could see that one of the two remaining cigars, the one in the center chamber, was sticking up in its slot higher than the other. Almost like he had thought about pulling it out for himself before stopping. *Mother Fucker* I thought to myself.

"Yeah, yeah, I left it inside. I took off so quick because I put it down like an hour ago. But it was still there. Guess I got lucky."

"Figured you were just running from the cops," I joked.

I had noticed cops patrolling the beach after he ran. At that point I had run out of time for small talk. With my eyes I motioned to the stool beside me. Robie lifted the cigar case cover from the bar, recovered the two remaining Monte Cristo #2s and, as I turned back to the bar for one final swig, he placed the complete cigar case back in my briefcase. I turned back, shut it, and headed into the house.

It wasn't long until I found myself on the stairs. Instead of crashing in the car and working for an hour or so before freshening up and heading to the office, there would be no sleep. There would strictly be work, once back in the limo, followed by a quick shower and my usual walk to the office. I got to the top and turned right, just as I was told. Looking back on it now, the time I spent walking down that dark hallway could have been ten seconds or ten minutes. I can't quite remember.

Eventually I came upon a door that was closed but had light escaping out into the hallway from underneath. I knocked.

"Who's there?"

The sexy voice was Angie.

"Rabbi Frank," I replied.

"Come on in rabbi."

I turned the knob and opened the door. Inside Angie was wearing nothing except a pale blue thong and her Jimmy Choos. Her feet were firmly planted on the floor and her strong, perfect legs were spread as she leaned, far, over the sink. Her head was turned back toward the door as she spoke to me.

"The party's just about to get started."

She motioned with her eyes for me to look down to her right. On the black marble counter surrounding the sink were two thick, long lines of coke.

I went inside and closed the door.

CHAPTER 14

I fell into the backseat of the limo at about three thirty A.M. My skin glazed over, I smelled of a mix of booze and Angie's scent. I opened the sunroof and leaned my head back as the chauffeur slowly pulled out of the driveway. I listened to the gravel underneath the tires as each pebble was spit backward as the rubber gripped the surface. The sky looked like smooth black granite. The stars popped like Christmas lights.

Once we eased our way onto the highway, I pulled my attention back into the car. The top two buttons on my shirt undone, my suit jacket folded on the seat next to me, I leaned forward and walked, crouched and fumbling, a few steps to the bar. My legs were further apart than normal as I tried to maintain my balance. I poured myself some Sapphire straight up over a couple of rocks.

Before I retook my seat, I reached into my briefcase and grabbed a CD, Rage Against The Machine's *The Battle of Los Angeles*, one of three emergency albums I keep with me at all times simply because one never knows what may arise. In case you're wondering, the other two albums are Coldplay's *A Rush of Blood to the Head* and the Beastie Boys' *Hello Nasty*. I popped the disc into the limo's Harman Kardon CD player then fell backward into my seat keeping my left hand, the one holding the cocktail, high in the air so as not to spill. With my right hand I grabbed the audio system's remote control and immediately hit play. From the crushing, precise sound of the opening drum beat I knew two things. I needed to skip three songs forward and I needed to turn up the volume.

I dropped the small remote on the seat next to me as "Mic Check," or track 4, started to pulse all around me. I took a healthy sip of my gin then lowered the windows, reaching my hand outside to feel the force of the air as it whisked by, extending into the passing night like ribbon from a "Just Married" sign.

Straining my eyes, I tried to make out where the earth and sky met in the distant blackness. As the world continued to furiously race by I became dizzy, so I returned my attention to inside the vehicle. Once I did I saw an image suspended in the air. Everything else had disappeared. It was a woman, seemingly Angie, just standing there at the exact moment we met with that perfect, sexy posture. Her tight shape covered by the same exquisite dress. Again I lifted the glass in my left hand to my mouth. The smooth crystal gently met my lips as I slowly took a careful, savoring sip.

Once the clear, cold liquid made its way past the back of my throat, I graciously accepted the satisfied smile that eased its way across my face. My eyes, moving consciously slow in order to soak in each detail, began to make their way up her enticing form. Her delicate, tanned feet strapped into those spiked Jimmy Choos. Her smooth, defined calves that so easily, gracefully blended into her athletic knees. Her beautifully proportioned thighs as they met the silky material of her dress. And so on. When I finally reached her neck I could feel the excitement of just a little while earlier, in Sam Archmont's bathroom, as nerve endings throughout my body were connected through bursts of desire. I was eager for just one more look into her eyes. Then —

I got to her face. Or should I say, lack thereof. This was the exact moment I realized just how much my drunken mind was fucking with me. The vision before me was faceless. Was it supposed to be Angie? I quickly rescanned her form. Was it Perry?

By six thirty Friday morning, showered, clean shaven, and rejuvenated, I was already hard at it when Jake came into my office. He was drinking from a Starbucks cup. A *New York Post*, folded in half, was under his arm.

"So, how'd it go?"

Jake has this innate ability to intertwine weather and fashion. His tie always reflects the mood of the day outside. That Friday morning was gray and dreary. Jake was wearing a Gucci tie with a simple pattern of brown and black.

"My meeting with Sam or the wedding?"

"Both."

"Productive for the meeting. Wild for the wedding."

"I'm sure. Let me guess. His wife stormed down the aisle, chest out and full of purpose, to Motley Crue's "Girls, Girls, Girls" like she was at work gunning down the catwalk for the pole."

"Not quite."

"Really."

"Nope. The song was Def Leppard's "Pour Some Sugar on Me.""

Jake took a sip of his coffee and sat down. At that moment rain could be heard starting to fall. We both glanced at the window as diagonal streaks of water began to fill up the glass.

"Tell me about the meeting with Sam. You get what you were looking for?"

"I absolutely did. Even though Sam stopped short of telling me that buy-back terms had been discussed, if not set, before title was transferred, he did tell me who's handling the deal internally. A guy named Jack Merrill. Once I told him why I was asking he told me he'd call the guy personally, ASAP, to see if he's willing to field any offers. Or at least listen."

"Who'd you tell him the buyer was?"

"I just let him know that he would have to trust me on their strength. Let's also say it didn't hurt for those old, big-ass ears to hear I was talking all cash."

We both paused as Jake absorbed my words.

"I should hear from him no later than ten this morning," I added. "How about you? How was lunch with Jagger?"

"As expected. The due diligence scenario freaked him out. He said it was out of the question, even assuming his family was willing to discuss parting ways with any of their interests. "

"He actually knows what the word diligence means?"

"Unfortunately, all too well. And you know how stupid people are. He lives his life in this constant state of paranoia that everyone and their mother are trying to put one over on him."

"Were you able to ease his concerns?"

"I told it to him straight. That we'd be willing to offer financial considerations for operating under such unusual circumstances. So he goes on to ask me what kind of considerations I'm talking about."

"What did you say?"

"I said, 'Easy there, young Jagger. You don't just expect me to empty my pockets, do you? You let me know that your family is at least willing to listen to what I have to say, I explain what type of consideration. It's that simple.' "

Jake took another sip of his coffee.

"That's when the moron missed his mouth and ruined his tie with dill sauce."

"So, what was the outcome?"

"Said he'd mention our conversation to his cousin Leo this morning."

"Ah, Leo. The other cheek of the ass."

"Their fathers are due back in town this weekend. They're golfing at Pebble Beach. No matter the general sentiment of all parties, Jagger said I can expect to hear from him first thing Monday morning."

"You think the two dickheads will actually tell the old men?"

"Of course not."

Jake began to lift himself out of the chair.

"Which is fine with me."

I knew exactly where he was going.

"Jagger and Leo don't tell them, it only confirms what we've known all along."

Jake's back was now to me. He was walking toward the door.

"That the old boys really are looking to sell," I responded.

Jake stopped in the doorway and turned around.

"You're not as stupid as you look, pretty boy. Sad, isn't it? How easy they are to read? You put the four of them together, you get one big fucking piece of Saran Wrap."

Jake sipped more of his coffee. Although he had intended on going back to his office, we ended up talking about Archmont's wedding for about ten minutes as he leaned against the frame of the doorway. I gave him all of the details from the hookah to the harp music to Angie. At one point he was laughing so hard he farted.

"Now, if that's not a sign of getting older." he cackled.

"Anything interesting in the paper?" I asked.

"Aside from the front page moving on from the drug addict actor who's missing?"

Jake took the paper from under his arm, took a few steps back into my office and threw it on one of my chairs.

"Take it. I already read it. Hey, what do you think of this?"

Here it comes, I thought. Jake's idea du jour. He may be a hard worker, but that doesn't necessarily mean because he wants to be. What he really wants is to come up with an idea that allows him to live off the royalties, and then kick back in a silk evening robe a la Hugh Hefner.

"Little miniscreens in coffins, right above the dead person's face. You send in a signal through a satellite, they spend eternity with their favorite channel."

I couldn't even respond to this one. I just stared at him as though I could see right through him. He turned and left my office.

"Rich people will pay for anything, you know that—" he said, his voice fading.

After he disappeared, I put my nose right back to it.

At about nine fifteen, we all met in Tommy's office to discuss how each of us had fared in the initial stages of the plan. As for Perry, she too had made solid headway. She had received a very clear message from James Auerbach. He fully believed the board was ready to play ball. He gave his word he would do everything he could to expedite any potential deal. His game plan was to speak with as many decision makers as possible, then report his initial findings and plan of direction back to Perry.

The mutual feeling was a strong one. Each of us had done exactly what we had set out to do. We were all focused, intense, buzzing. Our captain had jumped right in with both feet, as always, leading by example. With the skill and balance of a tightrope walker, Tommy was tending to a significant portion of our combined affairs. He was working for us because we were working for him and he was actually enjoying the work load. The energy of such fierce multitasking was making him feel like a young, deal-hungry animal again.

At 10:00 A.M. sharp I was by my phone. Sam Archmont was the punctual type. It didn't matter that he had had a wedding the night before, his own nonetheless. If he said he'd be in touch at ten, it meant he'd be in touch at ten.

Three minutes later Carolyn informed me Sam was on the phone.

"What's the deal?" I started. "A sixth marriage doesn't entitle us to a honeymoon anymore? What's the world coming to?"

"Please. I was probably asleep before you. Whether it was the booze or the fact I'm a hundred years old, I'm not sure."

Amazing. The old fella had been partying and boozing all night at his own bash. Now he was up talking shop like he was in his prime. I couldn't help admiring his old-school, balls-to-the-wall style. At the time, I couldn't help hoping that someday that would be me.

"You enjoy yourself, kid?" he continued.

"I did, Sam. I did. It was a fantastic party."

"Good. Then let's get to it. I spoke with Jack Merrill this morning as promised. And, also as promised, I filled him in on the necessary details. Now, he wouldn't disclose whether buy-back terms had been previously settled on. But, nonetheless, he's more than willing to sit down face-to-face with you."

Ah. Such beautiful words. There are few things as sweet as those ultraimportant, ever-revealing moments in the birth of a deal. One of those moments is knowing that the person who will be sitting across the table is genuinely interested. Their not knowing the deal about to be presented is a thousand times better than they had even hoped is another.

"That's good to hear, Sam. That's all I'm looking for, a little of Mr. Merrill's time."

"Well, he's happy to give it to you."

Of course he was. Whether it was because I was a cash buyer or merely someone who could expose his little cover-up scheme with Murdoch, it didn't matter either way.

"Is there any chance of my swinging by this afternoon? You know, before —"

"He's on the golf course," Sam cut me off. "He'll be unavailable all weekend."

"Did he mention how soon we could get together?"

"I explained to him that you were trying to adhere to an atypically fast-paced timeline. That understood, he still wouldn't commit to anything over the weekend. He has plans to be at his house on Nantucket with his family. He said he could do Monday morning in his office, early as you want."

Not bad at all. Sam had done great.

"Think about what time for a second," Sam continued. "I need to grab another line."

Sam put me on hold. Waiting for him to return, my eyes started wandering around my office. Eventually they stopped at the *New York Post* Jake had thrown on my chair. It was folded horizontally in half. All I could see was the paper's logo and the day's headline: JUNE EASTER EGG HUNT.

Again, I looked at the phone. Nothing. Within a millisecond I jumped up, grabbed the paper, and returned to the chair behind my desk. As my ass hit the leather I let the back half of the paper drop down, fully exposing the front page. Underneath the headlines it read: "Prized Fabergé egg, worth reported thirty million, stolen from U.S. Mission to the UN on East Side." Wow, I remember thinking to myself. Talk about balls.

I decided to read the first few lines of the article, which started on the front page in a column running down the right side. It began by describing the way it went down. It had happened at 5:14 A.M. the previous morning. It was an inside job by the consulate's chief of security who, seemingly unbeknownst to him, got caught on cameras even he didn't know existed. They had been installed by our government as their ultimate line of defense even against our own employees and security staff.

Fabergé Easter eggs. Many consider these little masterpieces some of the finest works of art on the planet; I know this because a girl I used to date was infatuated with them. Any time we passed a Barnes and Noble she'd drag me inside to thumb through the big, colorful coffee-table books about them. She even gave me the book as part of my birthday present one year so she could look through it when over at my apartment. They were designed by, and named after, Peter Carl Fabergé. In 1885, as Easter was to mark the twentieth wedding anniversary of Czar Alexander III and Czarina Maria Feodorovna, Alexander wanted a one-of-a-kind gift for his wife. At the time the work of a young jeweler, Peter Carl Fabergé, had recently caught Maria's eye. Therefore Alexander deemed young Fabergé the perfect man to be commissioned for such a special gift.

I should tell you right now that simply calling these things "eggs" doesn't do them justice. These little wonders are some of the finest, most masterful examples of transcendent art in all of Russian history. The shells are decorated on the outside with diamonds, pearls, and rubies. Opening the shells reveals their innermost secrets: miniature rings and crowns, picture frames and platinum swans; golden rosebuds and miniature ruby eggs. But it isn't just the precious gems and metals that account for the eggs' astronomical prices, it's the craftsmanship. One of the eggs even holds within it a small train, perfect down to the last detail. Or consider the *Orange Tree Egg*. When a key is pressed, a tiny, feathered, gold nightingale appears from the top of the tree, to sing and flap its wings. Each egg is its own story that plays out in some wondrous carnival for the senses. Some of the eggs are so complicated they took years to complete.

The article went on to say only forty-two of the original fifty eggs Fabergé designed for the czars had been accounted for by 1979. That was when two of the missing eight were found in the basement of an old, turn-of-the-century home in eastern Russia that was about to be torn down. But because there is such little information available on the eight missing eggs, at the time of the article they were still pretty much in the dark. Aside from a general description—it was made mostly of gold and colored with blue and white enamel, as well as a rainbow array of diamonds and gems—and the fact that the egg was a gift from Czar Nicholas II to his mother, Empress Maria Feodorovna.

In 1980 the two recovered eggs were sold at auction. *Danish Jubilee Egg* went for fifteen million dollars, but today the value is said to have gone up to somewhere between thirty and thirty-five million. The anonymous buyer loaned the tiny work of art to the U.S. mission to the United Nations in New York City for display indefinitely.

The article explained that a guy named Lawrence Hart, still at-large, had been the moron who actually thought he could have gotten away with something like this. As I chuckled to myself Sam's voice came through the phone.

"Sorry about that, Jonah. Had to take that. The missus wants me out on the boat by noon."

"It's fine, Sam," I responded.

"Now, where were we?"

As Sam continued to speak I couldn't help wanting to just see Lawrence Hart before dropping the paper. I felt I owed it to myself since I had read the first portion of the article. And it was at that moment, when I looked at the front page photo of the guy caught on camera leaving the scene of the crime, the rest of the world around me simply melted away. It was almost as if everyone I had ever wronged in my life had just lined up and each taken a free kick at my balls. The moron, known to the world as Lawrence Hart, was someone I knew. And not as Lawrence Hart.

"Jonah? What do you think about that?"

Sam's words were falling on flabbergasted ears. I dropped the paper on my desk. Feeling seriously uneasy, I found myself making a conscious effort to maintain my composure. With everything that surrounded me at that given moment, I had to remain steady. I had Sam on the line talking a serious multimillion-dollar real estate deal. I had people walking by my office at a steady rate, able to see inside because of the glass doors. And I had hundreds of scattered memory fragments from the previous evening stabbing at my brain.

"Jonah?"

Finally Sam's voice tugged me from my stupor.

"I'm sorry?"

"What time should I tell Merrill?"

My eyes began furiously surveying my office. I needed to get through this conversation unscathed, while at the same time beginning to address what was happening.

"Tell him, uh . . . tell him nine A.M. in his office," I pushed out.

"Done. Meanwhile, it's Friday in the summer, wonderboy. I imagine even you give yourself an afternoon off here and there. What are —"

I was done with the conversation. I had gotten what I needed, but more importantly my whole life had possibly just changed. I needed to keep Sam happy, but I also needed an immediate out.

"What's that, Carolyn?" I blurted out to no one. "You have him on line three?"

I refocused the direction of my voice toward the phone.

"I need to take this, Sam, but, as always, I can't thank you enough. Enjoy the weekend with your new bride."

"I will, Jonah. Promise me one more thing, will you? I want you to —"

"Thanks again, Sam. I really need to run, but I'll talk to you next week."

Finally I was able to hang up. Immediately I hit the intercom and told Carolyn I'd be down the hall for a minute, "down the hall" being the team's code for "in the bathroom." I grabbed my briefcase and took off.

CHAPTER 15

I closed the stall's thin, gray metal door behind me, but didn't sit down. I placed the briefcase on the floor and stood motionless. I decided that in order to move forward in the fashion I was going to need to, I first had to let go. To just force the shock out of my system in order to make way for the clarity, the acute sense of reason, I was sure to need.

While staring at the wall behind the toilet, I reached out with my arms and braced myself between the thin aluminum barriers as if I were being swallowed by a black hole. My body was trembling. I could feel all of my blood rushing toward my head. Just when it felt as if it might explode, I gulped down some air and adjusted my breathing to match my heart rate.

I sat down on the toilet, still with my pants buckled, and returned my mind to the newspaper that remained in my office. Like I said, I had previously seen Lawrence Hart. Only to me, he was John Robie, the putz who had almost stolen my cigar case the night before.

Now this was definitely fucked up. Unfortunately, it was the smaller issue of a larger problem. My greater concern was that of a certain image that was gnawing at me, haunting me more than all of the rest. Me letting Robie, the night before, place my cigar case back in my briefcase as I turned back to the bar for one last swallow of vodka. Still on the ground in front of me I opened my briefcase. My eyes caught the cigar case. My mind was telling me "no shot" because of the egg's dimensions and fragility.

I picked it up anyway. I held it in my palm, and gently moved my arm up and down like it was an actual scale. My findings seemed to confirm my initial notion, but I couldn't yet let it go. Remembering that there is room between the tops of the cigars and the top of the slide-off case, and that Robie had started to remove the one in the center, I squeezed the bottom of the chamber. The leather gave. I took off the case's top, pushed the cigar in the center all the way back down, replaced the top and tossed the complete case back in my briefcase.

I began to shift, rearrange the rest of the briefcase's contents. Then just like that I got the surprise of my life. It was a black leather rectangular box. It looked like one used for eyeglasses, only longer and a bit fatter, closer to a square. I started to open it. The first thing I saw was gray, spongy foam. I kept opening it. My heart began thumping. I started to silently beg, plead with no one in particular to show mercy and let the bloated jewelry box be empty. And just as I did, there it was, slap in the face confirmation of what I believed I already knew.

Given my surroundings, I realized the most unsafe thing I could do was start examining the thing. I closed the box in a rush and buried it as deep as I could in the briefcase.

I took a deep, calming breath, as I refocused. I needed to be myself. I needed to walk out of that bathroom as if everything was the same as before I had seen the newspaper.

I quickly splashed some water on my face. As I exited the bathroom, I did so with so many questions. Why me? Was it supposed to be me? Was it me because I was by chance at the same party as Robie? Was Robie really his name? Was Hart? Was I being watched? Did anyone else know what I had? Would people be looking for me? Was it safe to speak on my phone? Any phone, meaning my office, home, or cell?

I couldn't make sense of any of it. Thinking back now, my

biggest concern was definitely one of circumstance. Had I been brought into this because of improvisation on Robie's — Hart's — whoever's part? Or had I been part of some bigger plan from the beginning?

CHAPTER 16

I popped into Jake's office. He was on the phone.

"Can I borrow your cell for five minutes?" I mouthed to him.

Without answering or breaking stride in his conversation, he scooped it from his desk and flipped it to me. I quickly turned and headed for my office.

I closed the door behind me and settled behind my desk. I had received five e-mails just since I had been in the bathroom. As I began answering them, I entered the front desk number at my apartment building into Jake's phone. Considering I had absolutely no idea who or what was responsible for what was now surrounding me, I had immediately become security conscious. I decided I couldn't risk talking on any of my normal phones for anything other than what was, well, normal. I hit the send button. Clarence picked up on the other end.

"The Wellington."

"Clarence, Jonah."

"Good morning, Jonah. How may I help you?"

I needed to be subtle.

"Clarence, I need you to take care of something for me. A certain female flight attendant friend of mine may be coming to town tonight, depending on her schedule."

"Miss Tracy, Sir?"

Clarence and Parker knew all of my girls.

"That's right. Anyway, being that she's a Midwesterner from a small town, she gets a bit nervous by the fact that I only have one lock on my front door. I wanted to surprise her, so I —"

"Say no more, Jonah. I'll have it taken care of immediately."

As I was hanging up, the glass door to my office opened. In came Jake.

"Why did you need my cell?"

"I, uh, was about to go downstairs to Starbucks and I had a call to make. Mine's dead."

I needed to forge ahead.

"No matter," I began, throwing him back his phone, "I decided against it. What's the story with —"

At 3 P.M., after dealing for as long as I could, I decided it was time to get serious about two things. Examining *Danish Jubilee Egg* and fig- uring out how to safely hide it until I had some idea of what I was going to do. As I was packing up my office, deep in concentration, Perry came sauntering in.

"Taking off?"

"I am," I started. "I want to get a few errands out of the way before settling into my apartment for the weekend. Got a million calls to make. I need to get my due diligence team in place."

The three of us had been planning that whole week to use the upcoming weekend for nothing other than deal orchestration. Because of the time constraints we were under for Andreu, it was essential to have everyone ready to move on the drop of a dime. Roof inspectors, system inspectors, structural engineers, environ- mental inspectors, elevator system consultants, attorneys, just to name a few, all needed to be in place. About an hour before this conversation, when I was prepping to leave for the weekend, we had all shared our lists of who we planned on using. Contractors tend to be a great source for market information, so we did so to avoid overlap. We needed to be as careful as possible not to leak the fact that we, as a team, were in the market for other deals, when in each instance we had made it clear to ownership we weren't. Keeping inspection teams separate minimized our chances of anyone leaking another deal to any given owner.

"Don't forget about tonight."

Her words stopped me cold.

"Tonight?"

"Jonah! You promised me."

Fuck. Auerbach, along with his wife and some friends, at Pangaea's farewell party. I had promised Perry I'd go with her, and now she was even more fired up because she realized meeting Auerbach there could mean getting a jump start on what was to follow the week after. She wanted to see if he had any more preliminary information and wanted to further whet his appetite. I had promised. I couldn't let her down. I wouldn't let my attention to the deal slip. For all too many reasons.

CHAPTER 17

Outside the weather was for shit. Humid, gray, and sticky, although it had stopped raining. Even though I lived close, I was paranoid that by being on foot I could more easily be followed. I jumped in a cab.

I immediately acted snotty and affected to the cab driver. This way they leave you alone. I placed my briefcase on the seat next to me, opened it, and removed the black leather box. I had surveyed my situation carefully. I lowered myself, hunching forward like I was tying my shoe, in order to disappear from the views of both the driver as well as people on the streets. My hands, along with the box, were almost at my feet.

I carefully flipped the top open. As we moved through the city my eyes, shocked and locked, took in the most exquisite sight they had ever seen. Nestled into the gray foam, which had been cut precisely to hold the egg's form steadily, was *Danish Jubilee Egg* in all of its enigmatic glory. The antique seemed smaller than the paper stated it had been catalogued for auction, but was beyond magnificent. It looked like something you might see on an end table in one of the rooms of Louis XIV's castle at Versailles, something fitting since Fabergé's heritage, as well as much of his artistic influence, came from France.

The way the egg was secured, opening the case displayed a profile view. I optically scanned the mostly blue and white smooth enamel surface. There were tiny, intricate human faces and graceful gold vines. There were finely cut diamonds, rubies, and emeralds of different origins and colors. I noticed a base for the egg to stand on as well, something not mentioned in the article. It was made of the same materials and care as the rest of the piece and was topped off with three golden lions each on its hind legs. From the way the egg and base were positioned, their total length no more than six or seven inches, it was clear the mythical felines held the main attraction upright. As I continued my visual autopsy, I did so in sheer wonderment, questioning the whole time how someone could keep their hands so damn still.

The experience of being face-to-face with such a well-traveled, treasured antique was overwhelming. A rush of excitement, different from any other I had ever felt, had me near shuddering, gasping. The egg's beauty was so interesting, so thought-provoking, like a full moon glowing in the midday sky. Part of me wanted to hold it up and scream at the cab driver, "Do you see what I have! Have you ever seen something so fucking ridiculous?" My better sense kept me in check. *Danish Jubilee Egg* was simply mesmerizing. Over the top. Each delicate aspect, whether the placement of a gem or a precious carving, had been done with not just intent but immensely obvious, deep, pronounced care. The beautiful three-inch Easter egg was imperial, brilliant, intricate. To look at it was intoxicating, invigorating, stupefying. The details, right down to the tiny, light blue elephant on top, left me teetering on the edge of incomprehension. *Danish Jubilee Egg* was the core, the essence of art.

The cab stopped in front of my building. I jumped out. Without moving my feet, I put my eyes on the front door then looked to my right down the avenue. My instincts told me to hop back in the cab and head for the nearest precinct. My reality, past as well as present, reminded me that upstairs was my only choice. The cops, for me, were out of the question.

I headed inside. Parker had replaced Clarence, the norm by this time of day. He immediately opened the front door as I approached.

"Good afternoon, Jonah."

"How are you, Parker?"

I crossed the building's threshold. He scooted behind the concierge desk as he continued.

"Doorman Clarence left something for you."

He handed me an envelope.

"Thanks." I said.

"You also had some dry cleaning returned. Shall I hold it?"

"That's fine."

"Very good, sir."

After about forty feet, still paranoid, I made a sharp left down a hall that led to the elevators. I jumped on cab number two and hit PH. As the elevator purred upward toward the penthouse, I found myself stumbling through the pile of thoughts that had been dumped on my brain's floor. I'm not happy as it is when I'm not in control, but I learned something different that afternoon. I discovered that one of the most difficult places to be is that of not knowing who's actually in control at all. I couldn't come up with a definite course of action because I wasn't sure who was calling the shots. I thought, was it, in fact, me? Had I just altered some game, one I wasn't even asked to play, because of some ridiculous timing? Or was it someone else? Could it be? Was there really a chance that I, Jonah Fucking Gray, was being used as someone's pawn? Someone's chess piece? Could someone really be trying to pull my strings?

I stood in the hallway by my front door and put my briefcase down. For an instant I looked at the new keyhole hovering a few inches above the old one before I took out the envelope Clarence had left for me. I removed the key, looked around, and slowly let myself in. I was so tuned in with my senses it felt almost as if I were an intruder.

Once the door closed behind me, and I had locked the locks, I just stood there. As I heard Neo in the distance racing down the hall to greet me, I even went so far as to say "Hello?" out loud, like someone was just going to show themselves, just going to appear and in one breath make sense of everything. When Neo reached me, instead of dropping onto my back for our usual greeting, I scooped him up in my right hand using the briefcase still in my left for balance. As much as I wanted to just fall into the cushion of comfort that usually comes from being in my apartment, I couldn't. Not yet, not with everything that had just taken place. I began in the kitchen and briskly, yet carefully, moved from room to room making sure everything seemed cool. My eyes were peeled, the whole while Neo trying to lick my face. Once I made it through my bedroom closet I felt safe. I placed my briefcase on the floor, playfully tossed Neo onto my bed then fell next to him on my back. Immediately he jumped on my chest.

A couple hours later, after hiding the black box in a brown leather Ferragamo boot in my closet, I was down the hall in my office. My computer was on, as was my TV, which was muted because Lou Dobbs yammering away was clouding my thinking. There were files all around me yet my chair was swiveled around. I was staring out into the darkening city as it was pelted with rain. I was talking with Andreu Zhamovsky who was on speakerphone. I was bringing him up to speed.

"Exactly. Now that we have laid the groundwork, each of us will be using the weekend to get all of our due diligence resources in order. The goal is to have everyone ready to swoop in the second we have the green light and all parties are in agreement that there is a deal to be made."

"Or in our case, three deals," Andreu countered.

"That's right. As we get further along, if we're even lucky enough that each of the three parties takes our bait, we'll know which deal is really the one we want to pursue. The fact-finding process will shake out a front runner."

"Have the preliminary talks given you any kind of an idea?"

"About what?"

"Which opportunity may be the most realistic?"

"Way too early, Andreu. To tell you the truth, at the end of the day I think all three are doable."

"I love that about you, Jonah. That 'take no prisoners' American attitude."

"Isn't that why you came to me?"

I was doing my best to seem as normal as possible and keep it all together. Then, a click. Call waiting. I thought for a couple of seconds about if I wanted to answer it. I looked at the call waiting: unknown caller. Andreu's next sentences were instantly reduced to nothing more than props standing idly on the stage of my life. I heard nothing. Except, now, the second click. It dawned on me that perhaps it was someone who could shed some light on what was happening. If I was going to answer it I needed to do so. Stay even, I thought. Stay undisturbed.

"Hang on one second, Andreu. I have another call coming in."

I swiveled my chair around, returned my attention to my desk and made the switch.

"Yes."

"Jonah?"

A pretty voice. A new, yet familiar voice.

"Wow! Hey—"

It was Angie. I had only known her for about twenty-four hours, and hadn't seen her in about fifteen of them. But I already knew her voice. That sexy voice.

"How did...I mean, did I..."

"You dialed it into my cell phone. Remember, so I wouldn't lose it?" she said.

I didn't remember, which wasn't surprising. I was a party sandwich of liquor, weed, and coke when we had last been together.

"Actually, I don't."

There it was, that cute, sexy giggle. I slammed into multitask mode.

"Can you hold on for one minute? I just need to finish up this call."

"Of course."

I switched back.

"Sorry about that. Anyway, I think you should be completely up to speed at this point."

"Good. I appreciate your efforts of keeping me current, Jonah. Being this far away, it makes me comfortable."

"Please, Andreu, not a problem. Close communication is going to be essential for seeing this through," I replied. "Shouldn't you be getting ready to begin your night out just about now?"

"I should. And apparently since you'll be in all weekend getting us ready for battle, I'll need to be partying for both of us."

"Then get to it," I concluded. "I'll call you if anything comes up."

I switched over.

"Sorry about that. I was in the middle of something."

"Is it a bad time?"

"Not at all."

We paused.

"How was your day?"

"Nice," she replied. "I lounged on the beach and read. Probably unlike someone I know. Was your day as busy as you thought it would be?"

"You could say that," I replied, dryly.

"You know —" we both said simultaneously.

"Please, you," I went on.

"No, no."

"I insist."

"I had a great time last night, Jonah. I hope — I hope I wasn't too forward by inviting —"

"I'm sorry," I cut in, "don't you mean seducing —"

Again, the sexy laugh.

"You know exactly what I mean. I'll compromise, enticing."

"That works just fine."

"Then I apologize if I was too forward enticing you into the bathroom."

"Please, there's really no reason to be doling out apologies here. After what I was looking at when that door opened, I've never been so excited to enter a bathroom in my life."

"Well then maybe we can reenact the whole scenario again tonight."

I was confused.

"Aren't you out on the island?"

"Yeah, but I plan on heading into the city in a little bit. You know, since the weather is so gross. It's not exactly a beach weekend, so I figured I'd stay at the family apartment up on Lexington."

My pulse definitely picked up a notch, but I was having a hard time being excited.

"That's terrific. Really. But it's just . . . I . . ."

"A little too much enticing again. My fault," she went on, dejected.

"No!" I snapped back. "Trust me, this has nothing to do with you. Honest. I just happen to be involved in a deal that needs all of my attention this weekend. I promise you, nothing would make me happier than to be able to see you tonight."

Thirty-five million dollar egg. Billion dollar deal.

"But I just can't see you. Not tonight, anyway."

"I understand," she responded, forced strength in her voice. "Maybe we could get a bite tomorrow for lunch. Or maybe Sunday. I mean, you have to eat, don't you?"

She was right. And on top of that, it was important I remain normal in my demeanor as well as my activities.

"I do. Over the weekend for a bite definitely sounds like something I could swing."

As we continued to chat, I rotated my chair again in order to view the city. Rain was steadily falling, hitting the glass at all different angles from the suddenly gusting wind. In each drop I saw a different scenario, a different direction, a different fantasy. In each individual bead of moisture I saw a different possibility. One thing was for certain. Returning *Danish Jubilee Egg* was not yet a possibility. It couldn't be, not until I knew more.

CHAPTER 18

At nine forty-five I walked out the front of my building. Perry was waiting for me in the backseat of a chauffeured Town Car.

"Hey," I said as I jumped in. "You owe me one for this."

"Please, Jonah. Haven't you ever heard the expression 'taking one for the team'? Besides, since when don't you like an excuse to party a little bit?"

Not fifty feet after the driver pulled out, he stopped short.

"What is it?" I said, a touch nervous, as I leaned forward.

Looking at me as if I were a complete pussy he replied, "Red light."

I sat back in my seat. I turned my head, only to see Perry looking at me as if I was an imposter.

"Everything okay?"

"Fine," I laughed, shrugging it off.

"You sure? I mean you seem a bit jumpy," she tauntingly went on, sarcasm lining her words. "Not exactly —"

"Really, Per," I cut her off, "everything's cool. Just a little too much coffee today. Nothing some quality gin can't counter."

I paused before I continued.

"Where's hubby tonight?"

"Out with college friends. One is in from Arizona on business for the weekend."

"Are you sorry you're not with him?"

"Not at all," she answered. "They're annoying in a group. Besides, it gives me a chance to focus on what we're doing here."

She meant the business deal. But I couldn't, even in the middle of all the madness that was becoming my life, neglect what "we're doing here" also seemed to mean. We were meeting Auerbach, and his wife, who were going to be out with a few other couples at some swank hot spot. She had said she wanted me there for support, but the reality is these were all people she knew. And more important-ly, nothing that was going to be discussed, businesswise, was any-thing she couldn't handle. Whether Perry knew it or not, she had asked me to come along to fill the role of her significant other. I felt humbled, fortunate.

"What we're doing here," I repeated. "Right."

At that moment, as Perry turned and focused her attention out-side, I couldn't help looking at her form. She was wearing a tight, black skirt, a smart, white silk blouse, and a pair of killer heels. The slit up the side of her skirt went up mid-thigh, exposing a leg that I had trouble accepting belonged to a woman who had at some point given birth.

My cell rang. *Fuck* I remember thinking to myself as Perry's head swung back around. She caught me admiring her. I pulled the phone from the inside of my suit jacket, and looked at the caller ID. The number was unavailable. I had to pick up. She would have thought it was strange if I didn't.

"Jonah Gray."

"Hey, Jonah."

It was Angie again.

"Hey," I said, surprised. "What's up?"

"I'm sorry to call you again."

"Seriously, it's enough with the apologies already."

Almost on cue came the sexy laugh. Perry could hear that it was a woman. I could feel her curious stare.

"Anyway, I was wondering if you had any suggestions for Italian on the Upper East Side? My girlfriend and I are getting a bite and I felt like trying somewhere new."

She was a girl with a house in the Hamptons and an apartment in the city, but she needed suggestions for an Italian restaurant? The only thing she needed was to hear my voice again.

"Scalinatella," I responded, without a second's thought. "The best Veal Milanese of your life."

"Where is it?"

"Sixty-first and Third."

"Best of my life? You sound pretty confident."

"Don't I always?"

"Yes —"

She couldn't resist.

"— which completely turns me on."

We both paused. Then she asked another question.

"Where are you?"

Fuck. I had told her I would be staying in. She had gotten my cell number from my home's voice mail. It's on there because business people are always trying to get hold of me.

"I'm sorry?"

"Where are you? I thought you were working tonight."

I looked at Perry.

"I am working. I'm actually on my way with a partner to a meeting."

"At ten o'clock on a Friday night?"

She thought I was lying. I couldn't blame her.

"Look, Angie, I really am heading to a meeting. When I told you earlier I would be working —"

"Please," she cut me off. "You don't have to explain yourself, Jonah. Really, it's cool."

I could tell she was disappointed. And although I really did want to explain myself, I wanted to get off the phone even more.

"I really do want to see you," I countered, gently. "You have to know that. I'm just smack in the middle of something right now."

"Say no more, Jonah. Please."

"I really do hope you understand."

"Of course. Where's the meeting?"

Again, fuck.

"Pangaea," I said, knowing that the sound of this hot-spot

lounge would only give her more reason to doubt my story's authenticity. After years in business liquoring up models and movie stars, this was the joint's final night in business. It was their highly publicized, VIP only farewell party.

"Pangaea," she repeated, which is never a good sign. "Well, I hope your meeting goes well. I'll give you another try over the weekend."

While I was pissed at how the conversation had gone, I was relieved to be getting off the phone.

"Please do," I answered.

"Good night," she said.

"Good night."

I hit the "end" button on my phone.

"Who was that?" inquired Perry.

"No one."

"Didn't sound like no one."

"Remember when you said something about finding the hottest girl at Archmont's wedding, and visualizing you in her dress to compare?"

"I do."

"This was the girl I used for the comparison."

It was at this moment that I looked at my phone. I hadn't properly hit the "end" button. I put it up to my ear.

"Hello?"

I heard a click on the other end.

CHAPTER 19

My Sapphire and tonic felt sweet as it coated my throat. A Madonna remix blared through the space, which was a relaxing tango of velvet, leather, deep, rich colors, and dark lighting. Perry and I were seated around a secluded corner table with three other couples, most notably the Auerbachs. Between thoughts of the jewel-encrusted egg in my closet I listened intently to Perry's conversation with James, which had taken an unexpected turn. He was taking the position of "broker, then friend" as opposed to "friend, then broker."

"I told you, Per, Cantrol's board is more than willing to come to the table. But you need to know it'll only be because the right numbers have been offered. Not because you know what kind of apples my wife likes."

Perry laughed with obvious, intended sarcasm.

"The right numbers. James, we both know we're dealing with a couple of dinosaurs looking to unload here. 'The right numbers' are whatever you tell them they are, and we both know I'm coming in here offering figures well above market. Which, being the broker you supposedly think you are, should scream only one thing."

"Which is?" asked Auerbach.

"That I have a buyer coming in ready to buy. Not just ready to talk. An interested party that is willing to put forward a number noticeably higher than what it should be given the current market conditions."

Perry, giving him a chance to let the words set in, took a healthy sip of her Cosmo.

"Don't be a dolt, James. Don't fuck this up and start moving backward because you're not reading between the lines."

At this point, Perry was speaking to James as well as his wife. A smart move, since no man likes to, number one, look like a schmuck in front of his wife and, number two, let his wife know that his miscalculations could cost them both a boatload of cash.

"There's way too much of a payoff here."

Now, to drive her message home, Perry looked directly at James's wife.

"Your man, if he plays his cards right, could be one of the players to close a major deal this year. Which means, Catherine, you could finally gut and refurbish the Montauk house."

Perfect. It's all about knowing who's sitting across from you and Perry had hit James's nonworking housewife where it mattered most, her ability to spoil herself. Mrs. Auerbach now had a vested interest in her husband's potential deal.

I caught the waitress's eye and pointed to my empty drink. My eyes continued to drift, soak in my surroundings. I couldn't shake the desire to, every so often, check that no one unusual was looking my way, which was tough since people seem to curiously stare at me from time to time. I've graced enough business publications for people to have that sense that they have seen me before.

Everything seemed cool. There was one hot blond staring at me from across the lounge, but I knew from the way her tongue was fondling her sultry lips that Fabergé trinkets weren't her interest. Not too far away from her, on a burgundy velvet couch in a dark corner, two beautiful women, one with red hair and the other a blond, shared a passionate kiss, which I stared at simply because I'm a guy. Relevance? None, other than, looking back on it, I believe those were the only ten stress-free seconds of that entire day.

I brought my attention back to our table. I looked at the watch I had chosen for the evening, a Lange 1, strapped to my wrist. The time was 11:47 P.M. As the waitress put my drink down, Perry spoke in my direction.

"Tell James about Gerry Clauson over at Dillinger," she said.

Dillinger is an architectural firm we deal with regularly.

Before I had even had the chance to open my mouth, a multiple spilled drink incident at the next table, and the ensuing explosion of bodies springing up, captured my attention. I started to survey the faces of all the involved parties, but a hand touched my shoulder from behind me. I turned around.

"So this was who you were envisioning in my dress?"

It was Angie. She was angry, but damn she looked good. She was wearing tight, low-riding True Religion jeans and a form-fitting baseball T-shirt, white with pink sleeves, that said 'skank' on the front in glitter. On her feet were spiked Manolos, pink to match her T-shirt. I know, the fact that I remember this is a problem in itself. She continued, pointing at Perry belittlingly.

"Are you kidding me?"

Everyone, for obvious reasons, was clueless, shocked. Especially Perry, who was being taunted by someone she didn't even know.

"Jonah, what's going on?" asked Perry.

"Angie, what are you doing here?"

"I'm sorry, bad time? Am I ruining your meeting?"

I stood up.

"I don't think you understand—" I started.

"I understand perfectly. You're just another narcissistic fuck who thinks he's the earth's axis."

Any other night, if I was the person I am today, I may have agreed with her. But this night was different. I ignored her, even though, whether I realized it at the time or not, I had heard her loud and clear.

"Angie, if there's something you'd like to discuss—"

"You're damn right there is. I don't like being lied to."

That was it. I do not like to be embarrassed, especially by someone I barely know no matter how hot she is. And not only do I hate being cut off mid-sentence, she had just done it twice.

I turned back toward the people at my table and addressed the group.

"I apologize," I began. "Now if you'll all excuse me, I need to go educate this week's fuck-puppet as to whom exactly it is she's dealing with."

Small bursts of surprised laughter sprang from the table. Angie, shell-shocked, didn't move as I stepped away from the table.

"Are you coming?" I asked, shaking her out of her stupor.

Angie followed me over to the bar.

"How fucking dare you," she started.

I took a long sip of my drink then responded.

"Let me explain something to you. Whether you want to believe it or not, the dark-haired girl who you just insulted is Perry York, one of my business partners and one of my closest friends. The man next to her is James Auerbach, a prominent broker we're involved in a tremendous deal with. No one has lied to you. Furthermore, unfortunately for you, I am someone who doesn't take shit from anyone nor do I take kindly to being embarrassed. Now, if I say I'm going somewhere for business purposes, then I'm going somewhere for business purposes."

I paused for a second then continued.

"Do you know how you can tell?"

Nothing.

"Because if I'm going somewhere to fuck someone else, then I'll tell you I'm going somewhere to fuck someone else."

She said my confidence turned her on, so this must have been driving her crazy.

"Look," I continued, pausing briefly to throw back the rest of my drink, "I can't explain to you enough how truly great last night was for me. Not just the sex, but the connection. But, truth be told, I don't even know you."

"Tell me then what was all that bullshit about me being the girl used for your little fantasy comparison?"

"My phone was still on," I said to myself in a Seinfeld-esque moment.

"Yeah, your phone was still on."

"That, my dear, was nothing more than Perry, might I add who's married, and I playing with one another."

"Playing."

Her voice had retreated a bit.

"That's right."

"How so?"

"Well, to be honest, this is the point in the conversation where I'd usually tell you that it's none of your fucking business. But since you're so . . . let's go with persistent —"

Unable to hold it back, she smiled.

"— I don't mind explaining that we've been working closely together for seven years, and people in that position sometimes have a tendency to get close. Sometimes we play games with one another. What you heard on the phone, taken without the knowledge of how it fits into prior conversations, came across as an insult when in actuality I was complimenting you."

Angie's lip curled up as I got the bartender's attention.

"What would you like?" I asked.

"Grey Goose and cranberry."

I ordered the drinks then turned my attention back to Angie. I didn't have a choice. I couldn't afford to have some psycho rich girl stalking me. It was time to let her know exactly how things were going to be.

"Listen to me," I began. "There is a lot happening in my life, the deal back at that table included. Now that's not to say I don't have room for exploring something with you. But you need to know that in my professional life I always — always — appear as exactly what I am, which is the strongest entity, in every way, at the table. What you did tonight, in front of those people, completely undermines me, and I won't have it."

"Jonah —"

"I'm not finished. I'm going back to my business partner. Last night was sensational, but I don't have the time for some carrying-on little girl."

The bartender put our drinks down. I picked mine up then looked her dead in the eye.

"Relax, take a deep breath, enjoy your drink, and call me tomorrow."

As I walked through the hypnotic space toward Perry and the

others, I could feel Angie's eyes gouging into me. With each step, the reality of what had just happened sunk in further. Angie, a seemingly stand-out girl I had just met, had already shown, almost at record pace, the potential for becoming that psycho-possessive, lunatic, freak woman all men fear. As my ass hit my original seat next to Perry, she leaned into me as everyone at the table carried on with their conversations.

"I must say, a fine choice. Very classy girl." she whispered.

I knew it was coming, but I was in no mood.

"Later, Perry."

"Were you able to get your little plaything under control?"

I looked over at the bar. Angie was gone, her untouched drink left behind.

"Everything's fine. Let it go."

At two thirty A.M., wracked by both curiosity and concern as I sat in my study, I decided I needed to enhance my limited understanding about Fabergé imperial Easter eggs. Where did they really come from? How were they made? What and whom did they truly represent? I wasn't exactly loaded from the night's activities, but I was past buzzed, and edgy about leaving a Web trail on my home computer. On the other hand, I figured, the alternative was setting out to find an all-night Internet café and I was in no shape to be wandering empty streets alone with a still faceless foe potentially lurking. My internal debate continued. *This isn't the office*, I told myself. *This isn't some place where an IT guy is monitoring multiple servers and employee Web usage.* I was locked away in my apartment, no servers, just one high-speed cable connection to the Internet, where I was, in fact, the sole IT guy. My need for facts simply couldn't wait.

I pulled a couple nice hits off a joint, strapped myself in, and began touring cyberspace. The lights were off so Neo, sprawled out on the desk and snoring, his moist nose touching the edge of the mousepad, could get his rest. Around us, the building slept as well. All that could be heard was the gentle whirring of the apartment's air-conditioning unit against the calm of the outside night.

As article after article scrolled down the monitor in front of me,

I processed the information like a baby meeting his first puppy. Each nugget of information left me wanting a larger chunk. And with each chunk I found, I started to grasp the rich, regal history behind *Danish Jubilee Egg*.

Peter Carl Fabergé, son of a jeweler, was born in St. Petersburg, Russia, in 1846. His was educated in Germany, but most of his jewelry training had been in St. Petersburg, and by the age of twenty-four he was taking over his father's workshop. Later, brother Agathon, also a forward-thinking jeweler, joined him. The two formed a veritable team, and soon greatness began to take form as other fine artisans like Mikhail Perkhin and eventually Henrik Wigstrom joined.

While it was the Fabergé brothers who laid the foundation—created the forum—for such works of art, it is believed that others, amazingly, were responsible for managing the eggs' creation. Perkhin, a Russian goldsmith, became the House of Fabergé's leading workmaster in 1886, and supervised production of the eggs until 1903, when Wigstrom took over. Each had their initials inscribed to betoken the eggs under their care; MP for Perkhin—the Russian letter P actually resembles the mathematical symbol pi—and HW for Wigstrom. Some eggs were without initials, suggesting other possible supervisors than Perkhin and Wigstrom, but those that had workmaster initials also had Russian assay, meaning analysis, marks that showed the precious metals' purity measured in *zolotniks*. A *zolotnik* was a small Russian unit of weight used from the tenth to the twentieth centuries derived from the word *zoloto*, or gold. Roughly four *zolotniks* equaled one karat; 14-karat gold translated into fifty-six *zolotniks* and 18-karat gold equated to seventy-two *zolotniks*. Because the House of Fabergé had a number of separate shops, the final order of business was a stamp that marked the city of origin. St. George and the Dragon meant Moscow, and for St. Petersburg it was crossed anchors.

That night I learned that inspiration for the eggs came in all forms. While many were fueled from works of art Fabergé came across while traveling, many were simply predicated upon Russian history. There were eggs that depicted the Uspensky Cathedral and

the imperial yacht, *Standart*. During a time of war, the eggs served
as a tribute to the military and Red Cross. Others were dedications
to milestones of achievement, such as anniversaries and the completion of the Trans-Siberian Railway. Though no matter what the
source was for each egg's material, one thing was for certain: Easter
meant an extraordinary Fabergé imperial egg to be delivered as a
gift from the Czar to the Czarina. A tradition started by Czar
Alexander III and carried on by his son Nicholas II.

Moving full steam ahead, I decided to split the screen into two
windows. This way my eyes could bounce back and forth between
text and actual images of the imperial treasures. From the first
antique that came up on the right side of the screen, *Coronation
Egg*, I was immediately reminded of what was most interesting,
beyond all of the history and accolades, about all of the Fabergé
eggs. Their striking beauty. Just like when I had first laid my eyes on
Danish Jubilee Egg, *Coronation Egg* had me captivated. This particular egg, larger than any previous and dated 1897, had an enameled,
translucent yellow surface of golden starbursts—said by some to be
inspired by the empress's gold robe worn at her coronation—so
appealing, so lustrous, it appears as a giant piece of hard lemon can-
dy that would pleasantly melt in your mouth. To finish off the overall feel of the piece, bands of laurel spun from gold diagonally
crisscross the starburst field. Black, double-headed imperial eagles
appear at each gold band's intersection, each sporting a small pink
diamond on his chest. The surprise within the egg is a highly
detailed, incredibly proportioned miniature coronation coach less
than four inches long that in and of itself took fifteen months to
fabricate. As for the coach's interior, red and blue enamels were
used to re-create the upholstery of the original coach as to not leave
even one detail open-ended. The wheel rims were done in platinum
and the windows with etched rock crystal; all the wheels moved, all
the doors opened, and there was even a tiny step-stair. *Coronation
Egg*, like *Danish Jubilee Egg*, astonished me by its brilliance. I truly
could have stared at the picture until the sun came up.

I snapped myself from my dreamy little funk and looked for the
most important information, the tidbits that in fact authenticated

Coronation Egg, before continuing on. The information was right there in the description: MP (Perkhin), crossed anchors (St. Petersburg), and fifty-six *zolotniks* (14-karat gold).

I knew I should stuff as much information into my brain as possible, but I found it hard to resist the temptation to keep looking at more of the eggs before returning to the text. I minimized the window on the left, expanded the window on the right back to the full size of the monitor, and continued to scroll down. Some of the eggs, *Lilies of the Valley Egg, Gold Pelican Egg*, I vaguely remembered from the coffee-table books, while others like *Peter the Great Egg* and *Memory of Azov Egg*, I didn't recall whatsoever. Like one of my girlfriends walking by Luca Luca's store on Madison Avenue only to see the new spring dresses on display, my eyes were happily transfixed. For just as it is documented, as the years progressed so did the magnificence, creativity, and boldness of the eggs.

At 4:11 I kissed Neo's belly and headed for my bedroom closet. Once there I swooped in on the boot acting as a safe house for *Danish Jubilee Egg*, removed the black leather box, and went back out to the bedroom. I sat down on the bed and placed the black leather box in front of me. I went to open it, but just before I touched it decided that since this examination would involve actually handling the item, as opposed to just ogling it in the case, I needed protection against leaving prints. So I hit the closet again, opened a drawer that contained somewhere between five and ten pairs of winter gloves, and took out the thinnest ones, a black leather pair from Coach.

I repositioned myself on the bed, carefully opened the box, and, in an act I found both soothing and alarming, extracted *Danish Jubilee Egg*. I held the antique up in front of my face. Even though her strong, bantam beauty was enough to permeate the darkness, I still couldn't see the information at the center of my search. So I turned on one of end table's halogen lamps.

Searching for the critical markings, I looked again at the egg's base. And there they were.

Fifty-six *zolotniks*, which meant 14-karat gold. Crossed anchors for St. Petersburg, the location of origin.

My eyes kept going, looking for the head workmaster's initials. I couldn't remember what the two guys' names were. I thought, MW, H.P, M.W.

Perkhin and Wigstrom. The two sets of initials were MP and HW. But it didn't matter.

No MP. No HW.

No initials whatsoever.

CHAPTER 20

The following morning, Saturday, I headed out into the still resting city. The time was 5:02 A.M. The warm, fleeting breeze felt soothing as I hailed a cab. *Danish Jubilee Egg* was resting safely in its case, which in turn was neatly concealed in the half-empty Dunkin' Donuts box I was carrying.

Since returning from Pangaea some four hours earlier I had done nothing but read up on Fabergé eggs then sat on my terrace with Neo and a baseball bat taking the occasional snort of a bump or hit of a joint. The thought of turning the egg over to the police entered my mind, but I admit only briefly. They would never believe my story, and I couldn't risk that no one from the party would remember Robie Hart. I simply would have come off as an accomplice who'd suddenly grown a conscience. Besides, like I said earlier, for me the cops weren't even an option. Someone in my own history had made sure of that. So as much as I wanted the egg near, I needed to make sure it was safe.

After a quick cab ride up to 77th between Park and Madison, I hurriedly pushed my key into the front door of my father's four-story brownstone, which was passed down to him from my grandfather. I punched in the alarm code, shut and locked the door behind me then stepped into the main foyer.

To my left was the dining room, a boxy, high-ceilinged enclave with a long, golden oak table and an overly elaborate crystal chandelier. There were two Waterford candlesticks on the table, as well as a couple of others that matched a set atop the credenzas and buffets around the room's perimeter. The walls were covered with a cream-colored paper that contained vertically interspersed vines of soft, beige velvet. On the ground, in front of the head of the table's chair and slightly off to the left, was a buzzer that sounded only in the kitchen to summon the waitstaff.

To my right was the main living room, or as my father liked to call it "The Parlor." I took a few steps toward it and stopped in the doorway. The room was warm, rich. It had red-based, Far Eastern rugs covering most of the dark, Brazilian cherry wood-paneled floor and big, beautiful couches and loveseats made of thick yet soft auburn leather. The main coffee table had a brass base and a black-and-white marbled granite top, and matched the many end tables that were at all times, this moment included, adorned with an assortment of ceramic and glass vases full of fresh flowers exploding with color. The walls were spotted with an eclectic array of framed artworks from limited edition Maxfield Parrish and Andy Warhol prints to the haunting moonlit paintings of Ralph Albert Blakelock, one of which hung slightly off center over the fireplace. To my immediate left, snug against the center of the western wall, was a black Bombay-style three-drawer chest with a burnt orange lattice-work design. The complete works of Shakespeare, all thirty-seven plays, one hundred fifty-four sonnets, and miscellaneous verse stood on top held upright by simple bronze bookends. Next to them was an amber, lacquered porcelain lamp with a silk shade. Aside from anything to do with money, spending it or making it, these books were the only thing I ever remember my father reading. He loved them. So I loved them. So much, in fact, I was a Shakespeare legend with my friends in high school. The small, rare olive green antique books were lined up in the order they were written. On a few occasions I'd asked my father why he cared for the books the way he did. He always gave the same answer. "Someone we both know told me they're the perfect study in human nature." My mother, I figured. In the far corner was an old Steinway & Sons grand piano that I was told ever since I was a boy to stay away from. On top of the piano sat

Pop's prized collection of antique cigar humidors.

Once I had removed *Danish Jubilee Egg*'s box from the larger, less sturdy one, which I dropped off in the kitchen, I headed up the house's central staircase to the second floor. As I ascended in the darkness my eyes caught traces of the Ia (pronounced ee-uh) originals lining the wall next to me, drawings of wild animals done with the most intensely obsessive, almost *Rain Man*-like, detail. Each, whether it was a zebra or a tiger or a puma, was simply gray charcoal strokes on white paper. There were four separate pieces, and each was so lifelike, so ready to jump off the wall, it was almost startling. Even in the darkness the different animals' eyes were struggling to show an emotion, a story. My father, so I had been told, had come across Ia in his European travels around the time I was a young boy. The artist's work has been lining the townhouse's staircase ever since.

All of the common area floors were hardwood, so I was doing my best to be as quiet as I could. Once on the second floor, I headed straight for Pop's study. The room had a creaky, old door, so I decided to leave it open. My steps were no longer a concern since I was now on brown carpet. As I went for the desktop lamp, paranoia again grabbed hold of me and I began to ponder someone waiting for me outside, surveying the house. If this was in fact the case, they already knew I was inside. A light would give them not only my location, but the location of the egg.

I continued to navigate using only the predawn light. The room was in the same style of my own study, which made sense since I had copied most of it. The back wall was carefully speckled with framed photos of him and my mother, most of them black-and-white. On his desk a sterling silver Tiffany cup held some of his Writers Edition Mont Blanc pens, limited edition writing instruments crafted to honor some of history's greatest authors. It also contained a letter opener and a hand-held magnifying glass I'd never seen him touch. The pens are some of the finest in the world, and the only ones Pop ever liked to use. He always had one or two with him. They would bounce back and forth between his home study and his office. That morning I remember being able to see the sterling silver "snake" clip of Agatha Christie's 1920's-style tribute as well as the marbled, midnight blue cap of the pen designed for Edgar Allan Poe. Alexandre Dumas was there in the Tiffany cup that morning also, as was Dostoevsky.

On both sides of the pictures the walls were lined with book-shelves. Of the ones to the left, on a lower, out-of-the-way shelf, the last twelve books were attached to one another. They swung forward and out like some tiny door, exposing a 13" × 13" × 13" padlocked wall safe. It was nothing crazy, just something large enough to safely store cash, documents, jewelry, Fabergé Easter eggs, things that were home for assorted reasons as opposed to the safety deposit box at the bank. The safe had been installed by my father before I was even born. Even though only the two of us knew the combination, we changed it annually for safe measure. This year, my choice, it was 034050. The numbers, in order, of Stephon Marbury, Kurt Thomas, and Mike Sweetney, the only three Knicks worth shit for the future.

I knelt and slowly turned the dial to the appropriate numbers. The safe opened. The main chamber was empty aside from two watches, a gold Rolex Presidential and a gold Patek Philippe 10 Day, and two nice stacks of cash. I say main chamber because this is the true beauty of this safe: The rear, interior wall hides a second chamber. All it takes is a push on that rear wall, and it slowly comes forward from the top down.

After a quick push, the important goods were revealed. A stack of documents that are rarely touched and my father's "serious" watches: An F. P. Journe and a Vacheron Constantin, each a tour-billion valued at more than a hundred grand, and an old, silver Audemars that was a gift from my mother and the spark behind my theory on the untouchable Seamaster. When I was young, before he would dismiss my asking to see the watch altogether, he would say, "A good woman asked me, not you, to look after it." I figured from then on, like the Audemars, the Seamaster was a gift from my mother. Only the Seamaster, which he wore often, must have been engraved with something sentimental unlike the Audemars, which hardly ever moved. I never knew where he kept the Seamaster. It was never in the safe.

I placed my hands inside and dropped off the goods. I put the rear wall back into place. As I went to reclose the thick steel box, a voice emerged from thin air.

"What are you doing?"

"Fuck, Dad!" I jumped back.

"Relax there little girl."

"I didn't hear you coming."

He noticed, even though the safe was now shut, that the door was still open.

"It's not even five-thirty. Everything okay?"

"Everything's just fine."

"Don't bullshit me, Jonah. What are you putting in there?"

"Nothing. Signed tennis ball."

"Signed what?"

"Tennis ball. Andy Roddick, the kid who won the U.S. Open last year. I met him when I was out last night, and he signed a tennis ball for me. Anyway, I didn't want Neo to get ahold of it."

"So you woke up at five to bring it up here?"

"Please, Pop. I'm up because I never went to sleep. The rest of the donuts I just ate for dinner are in the kitchen for your breakfast. Anyway, don't sweat it. Go back to bed."

Pop didn't move. He wasn't buying the story.

"I know how you go out. And it's not wearing jeans like some goddamned bum."

He was fully onto me. But I couldn't drop the lie now, for his sake.

"What? I'm not allowed to go out casual?"

I opened the safe. He started to come closer. As the door swung back I stepped away making room for him. He kneeled down to have a look inside. Before reaching in, he looked at me.

"Unbelievable," I said. "I put on a pair of jeans, two hundred and thirty bucks by the way, and my credibility goes flying out the window."

Pop reached in and pulled out a tennis ball. The red autograph read Andy Roddick, only it had been signed by me. I brought it as a line of defense against him asking what was up. I didn't want to bullshit my father, but this was the last crap I wanted or needed him involved in. The less he knew, the better. Safe in its rightful case, *Danish Jubilee Egg* was tucked away inconspicuously under Pop's documents in the second chamber. The same pile of papers that hadn't been touched in what seemed like my whole life.

Pop walked me to the front door.

"You look like shit. Why don't you hunker down in your old bedroom for a few hours and sleep it off."

"Andreu's got me on a tight leash. I've got a lot of work to do if I'm ever going to put this deal together."

"You ever going to tell me the full scope of what you've got for him?"

Why not, I decided. Archmont's boy had agreed to meet with me, which meant the buildings were in play. Give the old man something to help him fall back asleep.

"Four Ninety and Four Ninety-five Madison. Lloyd Murdoch couldn't keep up because of some problems he's having. The bank took them back as R.E.O. properties after keeping their foreclosure status under wraps. Apparently Murdoch found some new money partners then let them swing back to Gallo thinking, after making sure the bank was whole, he would just purchase them again for prices that reflect this market. I'm thinking he had already made a deal before he even defaulted."

"You're going to steal them out from under him?" Pop deduced.

I winked.

"Slimy fucker deserves it," he went on. "I like it. But he's as much brains as he is asshole, Jonah. He's a smart man with the resources and guts for a good fight. It could get thorny so you need to move on him from the opening bell. You need to trust your reactionary instincts, let them guide you. There'll be time for cleaning—"

"— Up the mess later," I finished up. "I know, Pop."

"You're one hundred percent sure the buildings are within reach?"

"Perry and Jake have each come up with equally attractive scenarios. Because of the time constraints Prevkos has put us under we're working each deal as if it is the only one. We want each principal to engage with us as if they're negotiating with themselves, not each other. Once we've got our diamond, we simply discard the rocks."

"Can be a dangerous game, Jonah."

"Yes, it can. But not if the three potential prospects never get wind of each other."

"Who are the others?"

"Cantrol Petroleum and the Slevin clan."

"All heavy hitters. Just be careful here. Any of these people get wind of the fact you're playing with them, you could find yourself neck deep in —"

"Pop," I cut him off, looking at my watch. "Too early for anything that even approaches a lecture. Besides, haven't I made the right decisions so far in getting where I am?"

"And where's that, big shot? You let that kind of mentality stick around, you keep looking down at the ground from your little nest instead of looking up at the rest of the tree, you'll be knocked off faster than you can say 'has-been'."

"You're right, Pop," I agreed. "You know what I'm saying; I'm just tired."

Pop put his hand on my cheek, sighed, and gave me a gentle, affectionate pat.

"You're a good kid," he said.

Then he turned and headed for the stairs.

"Now try and get yourself some sleep. Sounds like you're going to need it."

CHAPTER 21

Neo and I took in daybreak on the terrace. It was a beautiful summer morning, not a white trace in the sky. Having simply tossed a couple of the donuts to make room in the box, I couldn't remember the last thing I had eaten, but I wasn't hungry. I hadn't slept, but I wasn't tired because I wouldn't allow myself to be. I simply had too many uncertainties circling. My laptop was open and files were everywhere. I was doing everything to keep my head in the real estate game, in the deal. Neo was curled up in my lap, twitching every so often as REM sleep took over.

I couldn't understand why no one had come looking for the egg. Frankly, it was making me uneasy because it just didn't seem possible. Had Robie or Hart or whoever the fuck he was, dumped it off on the wrong person? Was this even plausible? Had the authorities taken him into custody? Was he acting alone, which would mean I was the only one who knew the item's whereabouts? No way. A work of art like this doesn't get lifted by some poor schmuck who miscalculated. There had to be more, but I couldn't put my finger on any of it. All I knew was that the more I looked over my shoulder, the more I realized I was alone. Eerily alone.

I looked at Neo, envious of such innocence, and took in every whisker on his adorable face, every slow expansion of his breathing stomach. Something then occurred to me sending an unexpected jolt of reassurance, comfort through my veins. I hadn't done anything wrong. I hadn't plotted, schemed or planned any of this. I hadn't stolen anything.

I heard a ping. I looked at my laptop. Outlook had put up a reminder on the screen. It read, "Bungalow 8. Pinner's Bash. 11 P.M." Paul "Pinner" Luckman was L's pin-thin younger brother. He had snubbed the family business, but the two were close. "He's too smart for meat," L always said. Pinner had been an aspiring writer since we were kids and now his first novel was being published. The bash, being thrown by his publishing house, was to celebrate the book's release. Everything had gotten so crazy during the last week that I had completely forgotten about it. One thing was for sure. L would have killed me had I missed it.

11:45 P.M.

After a quick "what's up?" to Teddy, the bouncer, I headed inside Bungalow 8. Immediately, the jungle vibe enveloped me, and I dove in to the sea of hot women and top-shelf liquor. The lighting, purposely tricky, gave way to sexy shading and intriguing, inviting perspectives. Actresses and Page Six regulars were scattered about. I could feel eyes licking me, but not in an unusual way. I surveyed the area, and before even looking for Paul went straight to the bar located in the back of the space, giving the entire span of the lounge a good once-over. When I was satisfied, I went through the plan in my mind one last time. Say "hi" to Pinner, have a couple drinks, blame work, and get the fuck out.

I found L's brother seated at one of the tables lining the room's margins.

"Jonah," he yelled, jumping up from the huge couch that appeared to be swallowing him, extending his hand, and pulling me in for a "guy" hug. "I fucking knew you'd make it."

"Look at you, Mr. Goddamn Writer Man."

"Please. This business sucks. This publishing house is so fucking nervous right now about taking a chance on me. The last time they —"

We continued to chat for a few minutes. I went on telling him what an accomplishment this was, though I couldn't help laughing inside at the fact I probably made in an hour what he made in a year. All the while I let my eyes casually drift around the room. Then, out of the corner of my eye, I saw L.

After a few more minutes congratulating Pinner, L and I headed to the bar. We got a fresh round of drinks.

"What's doing? I've barely spoken to you since I saw you the other night."

"I know it. My fault, it's this deal I'm working on."

Keep it loose, real. Act normal.

"I haven't even been able to see any of my women."

"I'll bet you run into a few of them here," L responded.

He wasn't kidding. Definitely a possibility.

"I imagine, knowing you, the deal's going great. Am I right?"

"I don't know about great, but it's definitely going."

My phone rang. I glanced at the caller ID. Unavailable number. I didn't answer it.

"You're not taking a call? That's a first."

"I was in the Hamptons Thursday night for this wedding, and —"

"You were where?"

"Don't ask. Anyway I end up meeting the hottest, most seemingly unbelievable girl, getting wasted, and having unreal sex with her in one of the upstairs bathrooms. Crazy."

"And that was her?"

"I'm not sure, but I think so. I can't see her number. She's been calling all day."

I wasn't kidding. My phone hadn't stopped ringing since around noon.

"And, I'm sorry, what was the reason again that you're not getting that on the first ring and inviting her over?"

I noticed someone looking at me. It was some guy who looked about my age, sitting at a table with another guy and a few girls. He was dressed in a navy, three-button suit, but something wasn't right. He looked strangely out of place. If there's one thing I know it's suits, and his wasn't exactly befitting of Bungalow 8 clientele. The cut, the fabric, it was all too — cheap. Once I looked in his direction, he slowly turned away and rejoined his conversation. I couldn't put a finger on it, but something about him was familiar.

"Turns out she may be just a wee bit psycho."

"Ah. The lovely psycho. Let's have another shot," L suggested.

"Why not."

We threw down another Patron. I continued on in conversation, although everything had perhaps changed. I could feel my senses sharpen, get angry. Was it possible someone was not only tailing me, but watching me from such close proximity? When I found an appropriate opening I looked again for the same guy. Though I couldn't be 100 percent sure, again it seemed like he was watching me. Our eyes locked for a millisecond then he joined in with his table.

I wanted to be pissed. I wanted to walk right up to the guy and shake whatever truth may have pertained to me right out of him. But I couldn't. Not that night. If I was right, if this seemingly ordinary guy was in fact on my tail, I was in even more trouble than I knew. He was a huge question mark, and possibly an even greater exclamation point, all wrapped up in one.

"I'm gonna break in a few minutes. I shouldn't have even come out for this, but I didn't want to disappoint your brother."

"Are you fucking kidding me? Jonah, it's Saturday night. Since when can't you party till five in the morning and still get the deal closed?"

Since never. But, unfortunately, this wasn't only about the deal any more.

"Please, save it. Peer pressure isn't exactly the way to go with me. Anyway I'm going home to work. I'll be hammering away through the night."

Someone tapped me on the shoulder.

"Excuse me, Jonah Gray?"

It was a tall, knockout brunette whom I had never seen before. My defenses immediately kicked in.

"Perhaps. You are?"

"Jordan Ross. I'm a broker with Penchill Group. I don't mean to be so queer, but I just wanted to introduce myself. I've read a number of articles about your team. You guys really do some great work."

"Thank you," I said, eyes hunting.

"Can I buy you a drink?" she asked.

"Actually, Jordan, you caught me almost on my way out. But hopefully we'll run into one another again soon."

"Oh, well."

"Say hi to Ronnie Winger for me," I continued, referring to the CEO of her firm as I turned away.

Jordan, bruised ego and all, moved on. L was staring at me as if my face had just blown up.

"What in God's name is the matter with you? Did you, for some reason, not see how hot that girl was? That girl who just offered to buy you a drink, which, by the way, has still never happened to me once?"

"I've got to get going."

"Jonah, is everything okay?"

"Everything's fine."

"Since you need to be up all night, at least share a bump with me in the john."

"No thanks."

"Then tell me all about the psycho girl."

She was the least of my problems.

"Tell you what," I responded. "Let's go for that bump."

The line for the individual, unisex bathrooms wasn't too long. Once inside, L turned on the water, pulled a small, brown glass vial from his pants, and unscrewed the top. He then grabbed a tiny, Lilliputian-sized spoon from the same pocket and jammed it into the tiny jar. In one quick motion, L took a healthy scoop of the fine, happy white powder and held it under my left nostril. Using my finger I closed my right nostril and inhaled. The quick blast shot through my nasal canal, leaving behind its sweet, synthetic taste before settling in the back of my now-numb throat. L followed suit with a couple of his own quick shots to the brain.

"So I'm on the phone with my annoying mother yesterday, and

for a change I'm not paying attention. She tells me she wants the whole family to have dinner next week. Like I'm talking to you or something, I blurt out 'go fuck yourself.' "

We both cracked up.

"Quick," L shifted gears, "best cab driver name you've ever seen."

I realize now that L was never a good influence when it came to my drug usage. But as I stood there, staring at him in a funk, I realized that times like these were one of the biggest reasons I was so grateful for him. He was always able to get me to laugh or smile at the times I needed it most.

"Baljinder Fingjammer," I responded, zero hesitation.

"Please, I've seen a million of those. Baljinder, Sukwinder — that's nothing compared to what I saw today —"

L, enjoying the drama, stopped short.

"Which was?"

"Suchinct Pratoomtang. Fucking Pratoomtang! And he was singing Elton John, turban and all, at the top of his lungs. Where do these fucking guys come from?"

"Very nice," I sliced into him as I checked my nose in the mirror. "You're a modern day Archie Fucking Bunker."

"What's the deal with the turbans anyway? I mean, are there nice turbans and not-so-nice turbans? Can one Muslim walking down the street take a quick look at another Muslim's turban and be like, 'I used to know that guy. He must not be doing very well.' "

L turned off the faucet and we exited the bathroom to a couple curious stares. As we reentered the bumping belly of the club, we stopped at the bar at my suggestion for one final shot. I needed one last chance to evaluate the guy possibly tailing me. Two more shots of Patron were immediately placed on the bar. I slammed one down then took one more subtle look at my target. Sure enough, there it was. He started to look in my direction, only to be surprised by the fact that my eyes were already locked in. He awkwardly immersed himself into his table's conversation.

Then came the shockwave as I realized why this guy seemed

familiar. He was sitting next to us the previous night in Pangaea. I remember because someone at his table knocked a drink over and we all looked over at the commotion.

"I've got to go."

"Fine. Just promise to get this deal wrapped up ASAP. I need our partying schedule to get back on track."

I looked at L. He winked.

"I'll take that into consideration," I responded.

As I began to make my way toward the exit, I couldn't resist the urge to possibly get some answers. I knew that it wasn't the safest thing to do, but because of the coke I could almost literally feel my balls growing in my pants. Nothing stupid I told myself, just enough to help me decipher who this guy was. Besides, the place was packed. What was the worst that could happen? Before leaving Bungalow 8, I sharply came up behind the guy.

"Do I know you?" I asked quietly into his ear.

The guy seemed startled. He turned around.

"Excuse me?"

"I said, do I know you? Because you've been staring at me as if we know each other."

"I apologize, but I have no idea what you're talking about."

"So you haven't been looking in my direction?"

There it was. The moment of truth. The perfect question.

"I may have, but I assure you it was inadvertent. I'm sorry if somehow I made you uncomfortable."

Countered with the perfect answer. Fuck. I was right back where I started. Informationless. By this time the whole table had caught on to our conversation. I wanted to bring up Pangaea, but decided against causing even more of a scene and perhaps further endangering myself. I backed off.

"You all have a good night."

I stepped into my apartment and closed the door behind me. The front foyer was dimly lit. I could hear Neo's little feet trucking my way down the wooden hallway floor. When he reached me, he didn't wait for me to get on the ground for our usual greeting.

Instead he jumped straight into my arms. He licked my face furiously, and he was shaking.

My eyes spread open as if being propped with toothpicks. This was our sanctuary, mine and Neo's, and something had spooked him. I kissed his nose and put him back on the floor. Without pulling my vision from the foyer, I quietly reached into a nearby closet and grabbed from my golf bag what turned out to be my five iron. I began to make my way through the apartment. All I could hear were the sounds of the city beyond the walls. The weather was a bit glum, so Manhattan's evening sparkle was muffled beyond the windows.

The kitchen was clear. I grabbed a handful of Neo's treats then closed them along with my little pal into the guest bathroom, also clear, to keep him out of possible harm's way. I continued on through the apartment. The dining room was untouched, as was my study, so I kept going. The guest bedroom checked out too. It wasn't until I reached my own bedroom that I clearly understood someone had been in my place.

The TV, slightly louder than if it had been on mute, was tuned to NBC and showing *Saturday Night Live*. A few drawers were opened, as was my closet. Golf club cocked, I entered my bathroom to see my Jacuzzi had been recently used. But no one was in sight. The walk-in closet was intruder free as well. I looked through the glass doors onto the terrace. Not a soul. Now I was confused, yet relieved at the same time.

I returned to the front hallway and opened up the guest bathroom door. Neo was finished with his treats and just lying on the floor waiting. Upon seeing me he began to wriggle with excitement all over again.

"All right, pal," I said as I lifted him up.

We headed back to my bedroom. I was nervous, but calling the cops was out of the question. Thankfully, whoever had been there was gone. But, I thought, how the hell could they have gotten past the doorman in the first place? And for what—to take a fucking bath? I playfully tossed Neo onto the bed and buried him under the covers. He loved this game. He loved having to find his way out as

I pretended to impede his exit path. After about ten more minutes I kicked off my shoes and turned the TV to CNN. I upped the volume, grabbed the cordless, and headed over to the terrace doors. Neo jumped off the bed and followed me.

Once outside I walked directly to the patio's lip and put my arms on the banister. My eyes never strayed from the city lights, until:

"Jonah."

"Fuck!" I jumped.

"That is just the cutest little dog."

It was Angie. She was in a chair pulled back toward the building, out of sight if looking onto the terrace from my bedroom.

"You scared the — what the fuck are you doing here?"

"Your doorman let me up. I said I was your cousin. He just smirked and let me in. Guess he's been through this routine before."

I said nothing. I just looked around.

"Look, I'm sorry for barging in like this. But you wouldn't return any of my calls. I didn't know what to do."

"What to do about what?"

"About last night. About making an ass out of myself like some silly little child. I was completely inappropriate, and I needed a chance to tell you that I was sorry. I haven't had a real connection with anyone in a while and I went overboard."

I focused on Angie. She was wearing one of my Zegna custom-fit button-down shirts, yet only two buttons were fastened. It was white, and I could see my initials embroidered in black on the left cuff. She wasn't wearing anything else. A massaging flow of air brushed through the terrace, blowing the shirt almost completely up above her waist. She didn't flinch. I could feel her excitement growing as I looked at the top of her thighs.

"You had every right to put me in my place last night. I deserved that."

I could feel my eyes begin to squint with confusion. I was having trouble accepting that this girl found it appropriate to make herself at home in my apartment because she had been unable to reach me. At the same time my pulse was flat-out racing.

"What are you up to?" I asked.

Angie grabbed the cocktail she had fixed for herself from one of the small glass tables. She looked at the glass playfully.

"Only number two."

She downed a long healthy sip then raised the lit joint in her other hand, which had come from my ashtray, to her lips. She took a nice drag leaving her lipstick on the end of it.

"Can't we just pick up where we left off in the Hamptons?"

I wanted to. But as hard as this was all making me, I couldn't shake the feeling that something was fucked up. The timing of all of this was too perfect. The egg was still shrouded in mystery, yet all of a sudden here was this girl doing everything in her power to force her way into my life.

"Don't you want to kiss me again?"

She was possibly trouble, by chance a connection I thought, but alerting her to my suspicion was the potential for making things worse. She was in my home. And perhaps with a simple phone call others would be too. I decided my best option was to go along with this all being just about the two of us. Nothing else. At least for now, at least until I could get rid of her for good.

"Don't you want to feel my skin?"

I walked over to Angie. In my coked-up mind, which was wrapped in tequila, my goal was to keep myself secure and from triggering anything unexpected. She reached up and handed me the joint once I was facing her. Without another word I took a long draw as Angie unbuttoned my pants.

CHAPTER 22

Monday morning had arrived. Week two. As I strode up Park Avenue, the sky was so bright it felt as if hundreds of suns were scorching the earth. I stopped at my usual spot in front of Grand Central for a shoeshine.

Jimmy finished buffing my black Bruno Maglis and I headed into the terminal to take the route I walk when I need to use the bathroom. It was early afternoon in Moscow, so I decided to give Andreu an update. I dialed his cell number and hit "send." It rang as I walked. After only a few rings, as I approached my destination, I lost the signal.

I entered my usual bathroom, one that's out of the way and has a door so old it looks like a janitor's closet. As always for this early in the morning it was empty. I rehit "send" and walked right up to my favorite urinal. I put my briefcase down and situated the phone between my ear and shoulder. No answer.

Just as I was about to leave a message, someone gripped the back of my head as if it were a football and slammed my forehead into the marble wall. I never heard them enter the bathroom. The phone went flying. As I did my best to maintain my balance I was swung around and punched square in the face. I could taste the blood running from my nose into my mouth.

"The egg," the guy began, backing off. It was the guy who had been checking me out at Pangaea and Bungalow 8. "This same bathroom tomorrow morning. You show up without it and you're finished."

"I fucking knew it," I seethed.

With the quickness of a cat the guy charged me, pulled out a gun, and put it to my temple.

"I mean it, pretty boy. You show up empty handed, I put a bullet in your brain. You fail to show up, I find you, put a bullet in your brain. Simple as that. Understood?"

I said nothing.

"Six A.M.," he continued, then kneed me in the balls and high-stepped out of there. I took a couple of deep breaths, pulled myself and phone off the ground, turned on one of the faucets and cleaned myself up. I grabbed my briefcase and exited the bathroom.

I bought a large coffee at Starbucks, but before entering the Chrysler Center I decided to sit on one of the street benches along 43rd Street to gather my thoughts. The morning glare was gaining strength, and the number of people coming and going increased by the second. I touched my jaw. The pain had subsided considerably.

Soft punch I remember thinking to myself. Though the reality of being followed had come to an uncomfortable certainty, I was thankful to finally have something with which to work. And to tell you the truth, it was all quite a bit shocking. After all, we were talking about one of the most rare, valuable antiques imaginable. Yet here I was being threatened by some punk in a bathroom. Something didn't feel right. It was all too unprofessional. Or was that the idea?

By seven thirty we were all in Tommy's office forging ahead. Since I always keep new, unopened dress shirts and ties in my office in case of emergency — one of Pop's moves — I appeared clean and fresh as if my morning encounter had never taken place. Jake had the floor.

"I got an e-mail from Jagger this morning. There was nothing but a number, one both insulting and revealing. I assume it was the premium he wants on a per-square-foot basis."

"What's the number?" Tommy asked.

"I can't say. The lack of respect is too embarrassing. What I can tell you is that this number embodies both young Jonah's as well as my own suspicions. There is no chance in hell this number came from the old guys. Which simply means Jagger couldn't bring himself to tell them about the possibility of a deal once they returned from their golfing trip. My guess is that he and Leo came up with the figure after a few shots of moron juice."

"How do you plan to proceed?" asked Perry.

"Simple. I'll give them my number and one chance to get on board."

"If they don't?"

"Time being of the essence, I move on to Ray and Lawrence. They are who we need to be dealing with anyway. I imagine, at this rate, I will have heard back by the end of the day that my number is out of the question. Once this happens I approach the important duo in the family, get into some real numbers, and offer them a fair premium. By this time tomorrow morning, I will have acted appropriately in their eyes by approaching their sons first, and I'll be well on my way to getting my inspection team in place by the end of the week. Cake."

After a few more minutes of dialogue it was clear that Jake was dialed in and well on his way.

Perry went next.

"I'll just cut to the chase. Jonah was with me Friday night and saw that James is going to make me work here. I don't know, maybe he feels the board needs to see him break balls or something to earn their respect. I know how all you men can get. Anyway, I gave him a ballpark of what kind of number I'm playing with and told him to get the Board's consensus. I can't foresee any real stumbling blocks here. They need to sell. End of story."

"How about your inspection team?" asked Tommy.

"In place and ready to go upon my direction."

"And how about James?" asked Jake. "When are you supposed to hear from him?"

"Who the hell cares. Once I leave this office, I'm getting on the phone to begin riding him all day."

"Isn't he married?" joked Jake.

Perry sliced into him with unamused eyes.

"I plan on having a general understanding as to the comfort level of such a number by the end of the day, funnyman."

"Can you be sure the board will respond to Auerbach's inquiries so quickly?" continued Tommy.

"Not one hundred percent, but pretty close. I have done a serious job of outlining the timetable issue to James. He understands that things need to move unusually fast. Is he comfortable with that? I can't be sure. What I can be sure of is the fact that he understands I'm not yet looking for a formal written response. All I need is a general feeling out of his board, something that could greatly affect his own personal bottom line."

"Fair enough. Just be sure to —"

My cell phone rang breaking the meeting's rhythm. I immediately silenced the phone then looked at the caller ID. Unavailable caller.

Tommy continued, "Just be sure to keep him on your good side. I know you two have been close for a long time, but this would be one tough road to walk without his help. You hear what I'm saying?"

"I do, captain," Perry quipped. "Big business boards are made up of pompous assholes who usually only get where they're going because someone's leading them."

"Cute. Jonah, you're up."

"I —"

My cell rang again. Unavailable caller.

"You need to get that?"

I hushed the phone.

"I don't. Anyway, I have a —"

It rang for a third time.

"Fuck!"

Same unavailable caller, same noise suppression.

"Maybe you should —"

"Maybe nothing. I have a meeting with Jack Merrill from Gallo at nine. Until we speak I have nothing to report."

"How about—"

"All facets of my inspection team are fully in place. I spent most of my weekend making sure of it."

I glanced around, then looked at my watch.

"I need to get out of here. I don't want to be late to meet this guy."

I jumped out of Tommy's office. Perry followed me into the hall-way.

"Jonah, what's going on?"

I didn't break stride or look back at her as she tried to keep up.

"With what?"

"With you? Why the extra edge?"

"What extra edge, Per? Since when is my being focused cause for concern?"

"It's not the focus. It's the—I don't know—shortness."

Before I could turn into my office Carolyn stopped me.

"Jonah, I just got off the phone with someone named Angie. She wants to—"

"Got it, Carolyn. If she calls again this morning, which she will, I'm in meetings. All day. No exceptions."

Sensing Carolyn's angry, unappreciative eyes, I stopped.

"Sorry, Carolyn. Good morning."

Very important rule of thumb about New York City secretaries. They're all crazy. It is imperative, at all times, to keep them on your good side.

Perry followed me into my office. She closed the doors behind us.

"Ah. Now I see what's going on. The little plaything from the other night. What's the problem, Jonah? Having a little trouble taming this one?"

I didn't answer her. Not only because I didn't want to, but because as far as Angie went she was right. My cell rang again. I held it up. We both stared at it. My eyes turned to Perry. It was her invitation to leave.

"Fine, Jonah. Just do us all a favor and get this toddler under control."

She waited for a response. I didn't give her one.

"Whatever," she continued before leaving and slamming the door.

My eyes returned to the phone. As I stared at it, the annoying, outer space-like ring poking at my brain, images of both Robie and the guy from that morning in the bathroom blotted my mind. I had no choice. Angie wasn't going away.

"Jonah Gray."

"It's me. I thought after breakfast yesterday I would have spoken to you again."

Another Seinfeld moment. "It's me." No name. We'd been face-to-face three times in our lives.

"What? Are you going to try to tell me that it wasn't even better the second time around?"

"Angie, you can't keep calling and calling my cell phone."

"I know. I apologize. It's just that I didn't understand why you didn't call me."

Be careful, I reminded myself. Don't be angry, be tactful.

"I told you my weekend could only consist of a certain deal I'm putting together."

"So what was Saturday night? After you came home high and pumped full of tequila?"

"That was an unexpected surprise."

"I want to see you."

Call waiting. The call was coming from Gallo Booth West. I was supposed to have already left, which was why they were calling my cell.

"Give me one second. I have to take this."

I switched over.

"Jonah Gray."

"Good morning, Mr. Gray. Irene Gordon from Jack Merrill's office. I just wanted to let you know that Mr. Merrill is running about fifteen minutes behind schedule."

Irene Gordon had become my out.

"Can you hold on?" I asked without waiting for an answer.

I switched back.

"Angie, I have to take this."

"Jonah —"

"Really. I'll call you later."

"I want to see you."

"I'll call you toward the end of the day. We'll figure something out."

"You have my number, Jonah. You'd better use it."

CHAPTER 23

My first impression of Jack Merrill was that he seemed to be a very conservative, mild-mannered type. Turns out he was an arrogant prick. He was somewhere in his fifties wearing a gray two-button suit. He was finished off with burgundy braces, simple gold cuff links to match his gold Breguet, and brown bucks. We were alone in his beautiful Park Avenue office sitting at his personal conference table. A fresh pot of coffee, its aroma-laced steam rising, sat between us. The glare from the sun's rays bouncing off the glass table was the only light in the room.

"I have read about your team, Jonah. *Crain's*, *Real Estate Weekly*, you guys pop up all over the place."

"We do our best."

"Your best is pretty damn good considering what kind of market we're coming out of."

"Just trying to put something away for later, Jack. I imagine I don't have to tell you how quickly a poor market can come nipping at your heels."

"Amen to that, kid. You've been taught well."

Jack loudly sipped his coffee before continuing.

"Sam mentioned to me you may have a buyer for Lloyd Murdoch's Madison properties."

"That's right."

"What makes you believe that they're for sale?"

"Other than the fact that we're sitting here?"

Merrill thought for a second.

"That's right," he pushed out. "Other than the fact that we're sitting here."

"I know his financial situation. I know what position each of his holdings is in."

"And?"

"And cash is finite. Hence the reason that Gallo, a firm not in the real estate business, has ended up with these properties. End of story."

"What makes you so sure you have all the facts?"

"Again, we're sitting here, so having all the facts is irrelevant. What matters is that I have all of the important ones, which brings me to a question. Why has the security about this knowledge getting out been so tight?"

Merrill repositioned himself in his chair.

"Jonah, the goal of my getting together with you was not to discuss my dealings with another client."

"Then what was it?"

"To listen to an offer about a property that we may or may not be willing to sell."

"In that case, I have a very real buyer for both of them."

"Sam mentioned that. But you need to understand that we are still just getting our arms around these buildings, assessing our plans for them. Remember, they have literally just come into our possession."

"You mean you're honoring the grace period for Murdoch to get his shit together so he can make you guys whole then reclaim them."

"I mean we're getting reacquainted with them. We're doing our proper planning as I'm sure a man of your growing experience can understand."

Growing experience. Merrill was simply insecure about the fact that I was half his age yet making tons more cash than he was. He had read about my deals. He was jealous.

"They didn't grow legs or a dick, Jack. They're still buildings made from brick and mortar with a couple of issues that need some revisiting. Now I know due diligence is always part of any scenario, but things can always be accelerated under the right circumstances."

"Why the rush?"

"Sorry, Jack. I don't feel comfortable discussing the future business plans of a client. I'm sure you understand."

Merrill looked at his watch.

"I'll need to be on my way downtown shortly, Jonah."

I had made my point. It was time to back off, keep him interested.

"I understand, and again I appreciate the time you have taken this morning. I won't keep you. Let me just ask you one more thing. Did I mention my buyer would be willing to pay cash?"

"You did not."

"Well I meant to. Three hundred twenty-five dollars per square foot."

Before we had been talking. Now we were *talking*.

"How'd you come up with such a number?"

"Does it matter? At the end of the day you know as well as I do that no one out there would be willing to pay more than three fifteen, tops."

I had decided to play at $325. It was a fantastic price for the seller, but what he didn't know was that I had the leeway to end up even significantly higher if it meant getting the job done.

"I wouldn't be so —"

"Please," I cut him off. "My livelihood is defined by how sure I am of that. What you need to know is that there is a reason for the premium I'm offering. A very good reason."

Guys who pay cash are supposed to get a break. I was coming in with cash at top dollar. I could see the anticipation trying to burst through his chest like a fist punching its way through a plastic bag.

"Which is?"

"I need my inspection team on site by the end of the week."

"Seriously, Jonah."

Perry was annoyed with my choice of a lunch spot. I had asked her to meet me across the street from the Chrysler Center, on the lower concourse of Grand Central, at some little out-of-the-way Mexican joint. I was waiting at a small table in the back of the dining room. My back was against the wall so I could see the whole place like I was some mob boss.

"Why this place?"

"Why not? I felt like a burrito."

She took another look around, her eyes stopping on a stumpy busboy draped in greasy white linens.

"Well, it smells funky."

When she realized I wasn't responding she looked at me.

"It's just lunch, Per. No one's saying you have to move in."

"You're paying."

She finally took a seat and ordered an iced tea.

"So? How'd he respond?"

Over burritos and tortilla chips and salsa I filled Perry in on the morning's meeting with Jack Merrill. Perry then brought me up to speed as to the doings in the office. Tommy was apparently working on all cylinders. He had been transformed to his old firecracker self of a young broker and was getting off on the energy that comes with being in the trenches. Energy he had not felt in a while because he had the three of us. To no surprise, Tommy had all of our important, unfinished deals under control.

Perry spent the morning chasing Auerbach. By the time of our Mexican feast, the majority of Cantrol's board members had been informed of a potential buyer's interest and the kind of numbers they would be willing to come in at. Her confidence that she would have a sense of their initial reaction by day's end was high. As for Jake, he had submitted his number, as well as his one-time offer, to Jagger Slevin. He hadn't yet heard back.

My cell phone, which I had switched to vibrate, began dancing across the table. I didn't budge.

"I take it you're not answering that?"

Still I said nothing as the small rectangle slowly, intermittently scooted past my plate.

"What's the deal here, Jonah? I know your groupies sometimes have trouble getting over you, but this is a bit ridiculous."

She was right. As much as I wanted to answer her, I found myself unable.

"Seriously. All kidding aside. Everything okay here?"

No.

"Of course. All of a sudden you're afraid I can't handle some overzealous bimbette?"

"I'm not afraid of anything. I'm just saying —"

"You're just saying what?"

"That I know your eyes. And every time that cell rings, your ever-focused, unwavering eyes become instantly concerned. They look as if they're masking something. They start calculating, but in a different way than I'm used to."

I appreciated so much that Perry, saddled with enough of her own personal shit, wanted to dig. But in no way did I want to burden or endanger her in any way. Even if I had wanted to, where the fuck would I have begun?

"Tell me what's happening at home," I changed directions sharply.

"What do you mean? Everything's fine, Max is doing great."

"I'm not talking about Max. I'm talking about Brian."

"Brian. Oh, Brian's great. He's, uh, he's fine. Really great. You know, he's been really helping with Max, and, you know, he's been —"

Wrong topic.

"Perry —"

"No, really, he's been pretty terrific. He's been, like —"

She was now doing this crisscross thing in her side of Mexican rice with her fork.

"— he's been, you know, supportive in everything from —"

"Perry, honestly, we don't have to —"

"Yes, we do," she perked up, locking eyes with me. "We do need to do this."

She meant she needed to do this.

"I'm telling you, Jonah, everything's fine."

She had regained her composure, but it was forced.

"You just couldn't be happy, could you?" she continued.

"About what?"

"About the fact that I am finally one hundred percent focused on the task at hand. You just couldn't leave well enough alone. The other day you were insulted when I brought it up. But today it's important?"

She wanted to pretend it was about my selfishness. What she was pissed about was the real answer to my original question, the one about Brian and things at home.

"I wasn't insulted Perry. I was simply trying to —"

"I know, Jonah. Really, I do. Let's just —"

She was struggling to untangle her emotions. She grabbed her napkin from her lap and placed it on the table.

"Let's just get back up to the office."

By six forty-five I was on my terrace, alone. Parker had confirmed Angie hadn't tried to get upstairs all day. By this point I had made myself explicitly clear with my boys downstairs that no one, not even Cindy fucking Crawford wearing nothing but a teddy, was to be allowed near my apartment. The sun was still going strong. Neo was asleep on my bed; the doors leading inside were closed. I didn't have my cell, a newspaper, my computer, or CNN. I didn't have a joint, a drink, a bump. I had my thoughts.

I had gotten to the point that every moment not spent focused on the deal was on *Danish Jubilee Egg*. The more I thought about it, the clearer it became. I couldn't have ever been part of the plan. These people, if it was something larger than just the one guy in the bathroom, were just starting to get in touch with me seventy-two hours later. I figured they had needed some time to learn about who I even was. My life, my schedule, my circumstances, past and present. They needed to understand me, a good thing since I needed a little breathing room in order to better understand the landscape of the house of mirrors I had been dropped into.

When Pangaea-Man confronted me in Grand Central, he

never even pretended to have a clue about where the egg was, which simply meant he had no fucking idea. He'd tried to bully me with force, like some high-school thug. He had hoped to come off as controlling. Because he so obviously knew so little about the egg's whereabouts, he had simply come off as desperate, frustrated, not in control.

He didn't have anything to threaten me with. Think about that. He clearly had no understanding of the egg's whereabouts, yet he threatened me with my life. All killing me would have done was killed the sought information.

An eighteen wheeler, having trouble turning a tight city corner down below, started to blow its horn. I looked down. As I maintained my line of vision, I unbuttoned my shirt. I was overheating from the energy of my brain waves. The slight, uneven breeze gave me a much needed moment of relaxation. I began clinging to my confidence, speaking with it, reminding it that it needed to guide me. Especially since for me the reality of *Danish Jubilee Egg* was as stark as it was undeniable. Any wrong decision could be the last choice I would ever make.

CHAPTER 24

At five fifty-five the next morning, Tuesday, I was in the center stall of the desired Grand Central bathroom, door locked. My briefcase was on the floor. I faced the wall, standing there dressed in Brioni from head to toe like I was about to walk into a boardroom and negotiate a business deal. I figured Pangaea-Man for the punctual type. I was right.

Five minutes later the main bathroom door opened. I stepped out. "The briefcase. Now."

His attire was business casual, like some dot-commer having trouble facing the reality that we were, as a city, back in dress to the tits, kick-some-ass mode. Once he realized we were alone, he pulled his piece from inside his sport jacket.

"Why? You going to work for me today?"

He became furious. Like the day before, he stormed up to me not looking to waste any time. Without another word he clocked me across the face with the butt of his gun. I'd moved sideways, but he still managed to get me pretty good. I buckled slightly, then caught a glimpse of myself in the mirror. Blood was running from my nostril. A bit had sprinkled the collar of my white shirt.

"Fuck!" I yelled, straightening myself up. "Second fucking day in a row!"

I started for the sink.

"Do you have any idea how much one of these shirts costs?"

Pangaea-Man was in disbelief.

"Are you fucking crazy?" is the best he could manage.

"Put the gun down and see for yourself," I taunted him.

Again he moved in. He pointed the gun at the back of my head, no more than an inch away. We were now both facing the mirror, our eyes locked in the glass and staring back at one another.

"I mean it, pretty boy."

He nervously checked the door.

"I'll JFK your ass right now!"

"Okay," I conceded.

I put my hands in the air. I slowly turned around and began to head for my briefcase. Once I was a few steps away, I stopped.

"What the fuck are you doing, man?"

I turned around and faced him. I started to kneel. He was losing control, the control he had never fully garnered. Again, he quickly checked the door.

"I don't have time for this."

He stiffened his arm.

"I will fucking kill you!"

Once I was on both knees I clasped my hands behind my head.

"You already said that, so stop being a fucking talker. Pull the trigger."

I realized I was coming perilously close to the edge, but I needed full confirmation of just how right I was and just how far I could go.

"Go ahead. End my life because of a fucking diamond egg."

"You have no idea what you're doing here, man."

"Then kill me. Blow my head off."

Nothing. I started to stand up.

"You truly have no idea where it is. If you did, you would have just pillaged anything in your way to claim it."

I turned on the faucet. Pangaea-Man knew I was tuned in. Realizing he was pushing it with time, he put the gun back in his sport jacket. I didn't even look at him as I continued. I was more interested in cleaning my face.

"Now that we have that straight, I should also tell you I'm not looking to get myself killed. But I am a businessman."

"Meaning?"

"Meaning I have something you want."

My attention moved to my hair.

"And I am willing to give that something back."

Actually, at this point I didn't have enough of the facts to know if this was true. For the time being it was the way I needed to go. For now, I was simply looking to buy time.

"There's no such thing as something for nothing, pal. Not in this city."

"You don't know who you're fucking with here, man."

"Two million dollars, cash. You have forty-eight hours."

"You must be joking."

"You can't go to the cops, and you have made it clear that you have no idea what I've done with it."

I turned off the faucet, turned around, and stepped right to him, stopping three inches from his face.

"Do I look like I'm joking?"

The scenario was surreal. I feel filthy admitting it, but the rush was incredible. Seizing control here gave me a high I had seldom felt, a jolt of adrenaline so satisfying because it was all reactionary, all instinct. And it wasn't in a conference room.

"Two million for a thirty-five million dollar antique? Sounds like a pretty fucking nice price to me. Thursday morning. Same time, right here. New, crisp bills."

Crisp bills. I was getting into it. All of a sudden I was talking like I was in some cheesy, overrated Ben Affleck movie.

"Normal, everyday-looking luggage. I need some new pieces, so make them TUMI."

"You're out of your fucking mind."

Pangaea-Man was bewildered by my balls-to-the-wall style. Luckily for me, the guy was too stupid to realize everything had turned on him strictly because he had so weakly presented his case.

"Now I want to say be here by yourself, but I guess this doesn't really matter. After all, two guys, ten guys — if I'm not happy with what you present to me, simple. No *Danish Jubilee Egg*."

I grabbed my briefcase and started for the door.

"Thursday morning."

I left him there, standing in a pool of amazement. As the door almost shut behind me, I shouted, "And thanks."

I entered my office and closed the door. I threw my briefcase down. Before even booting my computer I fell into my cherry leather desk chair, holding up the day's *New York Post* in front of me. Robie/Hart, my mind had started referring to him as this by default, was on the third page. The headline read: SCAVENGER HUNT CONTINUES: FABERGÉ THIEF REMAINS ELUSIVE; AUTHORITIES CONFIDENT THEY ARE ON HIS TRAIL. I began reading the article. The motherfucker was still on the lam. Aside from insignificant circumstantial bullshit and hearsay surrounding the heist, there was nothing of interest. *Danish Jubilee Egg* was still officially missing.

I thought, why would Robie/Hart dish the antique off to me, but not pursue me?

Perry came storming into my office.

"Fucker!"

I fumbled the newspaper onto my desk. If she hadn't been out of sorts, she would have noticed she had startled me. She didn't notice or she simply didn't care.

"Per. What's up?"

I reached under my desk for my computer's on button.

"What's the matter?"

"I'll tell you what the fuck is the matter—Auerbach. That's the matter. I wake up this morning to the sound of him telling me the board isn't willing to entertain such an offer under such trying time constraints. Such trying time constraints! Do you fucking believe this guy? How dare he try to squeeze me! Most men would have, in the words of our esteemed colleague Jake Donald, 'blown a load' over the number that was put in front of them!"

Perry was going mad, steaming because she wanted the deal so bad. She was in crazy mode. As much as I loved it because this was where the team needed her to be, I was also loving it for more selfish reasons. She's beyond sexy when she's pissed—and yes, I realize I'm psychotic for taking notice with everything that was going on.

"Perry, take it easy. Come in and sit down."

"Seriously, Jonah. He has some nerve to be—"

I jumped from my chair and quickly moved toward her. She was wearing a black Armani pantsuit, flared subtly at the end of the legs and sleeves. Under the sport jacket was a burgundy satin button-down shirt with extra long sleeves coming out from underneath the coat. I grabbed her hand. The soft, smooth fabric mixed with the smell of her perfume sent a quick shock up my spine.

"Relax," I continued.

As if my hand grabbing hers gave her some sort of comfort, she immediately calmed down. As I led her to one of the chairs facing my desk, her sparkling eyes looked at me sheepishly.

"I'm fine, Jonah. Really. You don't have to—"

"Please, I'm a bit edgy myself this morning. The last thing I need is you coming in here yelling about all kinds of shit. Typical fucking girl. No ability to slow yourself down then look at the situation with some sort of objectivity."

Perry smiled.

"Ha-ha."

Perry was always intense, but she only jumped straight into irrational mode when she felt she was being slighted personally. Auerbach was her friend, and these types of things mattered more as of late because of the crap infiltrating her personal life.

"Good. You're smiling. Now, since when can't you figure out how to blow the doors off a lesser mind such as Auerbach?"

"I know, I know. It's just that—"

"He's been a friend for a long time, and you could do without the disrespect. Now, can we get back to the deal?"

"You're right," Perry conceded.

"What did he say?"

"That four hundred per square foot was out of the question. Even for cash."

"What is he looking for?"

"Four fifteen minimum. Says the board won't even listen to anything less."

"Who was asked?"

"James tells me two-thirds of the board received the number by the end of yesterday."

"Sounds like, if he's being up-front, he's with you more than you think."

"What makes you say that?"

"This isn't the board of some peep-show house on Broadway, Per. This is one of the largest oil companies in the northern hemisphere. From what you're telling me, James Auerbach says he not only got the word to two-thirds of the board yesterday, he's already heard back. Wouldn't you say he's responding pretty nicely to the time constraints you've saddled him with?"

"Well, when you put it that way, yes. Also considering that a number of the board members are overseas, albeit most of whom comprise the one-third unable to be contacted."

Perry thought for another second then continued.

"But these are educated men, Jonah. Four hundred per square foot is more than most —"

"Come on, Perry. You just said it yourself that these are educated men. The problem is that most of them are educated in areas outside of the commercial real estate market in New York City. What would an educated man be doing in this situation?"

Perry knew exactly where I was going.

"You don't really think James would be stupid enough to try and squeeze us here on a personal level?"

"Why not? He realizes that given the time constraints, we may not have a choice if we're serious about making a deal. And you just said it yourself, Perry, these are educated men. You didn't answer my question. What would an educated man do in this situation?"

"He would defer to his real estate specialist."

"Auerbach said that he already has a consensus 'no.' Do you believe him?"

"He's never given me a reason not to, Jonah. You know that. He's always been straight with us."

"Can you honestly tell me that the timing, as far as how quickly he heard back, doesn't concern you?"

"Trust me, Jonah, I asked him about that."

"And?"

"Because Cantrol has been exploring the option of selling, the board requires James to distribute a complete market analysis on a weekly basis just as they did his predecessor. They want to be ready to take action."

"And you think enough of these board members evaluate his materials thoroughly enough to respond this quickly? In less than twenty-four hours?"

"He wouldn't bullshit me, Jonah, especially with this. Look how much he has to gain here."

"Perry, the difference we're talking about simply sweetens his deal. Any halfway decent negotiator would take a chance at feeling out the bottom line. You know, a last ditch effort to fatten the pockets."

"I don't think so. I don't think he would come to me without approaching them."

"Want to know what I would do?"

"Do I want to hear this?"

"Find the least prominent board member Auerbach says he has been in touch with. Then give that individual a call."

"Jonah, he'll freak!"

"Two-thirds of the board within sixteen hours. I don't buy it."

Perry's disappointed eyes quickly bounced off my desk.

"Do yourself a favor, Perry. Find that board member and give him a call."

My intercom signal blared. I hit speaker:

"Clockwork, baby. Who's your daddy?"

"Any chance of losing the corny sayings this morning?"

"Negative."

"What's up?"

"My dick, after the news I just received."

"Lovely," chimed in Perry.

"Sorry, Per. Didn't know you were in there."

"Would it have mattered?"

"Of course not."

"And—" I continued.

"Just got off the phone with the Slevin duo. You know, the duo that's approaching rigor mortis.

"I take it you spoke with Jagger last night."

"Right on schedule, pretty boy. He got me on my cell while I was throwing back some Miso cod at Nobu. It was the resounding rejection I had been anticipating."

"How did the old boys respond?"

"Exactly as we expected. Intrigued is too soft a word. And just to punctuate how 'on' my instincts were, they couldn't say enough about my old school values; that the way to respect them was to respect their sons. In essence, I had the two fogies eating out of my hands. Albeit through a straw, of course."

"How'd you approach the number?"

"Same price. A different quote would have in effect come across as the real price, and this would have made the youngsters even more pissed than they're already going to be."

"And their thoughts on the timing?"

"They could give a shit. All they care about is cashing out. They told me they need a day or so to assess their plans, but they weren't fooling anyone. I swear to it that I even think I heard a high five. Picture that."

I actually tried to. The scene playing out in my head ended when Ray Slevin awkwardly missed and hit the deck with a thud.

"How about you two?"

"Perry seems to have—"

"Run into a minor snag," she interjected. "Nothing I can't handle."

She winked at me, her way of thanking me for helping her to channel her energy correctly.

"And you?"

I looked at my watch.

"I should be hearing something shortly."

"Time to play catch up, kids. Old Jake seems to be out in front."

CHAPTER 25

I was on speakerphone with Andreu Zhamovsky.

"I understand, Jonah. And don't get me wrong, it sounds like you are all making some serious progress."

"You have no idea what you have asked us to do, Andreu. Under the circumstances, I'd say we're moving fucking mountains."

"Didn't mean to steer us off course. All of the sudden you Americans have me nervous," he went on, chuckling. "I mean your country couldn't even keep their eye on that Fabergé egg. Maybe we should have kept that one over here."

"How do you know about that?"

"How do I know about what?"

"The egg."

"The whole world knows about it. I don't know if you're following any of this, but those damn eggs are like national treasures over here."

For obvious reasons, the conversation was turning in a direction that had me uncomfortable. Andreu was as pro-Russky as they get. I didn't want to think about how he'd react to believing I'd fucked with his homeland. Or maybe I was just being paranoid. Why talk of the egg? Why now?

"Andreu, you want to talk expensive egg memorabilia or are you ready to get back to business?"

"I don't mean to come on as unappreciative. I simply called to remind you that we're now into week number two."

"Off. You don't mean to come off as unappreciative."

"I'm sorry, Jonah?"

"Forget it. Look, I know where we are with time. What —"

Carolyn peeked into my office. I turned to her.

"What is it?"

She held out a small package.

"This was just delivered for you."

I wasn't expecting anything.

"Who is it from?"

"No return address."

I returned my attention to the phone.

"Give me one more second, Andreu."

I moved my eyes back to Carolyn.

"When I didn't see a sender I asked the messenger center downstairs where it came from. All they said was that it was dropped off by someone."

Great, a fucking suspicious package. Keep your cool, I reminded myself. Carolyn can be quite resourceful. Don't give her a reason to become curious.

"Not a problem, Carolyn. Just put it on one of the chairs."

"Andreu, as I was saying, I don't want you to become concerned with time. We plan on having inspections begin by the end of the week, as planned."

I was trying my best to forget about the package, but I couldn't. I was even making a concerted effort not to look at it. Eventually my curiosity got the best of me, and my eyes became glued to it as if they were fruit flies and the package was a sliced-open watermelon. I stood up, my vision deadlocked on the small brown box.

"What I need you to be focused on right now is the earnest money we're going to need to even get in the door. Your bank is ready at this point to transfer funds, I take it?"

"They are. Have you been in contact yet with Igor?"

"I have."

"Then feel free to use him as you need him. That's what he's there for."

I started toward the package.

"Now what I also need is for your attorneys to be brought up to speed. I will need them to all be on call twenty-four hours a day starting as soon as we get the green light for the first project. Even though our counsel, through power of attorney, will be handling everything from the contracts to the transfer of title, which, of course, you will be billed back for—"

"Cheap bastard," Andreu said with a light chuckle.

I looked at the box closely. It was small, about big enough for a softball to fit inside. There was nothing on the outside aside from my name and address written with a black Sharpie. My palms began sweating so I wiped them on my pants.

"— I will want your lawyers to have a look at everything simultaneously, as close to real time as that can be due to the distance between us, strictly for your comfort level. I know you trust me, Andreu, but this way there aren't any legal questions later on about the way we handled things. Any questions you may have can be dealt with immediately."

"I appreciate that suggestion, Jonah."

I took a semideep breath and lifted the package. It was light, almost as if it were empty.

"When do you plan on speaking with Mr. Merrill again?"

I returned to the chair behind my desk and sat down, still holding the small box up in front of my eyes.

"Shortly. Take a deep breath, Andreu. Go out and enjoy yourself, leave the business worries to us. I'll continue to keep you up to date. I'm going to switch you over to Carolyn now so you can double-check with her that we have all of the correct contact information for your attorneys."

"Remember, Jonah — Mr. Worldwide. We can't afford any snags. Let me know if you need something. Anything."

With that Andreu Zhamovsky was gone. I glanced at the door, knowing that even when I was alone in my office I wasn't really alone. I lowered the package and placed it between my feet, out of the hallway's view. I tore off the outer shell of thick, brown paper. Underneath was a plain, white cardboard box. I lifted open the top flap. Inside was some white tissue paper. I pulled it back, letting it drape over the sides of the box. When I found the object of my search, I became confused, startled. It was a lock of auburn hair, secured in the middle by a rubber band.

"Jonah?"

Carolyn's voice was coming through the intercom.

"What is it, Carolyn?"

"I have Angie on the phone again. She says it's urgent. She says you have something of hers that she needs to discuss."

I looked at the lock of hair.

"Put her through."

There was a three-second pause, then a beep. I pushed the button for line four and picked up the receiver.

"Why would you send me that?" I asked.

"Why won't you see me? You were supposed to call me last night. Why won't you at least try to explore what we could have?"

"You didn't answer me. Why would you send me that?"

"It's always about you, Jonah, isn't it? Everything is all about how it relates to you. What you can handle and what you can't, what you have time for and what you don't. Just like yesterday and just like the other night. You just profess what you want, what you need, and expect that the words you have spoken become fucking gospel."

"Why are you doing this to me?"

"Again, it's all about you."

"What do you want!?"

"I have never felt this crazy before, Jonah. This empty. Each time we make love —"

My mind was beginning to flip.

"That's not making love, Angie. That's called fucking. Straight up, lust drenched, substance-laden fucking. And as I have already mentioned, however narcissistic it may be, I am extremely busy."

"I wanted to hurt myself. Last night, when I was alone, after waiting for hours to hear from you, I had this urge come over me unlike anything I have ever felt before. I wanted to hurt myself. I was thinking about all the different ways I could—"

She paused, as if she were waiting for me to jump in. I didn't.

"—I could, you know—"

The situation was fully getting out of control. The deal, the egg, this girl. I needed to contain it. But what was really happening? I still wasn't sure if I was dealing with someone connected to the egg, or just some psycho who couldn't get enough of me.

I needed to be careful. I needed to tiptoe. I needed to, as always, be proactive. I had an idea.

"I'm not worth it, Angie. Really—"

"The other night at the wedding, Jonah, I've never felt that special."

"I find that hard to believe, Angie. From the second I met you, I simply took you for the beautiful, sexy, confident girl you appeared to be."

"I wish I was those things, Jonah. Unfortunately, I'm a little bit more insecure than that."

Gee, really? Is that so, you fucking sick, crazy, warped, hair-sending, possessed, twisted, psychotic, pathetic loon of a human being, who on the other hand is possibly just some damn fine actress trying to set me up?

"Look, I'm not bullshitting you when I say I'm in the middle of the craziest business deal you can imagine. But if it means that much to you, I can meet up with you this evening. Now I must tell you, I have a dinner appointment."

Get her in person, spend only a few minutes, douse the fire.

"But I'd be happy to meet for a cocktail around seven so we could talk about this."

"I'd like that, Jonah. I'm happy I sent you the lock of hair. I just wanted to put a part of me in front of you, something to remind you that I exist and I'm thinking of you. I'm happy I kept it simple."

I could literally feel myself move from nervous to terrified.

"As opposed to?"

I was almost sorry I had asked before the words had come out.

"I was thinking either my pinkie toe or ear. Maybe the tip of my tongue."

I couldn't fight the image of a tongue-tipless Angie spitting uncontrollably while butchering the English language.

"Something small enough to deliver, yet serious enough to send the message that nothing could hurt as much as what I'm feeling right now."

I picked up the phone and dialed. I waited for an answer.

"Sam Archmont."

"Any surfing this morning, young fella?"

"Sticking to indoor sports today with the new missus, if you know what I mean. She can't get enough of me or my Viagra."

"Well in that case, I'm sorry to bother you."

"You're never a bother, Jonah. You know that. I spoke with Merrill. He says the two of you had an interesting meeting."

"Depends on your definition of interesting."

"What'd you think of him?"

"I think he's a pussycat."

"Atta boy."

"Actually, Sam, it isn't Jack Merrill that I'm calling about."

"What's on your mind?"

"Your neighbors, the Sheppards."

"Good people, Jonah. What's the interest?"

"I'm curious about their daughter, Angie."

"Sweet kid."

"So you know her well?"

"I knew her quite well. She used to run the beaches along the back of our homes all summer long."

"So you haven't seen her in a while?"

"No one has, Jonah. She was killed in a car wreck about five years ago."

CHAPTER 26

At three fifty-five I was sitting in my office, ensconced in technology. Files and documents littered my computer screen. I had fourteen windows minimized at the bottom of the flat-screened monitor. The file that was open was in Acrobat Reader. It was a final draft of the contract between PCBL and the firm that would be responsible for the HVAC inspection of the Madison properties.

As I was sitting there, evaluating a document that was simply regurgitating terms I helped put together, I found myself doing something I had never before done in my entire professional life. I was pretending to work. Sam Archmont's little morsel of information had completely thrown me.

I had become paranoid to the point of believing that my office's phone and computer activity were possibly being monitored. A few minutes earlier I had used one of the vacant offices two floors down, the ones set aside for new administrative underlings brought on board, to do a little research on Angie Sheppard. I Googled her and, in fact, Angie had died not five but six years earlier one summer night in the Hamptons. She was close to her family's home when the accident happened. It was on Ocean Drive. Her BMW was crushed by an SUV being driven by a young guy more hammered than Eddie Van Halen at a bachelor party. The Angie I knew was not only a complete lunatic, but she was also a complete fraud.

"Jonah?"

Carolyn's voice came through the intercom, shaking me from my reflective, façade-driven state.

"Yes, Carolyn."

"I have Jack Merrill on line one."

I literally gritted my teeth. All I wanted was the solitude to examine what was happening, what I might have missed.

"Please put him through."

As I waited, I turned and stared blankly at the cardboard box I had thrown in my trash can.

"Jonah."

"Jack. How are you this afternoon?"

"I feel good. I apologize for not getting back to you earlier in the day, but I was still waiting on word from the final decision makers. I must say, Jonah, they found the offer very interesting."

I rolled my eyes. We both knew they were all probably doing their best to avoid the champagne corks being shot around the conference room.

"I can't say I'm shocked. Frankly, I'm amazed it took so long for them to agree that this purchase price for an all-cash transaction is a no-brainer."

"Don't get ahead of yourself, Jonah. I never said they had yet agreed on the purchase price."

"Please, Jack. I should probably mention that this call is being recorded. Don't force me to make you look like an ass when I play this for our peers, and show them you had the nerve to ask for a higher price. You know what has been offered here is the aggressive, overinflated price of a very eager buyer."

I wasn't kidding. The price I had gone in with was decided upon for one reason. To allow them to make a quick, easy decision.

"Not my call, Jonah. I'm simply the messenger on this one."

I could feel my real estate instincts starting to take over.

"You're the chief real estate advisor, Jack. Did you advise the final decision makers on just how stellar of an offer this was? Or did you not?"

We both knew the answer to that question.

"I acted in a manner most appropriate in terms of assessing the situation and guiding my company."

"Basically, that's code for saying you told them you had a serious buyer who you should take a chance on squeezing."

"The Madisons are two trophy-caliber buildings, Jonah. We're not just going to let someone come in and bully their way into taking them into their possession. Now as I mentioned, we have found the offer to be quite intriguing."

It was obvious I was dealing with a guy who must have had a joke of a poker face. I sensed myself clicking into warrior mode, entering that place that makes the great brokers stand above the good ones. It was all about the upcoming moments, ones I could feel were about to happen, that often end up making, or breaking, deals.

"But we need the number to be a bit higher in order to make this a priority."

"How much higher?" I asked, playing along.

"You tell me we have three thirty-five, and I can give you my word that we'll look to make this a priority."

My blood's temperature rose quickly. Three hundred and thirty-five dollars per square foot was not the issue. Some pretentious, wannabe big shot looking to take advantage of me was.

"I'll give you twenty-four hours, Jonah, to decide if you'd still like to move ahead."

Looking to exhibit the control that had come to define my life and that others were trying to take from me, I decided to show Jack Merrill the light and punch him in the face as my father taught me. Not just for the team, for the deal, but for myself.

"At this precise moment, Jack, twenty-four hours is a tremendous amount of time. I don't think I have it to spare."

I decided to show Jack Merrill who, in fact, was in charge.

"So here's my counteroffer. Take it or leave it."

"Jonah, just rewind here for one second. If —"

"You tell your final decision makers that I didn't come in at three twenty-five as a starting point. I came in offering you all three twenty-five as a fucking gift in order to get what I want, plain and simple. If you want to pretend that this was just some interesting starting point in order to churn out a few extra bucks, I'm fine to take my business elsewhere. Are you with me so far?"

Just like that, all of the craziness fell away from me, like the shiny robe from the back of a champion fighter upon entering the ring. It was ridiculous how much, if only for a few needed moments, I was enjoying myself.

"If I may get a word—"

"You didn't answer me, Jack," I continued. "Are you with me so far?"

After a brief pause, Jack Merrill finally got wise to the situation. "I am."

"Good. I'm not fucking around when I say I don't have the time for crap. Three twenty-five is the number, and you can forget twenty-four hours. You have ten minutes to get back to me."

"For Pete's sake, Jonah, you haven't even told me who the buyer is yet!"

"Given the fact that we're going to be paying cash, you should focus your energy elsewhere as this should be the least of your concerns. As I mentioned to you previously, they're spotless. Once you confirm for me that the number is accepted, both parties sign a confidentiality agreement, one I have already had drawn up, and we each start our due diligence. You'll have all the numbers and information you could possibly need, and you have my word that the strength of this buyer is what has given me the ability to come in as strong as I have. If you don't like the organization, which I promise you won't be the case, you can simply walk away. As an act of good faith, my client will deposit a hundred thousand dollars into your account to show we're not looking to waste anyone's time. We make the deal, you credit the hundred K against the final number. We fail to agree on terms, Gallo keeps the cash. As for Murdoch, that's your fucking problem. Now, have I made myself clear?"

"You have," he conceded, painfully, after a brief pause.

"Good," I said. "Two things. Number one, stop saying 'for Pete's sake.' It makes you sound terribly fucking old. Number two, the clock's ticking."

I hung up.

Nine minutes later, Carolyn informed me that Jack Merrill was on the phone.

"To begin with, Jack," I started, "I'd like to have my inspection team on the premises by Thursday morning."

CHAPTER 27

I walked into Pastis at seven ten. The Meatpacking District hotspot was already buzzing, the norm for a nice evening. The red tin ceiling, which is embossed with a smart, simple pattern, was highlighted by the clear light bouncing off the mustard-colored walls. The soft breeze from the city was rolling off the cobblestone streets and in through the windows lining the avenue. Above the bar, a wall-size mirror laid out the menu for all to see in white grease pencil.

My eyes scanned the crowd in a way that was becoming all too familiar. I remember at this moment feeling uneasy about the fact I could actually feel myself getting better at such subtle surveillance. The bar area, which is tight, was jammed with all types. People in suits, people in jeans, whatever. The only constant was that most of the crowd, speaking predominantly in European accents, was wearing bright colors.

Through bodies and suspended cocktail glasses I could see the girl pretending to be Angie at the bar. Somehow she had managed to save a seat for me. As I made my way toward her, I could feel all of the eyes on me becoming increasingly inquisitive as people realized I was the lucky one with the hot girl. *You should all only be so fucking lucky*, I thought, pissed.

"I took a nap this afternoon. I dreamt about you."

I sat down. Whoever this girl was, she looked delicious, as usual. Low-riding Seven jeans, sharp, plum-colored Yves St. Laurent heels, and a matching colored, tight-fitting cotton top. I hated myself for noticing.

"Lucky me," I replied.

I immediately got the bartender's attention and ordered a Sapphire and tonic. Then I quickly turned back to the imposter girl, locked eyes, and said, "Angie Sheppard died six years ago in a car accident in the Hamptons. Out with it."

Angie shot me the faint smile of a demon. It was a bit bizarre, revealing a glimpse of her potential psychosis.

"You think it's really that easy?" she asked.

"Whoever the fuck you are, you need to know that I don't have the time or the patience for this kind of drama."

"You have no idea what drama can be."

"Look this is all very cute, but I don't really feel inclined to sit here and trade war stories with someone who's seen *Fatal Attraction* one too many times. You need to tell me who you are. Then you need to understand what is going to happen when —"

"Look at you, Jonah. You really think you're that almighty simply because you know how to stuff your pockets? You know how to control the soulless shells of other money seekers?"

The irony from this comment, that I can now see, was amazing. This girl seemed to be as far from what I'd call stable or clear thinking, imaginable. At the time, all I could feel from such words was anger. What I couldn't — wouldn't — allow myself to see was such poignant, painful truth.

The bartender placed my drink down. I took a healthy sip and continued, "This is the last time I am going to ask. What is it that you want?"

"A fair chance, Jonah. A fair chance to have a real connection, a real life. Can you really sit there and deny what happened last Thursday night? Can you? The way —"

"I can't!" I broke in. "That's why I fucking hate you! You have no idea what kind of possibilities for my life you presented the other night."

I was curiously, surprisingly incensed. Indeed, I did hate her for being a liar and possibly a serious threat to my well-being. But that wasn't it. There was something else there, something more needy, more selfish.

"Seeing you standing there the other night at the wedding was mind blowing. It was almost like, as cliché as it sounds, for the first time I could feel what destiny means. I looked at you and I knew we'd click right away, like we had already known each other in a past life or something. I knew we'd click, and I was right."

I noticed that my right hand, the one holding my drink, was shaking, quietly rattling the glass against the bar. My emotions were unraveling. I quickly spun them back in.

"Every day I live with the fact that all of my conquests serve as nothing more than filler for the woman I really want. I also live with the fact that they serve as this filler because I have no choice since that woman for me is out of reach. The other night I actually thought you had proven me wrong. Instead you turn out to be nothing more than some sick joke, and I find myself chalking it all up to my senses being clouded by the booze and drugs that were running through my system. Trust me, I would never pretend to deny what happened. It was you who fucked with that. Not me."

She gently touched my hand, letting out a giggle, trying to win me back over.

"Jonah, you don't need to be so serious about —"

I pulled my hand away.

"What is it that you want?"

Again, the weird smile.

"What do you mean, sweetie?"

Could it be? Fuck! I didn't want to say it, but I had to.

"You're part of all this. That's why you were there that night," I said it out loud for the first time.

"Part of all what?"

I said nothing.

"What Jonah?"

"I want to see your driver's license."

"Don't have my wallet."

"Shocking."

I slammed down the rest of my drink.

"You are to stop coming near me."

"I'm afraid I can't do that."

"Why not?"

"Because I can't."

"Fine. To tell you the truth I don't even want to know your real identity. I have too much to worry about as it is. So here it goes. I have supplied my apartment building as well as the Chrysler Center with your picture. Each has been instructed to call the police first, me second, upon sight of you even near the premises."

"That isn't necessary."

Her face changed into a combination of sadness and restrained rage. All of a sudden it was as if I was actually staring into the eyes of Lucifer.

"I appreciate the input," I responded, sarcasm intended, "but I'm going with my instincts on this one. Your words, your tough little attitude, your fragile, kooky tone and mood shifts, none of it means shit. The moment I found out you were nothing but a lie is the moment you became an insignificant little insect to me."

I stood up.

"Understand that I'll crush you if I need to."

"I need access to you, Jonah. I need to be able to get to you."

"Go fuck yourself."

"I'll find your father, Jonah. Or perhaps your perky little partner, Perry—"

Infuriated, gripped, I sat back down, demeanor in check. I took out my Paul Smith pen from my inside jacket pocket.

"I would think twice about that if I were you."

I grabbed the cocktail napkin that came with my drink and started writing.

"Is that so?"

"It is."

"Why?"

I held up the cocktail napkin so she could read it. Matter-of-factly, it said, "Because I'll kill you."

Once I was sure her eyes had scanned, her brain had processed the words, I crumbled the napkin and held it in my fist.

More freaked out than I was letting on, I left. I still had no idea who the hell she was, and why it mattered to me, if it even did. Also, I had given no one her picture. Not my apartment building, not the Chrysler Center. It was all a bluff. The last thing I could do was willingly bring the cops into my life, no matter how much I was starting to feel that I could possibly use them. No matter how much I wanted to know who she was.

Knowing my visit would be short, I had a car waiting for me out front. It was my father's stretch, and Mattheau, Pop's Haitian driv-er of twenty-five years, was at the wheel. I would often call upon him when my father wasn't in need of his services and that night I was meeting my father at a restaurant a block from his office. Therefore, Mattheau was free.

I jumped in the back, and as quickly as the car pulled away I opened my briefcase on the seat next to me. Mattheau, an extreme-ly pleasant and accommodating man with cautious eyes, knew where we were going so there were no words spoken. I removed a small, emergency vial of coke from one of the inside compartments along with a fresh joint. In a perfect contradiction of drug use, a contradiction that mirrored some of the emotions stirring inside of me, I took a nice bump in each nostril then sparked the grass ciga-rette. A simple dose of "up" followed by a simple dose of "down." Coke to keep me aware, pot to scrape away some of the edge.

"Jonah, are you sure you want to —"

Mattheau had seen me grow up, from the money to the wildness to the drugs to the entertaining of women, therefore nothing about me fazed him anymore. He always kept everything he saw between us, which I rewarded every Christmas by giving him cash on top of what Pop gave him.

"I'm okay, Mattheau. Really. Crazy day."

"I know you're okay. It's just that when —"

"Mattheau, really. It's cool."

He retreated.

"Sure, Jonah. Of course."

One hand on the wheel, the other working the keypad of his cell, he returned to the tasks at hand.

"Yves?" I said.

He loved to "text" his only son. He looked at me in the rearview mirror and nodded.

"Tell him I say 'hi.' "

I always found Mattheau to be an interesting concoction of a soul. He had the manners of a topflight English butler yet the instincts of a lion for working Manhattan's infamous asphalt grid. He was soft-spoken and mostly an introvert. Even though he had a child of his own, at times he looked out for me like a guardian. Especially when he sensed I was acting reckless.

I cracked the window as Mattheau seamlessly attacked the city. After only a couple of drags, I put the joint out on the bottom of my shoe and threw both drugs back into my briefcase. My cell rang. It was Perry calling me from the office.

"What's up?"

"I'm here with Jake."

They were on speaker.

"I was just telling him about how you handled the guy from Gallo."

"You fucking stud!" Jake screamed.

"Just trying to make you some money, kid."

"I mean it, man, that's some kick-ass work."

I heard a quarter start bouncing haphazardly around Perry's glass desk top. Jake had missed.

"Sorry —"

"Where's Tommy?"

"At a broker party for Seven Twelve Third," Perry said. "God bless his young heart."

Broker party: bash thrown by the ownership of a property at the beginning of a big marketing campaign to lease available space. They invite all of the hungry power brokers in the industry to the building. Then they let them see the available vacant space first-hand, have some kind of testosterone-driven raffle—possibly a golf weekend in Hawaii or a pair of jet skis—and serve free booze. All of the players get up to speed on one another's deals, exchange some sensitive information, look for leads to infiltrate — you get the idea.

"You might say he's really submerged himself in this role of playing his younger self," Jake commented.

"Good for him and good for us," I replied.

"Always thinking with your wallet. That's why I love you."

"Where are you?" asked Perry.

"On the way to the Four Seasons to have dinner with my father. Tell me what's up."

"I think you may be right, Jonah. I hate that I did it, but I think you may be right."

"You called a board member."

"I called two. Both easily reachable, both in New York City. I also have a call in to another in Boston. His assistant told me that he'd contact me around nine tonight."

"That fucking prick," I bashed him.

"Tell me about it. I really didn't want to make that call, but I couldn't deny what you said. It just made too much sense."

"It was the right move, Perry. We've got a client to please. Collateral damage gets handled later."

"You got that right," Jake jumped in. "We simply don't have the time to be lied to. What this motherfucker did, after all these years you two have been friends, he deserves whatever he has coming to him now."

"Cantrol's board will slaughter him, Jonah. Think about it. Not only withholding an offer to them, but actually responding to that offer?"

"Not your problem, Per."

"I know that. I'm willing to put him against the wall for it. It's just that, I guess I'm disappointed."

"In what?"

"The fact that this could ruin him. Not just with Cantrol but beyond if it really gets out. All I wanted was to make sure the deal was moving along properly."

Perry's personal life was more than showing chinks in her

armor. Her remorse was nothing more than a by-product of her newfound loneliness. She was scared to lose anyone else, especially someone she had known for so long.

"And you did that, so let's keep moving forward," I pushed her.

"Definitely," said Jake.

Perry didn't say anything, which meant she had gotten the message.

"What now?" I continued on.

"I told her to not make any rash decisions until she hears from number three. Boston," Jake said.

"I agree," I countered.

"Once I hear from him," Perry continued, "if it's what we all expect it will be, I work through the night on a confidentiality agreement to be sent first thing in the morning and signed for individually by each board member. From there we move forward with the board and, hopefully, lose nothing more than these past couple of days."

She paused, then, uncharacteristically, quipped into the air to no one, "This is unfucking believable!"

"What's that?" I asked.

"I'm not sure."

"About—" I probed.

"What pisses me off more? The fact that James would so easily spit on our friendship or the fact that I've lost substantial time."

Perry wasn't kidding. She really wasn't sure. It's hard enough to swallow a real estate foe screwing with you in the first place. It must be a whole different story when it's a friend. On the other hand, Perry hates being thrown off schedule. She adjusts as well as anyone when it happens, but she hates it.

As for what happened between Perry and Auerbach, I wouldn't know. I've never given anyone professional, whom I remotely consider to be a friend, even one second to think that sticking it to me would be a wise move. So I thought about how I react to people who try to fuck with me in the business world, and I gave her the same advice my father once gave me.

"Let James Auerbach go, Perry."

"I know, Jonah. But when —"

"I mean it. Let him go, angrily. When you have, nothing will be more of a lesson to him than if this deal gets made in spite of his efforts. He'll have to think about it every day. Nothing will gnaw at him more. Perry, you need to steamroll over him. You need to knock him to the ground. And when he's down, you need to make sure his eyes are still open. This way he'll be able to see the sole of your shoe as it comes crashing into his face."

I walked into The Four Seasons on east 52nd street. Within one step of entering the space I was transported to the 1970s. Not the '70s of trippy colors and tight shorts, the one of elegance and taste. The one of growing American wealth and splendor. The Four Seasons was the same place to eat for the privileged today that it was then. Same smart hues, same subtly crisp Philip Johnson architecture, same timeless aura.

After walking upstairs to the dining room, I was immediately greeted by Julian Niccolini, of Julian and Alex fame. The two together are responsible for fuelling the restaurant's success from the beginning. Julian, the crowd pleaser, has a reputation built on his outgoing personality and charm, especially with the ladies. Alex Von Bidder, his reserved counterpart, has always been thought of as the establishment's lightning rod. Together, they make a formidable restaurateur team.

I walked through the narrow hallway, the one with the huge, earth-tone Picasso on the wall, then past the wine room and into the main dining area. The cavernous, high-ceilinged room was dimly lit, as it usually is in the evening. The warm cherry wood walls seemed to be absorbing, then evenly redistributing, all of the room's energy. The famous drooping, pink and bronze metal chain-link curtains gently shimmied in tiny vertical waves up and down the walls. Orderly, proper staff members glided about with little distraction. The square pool of cool pale blue water located in the center of the space muffled all of the room's voices into a single calm entity. I spotted my father, and a woman I had never seen before, sitting at our usual table right up against the pool's south edge.

A bit uneasy I sat down. I hated the fact that I had to be near my father, possibly putting him directly in harm's way, but therein lay the problem. He knew me better than anyone and would have become suspicious had I started blowing him off. One of the few constants in my life had always been our time together. In his eyes, anything that ever threatened that routine came across as erratic.

I shook my dad's hand.

"Jonah, say hi to Cesara. She's Spanish."

Cesara, who looked younger than me, had olive skin, huge breasts, and chiseled facial features. She wore a short, slinky black cocktail dress and three-inch heels. Her dark, lustrous hair was long and flowing. Her nose was buried in her BlackBerry.

"Hey!" Pop barked. "This is my son here! Finish up with your goddamned e-mails later."

Cesara mumbled something in Spanish under her breath. She hit the miniature keypad a few last times and lifted her eyes to give me a quick once over.

"Nice to meet you."

I could see right past her eyes into the smutty thoughts forming in her gold-digging brain.

"Stanley," she went on, her voice spiked with Latin flavor, "I really need to get back to these people. Since the two of you are probably just going to talk business anyway, I —"

"Yeah, yeah, just go," Pop quipped, as if he'd been through this exercise before.

Cesara jumped up. BlackBerry still in hand, she picked up her purse and cell phone, and scurried out of the dining room.

I sat down. A Sapphire and tonic was waiting for me.

"What's doing, kid?"

The dope had made my mouth a bit dry. I downed a third of my drink.

"Not much," I said. "Didn't know there would be three of us tonight."

When I arrived Pop had a few business papers out on the table along with one of my favorites of his Mont Blanc pens, Hemingway, but he was looking at a *New York Post*. He was taking one last glimpse at whatever article he had been reading as he put it aside.

"This egg thing is unbelievable," he said, nearly throwing me from my seat.

"Excuse me?"

"The Fabergé egg that was stolen from the embassy. Haven't you been following it?"

"Actually, not really. I haven't had all that much time for the news lately."

My insides began to simmer. I was surprised by my father's interest. His nose was usually buried in the business section. I had never thought of him as a current events kind of guy.

"Yeah, well, it's simply sickening to me that someone would steal something like this. I just don't understand it."

Shaking his head, he placed the paper on the floor next to his chair.

"Maybe it was Sam," he continued, smirking, as he took a sip of his drink.

"Sam who? Archmont?"

"You never know," he shrugged, half-kidding. "You know the story behind his going to prison? He was a dockworker. He stole some artwork that was headed overseas right out of the shipyard."

All of a sudden it felt as if my head had been placed in a vice. Then, in a blink's time, the Pool Room at The Four Seasons had become my own personal time machine. I was back at Archmont's wedding, standing at the bar. I could see, not well, only peripherally, Robie/Hart putting my cigar case back in my briefcase. And I could see the cops that seemed to be milling about on the beach.

I had requested — pushed for — that meeting with Sam that evening. I thought, had I simply fucked myself inadvertently, putting myself in the proverbial wrong place at the wrong time?

Pop looked at his Patek Philippe.

"How was your drink earlier?"

"Irrelevant."

"Where'd you go?"

"Also irrelevant."

"How come?"

"Pop if it's cool I'd rather just pass over it. Some bimbo who isn't even worth discussing."

"Fucking women," my father pushed out under his breath. "My lifelong dilemma. Of course, only since your mother passed, that is. Every day since has been the same crap, Jonah. They're too damn needy to want around during the day, and too damn warm and pretty not to want around during the night."

"Nice sentiments. James Brown would be proud."

"Joke all you want, Jonah. But for me there will never be another like your mother. That's why I don't waste too much time on any one girl. If they're young, have a tight ass, and look great in an evening gown, I keep them around right up until the time they get used to the lifestyle and start expecting things. Once they do, I'm on to the next. I keep my mind on making deals, I limit my exposure and possible commitment levels and have some great sex along the way."

Pop sloshed down a couple gulps of his drink.

"Trust your old man on this one, Jonah. I'm sixty-three in a couple weeks. I've lived a lot of years. You're entering the prime of your professional life. Keep dealing with the ladies the way you have been. Don't get too attached to any of them. That way you won't get hurt or sidetracked. That way you can keep closing deals, which is the only place your head should be."

Discussing our respective day's events, we jumped right into the atmosphere. Soon we were eating caviar and sampling different cognacs on the house, all the while my senses working overtime. It was obvious my father had no idea he was cohabitating with the missing Fabergé egg. Soon it was equally clear that no one out of the ordinary had contacted him. Nothing odd was happening in his life. I had always thought I could tell when my father was keeping something from me. That night I was sure he wasn't. Something that helped me loosen up enough to handle the moment.

I let the discussion turn to business, to Andreu, and filled my father in on how we were doing.

"By the way, how's Galina?" he detoured.

"According to Andreu she's fine. Still painting or doing whatever it is she does."

"What she does is paint, draw, and sculpt," Pop replied as he buttered a minicroissant, a grin spinning onto his face. "Never signs her work. Just dates it. Anyway, that's good. The two of them must have really bonded once Alexander died."

"I wouldn't know, Pop. Our recent conversations haven't exactly been dealing with family and affairs of the heart. A wise man from the Upper East Side once told me there's only so much time in a day. Know what I'm saying?"

Cesara eventually returned to the table. For dinner I ordered a sirloin steak topped with grilled onions, broccoli, and pureed truffle oil infused potatoes on the side. My father went with the fish special that night, scallops. Cesara had Dover sole. When we were about halfway finished with our entrées, something strange happened.

A man appeared at our table. I recognized him, but he was looking at my father. They knew each other from both being part of the Manhattan real estate landscape for so long.

"I understand you have a tee time at my country club on Saturday morning, Stan."

My father shot me a look before answering.

"You understand correctly, Lloyd. I'm playing with Halper."

"Watch out for number fourteen. She's an angry little bitch of a par three."

"How have you been?" Pop went on.

It was Lloyd Murdoch. The man who's empire I was infiltrating. Even though I had recently chumped him, I couldn't help respecting the fact he was smoking a cigar in a "no smoking" restaurant, like he owned the place. Monte Cristo #2 no less. Before answering, he turned his eyes to me.

"Better. I've been better."

I smirked at the guy menacingly. He was dressed sharp in Kiton from head to toe wearing a navy suit, perfect white spread-collar dress shirt, and gold well-knotted silk necktie. His feet were covered in Ferragamo. To most, without question, he looked successful. To me he looked like nothing more than a man trying to maintain an image that was in the process of fading away.

"Have you met my son?" Pop asked after introducing his date.

"Surprisingly, I haven't yet had the pleasure."

I extended my hand. I was surprised when he, without hesitation, shook it confidently.

"Jonah Gray."

"Stan, you might want to have a discussion with your son. A dialogue about certain unspoken points of ethics when dealing in property."

Murdoch took a nice draw of his cigar.

"Nah. I think he's doing just fine," Pop replied.

"Is that right?"

I looked at my father.

"Pop, why don't you tell your friend I'm sitting right in front of him if he has something to say to me."

The traces of blow swimming through my system took hold. I could feel cocaine muscles starting to grow underneath my shirt.

"I figured the discussion needed to be addressed as if you're a child since that's how you're acting."

I laughed then took a swallow of my drink.

"Does that kind of wisdom come from your previous real estate life? Or the recent one that has you overleveraged, on the verge of losing your buildings and realizing those who once had confidence in you no longer do?"

"You've got some fucking attitude on you, kid."

"You're damn fucking right I do."

"You better be careful. The game can be a tough one when you decide only to play by your own rules."

"What the fuck does that mean?" I asked, raising my voice.

"You know exactly what that means."

"No," I reacted, pissed, "I don't."

I stood up. We were now making a slight scene.

"You want to interrupt our evening and come up to us uninvited, you'd better be ready to answer me when I speak to you."

"There are certain rules that —"

"Save your fucking breath, pal. You have some kind of nerve coming over here and speaking to me like I'm some kid. It's an insult to me and it's an insult to my father."

Murdoch looked at my father. Pop put his hands up in the air and leaned back in his chair.

"You did come over to us, Lloyd. And I stopped fighting Jonah's battles a long time ago."

Murdoch was a bit embarrassed, but did a great job of keeping his cool.

"You blew it," I continued. "And you're angry because all you did was turn around for one second and a guy half your age came in and showed you the lesson of your professional life."

"You think so?"

"I know so. Let's see, how many hours actually was it that the bank had been holding onto the Madisons? I imagine that's the last time you leave something so precious to chance for even five minutes. Anyway, this all just happened. What, are you following me or something?"

I know a guy like Lloyd Murdoch probably dines at The Four Seasons once a week, but under the circumstances I couldn't help feeling a bit strange about the coincidence. Even though there was no conceivable connection between this chance meeting and my other situations, I threw my eyes quickly around the room while keeping my head as still as possible.

"Your arrogance could get you in trouble, Jonah," Murdoch said, smiling slightly. "You wouldn't be the first young hotshot to get ahead of himself in this business."

"Please, I'm on to your little game with Gallo. So you can take your unspoken rules and ethics and puke them up on someone else. When you look at me, you'd better see a broker willing to do anything within the confines of the law for his client. I've earned that. You let your eyes see anything else and —"

I sat back down as I continued.

"— well, I guess you already know what may happen."

Murdoch, with the resilience of a seasoned player, brushed my words aside. He looked at my father.

"Stan."

"Lloyd." Pop responded.

Murdoch didn't say another word to me then left.

My dad, amused, started eating again, though I could see his eyes looking me up and down.

"Don't you think you should have finished the job?" Pop asked. "You know, maybe grabbed a knife off the table and given him your best Iago impersonation?"

Shakespeare reference. *Othello*. Act five, scene one, when Iago stabs Roderigo.

"He deserved it," I snapped back.

I looked up from my plate. We turned to Cesara whose mouth was hanging open. Pop sliced one of his scallops in half. I looked around the room again.

After dinner, and a bit of the best Pear William soufflé known to man, I exited the restaurant and turned right. Once I got to the corner at Park Avenue, L was waiting for me at the bank of payphones. During dinner I had called him from The Four Seasons house line.

"What's going on?" he asked, handing me the box of a new cell phone. I never looked him in the eye.

"Just walk away," I said quietly.

I immediately threw my hand into the air to hail a cab, even though I was very close to home.

"Jonah, what are you talking about? What's the deal?"

The evening traffic was thin. A taxi came rolling to a halt in front of me.

"I mean it, L. Walk away. I'll call you tomorrow."

I jumped into the cab and gave the driver my address. When I looked out the window, L, stunned, still hadn't moved. I mouthed "thank you" to him just as I took off.

I opened the Samsung cell phone box. First I pulled out a fresh vial of coke, since I was running low, followed by a black Smith and

Wesson nine-millimeter pistol and an extra clip. It was small enough to fit into my suits' inside jacket pockets, yet strong enough to keep someone off my ass if they got too close. Because L's family is in a cash business he keeps a gun in his office, one in his home, one in his car, and one on his body. I've never been one to condone guns, but I've never been one to downplay their importance at the right times either. Unbelievably, my life had gotten to the point where having a piece on me simply seemed like the right thing. And, needless to say, L had one to spare.

CHAPTER 28

At 6:02 A.M. Thursday morning I opened the door to the ren-
dezvous point, the bathroom in Grand Central. Pangaea-Man was
waiting inside. He was standing in front of the sink farthest from
the door, pretending to fix his hair in case someone unanticipated
was to show up. Next to him were two large, black TUMI suitcases,
standing upright.

"Let's go," I said.

Before he could utter a single word I turned around and started
off. The door closed behind me. When I was about thirty feet away
the bathroom door opened again. He was quickly following me,
pulling both rolling suitcases behind him, one in each hand.

I led him outside. Once on the sidewalk I stopped so he could
catch up to me.

"What the fuck do you think you're doing?" he asked. "We had
a deal."

At that second, a black Mercedes-Benz limousine pulled up
beside us. I opened the back door.

"Get in."

Pangaea-Man froze. He definitely hadn't anticipated anything
like this, which is exactly why it was happening. He glanced around
nervously.

"What if I say 'no'?"

I walked up close to him, and spoke so only he could hear me.

"Then I get in the car, drive away, and you never see me or the fucking egg again."

Keeping my eyes locked on his I grabbed the handle of one of the bags. He grabbed the other. We both got in the car.

The black glass divider between us and the driver was up. I knocked on it three times, the signal for the driver to get moving.

"Where are we going?"

The truth of the matter was that we weren't going anywhere. Mattheau was at the helm of the car. These days Pop wasn't leaving the house before seven thirty I had instructed Mattheau to simply drive around until he received my second signal, and he willingly obliged, as usual, with no questions asked.

Pangaea-Man was sitting on the rear bench. I sat, facing him, on the bench situated under the driver-passenger divider. The two suitcases were awkwardly on the floor between us.

"Open one."

"Let me see the egg," he said.

"How about we stop the car and throw you and your fucking luggage to the curb."

"I just need to make —"

"Look, let's just cut the expected bullshit chatter," I cut him off. "I have a busy day. Now I promise you when I'm satisfied you took care of your end, I'll happily give you *Danish Jubilee Egg* so we can part ways. All right?"

Pangaea-Man clenched his teeth. He looked like he was ready to burst.

"You better not be fucking around with me, man. For your own sake."

"I know, tough guy. I'm really fucking scared considering you're so desperate you just jumped in a car with me."

I thought about pulling the gun in order to freak him out and maybe get some information. But I decided against it. If necessary, there would be opportunity for such drastic action soon enough.

"Now open one!" I said, pointing to the bags.

He wrestled one of the bags onto the seat next to him. He unzipped it and lifted the top up. I stood up in a crouch and, eyeing him the whole way, leaned in for a look. It was filled with stacks of fifty and hundred dollar bills. They were all brand new. They looked as if they had never been touched by human hands. The sight of this much cash made me feel two different things. For starters, I had only seen numbers, whether in business or in my own personal accounts, as funds passed from one stop to another. I had never actually seen this much cash money that I could actually hold. The feeling was unbelievable. The smell was as unique as the situation. It was like all of a sudden this giant tidal wave of possibility, of potential instant gratification, came slamming down on top of me like I was a sixteen-year-old walking into my first strip club. The second observation I made was the one that brought me back to the moment, the fact that Pangaea-Man was able to come up with this much fresh cash so quickly. It was obvious that he was dealing with a money player.

Or was he? Could he be the money player?

Before I addressed him, a question shot from one end of my brain to the other. Why the paradox? Why was someone with so much cash running a plan so sloppy that I inadvertently got dragged in? I still had no idea how I fit in to all of it. But I knew unless that fact became clear on its own volition, for now it would have to wait.

"What the fuck is this?" I asked.

"I'm sorry?"

I fell back into my seat.

"What the hell am I suppose to do with that?"

"I don't understand."

"Those bills. Are you kidding me with those?"

He looked as if he had just taken a bite of a hamburger, and unbeknownst to him someone had replaced the meat with shit.

"What? They're brand new."

"Actually, Copernicus, I was referring to the denominations, not the age of the bills."

He looked at the contents of the suitcase, as if he truly hoped staring would help him see what I was referring to.

"I have no use for hundreds."

Pangaea-Man returned his eyes to me.

"Why not?"

"Because they are the most easily traceable, dickhead. I guess I should have told you that I'll only take twenties and fifties. I just figured that any moron who had seen three cop movies in his life would have known this."

I leaned forward, aggravated.

"Just how fucking small time are you?"

I was talking completely out of my ass. I went into this morning encounter with only one objective, to buy time. If the bags had been filled with twenties, I would have told him I needed fifties and hundreds.

He slammed the suitcase cover down.

"This is the cash, you pain in the ass. You said two million, I delivered two million."

"Well I don't accept it."

"You what?"

"What don't you understand? I don't accept the payment. I'm not walking around with traceable bills because you have no idea what you are doing."

I don't believe this fucking guy, he must have said to himself, falling back into his seat. "Just because they're hundreds doesn't mean they're traceable."

"I don't like this any more than you do. I want nothing more than to give you back what you claim is yours so we can all just go on with our lives. But I'm not going to do so in a manner that puts me in harm's way. It's as simple as that. Now, you can either fix the problem or you can say good-bye to the egg. Clear?"

Pangaea-Man watched the city race by through the deeply tinted glass. He gritted his teeth.

"What do you want me to do?"

I knocked on the divider five times, Mattheau's signal to return to the spot where he had picked us up.

"Simple. Two million dollars in twenties and fifties, and I don't give a fuck if you need six suitcases."

"I don't have the time for this, man. And frankly, neither do you!"

The latter part of this statement had me near terrified, but I didn't want to break stride.

"Then take your head out of your ass and focus."

"You don't find a man standing around with six huge suitcases at Grand Central Station suspicious?"

"That's your problem," I said. "Get creative."

The limo pulled up along the same curb we had stepped in from. Pangaea-Man and his luggage got out.

"Tomorrow morning," I said as he pulled the second bag from the backseat. "This sidewalk, same time. That gives you another twenty-four hours."

"Don't you think twenty-four hours is a little unreasonable?"

I switched seats, jumping to the rear bench he had just vacated.

"Absolutely," I said. "Anyway, you just said yourself you're under the gun. I figure the sooner the better for both of us."

I pulled the door closed and we took off. I wasn't yet sure about how I wanted to handle *Danish Jubilee Egg*, so I had bought the little more time I needed. On the one hand, I admit, I'm human. I loved the idea of that much tax-free, cold cash in my hand. Also this way I would be free and clear of the egg and all of the trouble associated with it. But accepting the money made me part of the whole thing on a criminal level, and at this point I still felt I hadn't done anything wrong since I had no part in the actual *taking* of the antique, although the fingers would probably end up pointing at me.

The short answer for why I needed to buy more time was easy. Because of everything on my plate, I hadn't yet figured out which option made more sense.

"You are a serious ass, James. You should be thanking me."

"I should be thanking you? What should I be thanking you for? Going behind my back and making the board think you'd rather not deal with me?"

It was only six twenty-five. The floor was relatively quiet aside from the speakerphone shouting match going on in Perry's office. I walked in and sat down at one of the chairs in front of Perry's desk. She was standing, her body making gestures with the appropriate words as if Auerbach was standing right there in front of her.

"You should be thanking me for going to them as if I was doing so straightaway, bypassing you all together. Can you imagine how you'd feel if I had actually given you what you deserved and told them what you had done?"

"I never intended to be dishonest with you, Perry. You need to stop saying that."

"I came to you, as a friend and told you what I needed. I told you that timing was my main concern and something I was willing to pay a price for. You messed with that, lied to me, looked to juice me and, in the process, have now put me behind schedule. All I can say, James, is how fucking dare you call me and scold me as if I'm the guilty party here."

"Perry, you have no idea what it takes to deal with a board like this."

"Save it, James. You stand to make a huge commission here, not to mention the fact that your wife has already probably started decorating as we speak. You'd better watch your ass now. You fuck this deal up in any way whatsoever, in fact, you do anything that isn't in the best interest of seeing to it this deal closes, and I'll make sure you swing."

"Perry, Jesus! Now let's just talk about this —"

"I'm done talking for now, James. I have been instructed by the board that all real estate dealings are to go through you. They told me there would be a board consensus in the near-term, and that it would be coming from you. If I find out you waited one second more than you needed before calling me, I spill the details of what happened. Got it?"

"Perry —"

"Got it?"

Auerbach sighed, defeated.

"Got it."

"Good. Wouldn't want you to disappoint the wife now, James."

Perry hung up. Still standing, she folded her arms.

"Whoa!" I said.

"He never came home last night, Jonah."

"Who?"

Annoyed, she didn't respond. She just tilted her head to the left as though it were obvious.

"Did he at least call to tell you where he was?"

"Uh-huh, sure he did. At five o'clock this morning! He said he slept in the office. He said that he was working on some article and he's coming up on the publication deadline."

"You know, that doesn't necessarily —"

"He wouldn't e-mail it to me Jonah. I asked him to send me a copy, you know, for peace of mind, and he couldn't even do that."

"Don't jump to conclusions, Per."

It didn't sound good. As much as I wanted to forget everything else and help her I couldn't. I had become so consumed with the deal, and my own one million and one dramas, I only wanted her to remain focused, solid. She would have time, I told myself selfishly, to deal with her crumbling world later.

"What's the difference anymore?" she asked, bitterly. "All the conclusions point to the same fact. I married a complete asshole."

I wanted to forge ahead, into my own shit, into our deals, but I didn't. I couldn't. Perry, dejected, began sifting through the neat piles on her desk as she searched for something.

"Damn!"

"What are you looking for?"

"Electricity survey for the Cantrol property."

A red flag that I couldn't ignore went soaring into the air. Perry never misplaced anything, let alone a crucial document from a live deal.

"You want to talk about it?"

"It's just fucking electricity, Jonah."

"You know what I'm talking about, Perry."

She stopped and fell into her chair. I closed the door. Perry went on for a half hour about how it wasn't right, about how she deserved better. She went through peaks and valleys of rage, then disappointment, hatred, then faith. I simply sat and listened, realizing that I owed this to her.

"I just want the best for Max. You know that. He deserves to be protected."

"If you're that sure, then there's nothing that says you have to remain married. People everyday are —"

"You know this isn't that easy, Jonah!" she exclaimed, leaning forward in her seat. "You know who his father's best friend is. They will all make this beyond difficult for me. Maybe even dangerous."

"You don't know that, Perry."

"No, I don't," she went on, wilting back in her chair again. "But when I think of Max, and what he needs from me, I'm not even sure any of that even matters any more."

Mascara-tainted tears welled in Perry's eyes before one rolled down her cheek. She told me she was thinking, once and for all, of leaving him. For the first time I believed her.

When I returned to my office, to my mayhem, the day instantly got even worse. My other clients were seemingly all calling about their own respective deals. They were getting antsy by the fact they weren't hearing from me and they were curious why I had turned so much over to Tommy. I explained to them that Tommy's expertise was the most appropriate for the current stage of their deal, whatever stage this happened to be. I also told them that I'd be back on top of the situation again upon the current stage's completion.

Sprinkled in between these calls were fleeting moments of trying to decide about the egg. But just as my mind would get started I would again be interrupted. If not by clients or partners, then by other thoughts. Thoughts of the girl pretending to be Angie. Thoughts of the conversation I just had with Perry. Thoughts of if we were really going to be able to pull this deal off. Thoughts concerning my safety.

After getting back from the bathroom, where I inhaled a quick bump, my phone rang.

"Jonah Gray."

"Klyman tonight, punk."

"Oh Fuck," I sighed.

"Don't even pretend to tell me you forgot!"

Jake was calling from his cell. And, yes, I had forgotten.

"Of course not," I said. "I just have a lot going on this morning."

Dan Klyman was a rowdy guy around Jake's age and the son of Ken Klyman, one of our larger clients. The Klymans own a chain of eyewear stores across the country. Dan runs the West Coast operation. He comes into Manhattan once a year and always expects Jake and I to show him a good time. I wanted so much to get out of it, but the red flag this would have waved for Jake felt like too great a risk. I couldn't think. My mind was spinning too fast because of the coke.

"I . . . uh . . ."

"What's that?" asked Jake.

"What time again?" I said.

"Eight. Dinner at The Palm on the West Side then sandbox time at that new Penthouse Club. What's the matter with you? You set the night up."

Jake and I eventually hung up, which ultimately led my mind somewhere else. This was the moment I realized perhaps my drug use was starting to get away from me. My friends and I had always used all types of shit for fun, for avoidance. But now I was doing it to keep myself awake, to even my nerves, to pump my veins, to heighten and soften my senses. Now I was using them to literally help me function. Life during the previous ten days had changed drastically. My life had taken on a potentially life-threatening texture, but even though the times when I would party had vanished, my cravings had only gotten stronger. It had just cost me the opportunity to think on my feet, something I had always taken pride in, and get myself out of the situation. I had completely choked. I needed it to function, to make it through. I realized that it was all starting to get away from me.

By the early afternoon I was feeling uncomfortably confined in my office as well as in my head. I hated that outside circumstances were starting to dictate my life. As out of whack as everything had become, the calm surrounding me was eerie. The waiting for something to give or any sign of imminent resolution was becoming unbearable. I needed to get out. I needed to get away.

CHAPTER 29

I decided to head to the Madisons and check up on the progress of my deal. Once outside, I checked for the gun, which was in place. The sun was strong, so I put on my sunglasses, identified the shaded side of the street, which was another trick I learned from Pop when I was a kid, and headed uptown.

Park Avenue was bustling. The air outside was perfectly balanced and felt invigorating as it filled my lungs. Sharply dressed men and women were coming and going in all directions. Every important designer known to man was represented in some manner within eyeshot. Buildings that house the corporate headquarters for some of the world's most vital, significant firms lined both sides of the street. Men with perfect haircuts barked into cell phones as women dressed in perfectly contoured, feature-enhancing business suits that showed just enough skin to keep the imagination churning gave eyes as they walked past. It was a needling tease, a harsh reminder of my usual Friday afternoons in the summer that consisted of deal making, "beautiful people" watching, and powerful commercial properties.

I made my way past the corner of 50th and Madison, only a few blocks from my destination. The smell of hot dogs from a vendor's cart overwhelmed me as it hovered in the intersection like a mushroom cloud. I heard the growing rumbling of cars charge up behind me as the lights, in unison, turned green. I looked to my right. Half of the vehicles were assorted colors, half were the familiar yellow of a New York City cab. Then I almost slammed into one of my favorite types of tourists, the ones who, out of nowhere, decide to completely stop in the middle of a flowing sidewalk so they can wondrously look up at the surroundings. Part of me hated them while part of me envied their sense of wonder.

I walked into the classy, simple lobby of one of my deal's two buildings. Just inside the revolving door I stopped, my shoes' soles resting on the same gray, shiny marble that made up the rest of the three-story foyer. The calming, sturdy rock was laced with slight, faint white streaks. Two appropriately dressed men wearing blue suits—one a starter, or concierge, the other security—stood behind the centrally located concierge desk. Behind them on the wall was a huge oil painting of muted overlapping, black-and-white circles of all sizes over a gray background that matched the lobby's hue. On the wall to my left, only feet past the entrance, was a flat, touch-screen building directory.

My needed senses, the ones I had put in my pocket for a few minutes, returned in a rush. Behind my glasses I took inventory of the lobby. Once I was comfortable, I took them off and headed for the elevators. My first order of business was to see how they were doing on the roof. I knew I would be able to find Ron, the chief building engineer, in the building office on floor twelve.

Just as I was about to step into the elevator my phone rang. I didn't recognize the number. I stepped to the side and let the small group of awaiting passengers go ahead of me. It could be Angie, I thought. Or it could be business related. I let it ring. If it was Angie, I could simply hang up.

"Jonah Gray."

"I don't like being played the fool, Jonah."

It was a man's voice. I couldn't place it, but I definitely recognized it.

"Who is this?"

"My ties at Gallo are very strong, Jonah. I've spent many years cultivating them."

It was Murdoch.

"Perhaps in case such a day as this was to arise."

"How did you get my number?"

"Don't sound so surprised. Think for a second about how many mutual acquaintances we must have."

He was right. The number could have been in the hundreds.

"Look Lloyd, I really don't have the time for chitchat today. What part of our conversation last night was unclear?"

"You're a real fucking wiseass, kid."

"And you're very original. Are we finished?"

"The bank's going to want to keep the buildings with me, Jonah. You can bet on that."

People coming and going from the elevators kept filing past me. Murdoch was throwing out another feeble attempt at intimidation. It was almost pathetic.

"What I'm betting on is the fact that my inspection team is already swarming the building," I said. "Gallo is a bank, Lloyd. And economics speak for themselves."

"Meaning?"

"Meaning they'd rather deal with a class A buyer stepping to the plate with a bat made of cash than some debt infested has-been treading water."

"Don't even think —"

"Listen, Murdoch, you're keeping me from speaking with — well — anyone I actually deem important. You want the building, come and fucking get it. You got Gallo in your palm then call them. Not me."

"I already have, Jonah. So don't be surprised if you fall just short."

I felt a jab to the stomach. The boys of Gallo were players, and they were still talking to Murdoch even though we had the parameters of a deal in place. The rule of thumb is that when earnest money is paid, and a firm begins due diligence, it is the same as a handshake meaning the deal is the buyer's to lose. Merrill felt just as threatened by me as this asshole so I wasn't all that surprised.

"You fucking scumbag!"

"Real Estate is all about relationships, Jonah. You must realize that by now."

"I have an earnest money contract with signatures, Murdoch. You fuck with that, and I'll nail you and Gallo to the wall!"

"I have no idea what you're speaking of. I simply called to wish you good luck in your endeavors and remind you that failure is always a part of success."

The smug fuck had been around the block, so I knew I needed to be careful. We both knew he was short on funds, the reason he lost the buildings in the first place. I took a deep breath.

"Speaking of relationships, who'd you go groveling to for a bailout? Must have been pretty embarrassing, you know, since you work so hard to present yourself around town as such a big shot."

I was onto his game. I figured he'd found a money partner and was speaking quietly with Merrill and the boys at Gallo. Whether he knew the parameters of my deal or not. I couldn't be sure. Had Murdoch's group also proposed an all-cash deal as opposed to one involving other financial instruments? I couldn't be sure of this either. What I did know was that the guy was grossly underestimating me, which is the only reason he could have possibly called to rub his ongoing talks in my face. He should have just kept quiet.

He chuckled. "You churn ahead in such a brash, yet obviously naïve manner."

"Yeah, yeah. Look, you want to see just how naïve I am why don't you have a look at my bank account."

"Exactly my point," he continued.

"Here's my point. I castrate all comers young and old who underestimate me, and I'm a busy man. Don't call me again."

"Such words of wisdom. Is that all the advice you have for me?"

"It is. But I'll tell you what, I'll bring you along to the closing. This way you can actually watch as the buildings officially transfer to an owner who can afford them."

"Careful there, young one," he said condescendingly. "Often, the one who arrives right on time is the one who completely misses the party."

Sick of his voice I hung up, but instead of heading to the

elevators my legs started for the front door. His last words resonated with me. Ironically, not with regard to real estate.

I slammed the front door of my father's brownstone shut behind me. There was no time to wait for the elevator, so I charged up the stairs with the same thoughts tossing in my head as they had done the whole cab ride uptown. Maybe everything was playing out so calmly for a reason. Maybe certain powers and people, which I still couldn't put together, were doing just enough to keep my attention away from where it needed to be: *Danish Jubilee Egg.* Maybe Angie, Robie/Hart, and Pangaea-Man were all in on it together; maybe they had been pulling me here and there with locks of hair and bathroom visits on purpose. Maybe they were watching closer than they wanted me to think. Paranoia was working in overdrive.

Just as I reached the top step I slowed down. Pop's long-time housekeeper, Bea, was usually milling about this time of day. When I didn't hear her in the immediate vicinity, I continued in to the study. I thought of closing the door, but decided it was better to be able to hear someone coming down the hall as opposed to their turning the knob and walking in on me.

I crouched then opened the door of books. As I started turning the safe's dial, I couldn't shake off the feeling of defeat that was starting to creep its way up my body. Nor could I make sense of it. I had never been involved in anything like this. I was starting to feel as if I'd been had. I had heard a million stories. I had read a million books. This was always how it happened. Unassuming bastard gets blindsided, and he never saw it coming. My breathing sped up from the tension. It was as if I was about to win the antilottery.

The front chamber articles seemed to be intact. The only difference was that some of the cash was gone. My father, I thought. Hurrying, I pushed on the rear internal wall, revealing the second chamber. The watches were all in place, as were the documents, which I removed and placed on the carpet. As I reached back into the safe I could feel goose bumps raise on my arms just as a thin rush of sweat came to the skin's surface over my whole body. I took a deep breath.

As I pulled the black leather box from the confines of the wall, my confidence as well as my inner faith picked up where the feelings of defeat had left off. I flipped it open and stared mesmerized for a few moments at the work of art, absorbing its beauty. I hadn't seen it in only days, yet the mental image of how brilliant it was from the perfectly aligned elements to the piece of history subtly told had already begun to dull. It was that impressive.

I tucked the black box back in its safe house then picked up the documents to do the same. But as I lifted the surprisingly weighty stack of what seemed to be more like card stock than paper, I couldn't fight my curiosity. I had never once looked at these articles. But now they were face up in my hands and from the systematic chad markings to the different stamps and seals it became immediately apparent what I was holding. They were stock certificates. Only the words on them weren't in English letters. They were in the Cyrillic alphabet.

The hair on my arms stood on end. I lightly touched the surface of the topmost certificate and looked again at the typed Russian characters in the center of the sheet. There was something written in pencil, in my father's handwriting, underneath them. I lifted the document closer to my face. It read: SAPPHIRE PENDANT EXCAVATION.

Sapphire Pendant, I said to myself. *Sapphire Pendant.*

It sounded familiar, I thought. But why? Aside from the name of the booze I liked to drink?

Figuring it was Pop's English translation of the company's name, I moved on to the next. Same thing. Underneath the bold, centrally positioned Russian words was his penciled handwriting. The second read, CH. CHARIOT ENERGY INC. I could swear I had seen this one too. Just as I began whispering to myself, "What the hell —" it came to me. They were the names of two of Prevkos' subsidiaries, companies I had read about a number of times before while keeping up with our family friends' progress.

I barreled through the rest of the pile. THE NECESSARY MINING COMPANY, ALEXANDER GAS CONSTRUCT, M. ENAMEL ENERGY CON-

SORTIUM, EMPIRE NEPHRITE MINING AND PIPING. I had read about
them all. But as I came upon the name on the seventh and final certificate, I understood that there was perhaps an even deeper,
undoubtedly scarier, connection than I ever could have anticipated. The name of the last subsidiary was NORTHERN JUBILEE GAS
EXTRUSION.

Jubilee.

As in *Danish Jubilee Egg*.

I went back to the first certificate in the stack.

"Sapphire Pendant," I repeated again.

Then it hit me.

Hen Egg with Sapphire Pendant.

I swept into my apartment like a cyclone, Neo doing all he could to
keep up as I tore toward the living room. I went straight for the coffee table, more specifically the stack of five ridiculously oversized
coffee-table books on top of it, and removed the top one. It was the
self-serving birthday gift from my old flame Sharon. The cover was
shiny, still looked brand new, which made sense since the book had
only been cracked a handful of times. I tucked it under my arm and
headed for the study.

Once there, I placed my briefcase containing the stock certificates and the repossessed stolen antique on my desk and fell into
my chair. I put the book in my lap. For a moment I marveled at the
photograph on the cover, a shot of two imperial eggs side by side.

"Basket of Wild Flowers Egg," I whispered to myself, remembering the one on the left. It was one of Sharon's favorites.

Basket of Wild Flowers Egg was exquisite. Predominantly a silver
body covered with pearly enamel and rose-cut diamonds, the top of
the egg was an untamed explosion of colorful buds in full bloom.
Buds so lifelike, you could swear they were prime to be plucked for
a magical bouquet.

I opened the book and started to rip through. There it was just
as I thought. *Hen Egg with Sapphire Pendant*, produced in 1886.

I removed the stock certificates from my briefcase, revisited the second one, CH. CHARIOT ENERGY INC., and returned again to the book. *Cherub Egg with Chariot*, 1888. I proceeded to go through the full list of companies. As I did I confirmed what my instincts had already told me. Each of the seven company names on the Prevkos subsidiary stock certificates I was holding was derived from, in some way, one of eight Fabergé imperial Easter eggs.

The eight imperial Easter eggs that had gone missing almost a century earlier.

The egg unaccounted for was 1909's *Alexander II Commemorative Egg*. I booted my computer and jumped on the Internet to corroborate my thoughts about the subsidiaries. My thinking was dead on. Of twelve total Prevkos subsidiaries, eight were named after the missing eggs. The unspoken-for treasure's offspring was called "Alex Com II Exploration."

I closed the book and dropped it on the floor. I didn't move, barely breathed. As much as I wanted to collapse from the strain of trying to make connections from all of the information, something gave me strength. Something I couldn't ignore, something true. It was Tommy's voice. I could hear the thing he said to me six years earlier.

"There's one thing I demand of anyone who works for me, Jonah. One thing," he exclaimed before suddenly making it a point to stare into my eyes like he was trying to hypnotize me, "that you never — ever — pass up an opportunity to gain knowledge. Because in real estate, like in life, knowledge always wins the race."

I took a deep breath, picked up the book, and once again placed it in my lap. I concentrated on Tommy's words, words that professionally had worked nicely for me. I had run the real estate race with Tommy, Jake, and Perry as a team and won. But it was life's race, I was starting to feel, where I was perhaps lost somewhere in the middle of the pack.

I started at the beginning. Almost instantly miscellaneous information began to jump from the pages. There were the names of the two looted imperial palaces where the eggs had resided, Anichkov Palace and Gatchina Palace. There were the names of the two men believed to be the possible creators of the initial-less eggs, Piotr Derbyshev, an expert stone carver and one of Wigstrom's most trusted hands, and Nikolai Alexandrovich Petrov, the shop's utmost authority in enamel application. There were all types of arresting facts about not only the eggs and the players, but about the revolution and the era itself.

I knew that I had to keep reading. I knew from Tommy's teachings that I didn't have a choice. I flew through the eggs and their surrounding history, but as I whisked through the sheets of paper as fast as I could, I couldn't help getting stuck on some of the pictures. Strangely, surprisingly, Sharon's wandering seminars had taken on a new face. Her words, her desire to share something truly beautiful with me, no longer seemed as selfish as I had once thought. I was enraptured by the colors, the intricacies, and the materials. The meticulousness of each egg that used to seem tedious suddenly captivated me.

Finally, I came across *Danish Jubilee Egg*.

I looked at the black-and-white photograph, as well as the publisher's digitally enhanced supposed color version next to it, both of which paled by comparison to what I now possessed. It was one of only two of the missing eight imperial eggs with a visual record. There was mention of two smaller accompanying portraits, but since having the antique, I thought, I hadn't seen either. Then I realized since most of the eggs opened to reveal a miniature surprise they must be hidden in the egg's center.

I started on the text. Because it was, for so long, considered one of the missing, there isn't as much information available as there is for some of the others. But apparently, in basic terms, this Fabergé egg memorialized the most significant event of 1902 for Maria Feodorovna—her visit to Copenhagen to mark the fortieth anniversary of the ascension of King Christian, her father, to Denmark's throne. It also marked the death of Queen Louise five years earlier at Bernsdorff Castle. The egg was given to her by her son Czar Nicholas II. The two portraits contained within are of her father, King Christian IX, and of the king's queen, Maria's mother.

Once presented, *Danish Jubilee Egg* remained at Anichkov Palace until 1917. It then went missing after the revolution until the day it was found in 1979.

I looked for information on the critical markings, but there wasn't any. Not just for *Danish Jubilee Egg* but for any of the missing eggs. No *zolotniks*, no head-workmaster initials, nothing. Just more mystery.

CHAPTER 30

That night, after a raucous dinner at the Palm, the group of us headed to the new Penthouse Club on the West Side. It was Jake, Klyman, two of his pals who live in the city, and me. We were pretty liquored and drugged up. Even though I had realized I needed to curb this shit, I couldn't give Jake any reason to question me. But between the package from the girl still calling herself Angie and the stock certificates, my paranoia hit a whole new plane. Every once in a while I reached into my jacket and felt the gun just to make sure it was still there.

The five of us were given a prime table up front. Drinks were immediately placed all around, and before we could blink there were what seemed like five girls for every one of us swarming the table. Each woman's body was tighter than the next. One girl actually seemed to have a line of aqua-colored floss running between her legs and nothing else.

"Hey, Jonah, Archmont's wife working tonight?" joked Jake. "How about this one. A thin, retractable cord attached to cigarette lighters in cars? This way you can't lose the lighter under the seat while you're driving."

A hand appeared on my shoulder.

"How you doing tonight?" asked a forced, overly sexy voice. "I'm Shawna."

Shawna was a blond bombshell standing no more than five foot three. She had a tiny waist, huge fake boobs, orange skin from caked-on tanning lotion, and muscle tone beyond belief. Her bleached platinum hair fell to her waist and her green-color contact lensed eyes fought hard to connect with my own. She was wearing a barely there white bikini top that only covered her nipples along with her matching, leave-nothing-to-the-imagination thong.

"No thanks," I said, referring to the lap dance she was offering. "I'm just drinking tonight."

"Well, I don't think it's up to you."

Klyman, being straddled by a hot African-American girl, raised his martini glass to me.

"Your friend seems to think you may like me," she continued.

"Thank me later," barked Klyman.

He had prepurchased me a lap dance. I returned my eyes to Shawna. I couldn't afford to draw attention to myself by acting out of character. A quick dance, I figured, then I could remove myself from the table.

"Maybe just one," I said.

No sooner than the words had come out of my mouth was Shawna removing her top. Slinkily she began to dance in between my legs, gyrating slowly as she ran her hands up the front of her body and began to play with her hair. Her eyes were closed, and her knees slightly brushed the inside of my thighs with each of her seductive sways.

She then turned away from me. I took a sip of my Sapphire and tonic just as she decided to bend all the way forward, keeping her well-proportioned legs perfectly straight as she strategically positioned her ass right in front of my face. I was supposed to be focused on the results of Shawna's countless hours on a StairMaster. Instead I was dialed into a guy sitting across the way having a lap dance of his own. He seemed to be looking my way.

I turned my attention to Shawna again just as she swung around. She was facing me. She lunged forward, grabbing the corners of the chair out past my shoulders, then slowly slid the front of her body down my own until she was on the ground, kneeling in front of me. She ran her chest back up my crotch until her face was level with my own. Her hands now used my thighs as supports as she moved her mouth around to my ear. I could feel and smell her hot, minty breath as her lips parted and she began to speak.

"I know you," she said.

"I'm sorry?"

She moved closer until her lips lightly touched my ear.

"I said, I know you," she whispered.

I cocked my head a bit to the side.

"What exactly is that supposed mean?"

She giggled.

"It means I'm onto you, Jonah Gray."

I freaked and grabbed the back of her head like it was a grapefruit, forcing it in front of my face. Her ass knocked into the table, sending a few near-dead cocktails and beer bottles flying.

"What the fuck did you just say?" I asked through my teeth.

"Ow! You're hurting me!"

My grip was tight. Shawna grabbed each of my arms with her hands and tried to pry away my fingers.

"You're fucking hurting me!"

"Who do you fucking work for?" I continued as I suppressed the full scope of my anger.

"What are you crazy? Are you fucking crazy?"

The music was still pumping, but all eyes, from my table as well as others, were now on me. Instinct made me search immediately for the guy who originally had me suspicious. He was gone, and I couldn't make sense of any of it. I pulled her head in even closer.

"How do you know who I am?"

"Take it easy, man," Jake chimed in.

I never looked at him, even after hearing his voice. Then with unexpected force, Shawna managed to take a good swipe at my face as a last resort.

"Because I've read about you," she shrieked.

"Read about me?"

"That's right!" she yelled, catching me in the face the second time around and setting herself free.

Shawna shot backward and was now standing up. She was scared, embarrassed. She bent forward and at a loss for how to react, she attacked me with a few more girly swipes. I simply put my arms up to deflect her.

"What? Some dumb whore couldn't possibly have read about you in *Crains?*"

I swallowed hard.

"It isn't possible I'm putting myself through business school? How dare you, you fuck!"

I stood up. Before the bouncers could get involved, I bolted for the bathroom. Once inside I rinsed my face with cold water. I looked at my reflection in the mirror. Ashamed, scared of what I was becoming, I turned away.

Later, after getting home and sitting wide-eyed on my patio with Neo, I decided I was in desperate need of at least a couple hours of sleep. In order to slow down my mind, I drank three quick shots of tequila. The doors leading outside were left open for the spring breeze to dance in my bedroom. I fell asleep on my bed for what would turn out to be the only forty-five minutes of sleep that night. Neo slept on my chest.

During those forty-five minutes I had a dream. I'm not exactly sure where I was, but I was standing in front of a crowd of maybe thirty or forty people. No one was speaking. Everyone was looking intensely in my direction. And everyone, including myself, seemed to be wearing white.

I held a gun in my right hand and it was pointed at the side of my head. I pulled the trigger. A terrifying boom went blaring, tearing through the room, through my dream. My head snapped back awkwardly, like Kennedy's. Strangely, I wasn't dead. My head bounced right back into position. I was standing again, looking out into the same crowd. Only this time everyone was staring back with their own unique expression of terror. There was deep red blood splattered everywhere. No one was moving. I felt absolutely nothing.

I pulled the trigger for a second time. Then I awoke. Sweating hard, I sat up. Neo growled showing his displeasure at being disturbed. The room was dark, the surroundings strangely unfamiliar. Forget turning back. I didn't have time for looking back. All I could do, whether I liked it or not, was keep moving forward.

CHAPTER 31

On Friday morning, at five fifty, I was sitting in back of my father's limo. Dressed sharp, as usual, for my day, I read the *Post* as Mattheau took me to Grand Central. As I started to flip through, an article on page five jumped off the page at me. It was another follow-up about the egg heist.

My eyes began to speed ahead of my brain, devouring each word. The piece delved further into the life of Robie/Hart. He was from Syracuse, New York. His father, Nolan Hart, was a political science professor at Syracuse University. His mother, Lea, was a business administrator at nearby LeMoyne College. But from an early age Lawrence Hart was more interested in the arts and left central New York to pursue a degree in photography from Parsons School of Design in New York City.

Simple math, living in Manhattan plus no cash equals zero fun. So through his father's political science contacts, he got a job working the phones at the U.S. mission to the United Nations on the East Side. Right from the start it worked out well. By Hart's senior year he had spent so much time at the facility that he was helping out on weekends with security. After four years he knew all of the players, all the rules, all the drills. He knew what made our nation's UN home turf tick and what made it cringe.

And, perhaps most important, he found himself extremely trusted.

So, after being unable to land steady work as a photographer, he stayed on at the mission full time. A few years later he was put in charge of the entire security department. The rest, as we all know, is history.

The limo stopped, but my eyes remained glued to the paper. The article's closing fact, an afterthought used to solidify a potential insider's involvement, was more than a little disconcerting. At the time of *Danish Jubilee Egg's* theft the treasure was less than a month away from a trip to Washington, D.C. As a tribute to foreign relations, she was scheduled for display, indefinitely, in the rotunda of the U.S. Capital.

A knock on the window woke me. Like a deer surprised by headlights, my vision swung to the glass. It was Pangaea-Man. He must have recognized the limo from the day before. His face was right up close, his free hand covering the area between his eyes and the car as he attempted to keep the sun away and see through the dark tinted window.

My heart's pace stepped up a notch. I felt warm. I reached inside my jacket pocket to make sure I had my gun, which I did. Pangaea-Man, standing there with three huge, black canvas army duffel bags next to him on the sidewalk, knocked on the window for a second time.

I closed the paper and threw it down next to me. Nervous, I opened the door. I quickly retook my seat. I watched as Pangaea-Man flung the three duffel bags into the car. Then he got in as well and slammed the door shut after him.

We were now facing each other. The stuffed bags were between us on the floor, crisscrossed like three clumsily piled body bags.

"Here's your fucking money."

I knocked on the divider three times for Mattheau. We started moving. I kept silent. I was doing everything to keep my demeanor in check. On the surface I was poised, cool. Underneath my thick skin I was trembling.

"Those things are heavy," he went on. "Don't you want to check them out?"

As I looked down at the bags, my peripheral vision caught

Pangaea-Man reaching into his pants' pocket. The next moment was one I have trouble describing. It's almost as if my brain instantly vacated all thought. Everything went blank. I could no longer even hear aside from faraway sounds. It was as if I was under water.

I lunged at Pangaea-Man, startling both of us. By the time I reached him my gun was out in my extended nervous right hand. Using my left, I pushed him back into the seat by his throat, placing the point of the gun against the skin between his eyes. They crossed as he tried, in disbelief, to look at the revolver. He held his hands out to his sides, defenseless, as if subconsciously trying to show me there was nothing in them.

"What the fuck are you doing, man?"

"Whatcha got in your pocket?"

"I was reaching for a pack of smokes."

I reached inside his right, front pants' pocket with my left hand and pulled out a pack of Camels. I tossed them on the floor. It felt like something else was also in the same pocket, only deeper. I fished my left hand in one more time. This time, to my horror, I pulled out a NYPD police shield.

The hole that was becoming my life, slowly swallowing me, had opened its jaws even wider. I was free falling. There was no net. No escape.

"You're a cop?" I asked.

No response.

I pushed the thin, one-centimeter-wide steel circle farther into his skin. I could see his molars clenching through his skin as he winced.

"Fuck!" I blurted out, stone-faced, to no one in particular. "Fuck!"

I had no idea what was going on. My mind broke into a mad dash. Questions about conspiracy, mortality, and murder—mine or someone else's, I'm not sure — began buzzing around my now darkened mind like fireflies.

I took a deep breath in an attempt to harness my composure.

"What the fuck is going on?"

"Just relax, Jonah."

"Don't tell me to relax. Right now. All of it. Tell me every-thing."

"It's not going to work like that."

"Oh is that so?" I asked, alluding to the gun by simply applying a little more pressure.

"It is, Jonah," he responded. "It's not going to go down like this."

Suddenly, like I had reached into a hot oven forgetting a mitt, I felt scorched. Something about Pangaea-Man's voice and de-meanor were freaking me out. In the blink of an eye, he no longer sounded or seemed in any way like the hyper, unsure thief looking to shake me down. Now he was cool, trying to methodically garner control of the situation. The reason was an odd one, yet one I could easily identify and relate to. Exposing Pangaea-Man transformed him from hyper thief to a cop releasing a formidable concoction of instinct and training. Now I was in his boardroom.

I knew I needed to be wary. I also knew that if I had any chance of coming out of this situation unscathed, both literally and figura-tively, I needed to immediately demonstrate my control.

"Tell you what, I'll decide how it goes down. Now I'm not going to say it again. Tell me what —"

"I need you to put the gun down. I need you to relax."

What I needed was to establish that I wasn't going to be rolled over. I had a gun to the fucking guy's head and he still wasn't buy-ing me. Therefore it didn't take me long to understand that if noth-ing changed and that gun came down, I was in some unbelievable shit.

NYPD cop I reminded myself. Someone trained, when in dan-ger, to pounce on the first sign of weakness. I wasn't ready to kill anyone. But I knew I had to act like I was.

"Hold up your hand," I said.

Nothing.

I couldn't back down. I cracked the bridge of his nose with the butt of the gun. Before his head could even buckle to the side I caught it with my left hand, propped it back up against the seat and repositioned the gun between his eyes. Blood came streaming from a gash the gun left as well as Pangaea-Man's right nostril.

"I said hold up your fucking hand! Now!"

I was losing it. I had found my way into some profound state of conscious lunacy, a place where I had become so committed to protecting myself I was ready to lay it all down. I could actually see the anger growing inside of him, but it was obvious his better sense was holding it back. It was also obvious he had been around the block enough times to understand you'd better listen to someone when they have a gun to your head, no matter how seasoned you are.

He reluctantly held up his right hand. Without moving my eyes from his I grabbed his right pinkie with my left hand.

"Last chance, cop. You ready to speak?"

Pangaea-Man said nothing. By doing so, by challenging the sincerity of my words, all he did was harden my mettle. He was probing for weakness where there simply couldn't be any. I snapped his finger to the left like a twig. He couldn't help but to scream as it stuck out perpendicular to his hand. I swallowed hard and dug the gun in even farther.

"I think it's time to talk," I seethed, starting to scare even myself. "You agree?"

"Fuck!!! Fuck—okay, okay. I'll talk. I'll fucking talk. Ah —"

I backed off. I took my original seat across the way, gun still pointed in his direction. He gingerly probed his broken hand with his free one. He looked at the finger, then back again at me.

"You're either crazy or just rock fucking stupid assaulting a police officer like this," he pushed out between gasps.

"Please. Listen to you. A bit delusional, aren't we? You're no cop, you're a common fucking criminal running around and holding people up in public bathrooms."

"You won't be able —"

No weakness.

"Shut up and explain. I mean it. Enough bullshit. Start from the beginning. And do so understanding that you'll be wishing for only another snapped finger if I feel like you're trying to fuck with me."

Pangaea-Man took a deep breath and thought for a quick moment. I had snapped his digit without a second's hesitation and I now had a gun pointed straight at his face. He had no idea where he was going. He knew that he was all alone. He didn't have the antique. He had just placed two million dollars in cash in my car. He didn't have any of the power. I had *Danish Jubilee Egg*.

I had finally begun to demonstrate my control. I wasn't surprised when he started to speak.

"Aren't you concerned about the guys tailing us? Ah —"

He was having trouble sucking up the pinkie situation.

"I might have been if you hadn't held me up, threatened my life and produced two million dollars in cash. New York's finest my ass. You ever seen the movie *Bad Lieutenant?*"

The guy knew I had him. He left it alone.

"Who the fuck are you?" I continued.

The beach behind Archmont's house popped into my head again. Mentally I was zoning in on the cops. There was nothing clear. They had been too far away and I didn't have a very long look at them.

"Were you there that night?"

"Where?"

I stiffened my outstretched arm, which had started to relax.

"I don't know what you're talking about, man. I'm serious —"

"The Hamptons."

He paused.

"What? Look, I'm telling you, I have no idea where you're coming from with this. I'm telling you!"

He tended to his hand once again.

"Fuck," he mumbled to himself.

His response seemed genuine.

"If you're just some cop, where'd you come up with this kind of cash? Is it cop money?"

"Every drug dealer in Upper Manhattan and Queens are in business simply because we allow them to be. When I say jump they jump. They may cry foul, but believe me they're happy to oblige when they think about the alternative."

"What makes you so sure I have the egg anyway?"

"I know you have it."

"How?" I pressed him.

Nothing.

"I said how?"

Still nothing. Gun in his face and he still wouldn't answer. I moved toward him again. He just looked at me, with forced strength, in disbelief.

"I'll ask you one more time, cop. What the fuck makes you so sure I have it?"

Nothing.

With every second that went by the situation's seriousness elevated tenfold. I couldn't help feeling nervous, but at the same time I couldn't ignore the fact that my blood felt like it was beginning to boil.

It was crazy. Something started to take over. I want to say adrenaline, but it was something even stronger.

It was my father.

It was everything he had ever taught me about absolute power. Which now had me on the cusp of being terrified at the thought of not having it.

An incomprehensible reality washed over me. Only I couldn't figure out at the time what that reality was. It had me paranoid. It also had me wide-eyed, resolute. It had me at the highest peak of focus I had ever been in my life.

I dropped the pistol's aim to his groin. I had already crunched the guy's nose and busted his finger. He may have been a cop, but he was smart enough to understand that cooperation was now his greatest ally. He squinted, then lost control of his eyeballs, which bounced between my face and what was going on down south. Almost immediately he relocked his vision with mine, his last defiant moment before officially realizing he had surrendered, before fully accepting he was overwhelmed.

Which made two of us.

The tension was so thick that for those few seconds the only thing I could hear was the limo's air-conditioning system. His heart rate was accelerated and his nerves jangled uncontrollably. I could see it in his temples.

"Hold up your right hand," I went on.

He raised his damaged hand and I went for it. He said nothing until my hand tightly wrapped around his fourth finger. I didn't want to break another one, and I didn't think I'd need to.

"All right! All right!" he blurted out.

My left hand stopped, but remained in position to continue if needed.

"All right!" he barked. "Fuck!"

"What makes you so sure —"

"All right already, man. Fuck. You're completely crazy!"

"Explain. Now."

His wall was coming down. I could see right through his eyes into the pulsating blood vessels swimming around his brain. He had clicked into damage-control mode. He was ready to talk, salvage what was left of his interest in all of it.

I slowly retook my seat.

"Ah — someone told me," he said as I let go of his tortured hand.

"Who?"

"I don't know."

"Do we really have to go through this again?"

"I fucking swear," he pushed out evenly. "I'm being straight with you. I got the tip anonymously."

He gently rested his injured arm in his lap, accepting what had happened.

"How? Where? Was it a man or a woman?"

"Again, I don't know. I'm guessing a guy."

"You're guessing?"

"It was a note. It was dropped off at the precinct."

"What? It was — what kind of note?"

"What kind do you fucking think? It said you stole the antique egg that was all over the news. And that I had no connection to the person who sent the information."

I sighed.

"You expect me to believe that shit? You just think I'm going to sit —"

"I'm telling you, man. I swear!" he pleaded, "Nothing more, nothing less."

"All right, then where is the note?"

Ever so slightly he paused.

"The office. In my desk."

I didn't buy it. Precincts are busy, overcrowded. Cops are nosy. I pointed the gun at his balls again.

"I don't believe you."

"I'm telling you —"

"Five — four —"

"I'm telling you!"

"Three — two —"

"My pants! The note's in my pants!" he pushed out unable to take his eyes from the gun. "My other front pocket!"

He couldn't take his eyes from the gun. He was freaked by how low it was pointed.

"Slowly — and I mean fucking slowly — take it out and throw it to me."

He obliged in what must have been about one-quarter speed, fluidly like a slo-mo instant replay of Randy Moss making a fingertip grab in the end zone. The piece of cream stationery, folded once in half, landed between us on top of one of the duffel bags. Gun still aimed, I leaned forward, grabbed it, and sat back again in my seat. Eyes still on Pangaea-Man, I held up the piece of paper using my left hand and put it in front of my face. The paper's stock was thick, expensive. Once it was opened I shifted my eyes and scanned the words as quickly as I could. It read:

> I have no connection to you. I have randomly chosen you to receive the following information. *Danish Jubilee Egg* was stolen by Jonah Gray of Park Avenue. He works at PCBL.

I threw my eyes back to Pangaea-Man. The confirmation that I had been set up, part of this theft from the beginning, caused a fright so hard to explain that I simply won't even begin to try. The words continued to stab at me. I was even more confused. Something else was beating up my heart, like my ribs were using it as a punching bag. Something else had me on the brink of unraveling.

It was the note's handwriting. I felt like I had seen it before.

"I told you, man. Straight to the fucking point."

I moved my eyes back to the paper. I took another look at the writing, not the words but the penmanship. The subtleties, the spacing, I had seen it before. I knew I needed to shift my sight back to the cop, but I couldn't. Then, in a crushing instant like a baseball bat to the back of the head, everything, not just on this day but every day preceding, felt wrong. Everything seemed like a twilight-zone kind of scam.

The handwriting on the paper was my father's.

I forced my eyes back to Pangaea-Man.

"What the —"

My voice sounded nervous. I took a breath.

"What is this?" I asked.

"I just told you."

"How do you . . . when did you get this?"

"The day before you spotted me in that bar downtown."

Control.

I thought, *what fucking control? Can there really be a way this is even feasible? My father? A man I'd trusted my entire life?*

Could it?

I strained to keep it together even though I felt like a delicate tea cup dropped to a marble floor. Shattered.

Control.

What fucking control? I was dumbfounded.

"You know who sent it or something?"

Trained NYPD cop. He most likely had a gun on him and was just waiting for his chance, I reminded myself. I needed to regroup, but my mind started playing games. If it was my father, could he be conspiring with someone else? After all, he's the one who made reference to Archmont. But what if it was a set-up? What if it was easy to use Sam as the scapegoat simply because he was an easy target? Or, I thought, how about Andreu? After all, Prevkos' subsidiaries are all — or Angie? Or some combination of — How about my partners? They were the only ones I had told I was at the wedding. God damn, I thought, fuck Perry for all of her devil's advocate shit all the time!

I didn't want to believe my father could act like this toward me. What if his hunch about Archmont was nothing more than his usual good instincts? What if my father was the one being fucked with? What if we both were? I mean, who handwrites a note anonymously like this anyway? Aside from a —

I actually gulped in the middle of the thought.

— aside from a sixty-something-year-old real estate magnate with as little fear as he has computer skills?

Control.

Now more than ever.

Because this wasn't forgetting to leave out dog food or arriving forty minutes late for a closing because of traffic. This was a fucking crisis.

I blew off his question and forged ahead.

"Let me make sure I understand something. You got this anonymous information and instead of telling your precinct or supervisor or whatever you decided to hijack the egg and turn it into some cash."

"Something like that."

"Who else are you working with?"

Silence. No response.

"Sam? Angie?"

Still nothing. Not just nothing, an empty nothing, a submissive nothing. Because the realization of what this all meant to both of us was, mildly put, sobering. We both knew too much. We both knew too little. Above all, we both understood the complications of the two of us exiting the limo alive. I had the gun pulled and a keen grasp on the fact that had we both gone our separate ways, me with the egg and no explanation for its theft, I'd eventually, most certainly, be screwed.

I had no idea what my next move was. Right arm still extended, pistol poised, I began to slide the small, sturdy slice of vellum paper into my rear pants' pocket using my left hand. I kept my eyes on the cop, but I barely saw him. His face was nothing more than a bleary backdrop for the crisp image of the note that was still hovering in my mind.

As the sheet began to make its way through the thin slit in the suit's fabric, it got stuck. I dropped my eyes for the most split of seconds, but just as I did I was thrown back into the moment through an array of loud car horns. The limo swerved left then jutted right hard, tires screeching. As my free hand fought for balance, every muscle I have clenched up when we nicked the curb.

I inadvertently squeezed the trigger.

CHAPTER 32

Following a tumultuous three or four seconds Mattheau smoothly corralled the vehicle. My ears were ringing. Pangaea-Man, lifeless, was slumped back awkwardly on the rear seat bank, leaning slightly to the left. His arms were down at his sides, mangled finger no longer an issue. His left eye was gone. In its place was a hole from the bullet that went clean through his head and out through the small rear window, which didn't shatter since it was tempered glass. A narrow stream of blood flowed down his left cheek onto his shirt. The eye that remained intact was still open, staring straight ahead at nothing in particular. The extended gun was still smoking.

I froze. My mouth fell open. My breathing became ragged.

"Holy fucking shit," I whispered to myself.

Slowly I sank backward into my seat. I rested my arms at my sides, mirroring Pangaea-Man. Completely shell shocked, my gaze fixated, I tried to process what had just happened. What was yet to happen.

"Oh my fucking Lord," I squeezed out, still whispering.

In the midst of my ensuing perplexity, a question that was startling in its own right firmly took hold.

Had I really just done that?

Another humbling concept, query staggered me.

How many lives had I really just ended?

Feelings of loss, adrenaline, guilt, and relief became so tangible

I could almost taste them in my mouth. I had not intended to pull that trigger.

Thought fragments, scattered around my brain like puzzle pieces, slowly began to slide into place. I was driving around New York City in the back of a limo with two million dollars in cash from God knows where, a freshly killed New York City cop, and the gun that executed him covered with my prints. The magnitude of the situation firmly took hold.

I shook my head and forced myself to focus. My eyes squinted. I let out a slow, slightly choppy breath.

"Fuck," I said, sharply, this time a notch above a whisper.

I clenched my upper and lower molars so tight, as Pangaea-Man had only minutes earlier, that I could feel my flexing jawbones trying to blast through my cheeks' skin. In a flash, reality torched me like a campfire flame catching a marshmallow. I didn't have time to panic. I wouldn't have any more opportunities to correct wrong decisions.

My hands still shaking, I put the gun back in my jacket's inside pocket, never taking my eyes away from the dead man. Mattheau and I didn't exactly have a signal for what had happened. With as much poise as possible under the circumstances, I reached my left hand up behind me and started knocking on the divider. To my surprise Mattheau didn't lower it. I knocked some more. Nothing.

I would have yelled his name, but the rear of the vehicle when sealed off was nearly soundproof.

"What the fuck?" I mumbled to myself.

I reached for the passenger control button. The barrier slowly descended. As it did, I felt the car slowing down. I peeked through the divider. Just as my eyes crossed the threshold, Mattheau's hand clamped around my neck from out of nowhere like a bear trap.

"What are you doing?" I pushed out through gasps.

Mattheau was low in the seat. I remember being shocked that such a mild-mannered gentleman in such an odd position could garner such a stranglehold. His hell-bent expression both surprised and scared me.

"Jonah!" Mattheau exclaimed as he let go, his gaze bouncing back to the road in front of him. "Jonah, I'm so sorry! I —"

"Don't slow down," I continued, rubbing my neck. "Keep going."

"I thought...I heard a...I expected the other guy to come through here."

"Just keep going."

Mattheau, relieved that it wasn't me who had been shot, picked up the pace.

"Jonah, are you all right?"

He jerked his head right again to check on me. When he did he found me still staring at him in wonderment.

"I'm fine."

I quickly turned around and took another look at Pangaea-Man then the duffel bags. I dipped my chin and looked down at the seat under me before returning my attention forward to Mattheau. His eyes were shifting back and forth between the road ahead and the rearview mirror. He was trying to get a glimpse of what had happened behind me.

"I'm all right. Head back to the brownstone," I instructed him.

I hit the button and the divider went back up.

Speckled among the townhouses on the Upper East Side of Manhattan are a few with garages. My father's home is one of them. It had room for his two cars. His weekend Benz S600 convertible, always in the space closest to the door leading inside the house, and the limo even though it was usually with Mattheau. I knew Pop was still sleeping. Mattheau pulled in then closed the garage door behind us and shut the car's engine down. He had been a very loyal employee for many years and had always proved completely trustworthy. At this moment I couldn't have hidden what had happened from him if I tried. There was no choice. We both got out of the car.

Mattheau slowly walked to the rear of the vehicle, looking at the tinted glass even though there was no way for him to see through it. Then he saw the cleanly formed bullet hole in the rear window.

"Jonah, what happened?"

Neither of us said a word. Then he must have realized that not only had Pangaea-Man not gotten out of the car, he wasn't even stirring.

"What happened?" he repeated.

"I was just protecting myself, Mattheau. The gun going off was an accident."

Mattheau was processing, thinking.

"Why were you protecting yourself from this man?"

"It doesn't matter," I said rubbing my neck again. "All I know is that this is quickly becoming too much. All of it."

"Jonah?"

I started to pace. I ran through my options only to see how few there seemed to be. Mattheau leaned into the limo for a look.

"My God," he exclaimed with his head still in the vehicle before standing back up, "he was a police officer."

"This was not supposed to happen. I'm telling you. When he got in that car this morning, I had no idea he was a cop. I had no idea about a lot of things."

My feet stopped.

"I would never knowingly drag you into something like this. You know that!"

"I do know that, Jonah."

I stepped to the limo, ducked my head, and took in Pangaea-Man's face again. His lone eye was still beaming yet completely drained of life.

"Jonah," Mattheau went on, "perhaps your father would —"

"No!"

I snapped back into the upright position. The note. What did it mean?

"Forget about my father. Involving him won't do either of us any good. I'll just end up dragging him into my mess like I did to you."

"I understand your apprehension, Jonah. I do. But with all due respect, he knows —"

"I said no!"

I took a deep breath.

"I can't."

I had always treated Mattheau with the dignity he deserved. Honoring that, honoring me, he moved forward.

"What about the authorities? Are there other officers who —"

"No cops either. Yes, it was self-defense, but it's complicated. Going to the cops is just another dead end."

"I never said to go to the police. You didn't let me finish. My full question would have been, are there other officers who know the two of you were together?"

I thought for a second, but not about the question.

"What's going on with you, Mattheau? Why don't you seem the least bit scared by all this?"

"Because like you, Jonah, I don't have the time."

An overwhelming sense of guilt washed over me. Mattheau was a good man, a good employee, a good keeper of secrets. Which all made me realize one thing. This was one secret he shouldn't have had to keep.

"Go!" I blurted out. "I mean it, Mattheau. Take off!"

"What? Jonah, what the heck are you —"

"There's no reason you need to be a part of this. You can disappear into the house and I'll just . . . I'll just . . ."

"You'll just what?"

"I can handle this. You don't have to worry."

Mattheau looked at the door leading inside, but instead of moving he returned his attention to me.

"I can't take that chance, Jonah."

"What the fuck does that mean? I've earned your trust the same way you've earned mine! I would never let anyone think that —"

"You don't understand. It isn't about anyone thinking I was involved or not. It's about any of them, the police or anyone, thinking about me at all."

I didn't get it. I had nothing to say. Mattheau started for the driver's door, opened it, and reached inside. In one motion he pulled out the garage clicker.

"It is you who needs to go. Leave me to clean all this up."

"What the hell are you talking about?"

"I'll cover you, Jonah. I'll cover both of us. But the only way I can do that is if you leave. Now."

"How? Cover us how?"

"The duffel bags in the car and the contents of the cellar —"

The townhouse's cellar, a wide-open, unfinished space, was comprised of nothing more than a washer and dryer, a tool chest any of us hardly ever used, and my old high-school bench and weight set.

"— It's more than enough."

"Enough what?!"

He didn't answer me.

"How could you possibly have any idea how to take care of this?"

Mattheau held the garage clicker in the air as if to light a fire under my ass. I raised my arms in submission.

"Okay! Okay, fine. One more question and I'll go."

He nodded.

"Why?"

"No time for that right now, Jonah. But I'll tell you what —"

Mattheau finally clicked the button. The motor began whirring and the door began to rise.

"— Next time we're alone, ask me why I left Haiti."

I pulled my briefcase out of the car, crawled under the half-raised garage door, and dashed out into the city.

CHAPTER 33

The elevator doors closed behind me. My floor was barely stirring. Instead of my office, I headed for the bathroom. Once inside I jumped into a stall, locked it, and opened up my briefcase on the toilet.

All of the stress from keeping my emotions under wraps was starting to take its toll on my body. My mind was still sharp, acute, but I was starting to feel undeniably tired. I was used to little sleep, but this was different. My shut-eye the night before had totaled only minutes as opposed to hours in anticipation of my meeting with Pangaea-Man. I had spent the last hour or so adding cop-killer and obstructer of justice to my résumé. My mind and body were starting to play tug-of-war. My body was asking for a brief reprieve but my day was only just starting.

I needed time to figure out how to approach my father. I thought, *do I do a little reconnaissance first? Or do I just come straight out with it and ask him?* I needed to be sure.

I pulled my vial of coke from one of the leather pockets in my briefcase. I bounced a huge bump up each nostril. I closed the vial, put it away, shut the briefcase, and let myself out of the little drug pen. Once in front of the mirror I placed the case at my side.

I studied myself in the glass. I couldn't believe what was happening, what had transpired on so many fronts in such a short amount of time. I looked the same. In fact, I thought, I looked pretty damn good. I was exuding the kind of glow, confidence that went with rising up in the face of great challenges. I had chosen a terrific suit that morning. Canali head to toe. Three-button navy suit, sky blue herringbone shirt, and solid gold silk tie. Powerful. I took a deep breath.

I made eye contact with my image in the mirror. As much as I wanted to feel safe, the reflected room behind me appeared to be closing in, clamping down. I reminded myself that I still hadn't uncovered all of the facts, which meant an ironclad vision of how to get myself past all of this hadn't yet formed. I was definitely both exhausted and living in fear. But the show needed to go on.

I turned on the faucet and collected a small puddle of water in my hand. I snorted it up my nose to wash all of the coke down then let out a quick choking cough and headed for my office.

I closed the door behind me and put my briefcase down next to my desk. I usually took off my suit jacket when I was in the office, but had suspended that practice out of my need to have the gun as close to me as possible at all times.

Before settling in, I noticed a small, thin package on my chair. I leaned forward to have a closer look without touching it. It was sent to me with no return address. And it was marked with the same lettering as the initial hair package from the Angie Sheppard imposter.

Now she was really starting to piss me off. Instead of feeling nervous I became angry. I had recently joined the ranks of a death-row candidate while at the same time my team was still trying to close the deal. I picked up the package and tore into it fearing nothing.

It was a DVD of the movie *Fatal Attraction*. The fact I had thought and spoken of this movie when I was looking at her in Pastis made me uneasy. Fuck! I hated that she was actually paying attention to me! Just leave me alone!

There was a Post-It secured to the front of the unopened DVD package. It read,

Thought you might enjoy this since you feel like you are living it. Please give me another chance. Please. Don't make me do anything we'll both regret. Please.

Krissy

Krissy?

"What's that?"

I hadn't seen or heard Perry come in. She startled me. I straightened up, wide-eyed.

"Too much coffee again?"

"I didn't hear you come in."

I picked up my briefcase and placed it on my desk like everything was business as usual.

"What's your story this morning?" I went on.

I opened the briefcase and placed the DVD inside. I looked at my watch. It was 7:25 A.M.

"I didn't expect to see you for another twenty minutes or so."

I closed the briefcase and returned it to the floor next to my desk.

"Well there's this little half a billion dollar deal I'm trying to put together. My mother came by extra early to watch Max."

The deal. I still didn't know how to handle the deal. All I knew was that everything had to go on as business as usual. I couldn't let anyone, and that meant anyone, especially Perry, know what was happening with me.

"Hubby couldn't be there for him to wake up?"

"Hubby was out by five. And if it's all right with you, I'd rather not mention his name again today."

Point taken.

"Any word from Auerbach?"

"You might say yesterday's events served as a serious motivator. He called me late last night to apologize for the tenth time. In between pleas for regaining my friendship he threw in that the board definitely wants to make a deal and they seem very happy with the number offered. He explained to them that it was the number of a very eager buyer and that they should jump on it instead of trying to negotiate."

"The time constraints?"

"He outlined it all for them. He then said they'd have a consensus by Monday. I explained that I needed the weekend to get my inspection team on the premises, and that I didn't understand why so much time was needed if it was such an obvious no-brainer."

"What did he say to that?"

"That he was only concerned about being able to reach enough board members in such a short amount of time."

"And?"

"And I told him that I had a little story his board might find very interesting if he didn't figure out how to get me the go-ahead by the end of the day today."

Perry, dressed in a gray Armani skirt suit with a pink top underneath, sat down in one of the chairs facing my desk.

"Thanks, Jonah."

I sat down as well.

"For what?"

"For helping me to avoid being completely sandbagged by Auerbach. Normally I would have seen that coming."

"Is that so?" I asked, sarcastically.

"You know what I mean. It's just that these last few days have, well—"

"Don't you mean these last few months?"

Perry let out a semi-sad laugh.

"Besides, I thought you didn't want to talk about him today."

"I don't," she said back.

My cell phone rang. I looked at the caller ID. It was Krissy, formerly known as the Angie Sheppard imposter. Perry must have been able to tell from the look on my face who it was.

"What's this girl's problem?" she asked.

All I could do was raise my hand into the air and shake my head.

"Not now," I said.

My organs, my feelings, my soul, everything inside was dancing the tango. Yet in spite of all that was happening, I remember, ran-domly, feeling thankful for Perry. Thankful of the fact that her face could, even for a few needed moments as my mind was again speed-ing up, calm me.

"You know, Per—"

"What?"

I had started speaking without even knowing what I wanted to say.

"You should wear pink more often."

At that instance Tommy blasted into my office.

"My office, now!"

"What's going—"

"Now, Jonah!"

"What about Jake?" asked Perry.

"He's on his way upstairs," Tommy answered.

Two minutes later the four of us were in Tommy's office.

"Cold, buddy?" asked Jake, referring to the fact I still had my jacket on.

"Not now, Jake," scolded Tommy. "It's time for all of us to focus. We seem to have a potentially serious problem on our hands."

I sat there outwardly looking concerned, inquisitive. Inside I was a nervous wreck. Was this impromptu meeting about me? About Pangaea-Man? Was Tommy just keeping me still until the cops could get to me? Had Mattheau gone straight to the police? I shifted in my seat.

"I got a call from Ray Slevin at home early this morning. Said he couldn't sleep, so he decided to wake me up as well instead of waiting until we were all in the office."

Perry's and Jake's eyes shot nervously around the room. My eyes shot around also, as I pretended to be alarmed. In reality, given the alternatives, I was relieved.

"Do you know why?" Tommy went on.

"He was ecstatic about the boat load of cash he's about to make?" Jake said, looking to ease the tension.

"Not quite, smart-ass, but at the same time not entirely wrong either. You see, at first he was in fact excited about the number, and I want to stress at first. But something happened yesterday that apparently spoiled Mr. Slevin's mood."

Tommy took a slurp of his coffee.

"It seems, Jonah, that the roof contractors you have working on your deal decided not to honor their confidentiality agreement."

"I don't understand." I said.

"Well then let me spell it out for you. Contractors talk, Jonah. And the ones working for you apparently spilled the beans to some workers inspecting the Slevins's roofs for Jake. Apparently they had no problem whatsoever disclosing who they were doing the inspection for."

"Captain," I started, "I specifically explained —"

"Jonah, you were supposed to make it absolutely clear to all inspection teams that the confidentiality agreements in this case were of the utmost importance. That superiors were to make sure this message worked itself all the way down the line."

"This isn't my first time running a deal, Tommy," I reminded him, thrilled to have a reason to go to my happy place and unload a little steam. "I handled everyone exactly as I have always done in the past. Explicitly and professionally. I told them that I needed secrecy, and they signed the agreements claiming that I, we, had the privacy we needed. Need I remind you, Tommy, that the roof contractors I am using are a firm you introduced me to? I take personal offense to you attacking me and blaming me for the unprofessional conduct of someone else who can't keep their fucking mouths shut."

"Oh, fuck," Jake pushed out.

"Oh, fuck is right," Tommy went on, passing over my comments. "Ray Slevin called me this morning to say he was under the impression Jake had not been totally honest with him as well as his sons. He said he wanted to know if there was any truth to the fact that we were negotiating with others also."

"What did you say?" I asked.

"He already knew that you were looking to acquire the Madisons, Jonah. I told him the truth. I told him there were others, but that there was more to it than appeared. I figured it was already out there and would only put us in a deeper hole if I was to lie to him. Let me say, he was not happy."

"How did you explain the 'more to it than appeared'?" I asked.

"Thankfully I didn't have to. But that's why we're now sitting here."

"Oh, fuck," Jake squeezed out again.

"Can't we just put the fire out before it begins to get fanned?" asked Perry.

"The way I see it," Tommy started right in, "had he asked me, my instinct would have been to tell him that the new sellers had just come into the picture. That we hadn't mentioned them because we weren't even sure they were real until now. It's workable, but it changes the whole strategy."

"But that doesn't have to be so terrible, Tommy," Perry responded. "After all, playing the portfolios off of one another was an approach we discussed taking in the first place."

"But if you remember, Per," I added, "this approach often makes it harder to get what you want quickly."

Changing the rules in the middle of the game can be a serious risk, especially when it means adding unforeseen competition. For the seller, the skepticism and potential separation anxiety that goes with losing property in the first place gets compounded by the fact that the price is going down. People become so concerned they're getting snowed they unknowingly end up severely slowing down the process.

"It's the reason we decided to throw them all a premium and see if they'd ante up. Fuck, we didn't even force them to negotiate with themselves let alone anyone else."

"Pitting these sellers against one another definitely makes our lives harder," Tommy conceded.

"Well, do we even have a choice now?" continued Perry.

"No," Tommy said. "We don't. So here's my suggestion. It's already Friday, which probably means anyone whose opinion we even care about is already stuck in traffic on their way to the Hamptons. If anyone asks throughout the course of today, you simply say we aren't discussing anything with anyone aside from those involved in the deal. Period. If the principals involved call looking for answers, you tell them that it hadn't been mentioned because until today these other participants hadn't been deemed one hundred percent valid. When they want to know more, you tell them you're not at liberty to say because you haven't been handling the others, which, in each case, will be true since you've all spearheaded the deals individually. Then you simply get them refocused on their deal. We don't yet discuss how any of this may affect pricing until Jonah has a conversation with Prevkos and can determine which portfolio is the preference, and which is second choice."

Tommy turned to me.

"Your objectives with Andreu are pretty clear-cut, Jonah. Understood?"

"Understood, captain."

"Good. Once we have a full understanding of our direction on behalf of the client, we can regroup early Monday and blast into the week guns blazing."

"Hello."

"Good morning, Pop."

"Jonah, you really don't have to check up on me every —"

We went through the same routine each day and routine had to remain the same at all costs.

"You're a guy who's already had a heart attack and isn't getting any younger," I cut him off. "I don't do it just for you."

Only on this particular morning my call had a second objective.

"What's the story? Everything all right?" I went on.

"The story? I had to take a fucking yellow cab to work this morning, that's the story," he went on, chuckling. "Must be ten years since the last time I got in one of those."

"How come?"

"Mattheau showed up this morning with the limo's rear window blown out."

"You're kidding?"

"I'm not. He was stopped at a light and a truck's tire kicked up a rock that came crashing through. He called the body shop early, before I even came downstairs, and they told him to try and drop it off early before they got busy. They're farther uptown in the complete opposite direction of the office and I'm playing golf this afternoon with Alex Spencer. If I wanted to get to the office at a decent hour I didn't have time to wait around for a car service."

I paid unusually close attention to the intonation in his voice.

I wanted to ask him about the note. Or did I?

"Unbelievable," I said dryly, keeping my desired question at bay. "Anyway, it's good for you to take a yellow cab once in a while and remember how we commoners live. It builds character."

Mattheau was free and clear of my father.

"You got a lot on your plate today?" Pop asked.

"You might say that. You?"

"This and that, the usual bullshit."

His speech was even. I felt vulnerable, uncertain.

"So as you know I'm heading out to Connecticut early Saturday morning to play golf with Gary Halper," Pop continued, his voice carefree. "He's been begging me to see the new—"

I decided that it wasn't time. I knew more than anyone how sly my father could be. But I also knew he had never come close to trying to wrong me in my entire life.

I needed more answers.

At nine forty I was in Jake's office standing in front of his desk. Jake was standing behind it flipping a quarter into the air. We were on speakerphone with Jagger Slevin.

"I'm serious, Jake. Leo and I don't appreciate any of this one bit. We won't forget it."

"Jagger, don't be such a drama queen," Jake said. "You have to understand the position I'm in. I have a buyer that wants to move fast. While I respect that you and Leo are the two basically steering the ship over there," Jake said with a smirk, simulating the act of jerking off in midair with his right hand, "the fact remains today that your father and his brother are the ones who can pull the trigger on a sale. If this was strictly about having a triple A-rated tenant on the hook for a large block of space, you would be our guy."

"Then tell me. Why did you approach me in the first place?"

"I confess, Jag, that I was acting in a self-serving manner. You see, I understand that the older generation can be a bit stingy and unrealistic about certain things. You know, I get it that they like to think they still have a complete understanding of where the market is at all times. It makes them feel young. But the simple fact is that they don't. I know you and your cousin are both very market savvy, and that you guys understand the economic environment as well as anyone. My hunch was that you two would be able to see how ridiculously in your favor the deal we were offering was, and you'd get the ball rolling with your father and uncle before we even approached them. You are a smart man, Jag. I'm sure you can see my dilemma given the time constraints put on me."

"It's Jagger. Not Jag."

Jake fought not to laugh.

"And what's this about Jonah working on a deal to buy the Madisons?"

My ears perked up.

"According to my father, the two deals would fall into the same general price range. Is this a competing deal for us? Is he working for the buyer also?"

"It is a competing seller. But beyond that I really don't have too many specifics since Jonah's been handling them. To tell you the truth, they just officially stepped into the arena. That's why they hadn't previously been mentioned."

"Well none of us like what's going on here, and you can pass that on to your teammates."

"Duly noted."

"First you tell us we're dealing with a buyer that wants to remain anonymous then you guys pull this shit."

"One has nothing to do with the other, Jagger. We have showed you all of their necessary credit information and pertinent internal numbers, and they are coming to you with all cash. Since when does it matter who hands you a mountain of cash? They understand that the time parameters, along with their anonymity, is a bit out of the norm and they have offered a very generous premium in acknowledgment. I assure you that you have nothing to be wary of here. Your family's deal remains on the top of the pile."

"Well I may just have to suggest to my father that we pull it off that pile."

Thankfully there wasn't any real cause for alarm since we knew where the important Slevins stood on all of this.

"I can't tell you what to do," Jake said, perfectly poised. "But I will say that I really think it would be a foolish move. There is a deal to be made here, Jagger. Your father and his brother, annoyed as they may be, understand this. You are being pursued by one of the most prominent companies in the world. They are very ethical and they are very fair when it comes to business terms. We stay focused here and your family makes out as well as they do. Remember, the timing's nice for your family. We both know this market still has a ways to go."

"Unfortunately the buyer isn't my concern when it comes to ethics. Your team, especially Jonah, has a reputation for bending the rules."

"The only reputation I'm aware of, Jagger, is the one that we know how to close deals. We always play by the rules. We just usually tend to find, as our statistics show, that the competition isn't up for the challenge."

"You just better not be screwing around here, Jake. I mean that. My father smells trouble. Just hope for your sake that his message was Tommy's wake-up call."

"Easy with the threats, young man. It appears you're getting all worked up over nothing."

"You just make sure everyone's playing by the rules over there, Jake. Otherwise you guys better watch your asses."

I walked back into my office staring at the caller ID on my ringing cell phone. Krissy was still on the prowl. Carolyn's voice came through the intercom.

"Line two, Jonah."

"Who is it?" I said as I rounded my desk.

"Andreu Zhamovsky."

I pulled my eyes from the cell phone.

"Put him through."

I only had one second to channel my energy correctly, and focus.

"How are we today, Jonah?"

I had to continue to show Andreu that he had my full attention, that I had no reason whatsoever to deviate from our mutual goal. I had worked too hard to get where I was. I wasn't about to piss away the biggest opportunity of my professional life because someone was looking to frame me. I definitely had some questions for my old friend, but I was still too short on answers. All a desperate interrogation would have done at this point was possibly cause a problem where there wasn't one. For all I knew, Andreu could have been the one being set up. I just didn't know. The stars were beginning to align. I just couldn't yet see in which direction.

"I can only speak for myself, Andreu. And I'm well."

The initial words were the toughest.

"Good, Jonah. Good. I just wanted to check in before the weekend. I'll be on the yacht until the early afternoon tomorrow and the reception can be quite poor."

I had a job to do.

Numerous jobs to do.

React.

"Everything seems to be going as well as we could have hoped for. You can go out onto that ocean without a worry."

"Is that so?"

All he needed to know was that I was busting my ass and focused on the prize.

"It is. Our third and final inspection team should be in place by the end of the day. Now, insurance."

"Insurance. What do you mean insurance?"

"I mean there are a number of insurance issues. Liability insurance, property insurance, workmen's comp—the city even wants owners carrying terrorism insurance because of those fucking cowards in the airplanes. I have one of PCBL's risk consultants evaluating each potential portfolio in order to make an assessment of what type of coverage we need to have in place. Now once his recommendation is established, he will forward them to—"

In his mind I shouldn't have had any reason to deviate from the importance of the deal, so I didn't. I rolled right into a sermon about each aspect of where we were, and dove into the topic of insurance as if I were a professor on the subject. Why, as a commercial property owner, you have insurance. When you have insurance. When you don't have insurance. How insurance works. Why insurance works. The number of different areas of coverage offered. The reasons for so many different areas of coverage. The reasons some of those areas are essential while some are complete bullshit. Why dealing with insurance firms usually sucks. What insurance costs. What those costs entail. I probably bored the shit out of him, but business talk served two very important purposes. Momentarily, it kept me in a safe place and kept any suspicions at bay. Time would eventually run out.

CHAPTER 34

That night, after leaving the office, I locked myself in my apartment. I even went so far as to secure a chair under the front door knob. CNN was on the sixty-three-inch plasma, muted, in the barely ever used living room. I stared into the unlit fireplace, which I swore each winter I'd use and never touched. I was concerned about Mattheau finishing the job.

We never discussed if he was going to call me again that day. Since I hadn't heard from him I decided solitude was best. I didn't know what to expect. Would Mattheau have taken care of the problem or would everything unravel? I was still in my suit from the day, minus the jacket and shoes. The landline's cordless phone as well as my cell were both on the couch next to me, as was the gun. To my other side was a sleeping Neo wrapped in one of his favorite blankets. On the portion of the glass coffee table directly in front of me was a bottle of Patron Silver, a shot glass, my coke vial, and a tiny spoon. The intermittent drinks of booze were intended to take the edge off. The coke was to keep me awake in case of a call from Mattheau.

I sat there in silence. Then I leaned forward, picked up the miniscule scooper and hesitantly held it up to my nose. Before inhaling I just stared at it, hoping I would have the strength to put it down. It wasn't long until I gave in and blasted the fine powder up my nasal canal.

The tug-of-war between my mind and body continued. With each additional dose of either substance, more men simply jumped onto either side of the rope. I was exhausted but awake. My nerves were shot. There was nothing to do but wait. Lou Dobbs was silently speaking with Dick Grasso. Underneath them was a caption that read "New York Stock Exchange Chairman Comments on World-Com Accounting Scandal." About nine o'clock my cell rang. I leaned over it to see the caller ID. It was Krissy. For the hundredth time that day I silenced the ring.

As I leaned forward to replace the coke spoon, my ass accidentally hit the mute button. Grasso beamed to life.

"It's not necessarily about looking at the dollar amounts, Lou. It's about looking at where the money was. And why someone wanted you to see it there —"

My head lifted as if Mr. Grasso was speaking directly to me. I tried to hold onto the words but they were getting caught in the new ones completing the chairman's thought. I scrambled for the Tivo remote and backed up a few frames.

"It's not necessarily about looking at the dollar amounts, Lou. It's about looking at where the money was. And why someone wanted you to see it there..."

"Why someone wanted you to see it there," I repeated.

Grasso continued on but I no longer heard him. All I heard was the sound of my own voice in my thoughts. Timing, working for or against me, had until this point seemed to be the key to the entire, still unidentifiable, game. Only now, because of Dick Grasso's words, I had the timing of something else to look at, something that hadn't until this moment popped.

It was natural by this point to think the three weeks Andreu had given me to complete our deal was a concern. Now, it occurred to me that perhaps the timing of the deal, meaning the actual buildings changing ownership, wasn't what begged to be examined.

Perhaps, as Mr. Chairman had suggested, it was the timing — more important, the placement — of the money.

I looked down at Neo, the phones. Neither stirred. Mattheau passed through my mind again as did someone I hadn't seen in a long time. Someone unexpected. Someone I had once trusted who disappointed me. Someone, it chillingly occurred to me, I had no choice but to find.

I picked up the cell. With a quick touch I entered my address book and hit "S."

Stern, Ryan.

I hit "send." Within seconds I heard his familiar voice.

"Ryan Stern."

Ryan Stern. Executive vice president of institutional services at Salton Lynear Bank, the firm housing the Prevkos' deal funds.

"Ryan, it's Jonah."

Ryan knew me well. He was just surprised most likely because he never thought he'd be on the receiving end of a call from me again.

"Jonah. Wow! I, I'm—"

Maybe everything does happen for a reason, I thought.

"Where are you right now?" I asked.

I paced on the corner of Broadway and Eighty-third Street. I had stripped myself of the tie, but in an attempt to keep myself together I checked and straightened the collars on both my suit jacket and shirt. The breeze was stronger than usual. A whispery, baby tornado swirled a wrapper in the middle of the street. About a quarter to ten Ryan emerged from the restaurant. He located me and we walked toward one another.

"Jonah."

He put his hand out. I reluctantly shook it.

"Been a long time, Ryan."

"You're telling me. Must be two, maybe three—"

"Two years, seven months, sixteen days since they decided not to charge me."

He briefly looked away as he inhaled my comment before turning back.

"You know I never meant for any of that to happen, Jonah. I was told—"

I cut him off. "That the cash was in the account, which meant the termination agreement had gone into effect. I know. Only it wasn't. Because of you I told Murray —"

Murray-Reed Financial Partners, one of the largest hedge fund groups in the world and my former client.

"— to sign their leases and wire a sixteen point seven million dollar deposit for space that wasn't even theirs to an account I had access to."

"The story never changed. When I called Ian —"

"I didn't count on Ian for information, Ryan. I counted on you. Because I did there's an angry Special Agent Simon who'll be waiting for his chance to pounce on me until the day I die. Your fuck-up had me in so deep I actually slept on the floor of my closet to see if I could handle a jail cell."

"Jonah, now —"

"Just because I didn't take you down doesn't mean I couldn't have, Ryan. I covered for you huge. We both know it."

"I never asked you to."

"By not coming forward, I'd say that's debatable. Anyway, I did. I hope you don't make me regret it."

Ryan, looking back toward the restaurant, jammed his hands deep into his pockets.

"Jonah, what is it that you want?"

Twenty minutes later Ryan and I approached the world headquarters of Salton Lynear Bank, a chiseled, imposing monstrosity on Park Avenue that soars into the sky. Built in 1972, primarily with concrete and steel, the property is finished with a black glass shell that plays with whatever city light it can pick up, even in the night. I looked up at the square, three-tier wedding cake. I can still remember, past the black building, being able to see the thin black clouds moving through the black evening sky.

"You want to wait out here?"

You'd be surprised how lively a building like this could be on a Saturday night, the result of having thousands of employees. I could hear it in his voice. He didn't want me coming through security. Unfortunately for him, we had already been on high-resolution digital camera for at least a hundred feet. Anyway it didn't matter. I wasn't letting him out of my sight until I had or didn't have what I needed.

"Why don't you just give me the name you want me to look up?"

"Are you kidding me?"

Two weeks earlier Salton had completed the six-month process of relocating their corporate headquarters.

"And not get a chance to check out the new offices?"

I followed Ryan down a bright, crisp, new-smelling hallway.

"So?"

"Zhamovsky," I answered as I vacantly browsed the craftsmanship.

"What?"

I snapped back to Ryan.

"What's that?"

"I said 'so'? What do you think about how the offices turned out?"

Gratuitously I scanned the place one more time as we walked. Light gray, sterile, wireless, beaming.

"Offices."

"What was that you just said? Za-what?"

"Zhamovsky. The name our search starts with."

Ryan flipped the switch to his corner office. It was at this moment I couldn't ignore, even for one second, how tight the place had turned out.

"Damn."

Mahogany in all the right places. Top of the line light fixtures. Plasma-screen video conference center. Two soft, leather couches around the glass coffee table that matched his desk that so nicely displayed the framed pictures of his family.

"Core Architecture and Design."

The firm who designed and built the space.

"I knew I should have been giving them more business."

Ryan had nothing with him so he went straight for the chair behind his desk. He reached under and booted his computer.

"It needs a second."

Awkward silence.

"What's going on, Jonah? You in trouble?"

"Don't worry about it. Not your concern."

"Maybe if —"

The machine beeped; I charged around the desk just as the company's internal home page appeared on the monitor.

"Do you really need to stand over me like this?"

"Don't for one fucking second think I trust you, Ryan. I don't. This goes my way. The quicker you satisfy me, the quicker you go back to your wife and try to justify whatever bullshit excuse you gave her why you were leaving the restaurant. You with me?"

The log-in page was waiting for his username and password.

"Log in."

He did. Off we went.

"Who is it you want information on?"

"Andreu Zhamovsky."

I spelled it. He started typing.

"He's a big corporate player out of Moscow, and we're involved in a deal. We both have access to the same commercial escrow account so I know he's in your system. What I don't know is if he has any other accounts here. Personal or professional."

A little more typing, a couple of clicks of the mouse, and there was his name surrounded by all types of number sets and corporate financial jargon.

"There! Zhamovsky!" I barked.

"Yeah, but —" he continued to examine the screen, "he's only associated with one account here. The one you were talking about."

"You sure?"

"One hundred percent."

"Fuck!"

Having been hunched over trying to get a good look at the screen I straightened myself up and kick-started my brain. I thought back to when everything began.

"Last week, Monday," I thought out loud, "check the date and go back to last Monday. Maybe Sunday and Tuesday also. Let's take a look at all the Russian-based accounts, personal and business, opened those days."

Ryan said nothing. He didn't type. He just slowly turned around.

"Are you kidding me? Jonah, we're one of the largest fucking banks in the world."

I turned and faced the window. The building directly across Park Avenue looked like a checkerboard from scattered office lights. I closed my eyes, squeezed them shut in hopes, ironically, of seeing.

Fuck.

Think.

React.

"Tuesday!"

"Tuesday?"

"Last Tuesday. It was the day after I told him which bank I'd be—"

I opened my eyes and turned back around.

"We need to look at last Tuesday. We need to go through all Russian accounts opened that day."

"Jonah, I just told you—"

"My way, Ryan. Remember that. I can't leave until I'm satisfied, which means I'm prepared to sit here until the office starts filling up Monday morning if I have to."

Again Ryan typed. Because we were talking about Russian-based accounts being opened on one specific day at one specific institution in the U.S., the search wasn't too bad and took little over an hour with only one problem. No sign of Andreu.

Ryan took his hands from the keyboard.

"Look, maybe if you just go home and think—"

"I'm not satisfied yet, Ryan," I said as I moved out from behind the desk, "which means neither of us is going anywhere."

I turned my back and moved toward the couches at the far end of the office.

"Jonah, just listen to me."

I was trying to think.

"Just be quiet. I need a second."

"Jonah—"

I heard Ryan lift out of his seat. That's when the coke flowing through me, along with the roaring paranoia, took hold. I swung around, pistol extended.

"Holy fuck," Ryan sputtered, sheepishly raising his arms at the elbows.

I was as surprised as he was.

"Just sit down, Ryan. I'm serious."

I looked at the gun. Then I dropped my arm.

"Just sit back down."

He did. I put away the piece and took a seat on one of the couches where I could see him. We both sat in silence for a few seconds, Ryan staring at the computer, me staring at Ryan.

"I can't believe you just did that," he squeezed out.

He raised his chin, looked my way.

"Jonah—"

"Ryan, I'm sorry," I cut him off, putting my hand up. "I am. Just—"

Boom.

Thunder and lightning cracked my skull all at once.

I stood up.

"American accounts."

After all, the money was coming here. The venue for my thoughts, difficult as they were, quickly became standing room only. First there was my father. I could see him implicating Archmont at The Four Seasons as clearly as I could see the Russian stock certificates. Then there was the timing of my showing up to Archmont's wedding. He knew I was coming. Had he set me up? Had Angie? She had entered the beach house and made full eye contact with me almost on cue just as I was about to leave. She then immediately took a cell phone call. There was also, of course, Andreu, who had—

Fuck!

"We need to go through all American accounts opened that same day, both personal and corporate."

I started again for the desk. Ryan instinctively cowered back in his chair which, although I couldn't tell him, made me feel terrible.

"Don't worry, Ryan. I mean it. I have no intention of hurting you. I just —"

I have no intention of hurting you I repeated in my head, shocked by such thug-like verbiage. What had I become?

"Just American accounts. Please. From that same day."

Four hours later, done with the corporate accounts and well into the personal ones, the screen was starting to make my corneas sting. I was sitting in my own chair next to Ryan's as I grappled with the thought of calling it a night and sucking up the fact my instincts had been wrong. Only just as I got ready to put the miscue behind me, something clicked. A name that seemed familiar, seemed to mean something, appeared on the monitor.

"Stop."

I sat up in my chair and leaned forward.

Pavel Derbyshev.

"Derbyshev," I said out loud. "Derbyshev. Why do I know that name?"

The fact it was a Russian name on a personal American account opened on the day in question was interesting in its own right. It felt like something more. It felt like I had just literally seen or heard that exact name.

I shot out of my chair sending it straight into the wall. Pavel Derbyshev, same last name as Piotr Derbyshev who, according to the history, was one of Henrik Wigstrom's most trusted hands at the House of Fabergé. One of two craftsmen believed responsible for creating the eight eggs that would one day go missing.

CHAPTER 35

After returning home somewhere around four and crashing in the living room, the landline rang at 8:02 A.M. My eyes sprung open only to close again about halfway. The sun's fury was beaming, splintered, as it came knifing into the living room. My shirt was sticking to me. I was warm. To my left, Neo was still asleep, his white fur shining from the glare as his chest moved rhythmically.

I looked at the caller ID. The call was coming from my father's townhouse. Moving as fast as I could I answered it.

"Hello?"

"Jonah, it's Mattheau."

I sensed trouble in his voice.

"What is it, Mattheau? What's wrong?"

He paused, so I continued with caution. I was concerned about speaking on the phone.

"Was the . . . how was . . . is . . ."

"All is well," Mattheau said, taking my cue.

I should have been relieved, but I felt there was more. Was something going on between my father and Mattheau? Had I been wrong to trust him?

"You need to come to your father's, Jonah," he said. "Now."

I didn't answer him.

"Now Jonah. I promise. It's all right to come here."

"What's the . . . when was . . ."

"Jonah. Come now!"

Mattheau spoke with honest urgency. I grabbed the gun and cell phone on my way out.

The Upper East Side is quiet early on a Saturday morning, especially in the summer. The rear windows of the cab were down and the city whooshed by. I tried desperately to figure out what could possibly be happening. I couldn't.

As we pulled around the final corner I was surprised, frightened by the fact that there was apparent commotion going on in front of the home. When the cab stopped I handed the driver a twenty for a five-dollar fare telling him to keep the change. I looked out the window again once more before opening the door. Faces were looking back. If I had taken off at this point it would have been suspicious. I forced myself out of the car.

I had not anticipated the scene ahead. There were cops wearing the familiar blue uniforms, and others in street clothes with their shields in full view. Detectives, I presumed. I thought, did Mattheau fuck me and go to the cops? I started looking for him, the bags of money, Pangaea-Man's remains, anything related to the crime.

A plainclothes detective was calmly walking toward me at the moment I noticed the police line by the front door. Mattheau saw him coming toward me and started my way as well.

"Can I help you?" the cop asked.

He was calm, matter of fact. No colleagues following him. No gun drawn. He genuinely had no idea who I was. There I stood—murderer, conspirator, thief, illegal gun carrier, illicit drug user—and this fucking cop was clueless. So clueless, in fact, that he had just asked me if I needed his help.

"I live here," I started. "I mean, I used to. It's my father's house."

Mattheau reached us. I addressed both of them.

"What's going on?"

"I'm sorry, Jonah," Mattheau said, turning his attention to the front door area and back again. "I couldn't tell you over the phone."

"Tell me what?"

Like a slap across the face, I then realized the only reason in the world Mattheau would have brought me back to the house that morning was my father. Either Pop knew what was going on or something had happened to him. I looked again toward the front of the house. Before my eyes, the yellow of the police line became brighter than the rest of the scene, like it was doing all that it could to become fluorescent. Like it was doing all that it could to tell me something. I found myself drawn toward it.

"No," I said, quietly.

I slowly started in the direction of the front door.

"No," I said again.

"Jonah, I don't think you —" started Mattheau.

The cop put his hand on my shoulder. I swatted it away and darted toward the police line.

"A little help," the cop yelled to the others.

Everyone's attention was pulled toward me as I headed in their direction. They were all staring at me though I barely noticed any of them. I just felt them, their concern, their desire to protect me, as I made my way. At one point I almost lost my balance, but I kept going without hesitation, never even dropping my chin. The feeling of disaster in front of the townhouse, all of which I felt was being funneled toward me, was beyond palpable. It was downright telling.

As I approached the landing I saw a white sheet draped over a lifeless body. Blood had seeped through the thin fabric toward one of the edges. A few feet before the yellow tape, arms began to grab for me, brace me, from all angles.

"Pop!" I yelled as my momentum was halted. "Pop —"

I continued my thought silently. *What the fuck did you do?*

I only wanted to peel back the sheet and have one quick look underneath. It was all of the hope I had left of seeing that it wasn't what I thought; that I would get to see my father again. These cops, these arms, they were all trying to restrain me. I started to fight.

"No!" I yelled once again.

This couldn't be the end. We had unfinished business.

I grabbed at random forearms, and remember trying to literally pry them from my body.

"No fucking way!" I went on, saliva spraying from my mouth with each disbelieving, angry word. "No fucking way!"

"Tell me your full name."

Fifteen minutes later I was leaning against a black-and-white parked by the curb. I was standing with a detective. Two officers dressed in blue stood talking a few feet away between me and the crime scene. They had been placed there in case I made another break toward my father, who was still technically part of the physical evidence.

Pop had been shot twice in the head as he came out of the townhouse. He was leaving early for his golf game in Connecticut. Mattheau was waiting out front in the limo when it happened. When he heard gunshots, for the second morning in a row, he ducked down for safety. There were three shots. Two found my father's skull while the third was found embedded in the front door, also head high. According to Mattheau, he looked up when he heard a car tear away. His eyes searched for my father who was lying lifeless on the ground. By the time he thought to look at the vehicle it was already too far down the street. All he remembered was the fading rear end of a dark car.

I spotted the limo on the street. The rear window was properly intact.

"Jonah Gray."

"Middle name?"

"I don't have one."

"Any brothers or sisters?"

"No."

"How about Mom?"

"Died when I was young."

"How young?"

"Five years, three months, two days."

"So it was just the two of you."

"That's right."

"You two close?"

"Yeah," I answered, unsure now if this were even true. "We were."

Detective Tim Morante was in his late thirties. He was wearing jeans, black Kenneth Cole shoes, and a solid, royal blue button-down shirt, sleeves neatly rolled up. His eyes, hair, and skin were all dark. His shield dangled low around his neck secured by a thin, silver chain. He didn't come across like the detectives I was use to from the movies. He was well kept, properly groomed. And he didn't take notes as I spoke. He just listened.

"Jonah, what did your father do for a living?"

"He was a commercial real estate owner. Office buildings."

"It seems from the looks of things that he lived a very nice lifestyle. Had he been in this field for a long time?"

"My whole life. His whole life."

My eyes drifted again to the front of the house. Pop's body was still lying there, covered like some dog that had just been hit in the street, as crime-scene investigators evaluated, assessed the crime scene. There was a gurney waiting nearby for when the green light was given for his removal.

"Jonah, I'll be frank with you. This crime screams premeditation. There were three shots fired in the direction of your father's head. There is no evidence that anyone tried to break into the house and nothing was taken off of him once he went down. His watch, his wallet, nothing. According to the limo driver, as soon as those shots were fired a car was out of here in a hurry."

I returned my attention to him. I knew where he was going.

"You're thinking it was a hit," I said, saving him the trouble of having to find the right words.

"Did he have any enemies?"

"No," I shot back, careful not to hesitate.

"Had any deals recently —"

Keep the cop at bay, I reminded myself. Get where you need to go.

"My father was a good man, detective. An honorable man."

The word, honorable, passed through my windpipe no easier than a poorly chewed hunk of meat.

"Ask anyone in the real estate community and they'll tell you the same thing."

"Anything happen lately in his business dealings that seemed out of the ordinary?

"No," I shook my head. "Absolutely not. We talked real estate almost every day. He told me everything."

"So you don't even see the slightest possibility —"

"No!" I snapped, before gathering myself. "No. I'm telling you, my father was by the book when it came to business."

"So who then would have wanted to do this to him? Can you think of anyone? Maybe if not in his professional life, his personal life?"

I gently shook my head "no."

"How about you?" the detective went on.

"Me?"

"You said the two of you always talked business. Are you in real estate also?"

"I am."

"With your father?"

"No."

"Then in what capacity?"

"I'm a broker with PCBL."

"I see," said the detective before pausing for a few seconds. "Tell me a little about that."

"About what?"

"Your job."

I sighed.

"Detective, is this really necessary right now?" I asked extending my arm and gesturing toward my father's destroyed body.

"I promise to make it quick. Tell me about your job."

"Simple. I make deals. I represent owners as well as tenants, depending on who needs my services."

"Deals ever get hairy?"

"Sometimes," I said. "Sure."

Stay calm, I told myself. Let him go down that road. It's going to happen eventually, so just let him go down that road. Stay cool and get it over with.

"How about you? Any enemies on your end?"

React.

"None that I know of."

"None at all?"

"Nope. I mean —"

"You mean what?" he prodded.

"I mean sometimes deals can get pretty edgy, but nothing that has ever gone past a conference room. My dealings are all with top-level executives, principals and CEOs. Why?"

"Formality. I just need to gather as much information as I possibly can."

"Look, are we almost through here?" I asked.

"Almost. I appreciate you cooperating. This must be very difficult. Now, I just need to know where you were last night. Again, formality."

Fuck.

"I was at home by myself," I said confidently, as if I hoped that would suffice.

"Do you often spend Friday nights at home alone?"

"No. Yesterday I wasn't feeling well so I left my office early in the afternoon."

"Where's your office?"

"Chrysler Center. I spent the rest of the day and most of last night on the toilet battling some stomach thing."

"Is that why you're wearing a suit this early on Saturday? You haven't changed from yesterday?"

Christ, I thought. The fucking suit.

The gun.

"That's right," I answered. "Never quite had a chance."

I was pissed by the fact that I was being questioned as a possible suspect. Pissed, that is, until it dawned on me that if I was wrong about Pop, I was possibly responsible for his death.

"And where is your apartment?"

I gave him my Park Avenue address that in the long run I knew would help me out. It was obvious right away I had cash on my own. A little research on the detective's part would uncover the fact I was self-made, to some degree, thus lessening my potential motive.

"My building lobby has cameras, detective —" I said.

I looked to bolster my alibi and lead him away from the night's devilish hours. Those hours that if you get caught lying about where you are, the reason's never good.

"You can see when I came home yesterday as well as the exact time I left just a few minutes ago."

I looked again to the front of the house. Two men lifted Pop's limp body onto the silver rolling table. Another detective, along with Mattheau, was coming toward us. I turned back to the detective.

"Look," I continued, trying to close out our little question and answer session.

I moved myself away from the car and stood up straight. Then I deliberately stared Detective Morante in the eyes as I spoke, as if I was in my office trying to put the finishing touches on a deal.

"You just tell me what I need to do in order to help you figure this out," I said.

I looked again at the two approaching men, but still spoke so only Morante could hear me.

"I need to know who did this."

"Anyone have a key to get in the house?" asked the second detective once they arrived.

"Jonah?" Morante asked as he turned to me.

"I don't understand? I thought you said this was a hit?"

"It most likely is. But we wouldn't be doing our job if we didn't make sure. The reason for the hit may lie within your father's walls."

An image of the cash filled duffel bags blanketed my mind like one of those tarps they pull over center court at the U.S. Open when it starts to rain. Then I saw Pangaea-Man. I felt myself becoming very nervous.

"Do you have the keys on you?"

I wanted to say no, even though I did, but had enough sense to know how fucked I would have been to get caught in that lie.

"I do."

Going into the house with these guys sounded as good as dragging my tongue across a plate of live bees. I located the front door key and handed the key chain over to the second detective.

React.

"I want to see my father," I blurted out, not knowing if this was even true, if I could possibly handle such a thing.

The detectives looked at each other.

"I don't think that would be a good idea," said detective Morante. "He hasn't been properly —"

"I don't care," I interrupted. "I want to see him."

Still, no movement.

"I need to identify him, don't I?"

"You may want to see him after he's been cleaned up a bit."

I wasn't ready for them to enter the house.

"I want to see him now. No buts."

The two detectives took the lead toward the body. Mattheau and I followed. The gurney was next to the vehicle it was about to be lifted into. Desperate, I discreetly flipped open my cell phone. With one hand, low at my side, I put it in text mode and typed in two words: BAGS, BODY. With the simple press of three more buttons I sent the message to one of the numbers in my phone's memory then switched my ring to vibrate.

A few seconds later, as we reached Pop, I heard Mattheau's phone ring. My father was now in a black body bag, and as one of the paramedics went for the zipper to give me a look I sucked in a deep, loud breath. My goal was to draw the detectives' attention toward myself instead of the low-pitched chime coming from Mattheau's phone.

"Are you okay?" asked Detective Morante.

Out of the corner of my eye I could see Mattheau stepping away from the crowd. I knew how often he "texted" with Yves, so I figured this was my best hope of communicating with him free of suspicion.

"You know, Jonah, you really don't need to do this right now," he continued.

Mattheau was clear.

"I understand that," I responded. "But I want to."

The detectives stepped away and Morante gave the paramedic the go-ahead with a nod. Just like that, the zipper was tugged at and the little metal teeth separated. To say I was unprepared for what I was about to see is a gross understatement.

Pop was a fucking mess. It was as if he had put his head down on a table and let someone take a few good whacks at it with a sledge-hammer. His features were still discernable, barely, but the area from his eyes, including his right socket, and up was completely unrecognizable. Not just of him, but of a human being. The top of what use to be his head was a stew of skin, bone, hair, blood, and brain matter. Because of the devastation, and the fact that his facial lines no longer intersected as they once did, he was expressionless. It was simply the most horrific sight I have ever seen.

I started to tremble. I could feel my face, my lips stiffening as they tried to fight the oncoming tears.

"Oh my God, Pop," I whispered. "Oh my God —"

I gently placed my right hand on his chest, my palm and his body separated by the temporary coffin between us. My eyes sprinted back and forth over his face frantically.

I whispered again.

"What the fuck is happening?"

About thirty seconds later my cell vibrated. I discreetly managed a look at it. Mattheau had successfully text-messaged me back. One word: CLEAR.

After seeing my dad, I escorted the two detectives through the different floors of the townhouse for about an hour. They told me I didn't need to stay but I decided to anyway. I could still feel Pop's spirit all around me, and I was reluctant to let that go. Knowing the bags of money were gone put me at relative ease. As for the evidence of the murder, according to Mattheau there were no worries there either.

What I saw on the desk was what actually caused my heart to speed up.

It was a letter that had recently been started. It was to me, and it was among the mess of Pop's business papers. I peeked at the cops. They were looking at the pictures on the wall. So I scanned it in an instant before discreetly covering it with a set of financial statements Pop must have been reviewing for a possible new tenant. The letter read,

> Jonah. When it comes to how much you and the memory of your mother mean to me, just open your heart. That aside, reading this will hurt you as much as writing it hurts me. There was a time..."

That was it.

Pop must have just started it when Mattheau had shown up to take him to Connecticut.

I also took special notice of the stationery. It was cloud white, not cream, and it was both longer and wider than that of the mysterious note.

CHAPTER 36

We had just pulled away from the townhouse. Mattheau was giving me a lift home. As we were leaving the first news team was pulling up, which was inevitable. A rich, well-respected real estate man, gunned down mafia-style on his own front stoop, wasn't exactly the norm for the quiet and affluent Upper East Side of Manhattan. It would only be a matter of hours before everyone I knew, personally as well as professionally, was aware of what had happened.

I let out a long sigh as I leaned my head back on the seat. My eyes were still opened, looking straight into the gray of the roof's interior. I couldn't believe I had just stood in the bedroom of my youth carrying a gun used in a recent homicide. I was distraught on a level I never even knew existed. I wanted to cry more, but why? I wanted to smile at some memories I had of Pop, but why? I wanted to scowl at the thought of standing in front of my father's murderer, but why? Was I better than whoever had done this?

"What'd you do with the cash?"

"I consolidated it into two of the duffel bags. Then I took them to my home figuring they would be out of the way there, at least for now. Since the bags weren't filled to their limit and I only needed one to —"

"Don't! Mattheau, please. Don't. I don't want to know."

We both paused.

"Jonah, what would you like me to do with the money?"

"That's up to you. I can't have it anywhere near me. You want to burn it, burn it. You want to spend it, spend it."

"I couldn't, Jonah. I mean —"

I sat up and looked forward into the rearview mirror. Our eyes met.

"You've earned it, Mattheau. Really. And I don't just mean with this mess. Besides, I think it belonged to some drug dealers. My guess is that you'd find a far more worthy use for it than they would. A better life. You've paid your dues."

Mattheau thought hard then slowly started to shake his head.

"I don't know —"

"I think you should keep it. You want to drop it in some bum's coffee cup, that's up to you. Like I said it's yours now."

Mattheau nodded.

"Jonah, is all of this related to what happened yesterday?"

"I don't know," I answered, honestly. "I truly don't know."

I looked to my right out the window.

"Tell me about Haiti. Why did you leave?"

Mattheau began to clam up. Just as I was about to remind him he promised, he spoke.

"Do you know much about Haiti, Jonah?"

"Besides that it shares an island with a country that breeds base-ball players, no."

He sighed.

"Government in Haiti has always been a tricky situation. A dangerous situation. I, unfortunately, added to that instability and betrayal."

"How so?"

"I was born in 1957. Coincidentally, that was the same year a doctor named François Duvalier, or 'Papa Doc,' was elected presi-dent at a time our country was coming out of a very dark period. He was a prominent public health expert. He was a perceived believer in black power, one that both the U.S. and Haitian armies backed. Once he started his reign, his true intentions came to light. He changed the constitution to solidify his power and set out to build a family dictatorship. He rid the military of U.S.-trained forces and replaced them with younger, loyal soldiers. Naïve soldiers —"

He stopped.

"You were one of those soldiers?" I pressed him.

"No. I was part of a rural militia, known in Creole as 'Tonton Makouts,' created to maintain power outside the capital at any cost. By whatever means. I served under Duvalier's son. A man less angry than his father, yet dedicated to the same vision."

Mattheau locked eyes with me again in the mirror.

"I saw some terrible things, Jonah. I did some terrible things, things I swore I'd never do again unless it was absolutely necessary."

"And this was necessary? Cleaning up my dead guy?"

"It was."

"Why?"

"Because I have more experience with this type of disposal. I mean, I was a little bit rusty after all these years, but —"

"That's not what I meant."

"I know."

"Then why?"

"I was a young fool, Jonah. A boy working for the government looking to uphold the only thing I knew. I killed many men. Women too, tortured them. The only way I was able to carry on doing so was by never allowing myself to be in the position to hurt a child. One day I was in that position and I couldn't go through with it. Before I knew it, knowing I would soon be hunted by my own, I was fleeing my family and country for the United States. Because I knew, if I kept my mouth shut, it was a place I could start over again in peace."

"Which is exactly what you did," I deduced, "in anonymity. But the only way it would have worked, based on your background, was if the government never knew who you were or that you were even here."

"The police can't know who I really am, Jonah. You're not the only one with secrets. We all have secrets."

*   *   *

I shot through the lobby of my apartment building.

"I don't want any visitors today," I shouted back to Clarence just before jumping on the elevator. "Not L, not my partners, no one."

Just as the cab doors were about to close I heard my doorman calling back.

"Does that include your father?"

I opened my mouth to answer, but nothing came out. Then the doors closed.

Once inside my apartment I locked the door and again secured a chair under the knob. I heard the pitter-patter of a charging Neo. I fell to my knees. He jumped into my arms. I started to cry. Wriggling with happiness to see me, he licked away my salty tears. I remember feeling so alone, like all I had in the entire world to hold on to was this six-pound fluffball. I had to do everything I could to keep from inadvertently squeezing the life out of him.

Life was no longer just about money, partying, deal making, and women. Life had become about life. And death.

Paranoia wasn't far. Soon it tackled me from behind. I put Neo down and immediately headed past the kitchen and living room toward the main hallway, eyes peeled. Just as I did my cell rang. It was Krissy.

Instinct pulled me out onto my terrace in a boiling rage. I wound up to throw the fucking phone, once and for all, over the side of the building and out into the city below. Enough of the stalker. Enough of the games. My mind was filling up with too many complications and scenarios, too many facts and questions. I wanted to smash the goddamn phone into a million little pieces so it would finally stop ringing. I wanted to somehow start trimming away the fat and finding my way to the meat of everything that was going on.

I ran to the edge of the balcony and launched the phone as hard as I could nearly throwing my arm out of the socket. Only I never opened my fist. Throwing the phone overboard from the sinking ship that was becoming my life wasn't the answer. It couldn't be the answer and I knew this. In truth, I had no idea at this point what even the next five minutes of my life held for me. I couldn't be caught with absolutely no means of communication. And I still didn't know if Krissy had anything to do with Pop's death or not. In short, I just didn't know. About anything.

My mind was consumed with my father and the barely begun letter on his desk. "There had once been a time when"—what? Could it possibly have been that in some twisted way, for some twisted reason, he was trying to protect me?

I headed back inside, leaving the terrace doors open, and sat on the edge of my bed. Again I saw Pop. Not just an image of him, but a collage. One that spanned my whole life. His smiling face that beautiful spring day in Philly when I graduated from college. His frustrated scowl after ruining his tie with a drop of coffee. The fury in his eyes when he fought with another patron over a seat at *Phantom of the Opera* before being escorted out by the police. His elation when he closed a terrific deal. There were as many fond memories as there were shitty ones, but up until this point they had been our memories. Now they were just mine.

The next dilemma was Pop's burial. Because of my situation, the last thing I needed was some huge funeral. It made me an easy target. On the other hand, everyone would expect a big funeral. To minimize such a ceremony when there would, no doubt, be many looking to pay their respects would only cast further suspicion. I wasn't ready yet for what happened to my father to become public knowledge. At least not without a plan. The more I looked at all of the facts, the more I stressed. I was afraid to leave. I was afraid to stay.

I was pulled from my stupor by something rubbing against my shin. It was Neo, holding a mini-tennis ball in his mouth, asking me to play. I grabbed a pillow, fell back on the bed, placed the pillow over my face and screamed as loud as I could.

I don't really remember the rest of Saturday. More than anything, I wanted so badly to speak with L, Perry, Jake, the people in life I cared most for, had always trusted. I only wanted to explain everything to them, what made sense, what didn't, but by this point I couldn't rule out anyone's involvement. If they weren't part of this then I had already possibly put them in harm's way. I realized that letting them in on the game could pose a serious threat to all of our lives. The second I fucked with the continuity, normalcy of my life the greater the chances whoever was pulling the strings would be onto me or know I was onto them. I couldn't trust anyone. I was completely alone.

CHAPTER 37

S<small>UNDAY</small>

Neo barked. I jumped.

"Who's there?" I asked, sitting up, gun cocked.

I was alone with my hangover. I looked to my right and saw Neo standing just inside the doorway to the apartment. It was dark outside, stormy, and the sky had just opened up. The rain was loud, slapping against the building. I looked up through squinted, blood-shot eyes into the gloomy sky. The water felt cool as it covered my skin.

Neo was simply yelling at me to come inside. I looked at my watch. It was one P.M. even though it looked like dusk. I lifted myself up only to remember that the previous day my father had been murdered. Just as my legs started to wobble, a bone-jarring clap of thunder came roaring from above. I jumped inside and scooped up Neo who was now barking more excitedly.

I closed the doors behind me, muffling the sound of Mother Nature's fury, and headed for the bathroom. I placed Neo on the marble countertop so he could lap at the water running from the faucet while I brushed my teeth. I put my gun down on the brushed stone surrounding the sink. Neo licked it.

The questions kept relentlessly attacking. Where did Angie fit into any of this? Or my father? Or Derbyshev?

My head instantly began throbbing again then I remembered something. The dream from the other night, the one where I unsuccessfully shot myself in the head. When I pulled the trigger for a second time I woke up. For some reason, to think of it now, it felt hopeful. It suddenly made sense.

I fled the bathroom only to return seconds later. Without another thought I emptied my vial of coke into the toilet and threw my weed in on top of it. For a second I watched the sticky green plant float on the water's surface as the fine white powder dissolved underneath. Then I flushed it all down.

How was I to get my life back? *Could* I get my life back? I needed answers, and I needed them fast.

I dropped off Neo at Lucy's, the old, crazy animal woman who owns the other penthouse apartment in the building. She lives alone with two dogs and three cats. Neo would be safe with her. Finally, I gathered the things I'd need in the next twenty-four hours.

My briefcase. My gun. My cell. My nerve.

I peeled the tarp back over the vehicle, going from front to back, letting the fabric fall on the ground. The vehicle, a white, 1973 Porsche 911 Carerra RS—Limited Edition, with the word 'Carerra' written across the bottom of the door in orange cursive, was truly one of the meanest, most vintage cars you could possibly imagine. Both the exterior as well as the interior of the car were designed with one focus in mind, to win. It was simple and aerodynamic, functional and goal-oriented. Inside there was nothing fancy, just the necessary dials for gauging the machine and the road along with the stick and clutch. The single amenity was a Nakamichi stereo system. In short, within the world of muscle cars and racing, this vehicle was a fucking animal.

Sorry we weren't heading to Lime Rock Park for a little racing, our usual weekend destination, I placed my briefcase on the passenger seat, jumped in and closed the door behind me. Immediately I slid the key into the ignition and tried to turn the engine over. She wanted to start but needed another go. I turned her over for a second time and she finally rumbled steadily, forcefully to life. I rolled out of the garage. Once I emerged from underneath the building, and crept up to the curb, I looked both ways nervously. I tore out into the dark, rain-soaked city.

I had one stop to make before starting my solitary journey. The townhouse. The memory of seeing my father's handwriting on Pangaea-Man's note was gnawing at me, and I couldn't for the life of me fend off a feeling. Even though Pop was harsh toward me at times, I truly believed deep down he loved and respected me. He wouldn't have tried to screw me like this.

My wipers swept water furiously as I headed uptown. Before going any farther, I knew I needed to reach out to those who would be looking for me, if they weren't already, and kill the possibility of an FBI search party hunting me. I placed my cell's hands-free receiver in my ear and dialed L.

"Jonah!"

"Yeah, L. It's me."

"Jonah, I'm so fucking sorry about what happened. I came by the apartment but Clarence —"

"I know, I know. I told him to —"

"You told him to what? Jonah, tell me where you are. I'll come to you."

"No L. It's not that simple right now and I don't have time to talk."

"Jonah, what the fuck is going on?"

"I'll fill you in. Really, I promise. But for now I just need you to trust me and do me a favor. Can you do that?"

"Of course. Whatever you need. If it's about the funeral, I can —"

"Carolyn's on the funeral arrangements. Campbell's on the Upper East Side, Tuesday morning."

"Then what?"

"I'm going to disappear for about twenty-four hours so I need you to call Perry. Her cell number is nine-one-seven, five-five-five, six-six-four-one. Tell her I'm okay and that I want her to have PCBL issue a statement on my behalf that notes the funeral as well as the fact I would appreciate everyone, press included, to allow me to grieve privately. Then tell her I'll be in touch shortly."

I stopped at the corner before making a right on Pop's street. I slowly moved up, just enough to see the whole block. Toward the other end a cop car securing the crime scene area had its head and tail lights on. I waited, hoping it was doing a quick drive by. Fifteen minutes later I was still waiting.

There was no telling how long they'd be stationed, and I wasn't exactly in an inconspicuous car. I looked at my watch. I looked around the drenched intersection.

"Fuck!" I yelled as I slapped the steering wheel with both hands.

I needed a reason to approach the house. Or they needed a reason to leave. I threw all kinds of unlikely scenarios around, but nothing seemed plausible. Then my eye caught the rearview mirror. More importantly, I noticed the pay phone on the corner behind me.

"Nine-one-one Emergency Services," answered the calm, female voice.

The rain had picked up again. The small umbrella I kept in my car could barely shield me. My heart was beating so fast I could barely talk, but whether I liked it or not I was all in. To not say a word could have meant squad cars at this very pay phone within minutes.

React.

"Emergency Services," she said again.

"Yes, I . . . I just wanted to report what I think may be a robbery that's going on," I responded in an altered voice, one I hadn't planned on but now had to run with.

"A robbery, sir?"

"That's right. Over on Lexington."

I gave her a location only a couple of blocks east.

I hung up, jumped back in my car, watched and waited.

"Come on," I whispered, hoping the cops in front of the townhouse would be closest to the scene, "come on."

Sixty seconds later the patrol car pulled away.

I pulled into the garage, pressed the button on the remote and watched in my rearview mirror as the door lowered and sealed me from the city like a tomb. I got out and headed for the door that led from the garage inside. As I did my mind started to ask the same question over and over. "Where does it make the most sense to look first?"

It wasn't long until I was standing in Pop's closet. I felt conflicted standing in his personal space, as if I were intruding. I wanted to feel reassured from the sight of his perfectly pressed suits and bold, beautiful ties. But I didn't. I couldn't.

The few-minute search through his drawers and racks proved fruitless, so I moved onward to the study. Once there I immediately went toward the safe, got down on one knee and swung open the book door. My mind had become consumed with the possibility I had missed something in the second chamber. But as I started to turn the dial it dawned on me he never would have kept anything in there he didn't want me to see. I often borrowed his watches, so he knew I used the safe.

I closed the book door, jumped up, and took the seat behind Pop's desk. I did a quick once-over of all of the papers on top. Everything seemed to pertain to business. Once again I checked out the letter he had started to me to see if I had missed anything. I hadn't.

I gently pulled out the top drawer, the one that was front and center. I started to rummage through, pushing aside everything from Eclipse gum and highlighters to a calculator and a staple remover. Nothing. I closed the drawer. Next I pulled out the bottom drawer on the left side, which was a file drawer. I started to thumb through each individual file. There was one for townhouse maintenance issues/activity, one for Mattheau, one for me, and everything in between. Then my eyes fell on the second to last file in the drawer. The one simply labeled IA.

The last item in this particular folder was an ordinary sheet of nice, letter-sized, expensive white stationery. It didn't seem to have the usual typed or handwritten letters on it that I would have expected. It looked as though it was serving as the backdrop of a drawing like those lining the staircase. I lifted the file from the drawer to have a better look. When I did, a key ring fell from it onto the desk.

I picked it up. There must have been ten, maybe a dozen keys on the simple metal o-ring. No two were the same and they looked old, antique. A couple wore a little rust. They were small, unusual, and unlike any I had ever seen.

"What the hell—"

I scanned my brain, but simply had no point of reference. Pressed for time I carefully placed them in a corner of my briefcase. Then I moved on to the piece of paper that had originally caught my eye.

It was a typical Ia drawing. Charcoal strokes supremely lifelike and shaded to perfection. Only this picture wasn't of any animal from the wild. It was of an infant. I turned the sheet of paper over. There was a note. "Look close. Closer than you've ever looked before."

I turned the drawing back over. Like the first time I looked, I saw a baby. There was a half exposed rattle poking in at the top border. I moved the paper to my face and forced my eyes, straining them. I started at the top of the kid's head. Honest gaze, square shoulders, something was familiar though this was a face barely formed. I held it a little farther away and tried again. Nothing. Frustrated I looked up. My eyes stopped on the magnifying glass standing with the pens in the Tiffany cup.

I stood up and laid the drawing flat on the only vacant part of the desk. Once I gauged the distance for maximum clarity between the glass and the rendering, about two inches, I began my inspection slowly moving again from head to toe. The picture was now so close the form was gone. All I saw as I moved the magnifying glass was paper dusted with charcoal, a charcoal swath allowing a trace of paper to peek through or something in the middle. It didn't take long to reach the baby's feet. Still nothing.

I stood up. Look closer, I reminded myself.

Closer.

See what you're not seeing.

I leaned over again. I locked in on the item I had barely

noticed, the item easy to miss, the rattle. I returned the glass to the paper.

The immaculate shading left no doubt the shiny barbell-shaped noisemaker was sterling silver. The center of the rattle, or the part of the handle showing just where it entered the picture, was engraved with the initials A.G. Initials that meant nothing to me. I brushed this aside and kept looking. I noticed letters woven silkily into a mid-range gray hue running along the inside of the bulbous end. They were a hint darker than the gray surrounding them, but very clear. They formed a single word.

"Ours," I said aloud.

I scanned the entire piece but found nothing more. I pondered this word and saw something else I had missed. The year 1974 was written in the bottom right-hand corner. A surge of nausea jumped me. Something felt wrong.

I heard my father's voice.

"What she does is paint, draw, and sculpt," I remembered him saying just nights earlier at The Four Seasons. "Never signs her work. Just dates it."

The room started spinning. I was scared to move. Scared to breathe. I frantically scoured the drawing, both front and back, for someone named Ia's signature. I didn't find one.

I dashed from the study and stopped on the main staircase, squarely in front of the first Ia piece entitled *The Zebra in the Brush*. I looked for a signature. What I got was the year 1980 written in the bottom right-hand corner. I moved down the stairs and checked all four pieces. No Ia. Just years.

I headed upstairs, dazed, and fell back into the chair. Forget it being unreasonable, Galina Zhamovsky and Ia being one in the same seemed downright impossible. Only until I paired the cryptically placed "Ours" with the initials on the rattle.

A. G.

Andreu Gray.

Born, like myself, in 1974.

The situation unfolding before me was simply beyond my comprehension. Mouth agape, running on instinct, I held the drawing up higher so the little bit of natural light in the room could pass through it. Something inside me wanted to examine it further, as if something else would be there waiting to jump off the page. There was.

The watermark in the center of the paper was in Russian. I processed this. Started to fill in the blanks. The reality shook me to the core. I quickly took from my pocket the note sent to Pangaea-Man. I held it up.

This note too had a Russian watermark.

A car started coming down the street. I jumped from my stupor, the pieces of paper falling to the ground, and ran to the window. It was a Lexus. It didn't stop. Fearing the cops would be back any second, I needed to get moving. I could sort this all out once I was clear of the house.

On the floor, in the corner of the room, my eye caught Pop's cell phone, which was attached to the charger that was plugged into the wall. I scooped it up and jammed it in my pocket. I needed to leave, but something was keeping me from doing so. I looked to the safe. It was secure. I started to look aimlessly along the walls. *What?* I asked myself silently. *What the fuck are you looking for?* I would know if and when I saw it.

Another car roared by. I didn't move to the window this time. It passed and I let out a short sigh of relief. As I turned back, my eyes settled again on the desk. I sat back down.

I began to furiously go through the drawers on the right. Once I opened the second one down I knew I had found what I was looking for. It was Pop's contact book. He had tried to move to the new technology, but had remained stubbornly steadfast in his insistence of keeping his handwritten leather-bound book rather than moving his contacts to a wireless device. There were too many to bother with. My father knew more people, probably in the business world alone, than most individuals meet in their entire lives.

I grabbed a pen — Edgar Allan Poe — and a piece of paper and threw the contact book on top of the desk. Had he maintained contact with Galina Zhamovsky in private all these years?

I started at G. Nothing. Next I went to Zhamovsky. I found all of Andreu's father, Alexander's, information. His numbers at home, the office, on his yacht, all from before he died six years ago. Nothing for Galina.

I looked at the picture again, the sketch of the baby that seemed to be staring up from the floor at me, making direct eye contact.

Ia.

I flipped to I. Sure enough there were two numbers. My heart racing, I jotted the numbers down, stuffed the piece of scrap paper in my back pocket, and put Pop's contact book back in its rightful place. Then I closed the drawer. The two sheets of Russian paper that were still on the floor were the last order of business. I picked up the note sent to Pangaea-Man and placed it in my back pocket with Ia's phone numbers. Then I retrieved the charcoal drawing of a baby Andreu. Before I put it back, I took one long, last look at it. Devastation turned to anger.

CHAPTER 38

I headed south on the New Jersey Turnpike. The distant landscape passed both sides of the car smoothly as if on conveyer belts. It had stopped raining so I lowered the windows. The moist highway air swarmed me like yellow jackets working a hive. I didn't bother with any music. I just drove in silence, careful not to speed, and listened to all the passing cars.

I was more than shaken up. I suddenly had a Russian half-brother, someone I had known for most of my life, someone my father knowingly allowed me to take on as a friend. Both secrets and new characters alike were entering stage left faster than I could handle. Each frustrating, disappointing step forward seemed to only turn into a giant step sideways. In between nervous glances toward passing eyes, I looked out at the lush countryside in the distance. I just wanted to feel the air entering, then leaving, my lungs.

Two and a half hours later, still driving in silence as I merged onto I-895, I finally pulled my father's cell out of my pocket. It was T-Mobile. He used this service because he swore it had the best worldwide plan and reception for his international calls, something we both agreed on. I slid the piece of scrap paper with Ia's phone numbers from my back pocket and dialed the first one.

Just as the sun showed itself, teasing me as to what a beautiful day it could have been, the line started to ring those long, deep-pitched, hollow-sounding international rings. As I waited, my mouth began to feel as if it were lined with cotton. I wanted so much for her to pick up, almost as much as I didn't want that very same thing.

No answer. Just as I was about to end the signal I heard a voice. "*Privyet.*"

I had heard her voice a number of times before. It was unmistakably Galina Zhamovsky.

After a brief pause I answered her.

"Mrs. Zhamovsky?"

"Yes?"

Her Russian accent was extremely rich. I couldn't even begin to try and duplicate it.

I was hesitant.

"Galina?"

"Hello — yes?"

"It's Jonah Gray. I'm calling from New York.

Silence.

"Galina?"

"Yes — yes, Jonah. I'm here. I'm just very surprised. It's the middle of the night here."

"Ah —"

I paused as if checking the time.

"— I'm sorry. I was so focused on calling you the time difference slipped my mind."

"Is everything all right?"

"Everything's great. In fact, working on this deal with Andreu is what made me think to call you."

More silence.

"You are aware of Andreu and I working together, aren't you?"

"I . . . yes. I mean, he . . . I don't really get involved with the Prevkos affairs."

"Really? I remember you always a part of my father and Alexander's business discussions. When I was young, no matter where we'd meet up with —"

"That was a long time ago, Jonah."

"It was. Anyway, Pop's birthday is coming up. There's this

European artist he likes, Ia, who does these amazing illustrations of animals. I figured your ties to the artistic community in that part of the world could help me find him. It's the perfect opportunity to help Pop grow his collection."

"Is that so?" she asked after a pause.

"You think you could help me find one of his larger works? There's a great spot for it in Pop's living room."

"Jonah —"

"Maybe not his absolute biggest, but something close."

No response.

"Galina?"

Nothing.

"Galina?"

"Yes, I'm here."

"Can you help me with this?"

"Jonah," she cut me off, "I don't mean to be rude, but it's late."

"Of course. I apologize. What would be a good time to —"

"I'm sorry, Jonah. Good night."

She hung up.

Fuck.

I dialed her number again. On came her Russian voice mail. I had lost her. Most likely, I figured, because she wanted to speak with my father. I ended the signal before trying the number one last time.

Nothing.

I knew the ride to Baltimore well, only needing my MapQuest directions once I hit the Baltimore Beltway Outer Loop. One of my clients was based there. A couple years earlier they liked the team's work with their Manhattan satellite office so much they asked us to handle relocating their four-hundred-thousand-square-foot head-quarters. For a few months the team flew there on Monday morning and back Monday night. I would leave on Sunday. It was summer, so for me it was a perfect opportunity to let both myself and the car out on the highway. At the end of the day Monday, as they headed back to the airport, I headed back to the open road feeling more like a bird, between the stars and the wind, than anyone ever has enclosed in an airplane.

Just before eight P.M., the directions and the printout from Ryan's office on the passenger seat, I slowly made the final turn into Phoenix, Maryland, one of Baltimore's many suburbs. I was headed toward Jarrettsville Pike. There I would find the home of Pavel Derbyshev.

Always get them in person.

I could barely see the house because of the high gates and trees surrounding the sprawling property. All I could tell, from the points and towers toward the top of the structure, was that it looked like a big castle. I followed the quiet, rising street of über-rich suburbia as it slightly veered to the left. As I came around the bend, the gates of the estate started to open.

The strong sun was about to doze off, creating a wicked glare on the horizon. I squinted and focused on the road. In the blazing rearview mirror I saw a large limo, I figured a Bentley or a Rolls, leaving in the opposite direction. I turned and followed it.

Having never followed anyone before, I had no idea how far to stay back. Overly cautious, I almost lost him twice at the get-go. I threw on my sunglasses looking for any advantage. After a few minutes I found what I determined to be my safe zone.

The ride into the city was uneventful. I was worried at first about the traffic impeding my pursuit but it turned out to be a helpful boundary. After twenty minutes or so the limo turned onto North Calvert Street and pulled up to the valet at a restaurant. The place, one of the most upscale in Baltimore, was called Prime Rib. I had had a number of power meals there myself.

I pulled to the right of the street and stopped. The limo's chauffer got out of the car and started for the opposite side passenger door. I shut my engine down, checked my jacket pocket for the gun, and made my move.

I jumped from the Porsche and strode briskly toward the front of the restaurant. The chauffer opened the limo door. Just as I reached the car, a very tall man stepped out. He was alone.

"Excuse me, Mr. Derbyshev?"

Both men looked at me. The chauffer took a protective step in front of his boss.

"Mr. Derbyshev?" I asked again.

"Who's inquiring?" asked the chauffer.

I knew from Ryan's information that Derbyshev was an older guy, but this I never would have guessed. He looked like a fucking count or something. He stood no shorter than six foot five, had a long face with a huge nose, and a full head of silver hair. He wore a navy pin-striped suit, black alligator shoes, bright red ascot, and had an overcoat thrown over his shoulders like a cape even though it was in the high '70s. Once his chauffeur spoke, Derbyshev turned his attention back to the restaurant as if the inches I stood below him represented more than just height.

"That's for Mr. Derbyshev's ears. No one else," I responded.

Derbyshev started for the restaurant.

"Sir, excuse me, sir, I really do need to talk to you."

He kept walking. I took a step toward him. His chauffeur cut me off.

"Please, Mr. Derbyshev," I continued, "it's extremely important…"

"I imagine it is," the tall man stated in a heavy Baltic accent, never looking back or breaking stride. "Why else would you follow us in such a ridiculous car? You may as well be driving a fire engine."

I shrugged off the flip comment. He was getting closer to the front door. I couldn't let him disappear inside.

"Andreu Zhamovsky!" I desperately blurted out.

The man stopped dead in his tracks. He didn't turn around. He just stood there. I looked at his car and chauffeur again then returned my eyes to his back.

"Only three types of men get driven around in the back of a Bentley, Mr. Derbyshev. Smart, lucky, or corrupt."

Finally he turned around. His large, sunken eyes glowered at me.

"Depending on how you're involved with Andreu, there's a very strong chance I can either make or save you a lot of trouble. Isn't that alone worth five minutes?

Pavel Derbyshev received a king's welcome. Not two feet inside the building the maître'd stormed him, as did his pretty young sidekick who removed Derbyshev's overcoat. They all said their hellos. We were then led from the dimly lit entranceway past the coat check and bar toward the more vibrant, swank dining room. Boris, the chauffeur, had come in with us, no doubt to keep an eye on me. He walked ahead of us and settled in the lounge.

The dining room was dramatic, a true throwback to a supper club in 1940s Manhattan. A tuxedoed waitstaff tended conscientiously to all of the patrons, who were sitting in leather high-back chairs. Naughty Louis Icart lithographs adorned the black-lacquered, gold-trimmed walls. Soft sounds hummed from the piano and bass. There was a timeless feel of elegance.

We cleaved our way through savory smells of steaks and seafood and were shown to Derbyshev's table in the rear.

"A drink to start off?" asked the host, waving our waiter over as we sat down.

"Just the wine list, Bernard," Derbyshev said, "and a bottle of still."

Bernard hurried off and we settled in.

"You often dine alone?"

He was in no mood for small talk.

"Your five minutes are ticking."

"You've never banked with Salton Lynear Bank before," I jumped in. "Twelve days ago you opened an account with them for the first time. Why?"

"What's your concern with it?"

"My concern is that the name Andreu Zhamovsky seems to ring loud and clear with you."

"And?"

"Your partner may be trying to set me up. If he is, that means you're possibly an accomplice."

"What's your name?" he went on, dismissing me.

"You tell me," I snapped back. "You expect me to believe you're working with Andreu and you don't know?"

The waiter returned with a large bottle of Fiji water and poured each of us a glass.

"I don't — work— with anyone. I buy and sell people, interests, things. I'll ask you one more time or this meeting is over. What's your name?"

I took a sip of my water.

"One-five-eight-six-two-six-four-seven-two. You want a name, that's my fucking name."

Nothing.

"I can do a lot better than your social security number and recent banking history," I bluffed. "And I'm ready to take you down if I have to. You sure my name's still so important?"

"What is it that you want?"

"I've done my homework, Pavel. The day after I told Andreu where we'd be parking his cash, a corporate account for a private company called Partners International opened at the same bank. A corporate account in the care of — in the control of — Pavel Derbyshev. A man with the same last name as Piotr Derbyshev, who, considering what's been happening in the news —"

"I never expected to see that," Derbyshev interjected.

"See what?"

"That *Danish Jubilee Egg* had been stolen. I was just as surprised as you were."

"Bullshit! You and Andreu —"

The waiter appeared again so I clammed up.

"Have you decided on a bottle, sir?"

He hadn't looked at the wine list.

"Bring me a bottle of the 2001 Chateau Mouton Rothschild."

He looked from the waiter to me.

"One glass. We're almost through."

The waiter moved on.

"You and Andreu are planning to . . . to . . ."

"To what?"

"The only reason you would have opened an account when you did was because you were expecting funds. Because you were —"

"If you had done the homework you claim to have, you would have learned that I single-handedly built a shipping empire," he cut me off, leaning in towards me. "My firm has accounts all over the world."

"But you've never before banked with Salton. Ever. Why now?"

"That would simply be none of your business," he went on, leaning back again. "I don't answer questions about my personal affairs from people I don't know. The reason you're sitting here is because you said you could either make or save me a lot of trouble. I suggest you tell me how. Or you're on your way."

"I'll go to the cops," I bluffed further. "Tell them what I know and let them fill in the holes."

"No you won't. Because from the trouble it seems you've found yourself in, you would have already if it were a viable option."

Derbyshev, to my surprise, stood from the table. With a quick step he was at my side looking down at me.

"I'm a businessman," he stated sternly, "I make deals. What Andreu and I are doing is just that. We're making a deal, completing a transaction, one that doesn't concern you or *Danish Jubilee Egg*. Now it's time for you to go. When I return from the restroom, I expect you to be gone."

Derbyshev turned and started to walk off. I was so hot I became cold. As much as I wanted to run up from behind and tackle him, my gut was telling me this was a guy with the game plan to back up the talk. As I struggled to come up with my next move, Derbyshev turned back toward me.

"By the way — smart."

I was confused.

"Smart?"

"That's right. I get driven in the back of a Bentley because I'm smart."

Sitting there I anxiously eyeballed the dining room. I looked in the direction of the lounge but couldn't see Boris. I returned my attention to the table and had a stare down with the bread basket.

Fuck.

I wasn't going anywhere. I had just driven three and a half hours out of sheer desperation in order to get some answers. Somehow I needed to pry something, anything I could, from the guy. Somehow I needed to get some leverage, I needed to —

A nervous warmth engulfed me as I identified my best shot at success. I jumped from my seat and started back through the restaurant. I came to a fork. Right led back to the establishment's exit. Left led to the restrooms. The thought of leaving empty handed was near crippling. I reached into my suit jacket and felt for my gun. At that moment, scared shitless, I realized left had never been more right.

Quietly, I entered the men's room doing my best to control my breathing. The black tiles and art-deco chrome moldings instantly took me back to a time of old-world thugs. A textbook combination of antiseptic and air freshener filled my nose. Straight ahead a scrawny old white guy in a weathered tux was straightening the sink area with his back to me. He had no idea I was there. I swung my vision left, catching my own stare in the mirror along the way.

Derbyshev was facing the wall at a urinal. Once I realized he was the only other one there, I took a deep breath and rushed up behind him. I put the gun directly to the back of his head.

Talk about coming full circle.

"I don't want to hurt you," I started, unable to fight an image of Pangaea-Man.

Movement to my right. Leaving the gun in place I checked the attendant. He was tiptoeing toward the door.

"Not another step."

He gasped, turned to me, and threw his arms up.

"I mean it."

He couldn't speak. He just nodded.

I returned my eyes to the Count's silver hair.

"Tell me about the transaction with Andreu Zhamovsky."

Nothing.

"Tell me about the transaction and why it involves me."

Nothing.

"Now!"

Tick. Tick.

I checked the old guy. He hadn't moved.

I grabbed the back of Derbyshev's head and put his face into the wall as I simultaneously jammed the gun in farther.

Get what you need.

"A man named Piotr Derbyshev, same last name as you, is believed one of two men who could have crafted eight Fabergé eggs that went missing in the Russian Revolution. Six of those eggs have never been found, but two resurfaced in 1979, one of which is in the news for having been stolen. Andreu Zhamovsky's company, Prevkos, has subsidiaries named after those eggs, subsidiaries my dead father has a ton of stock in. You and Andreu are involved in a deal."

I pushed the gun into his hair, skin, skull even further.

"So I want you to start talking. I only said that I didn't want to hurt you. I never said I wouldn't."

Nothing.

Fuck!

Tick. Tick.

Instinct taking over, I moved the gun to his shoulder not easing up even the slightest bit on holding his face to the wall.

"Fuck it," I gushed dejectedly. "I'm not leaving without information. Maybe you'll believe this. Three —"

I was in full improvisation mode.

"Two —"

I thought, what happens when I hit zero without a response?

"One —"

Was I more prepared to shoot or not to shoot?

"Different!" he blurted out.

"Different. What's different?"

"The eggs. We're dealing with different eggs. I was surprised *Danish Jubilee Egg* was stolen. I have no idea who you are."

I moved the gun back to his head.

"Tell me about the deal."

"I'm selling Andreu a different egg."

"Which one?"

"*Necessaire Egg.*"

"You said eggs. Plural."

"I didn't mean to. One egg."

Voices were approaching the bathroom door. I looked to the attendant.

"Lose them, now," I barked, "Tell them you're cleaning up some puke."

The guy was frozen solid.

"Now!" I urged him through clenched teeth.

He moved to the door and opened it a crack like a woman who'd jumped from the shower. To my relief he lost them. He retreated back into the room and resumed his stance.

"You're selling it to Zhamovsky?"

"That's right. That's why I opened the account. You have no idea how many people would like to stake a claim on these items. Andreu knows as well as anyone that these eggs need to stay under the radar, just like any cash associated with moving them."

"One less transfer of funds between banks means one less stop of the cash on a federal server," I deduced. "To shift the money from Andreu's account to yours, in the same bank, is simply a book transfer. No other bank. No federal server."

"Very good."

"How did you get ahold of it? I mean, how — if —"

Something wasn't right. These eggs were said to be worth thirty to forty million each and we were dealing with a substantially larger amount of cash. Then —

"Oh shit! Oh shit!"

It hit me.

Eggs. Plural.

This much money could only mean one thing.

I threw the gun in my pocket as I headed straight past the attendant for the door. I opened it and walked through. Boris was coming my way. I ducked back into the men's room, gun out again.

The attendant immediately assumed the position. Derbyshev,

on the other hand, was now facing me. And he was pissed. Past him I could see a shade, not too far from the ground, pulled over what I figured to be a decent-size window. Life had become all about seconds. I needed to get to that window.

Again, as I shook my suit jacket off while maintaining my aim, I faced that question. Did I have it in me to shoot?

His chauffeur would be coming through the door any moment. Time had run out.

So I let him have it.

Boom!

I kicked him square in the groin sending him crashing to the floor. All it took was the pull of a string to yank the black vertical blinds wide open. I rolled the pistol, like brass knuckles, into my fist, which I then wrapped with my jacket forming a makeshift boxing glove. With a pop, the glass exploded. The center was clear but the frame still contained big chunks of sharp edges. I took a few quick jabs at what remained. Most of the pieces fell just as I turned my head at the sound of the bathroom door opening.

The window was only a few feet off the ground, no higher than my chest, so I literally propelled myself through it like a missile. Unscathed, I hit the ground and bounced up running. I darted around the building then down the street toward my car. Halfway there I looked over my shoulder. Boris was coming after me. Whether he followed me through the window or came back through the restaurant I couldn't be sure.

Calm, I told myself as I reached the Porsche. Be calm. I jumped in the unlocked car and unwound the jacket from my wrist, throwing it on the passenger-side floor. I tossed the gun on top of it and checked Boris through the windshield. He was gaining. He had a gun out.

"Calm," I whispered to myself.

I pulled the keys from my pants pocket and started her up. Within seconds I was on my way. I flew past the approaching chauffeur who had his arm extended. I ducked, bracing for impact.

He never fired.

CHAPTER 39

Around midnight, as I steadily moved up a straight stretch of the New Jersey Turnpike back toward Manhattan, I picked up Pop's cell phone. I looked at the printout from Ryan again. Derbyshev's home number. I dialed and hit "send."

"Hello?"

I wasn't surprised to hear the Count's voice. I figured his staff had either left or retired for the night.

"How many eggs is it, Mr. Derbyshev?"

"This is an unpublished number. How…"

He tapered off, probably remembering I had his social security number.

"You said eggs, plural. More than one. How many are there?"

"I have nothing to say to you."

"Zhamovsky's going to fuck you."

"Ridiculous," he scoffed.

"Is it? How well do you know him?"

No response.

"Mr. Derbyshev, if anyone here should be worried about trusting the other it's me trusting you. Take my word on that, especially given our little confrontation. Andreu's going to seriously work you. You give me a couple minutes, answer a couple questions, I think you'll understand that."

Derbyshev thought on it.

"You're expecting close to half a billion dollar payday, aren't you?"

Silence.

"Mr. Derbyshev?"

"How do you know all this?"

"It doesn't matter. I'll tell you what Andreu's up to if you help me put this together. Tell me about the transaction. Because for the life of me, I can't figure out how the money lines up. If—"

"All six."

"All six," I repeated, knowing full well what he meant.

Six eggs. The six imperial Easter eggs supposedly never found.

"Piotr Derbyshev was the mystery egg maker."

"He was," the Count conceded, finally realizing he had too much to lose to not give me a chance. "I have spent my entire life gathering the ones thought to be missing all these years. His grandson, my own father, tracked them for a while and kept records. As a young immigrant I simply made my sole goal in life to get rich so I could pick up where he left off and continue our family's quest. With so little information or records concerning their whereabouts, it feels like I had to touch every corner of the world to bring them back. But I did. All six."

"But how? I mean—who, or—where were they? How did they survive? Because it is my understanding that when the royal family was overthrown—"

"Does the name Maria Feodorovna mean anything to you?"

The Russian empress for whom many of the imperial eggs, including all eight that went missing in the Revolution, were made.

"It does."

"Fascinating woman with a terrific eye for talent. The kind of woman who would fight for what she believed in. The kind of woman who would stand up for those she made a commitment to."

I didn't get it.

"Mr. Derbyshev, I'm not following."

"The Czarina Maria Feodorovna loved all of the eggs presented to her, but it was her keen eye that identified Piotr Derbyshev's contributions to the eggs as superior. She asked Henrik Wigstrom herself for Derbyshev to have the opportunity to lead the creation of some eggs. When the revolution happened, Alexandra Feodorovna had her servants round up as many of the Derbyshev pieces as she could out of an obligation to someone she believed in. All eight of his creatioins were saved. Two were stolen soon after, not to be found until 1979 in Yakutsk."

"The two sold at auction," I filled in.

"Precisely. That's how Andreu got to me in the first place. We have a mutual acquaintance who possesses one of the other two — obviously you know which one. I've been trying to buy it for years. This person told Andreu where he could find me."

"But then why would you sell them to Andreu? After just telling me yourself you had to reach to the corners of the world to bring them home?"

"I never planned on it. Andreu approached me about it, but I said no. Unequivocally, no. He said he'd give me top dollar, forty million per egg, and I still said no."

"So what made you change your mind?"

"His offer doubled. Eighty million per egg."

Eighty million multiplied by six equals four hundred and eighty million. An amount right around Andreu's price range for our deal.

"Finally, I thought, what better legacy could my great-grandfather have than that? Than fetching almost half a billion dollars for the craftsmanship of his own hands?"

The count had come through. I owed him.

"Mr. Derbyshev, when did Andreu tell you the transaction would actually take place?"

"He said he couldn't be sure, but —"

"But within three weeks?" I completed his thought.

"That's correct. Within three weeks."

"Did Andreu ever tell you where the cash he would be using to buy the eggs would be coming from?"

"Coming from? How do you mean?"

"Andreu Zhamovsky is the chairman of Prevkos, Mr. Derbyshev."

"I know this."

"But did you know he's using his shareholders' money to buy your precious eggs, and not his own? Why else would he be funneling a half billion dollars of his company's funds into this country through a real estate deal with me?"

Nothing. I continued.

"I'll tell you why. Andreu didn't tell you to open an account at Salton to avoid another transfer. He did it so he could set you, someone with an account under the same roof, up when the Prevkos cash went missing. Public money supposedly being used for the purchase of New York City real estate and not the purchase of antiques neither of you can talk about but that will already be in his possession. A little matter of them, technically, being stolen property belonging to the Russian government."

"That can't be right."

"Oh no? Why else would he be bringing the perfect amount of cash into this country through the deal we're working on?"

"Andreu Zhamovsky is a wealthy man. I'm sure he has —"

"No other bank accounts whatsoever. Not one, at least with Salton Lynear Bank, the institution Andreu told you to open an account with. The institution Andreu told you his funds would be coming from."

Derbyshev paused.

"Why should I believe you? About any of this?"

"Because I'm the only chance you've got. You call Andreu Zhamovsky and tell him about this chat, we'll both learn that the hard way."

I ended the signal and tossed Pop's cell on the passenger seat. Within seconds it rang again. Unavailable caller.

"Forget to tell me something?"

"Jonah, why are you using this line? Where is your father?"

It was Galina Zhamovsky. I was caught completely off guard.

"My father is dead, Galina."

Silence.

"He was shot outside his townhouse yesterday."

"Oh my God. No!"

"I need some answers."

"He was . . . this . . . he . . ." she went on, her stunned voice dwindling away.

More silence.

Click.

She was gone.

The highway, still running straight but over a knoll, started to lose elevation as I hit the crest. A wall of stars in front of me, my mind returned to Andreu, our deal, the timing of everything.

Three weeks for the real estate transaction.

Less than a month before *Danish Jubilee Egg* was to be moved to tighter security.

Andreu was looking to corral these eggs, a group of six and another of two, respectively, that seemed to have gone separate ways. Plain and simple. The perfect collection. But while the nature of our property transaction perhaps now made sense, there were still so many unanswered questions. Questions like, why me? Not for the cash, now obvious, but for being the one planted with the now-famous egg less than twenty-four hours after its theft? Or the stock certificates? What was the connection there?

I pulled off the highway to a rest area and stopped next to a pump of premium. I turned off the car. Sitting there, windows still down, I listened to the fans as they continued to run underneath the hood against the backdrop of the country calm. She was coming down from her workout, settling. After gassing up I headed into the MobilMart for a bottle of water.

The place was empty. The wiry kid behind the counter couldn't have been a second over fifteen. I grabbed my bottle and placed it on the counter.

"Anything else?"

There were still some copies of the previous day's paper on a plastic, rolling *Star Ledger* rack to my right.

"Ledger."

Back in my car, constantly checking all mirrors, I slowly rolled into a parking spot off to the side. I unfolded the paper. I found it on page five next to a column about the still-missing actor. FALLEN MANHATTAN MOGUL INQUIRY MOVES FORWARD.

I started to read, but it was mostly the same facts I had already seen. I started skimming. More information on the evidence, the bullets, the body, and the testimony from Mattheau about the car that sped away. The cigar ash. The supposed timeline. Where my father was going so early. Why he —

Double take.

Cigar ash?

According to the article, a long cigar ash was found in the street in front of the townhouse, something authorities have deemed relevant because it was where the car supposedly sped away from "according to the testimony of the deceased's chauffeur."

The compact cockpit felt like it was closing in on me. My body temperature began to soar. I could see a snapshot of his fucking face like a Polaroid tacked up on the corkboard of my brain. I had seen him smoking just days earlier. Lloyd Murdoch, that bastard who knew Pop was leaving his house early Saturday morning for a tee time. He probably just sat there in the back of his limo, his arm hanging out the window, as someone with solid marksmanship took the shot. When the car jerked as it took off the ash from his cigar must have shaken loose. I closed my eyes and felt chills as I watched a reenactment of the possible scene in front of the townhouse. What a sadistic prick, I thought. Not only did he hire the hit as a message to me, he made sure he was there to watch it go down.

Pop had literally gotten caught in the cross fire.

But was it he, ultimately, who had helped load the weapon?

Parting the night, I glided toward New York City on the final leg of my journey. I was tired, angry, paranoid, yet undeterred.

Through all of the mixed emotions, through all of the anger, one thing was for sure. Andreu was looking to gather the missing collection of eggs, which made something else, so I thought, all the more clear.

Danish Jubilee Egg now didn't seem to be about me at all. She seemed to be part of a bigger plan than I originally thought, one that most likely had Robie/Hart hired, for lack of a better word, by Andreu to steal her to go with the other missing treasures. As I had learned days earlier from the newspaper, the egg hadn't been stolen even twenty-four hours before I had been saddled with it. Plus, Robie/Hart had been caught in the act on camera. These two facts pointed to one conclusion. Robie/Hart must have learned about the government's hidden cameras. A rapidly slamming window of opportunity was the only explanation for him following me out to the Hamptons to plant the egg on me at a crowded wedding. Because the antique was scheduled to be moved to the Capital so soon, the heist couldn't wait and they moved to Plan B. I conveniently became that plan. Andreu knew, for at least three weeks, I wasn't going anywhere. He had made sure of it, which meant I was ripe to hold onto the egg until later retrieval. All Robie/Hart had to do was track me down, plant the egg, and disappear. Enter Pangaea-Man.

As I came down, around the ramp that led from Jersey into the Lincoln Tunnel, I looked out to my left at the entire Manhattan footprint from Harlem to where the Towers use to reign. Even though it was the middle of the night, a dense ball of light hung over the island, the result of intense wattage flowing below. Thankful is the first thing I remember feeling for that energy. I couldn't help marveling at the fact such a jagged skyline could seem so orderly.

I felt relief that my partners didn't seem to be involved. I couldn't handle that level of betrayal. Not now. The stars were continuing to align, but I still had questions. How well did I really know Andreu Zhamovsky or what he was capable of?

Did I know him at all? My own half-brother?

My lines kept getting crossed between the note in my father's handwriting and the fact the watermark on that same note was in Russian. Is that why Galina hung up when I told her my father was gone? Was it possible she knew what was happening but was afraid of her own son?

At the bottom of the ramp I swung around to the right and shot through the toll using one of the EZ Pass lanes. Within seconds the tunnel linking the two states swallowed me. When it did, something dawned on me.

Someone once said that out of chaos emerges patterns. What if it didn't, I thought. What if chaos was to remain just that, chaos, but you were able to create the patterns on your own, without anyone knowing? What if you were able to define the emerging order of events into a pattern that only became apparent to others after the consequences of such events were already irreversible?

I had been forced to play someone else's game. So, I thought, maybe it was time to tweak the rules. Still wary of using my cell unless I absolutely needed to, I picked up Pop's, dialed a familiar number, and hit "send."

"Jonah!" L pushed out, trying not to sound asleep.

"Sorry to wake you, pal."

"What the fuck is the matter? You okay?"

"I'm fine."

"You said you'd — for twenty-four hours."

"I know what I said, L. I'm okay. Really."

"You're not selling me. Tell me where you are."

"It doesn't matter."

"I knew it. I knew you were in serious shit once you asked me for that gun."

"I didn't want to lie to you, L. You know that."

"Of course I do."

L paused before going on.

"I'm so sorry about your pop. The whole thing's so fucking awful."

At this moment I was treading water with regard to how I felt about my father. I said nothing.

"I wish I could bring him back for you, man. I'd be a liar if I said I know how this must feel."

I knew L was trying to help, but I didn't have the time or the stomach.

"I appreciate it, L," I stopped him, "but I'd really rather not get into any of that right now."

L obliged.

"How serious is the trouble you're in? And be honest."

It was time to trust my oldest, closest friend. My best chance for him to come through on my upcoming request was to convey the severity of the situation.

"Life and death I think."

"Oh fuck," he said under his breath. "Tell me where you are, Jonah. Let me come help you."

"It's out of the question."

"Why?"

"Because it has to be."

"I don't understand. What's so fucking —"

"L! Please! Don't you think you're the first person I would have called if it was at all, even the slightest bit, possible?"

He said nothing.

"If you truly want to help, just listen."

L let out a big, drawn out sigh.

"What do you need me to do?"

"Tell me the name of the loading dock guy we always laugh about who works for Plotkin."

Plotkin, whose facility is across the street from L's, is another meat distributor and one of Luckman's primary competitors.

"The who?"

"Come on, L, the fucking shady Mexican guy we laugh about who spends every other six months in jail. The one who always comes looking to you for a job but always gets hired back across the way when you say no."

"Oh, you mean Hernando, the one who helps smuggle illegals into the country?"

"Yes! Hernando!"

"What the fuck could you possibly want from him?"

CHAPTER 40

Early Monday afternoon, draped in fine Italian fabric and briefcase in hand, I stepped through the door and onto the sidewalk in front of my apartment building. Everything from the pistol to my sunglasses to each hair on my head was perfectly in place. Under the hot summer sun I made a right to head uptown. Just as I did, to my surprise, was an approaching Detective Morante.

"Good afternoon, Jonah. You have a minute for me?"

He looked just as he did the first time I met him, neatly dressed, almost stylish. A nicely pressed navy blue button-down was tucked into his nonpleated charcoal pants and finished off with brown leather shoes that matched his belt.

Remaining calm I looked at my watch.

"I'm on my way to a meeting."

"Yeah, I can see that," the detective responded slowly.

"Is there a problem?"

"No," his voice snapped back, his arm dropping back to his side, "I'm just surprised to see you jumping back into work so quickly. You know, with everything that's happened over the last few days."

"Yeah, well, it hasn't been easy. Keeping busy is best. It's how I deal."

"I guess that makes sense. I mean —"

The detective turned slightly to his left and threw his arms out in front of him, palms up, as if presenting my apartment building to me.

"How else do people come to live like this?"

I looked dryly at the property, then back at Morante.

"I have somewhere to be, detective. What is it that I can help you with?"

Detective Morante returned his angle, focus, to me.

"We're doing a full inventory of the crime scene, standard procedure in all homicides, and we've come across a cell phone A/C adapter plugged into the wall in your father's study. Only, there was no phone. You have any idea who may have removed it?"

Fuck! All I had meant to do was duck anyone listening in on me.

"Because," the detective went on, "it seems there's been some activity on the line since after his death. And if —"

A bit of sweat began forming on the back of my neck and it wasn't from the sun. If push came to shove, L and Galina could be easily explained. My best friend and, as I had just learned, my father's Russian mistress whom I felt the need to confront. Although then there was Derbyshev, which meant a whole new world of shit Morante hadn't learned of yet. That's when it hit me. A preemptive strike appeared to be in my best interest.

"It was me, detective."

If they knew it was me who took the phone then perhaps they'd have no need to check the identities behind the called numbers.

"Really. When?"

"Friday afternoon. Before I headed home from the office early I stopped at my father's townhouse to pick up some business papers I left in his study. Once there I realized my phone was about to die. Even though I felt like shit, I still had some time-sensitive calls to make on my way home. Pop told me to take his phone."

"Is that right?"

"It is."

I looked at my watch again.

"Detective, I really do need to get going."

"I understand, Jonah. You're a busy man. I just have one more question."

"About?"

"A couple of items in your father's basement."

"Like what?"

"For starters, the set of free weights. What can you tell me about them?"

"I used to lift with them in high school."

"High school."

"That's right."

"You haven't touched them since?"

"I don't believe so. Maybe a couple of times when I was home in the summer during college, but —"

"But what?"

"Detective, I'm not sure I understand your question."

"My question is I'd like to know if you can tell me why a couple of them are missing."

"Missing?"

"That's right. The weight set you have down there isn't only a damn nice one, but according to the manufacturer you have the complete set, both dumbbells and plates. Only, two of the barbell plates are missing. Both of them thirty-five pounders."

The manufacturer. Morante had just informed me, no doubt intentionally, he was digging.

"Like I said Detective, it's been a lot of years since I used them."

"Huh," Morante grunted, turning his attention to the passing traffic. "So I guess you wouldn't know much about the tool chest either."

"I don't know what you're talking about."

He returned his stare to me.

"You don't know about a tool chest?"

"No, I mean . . . yes . . . that's not what I meant. Of course I know about the tool chest. It's been down there my whole life."

"You use it lately?"

"No."

"Did your father?"

"I have no idea."

"Interesting. Because like the weight set it is of top quality, and also missing a couple of vital elements. Such as a pair of pliers and a saw."

My thoughts spun to Mattheau. His desire to dispose of the body and his hidden yet savage past. The more I wanted to now understand what he had done, the more afraid I knew I'd ever be to ask him.

"Detective, what does any of this have to do with my father being shot?"

"Probably nothing. Like I said, a complete understanding of the crime scene is standard procedure. It's just that, judging from your father's lifestyle, he doesn't exactly strike me as the handyman type."

I was nervous from the direction the conversation had taken. An inquiry of my own was all I could do to regain my footing and show the good detective he hadn't rattled me.

"Detective, while I have you here, I actually have a question of my own."

"Oh yeah," he shot back, humoring me, "what's that?"

"The cigar ash. The one that's been discussed in the papers."

"What about it?"

"Are you sure it was from Saturday morning?"

"We're running tests to determine that."

"Wouldn't it have blown away? Or couldn't it have come from somewhere else on that street?"

"At first you would assume either of those scenarios to be true, but that morning was so still our CSI team decided to check out the rest of the blacktop in front of the townhouse. Sure enough, not six feet from where the ash was found and your father's chauffeur said the car sped off, was a small patch of the same ash embedded more firmly in the tar, probably at the point of contact where it original-ly fell from someone's cigar."

I was confused by Morante being so forthright, then figured he was trying to freak me with the department's prowess in the area of scientific fact-finding.

"I see," I said, trying to remain calm.

Fucking Murdoch. I knew it.

"Jonah, did your father ever smoke a cigar?"

I quickly saw my opening.

"He did."

Here was my chance to lead the detective away from Murdoch so I could have him all to myself.

"In fact often, on summer weekends after returning from dinner, he would light one up and take a walk around the neighborhood. Maybe your crime lab could see if the ash found was from the kind of cigar he smoked."

"What kind of cigar was that?"

"Monte Cristo #2."

"How about you Jonah?"

"How about me what?"

"You ever smoke cigars?"

It felt as if someone had jammed a racquetball down my throat. I couldn't lie. All he needed to do was ask one person familiar with me and I was screwed.

"I do."

"Ever smoke Monte Cristo #2s?"

"Sometimes."

We parted ways, me heading uptown and Morante looking to cross the street. Before I was twenty feet away the detective yelled to me.

"By the way, Jonah, I forgot."

"What's that?"

"I think you know a friend of mine. Spencer Simon."

Just his name was enough to make me feel like a heavy-duty strap, the kind for securing an unruly mental patient to a gurney, was tightening around my chest. I didn't respond.

"He told me to mention you're in his thoughts. As are his hopes of a speedy resolution to all of this."

CHAPTER 41

I stepped out of the elevator onto PCBL's main floor in the Chrysler Center, a complete bat out of hell, albeit in mind more than body. Physically I was doing my best to remain alert, motivated, but not overly high-strung. My demeanor, my energy, was the opposite of what anyone I was going to encounter would expect. It was important I didn't blow my cover. It was essential I didn't appear hysterical by overcompensating. Inside, I was fucking bursting with anticipation. It was time to lift those up who deserved to be lifted. And it was time to swat those down who deserved to be crushed.

Cautious of being tracked, I felt I needed to pick my spots and keep moving. Everything that was about to occur had to happen expeditiously. I pushed my Bruno Maglis down the sophisticated hallway, the past two weeks chasing me, nipping at my heels. Poised, posture intact, I never looked over my shoulder. I simply moved forward wearing the mask of a strong man struggling to hold my chin up like a professional and return to my responsibilities. Truth be told, my grieving had happened in my apartment and en route to and from Baltimore. By this point I was insensate. I was nothing more than a thick, sharp, lethally pointed machine ready to bore into the eyes of those who had screwed me.

It was three P.M. when I entered the office following a quick shower in my apartment. I came in late because I wanted to keep my schedule fresh, my whereabouts unscripted. Unable to speak, touching the corner of her eye with a well-used Kleenex, Carolyn rose from her desk and wrapped her arms around me. I anticipated condolences and hugs that afternoon, so my pistol was in my brief-case that I was holding in my right hand.

"I'm so sorry, Jonah," she said into my ear through a sniffle.

"I know you are, Carolyn."

"Don't worry for a second about tomorrow. I've taken care of everything."

"I knew you would."

Still hugging me, she put her face in front of mine.

"Do they have any idea who did this?"

I shook my head "no."

"They don't."

She put her head back on my shoulder and gave me another squeeze.

"If there's anything I can do, anything, just let me know. You name it."

The serious tone made my jaw lock.

"I'm okay, Carolyn. How about you? Any of your numbers come in?" I asked, looking to break the tension.

A brief chuckle fought through her tears.

"Scratch off over the weekend, a thousand bucks," she replied, humoring me.

We separated.

"Actually, Carolyn, I'm going to have to take you up on that offer sooner than you think."

Carolyn, curious, took her seat.

"Whatever you need, Jonah. What's up?"

Action.

I looked around. I crouched down, my knees bent to the point I was looking up at her. I placed my hand up on her desk for added balance.

"I need your help, Carolyn. I know this is going to sound crazy, but I don't have the time to explain. I don't know who else to turn to. It is definitely the most important thing I've ever asked of you."

Carolyn shifted her eyes.

"Jonah, what's going on? You're scaring me."

"Don't be scared," I said quietly. "I need you to keep your voice lower. Everything will be fine if you help me."

Carolyn looked around, as if waiting for someone to pop out from under a desk to guide her. No one ever popped out, so it was time to lay it on. Years of gifts, astronomical bonuses, extra vacation for her efforts; all of this was about to benefit me in a way I had never planned.

"If you follow my instructions you won't be in any danger. And you could end up saving my life."

Carolyn's eyes turned from scared to determined as loyalty began to overrun apprehension.

"From the person who killed your father?" she whispered.

That's the fucking spirit, I thought.

"No time for questions," I said back to her. "All I'm asking you to do is make some phone calls."

"Phone calls?"

"That's right. Simple phone calls. But they need to be made from phones untraceable to you. Random pay phones."

Carolyn was silent. I could tell the mention of her having to maintain anonymity had her insides twisting.

"It would mean the world to me, Carolyn. And I promise to make it worth your while."

Sensing my true need, Carolyn took the bait. Jumping in line with the program, she nodded her head ever so slightly "yes."

"Here's what I need you to do —"

Once Carolyn had her marching orders I headed down the hall. Perry's and Jake's offices were empty. I figured if they were in the office at all, they were in with Tommy.

I took two steps into Tommy's office, closed the door behind me then just stood there. I put my briefcase down at my side. The three of them stared at me in complete disbelief.

"Jonah, where have you been?" asked Tommy.

"It doesn't matter," I answered.

"Are you all right?" followed Jake.

It was odd to hear Jake speaking in such a caring, earnest tone. It was so unnatural. I looked him deadpan in the face.

"I'm fine."

"Jonah," Tommy continued, "it's understandable to take time for —"

I turned my eyes to Tommy.

"I mean it, Tommy. I'm all right. Anyway it doesn't matter now. I'm ready."

"Ready for what, Jonah?" he asked.

Easy does it, I thought to myself. Stop thinking out loud.

"Ready to take care of business."

Without a word, Perry stood up and walked over to me. Like Carolyn, she wrapped her arms around me as she fought tears. Jake and Tommy then followed. Within seconds the four of us were in a group hug like a rock band ready to take the stage. For a few moments I closed my eyes and absorbed their love as I hugged them back.

"I appreciate it, guys," I said. "Thank you."

I meant it. I knew they must have had so many questions, concerns.

"We're here, Jonah," Perry said, her cheek still pressed against me. "Just know that we're here."

After a few more seconds, as we started to break apart, Perry grabbed my hand so tight I could almost feel our palm prints interlock like zipper teeth. I turned my eyes toward her. I mentioned earlier that one way to gauge two people's closeness is through what they're willing to say to one another. Right there, perhaps more than ever, I was able to put my finger on what made Perry so special. Her ability to speak to me without ever having to say a word.

We took our usual spots. The sunlight, hitting Tommy's windows just right, filled the room. I took my jacket off and folded it over my knee as I sat back.

"Let's talk about the deals," I said. "What's happening?"

Nothing. Just glances.

"What?"

"A couple of issues have come up," Tommy said. "Nothing you need to worry about."

"What kind of issues? It's only Monday afternoon," I said. "What could have happened since we all closed up shop Friday night?"

Again, nothing.

"Asbestos," Jake said.

Our eyes all moved toward him. Perry's and Tommy's eyes were surprised, mine were appreciative.

"Where?" I asked.

He looked at Perry and Tommy who both seemed annoyed he had bothered to burden me with any of this. He sucked in a breath as he thought about answering then blew them off.

"Two of the Slevin properties."

"Six of the seven properties were built in the forties and fifties. We talked about this. You said you asked the two old birds straight out."

"I did."

"And they said we could expect to find a bit."

"Traces, Jonah. They said we might come across traces."

"Okay, traces."

Then I got it.

"How much was there?"

"A lot more than we were expecting to—"

"Jake—"

"To the untrained eye, one might think they constructed the entire fucking building with it."

I was speechless. But more from the fact I was most likely responsible for the three pits in their stomachs than the information. I knew the feeling of a career-altering deal taking a potentially dreadful turn as well as anyone. On top of that, they were dealing with real-life issues that they weren't even aware of on top of business. Again, courtesy of me.

"Wow, that bad," I said.

"That bad. Coldwall, the environmental consulting firm, hit

these two buildings over the weekend. They were numbers five and six of the seven, which means there's even one left to go," Jake explained. "I got the call about it around seven this morning."

"Is there any possibility of removing all of it?"

"What's the difference?" he continued.

I knew there wasn't one.

"There's no way for us to have it handled the way the government tells us we have to in the time frame we've been dealt, and we can't be telling our clients to close on buildings that are rife with asbestos. It kind of —"

"I think he gets it," Tommy interjected.

I wanted to open them up to my suspicions, but I couldn't. Until I knew more, I needed everything to remain the same. For their sake.

"It's all right, Tommy," I said. "Really. The way I see it, why hit the panic button when we don't know all the facts? It's not our job to know if and when the asbestos can be removed, it's theirs. So tell them before they do anything else to give us a proposal for getting rid of it all as fast as possible."

"Jonah, you know as well as anyone how expensive it will be to tackle something like this. And either way there's minimal chance they'll even be —" Jake went on.

Tommy cut him off.

"We're having them look at it right now, Jonah. I happen to agree with you."

"You said there were issues, plural. What else?"

"A little something with Cantrol," Perry pushed out.

"How little?"

"Let's just say that Gerry's team came across something of interest."

The strategy department of PCBL was comprised of different teams that evaluated potential deals. Gerry headed up our favorite group. Perry got to use them since they had the most experience with huge, trophy buildings.

"What kind of something?" I prodded. "A lease-related something?"

"Not exactly."

She had hoped to leave it at that.

"Perry, then what?"

"It's nothing you need to worry about, Jonah. Really."

"Perry?"

She looked at the other two. She was trying to protect me, which I didn't deserve, from thinking my precious deal was coming apart at a time I was so vulnerable. I felt like such a dick. I swore to myself again, right then and there, that I was going to make it up to them. I promised, on my mother's grave.

"Perry, I need to have my head in this game right now. So please, tell me."

"A lawsuit, Jonah. A thirty-something couple and their two-year-old daughter. The parents died last summer when one of the elevators dropped thirty-three stories with them. Somehow the child survived."

"Holy shit," I whispered. "Why then…how…why didn't we—"

"They didn't come from much, so the surviving family agreed to keep it quiet if they were compensated fairly. Cantrol didn't want to get dragged into court and into the news, so they agreed. The settlement is still being negotiated."

At the exact moment I entered my office and closed the door behind me, Carolyn came through on the intercom.

"Line two, Jonah."

"Who is it?" I asked as I put my briefcase down on the floor behind my desk.

"Andreu Zhamovsky."

Never before had one name stirred so many emotions. I wanted to blast him. I wanted to reach through the phone and choke him. I couldn't, not if I was going to win and come out of this unscathed. Plus, the best chance I had for keeping my partners out of trouble was to keep Andreu happy and thinking he was still in control.

"Put him through."

"Jonah?"

It was a voice I had heard so many times in the past. That morning, sodden with deception, it sounded different. Or perhaps I was just hearing it different, gauging it with the bias of someone who'd been had.

Almost.

"Good afternoon, Andreu."

I looked at the platinum Lange 1 strapped to my wrist.

"Or is it good evening?"

"I'm so sorry to hear about Stan," he jumped in. "What happened? Why didn't you accept any of my calls this weekend?"

I heard ice cubes clash through the phone as he took a sip of a drink.

"I've had a lot to deal with. Thank God for your new real estate endeavors. It's been the perfect excuse to keep my mind occupied."

"How can I help?"

"By letting me stay focused on what we're trying to achieve. I have enough shoulders to cry on."

"It's okay to take a step back, Jonah."

The "buddy-buddy" thing had become very old, very fast. Business as usual, I told myself.

React.

"I appreciate the concern Andreu, but my focus is on the deal. Not just for you, for me. If a step back was what I needed I would have taken it. What I need is to forge ahead."

"Whatever you say, old friend. If that's what you want."

"It is," I shot back.

"Then forge ahead it is. Please, the details."

Like he gave a fuck. I could have told him the details involved one of the buildings being a lair for some priests and young boys. It didn't matter. What mattered was that he still thought I was in the dark. Which, on the contrary, was exactly where he now was.

"The inspection teams are all rolling along smoothly with even less obstacles than expected."

"And this surprises you?"

"Actually, it does. Things always come up like sloppy or inaccurate property management record keeping, environmental issues, unforeseen building system problems, undisclosed tenant and leasing issues, etcetera. Here we've been quite fortunate. Each potential deal only has minor hurdles."

"How minor?"

"For example, the Park Avenue Slevin portfolio seems to be showing some signs of, how would I describe it, trace asbestos in certain areas."

"And this is minor?"

"It is, happens all the time in buildings this old. So what we'll do is work the cost of the asbestos abatement, or removal, into the overall purchase price, which will simply decrease the total value on a per square foot basis by a couple of cents. Then we'll use these savings to handle the problem ourselves instead of tying up the transfer of ownership by having them deal with it. Piece of cake. After all, the goal here is to have all of them thinking we are ready to buy, even if it means handling some little, minimal risk annoyances on our own, is it not?"

"It is, of course."

"At the Cantrol building one of the leases turns over, expires, earlier than we were initially told it would. Nothing more than shoddy record keeping. Are the differences in dates glaring enough that they could jeopardize the deal? Absolutely not. Again it is something that needs a bit more attention so we can account for it correctly in the final purchase price."

"But you're not concerned. Correct?"

"Correct. So I need you to give your friend Igor Larionov a call in the morning."

As far as I knew, Andreu still had no way of understanding I was completely dialed in. Therefore he had to continue playing the deal out on my terms until he had what he needed.

"He needs to be aware that I may contact him shortly with regard to placing some more funds in escrow here in the States. For timing purposes."

"Not a problem."

CHAPTER 42

My eyes observing from behind my sunglasses, my gun, once again, inside my jacket, I headed into the sun-drenched city. As much as I wanted to accept that I was as alone as I believed, the fact I had originally been onto Pangaea-Man tailing me, and rightly so, still had me freaked. I headed uptown on foot.

I took out my cell phone. I had a laundry list of client calls to return from the previous three days, some relating to my father and others regarding the fact that, whether it was the point in their respective deal where Tommy's expertise was needed or not, they were starting to feel as if I had disappeared. Just as I was about to return the first call, I stopped. Paranoia returned. I felt as if somewhere, just around a corner, trouble was waiting. Once I got to Madison Avenue an uptown bus pulled alongside of me. I reached into my pocket, grabbed my wallet and pulled out my Metrocard. Then I jumped on.

The giant steel tube used for shuttling city types around the five boroughs like cattle began to move. I've always hated public transportation, but subways had often been my saving grace for making meetings. Midday traffic in Manhattan is nothing short of brutal. Because of this fact, coupled with my schedule, cabs or car services were often out of the question. That said, I had minimal experience with city buses.

Very few people were speaking. All I could hear was the

whirring of the engine. The huge vehicle bobbed slightly up and down like a boat moving along the water. The floor was dirty. The blue plastic seat under my ass felt hard, unforgiving. Again, just as I was about to start dialing, I stopped. The faces all around, paying no attention to me, had me captured. Behind each one, I thought, there was a different story from the next. I wondered if any of those stories were as fucked up as the one behind my own.

In the rear was a pretty, young mother with her little boy. As I looked at them I remembered the day a couple of weeks earlier in Au Bon Pain with Perry. She was so enamored with the innocence of the beautiful little girl in the store that day. How had things gotten so crazy? So out of control? I wanted to reach for the little boy in the back of the bus. I wanted to tell him so many things he was too young to understand.

I looked down at my cell phone. As I thought about the calls I needed to make I started laughing. A few faces turned towards me. Who the fuck was I kidding, I thought. Like any of it even mattered anymore.

Pop's townhouse was still technically a crime scene, but by this point most of the evidence had been either gathered or examined. Still, there was a uniformed officer in a squad car out front keeping an eye on the place. Because I was on foot, and since I had already used the 911 scheme, my choices were minimal. I was already walking down the street, which meant he may have already seen me. Time was ticking. I couldn't rewind. I couldn't duck around back like high school and sneak in the kitchen door. Confidently, as if I had nothing to hide, I walked up to the black-and-white and knocked on the window. I told him who I was and that I needed something from the house. He said he needed one second then he rolled up the car window.

He picked up his cell and made a call never once taking his eyes off me. I acted as if I didn't notice. I opened my own phone and pretended to be listening to my voice mail, and even went as far as to pretend I was speaking with someone. After a few minutes his window went back down.

"That's fine," I said to no one. "Just have Carolyn put it on my desk. I'll have a look at it when I get back to the office."

I hung up.

"Sorry about that," I continued.

"What was it you said you needed to get?"

"Just some paperwork I left here last week."

Surprised by my easy access I closed the front door behind me. All of the lights were off. The house felt so empty. Not just devoid of life but stripped of its soul as well.

Keenly aware of my mission, and the Ia originals hanging on the walls, I steeled myself and headed upstairs. Everywhere I looked I was reminded of Pop. Through the years we had had so many important conversations. With each room I passed, and each piece of furniture I looked at, I could remember a different discussion and could remember his eyes as they responded to the nature of our words. I could hear his voice, his snarl as well as his laugh. I reached the study and planted myself in the chair behind Pop's desk. I grabbed one of the brass handles and pulled it hard, sliding the file drawer all the way out. There had to be more, I thought. There had to be. Aside from his connection to Galina, Pop was somehow, between the note and the stock certificates, tied to the missing eggs that were connected to Andreu Zhamovsky and Pavel Derbyshev. There had to be more. If there wasn't, why was my father writing me what promised to be some sort of explanation in the midst of all this?

I started rifling through the files. Each time I heard a car come down the street I stopped moving, breathing, until I was satisfied it wasn't slowing down. When it passed, I jumped back in with the same fervor I had started.

No different than a computer search, I decided to go with key words. The first was "Andreu." My fingers went to work but quickly came up empty. Next was "Prevkos," and while there was a hell of a lot of information in this file, from annual reports to news clippings, there was nothing relevant in terms of my search. I scratched my head. "Eggs," "Fabergé," "Zhamovsky," "Galina" again, nothing.

Fuck.

"Derbyshev," "Pavel," "Baltimore," still nothing.

As the pit in my stomach grew at an unsettling rate, it became all too clear I wasn't getting anywhere. I started to broaden the search. "Missing," as in missing eggs. "Other," like other son. "Mystery," for mystery man in Baltimore. "House," as in House of Fabergé.

Nothing, nothing, nothing, nothing.

I slammed my fists on the desktop and looked at my watch. I was supposed to be grabbing some papers. Time was running thin.

"Screw it," I said out loud.

I started at "A" and flew through the entire alphabet as if someone had hit the fast-forward button. When I reached the end, having gained nothing, I angrily slammed the drawer back into its slot. I jumped from the seat and raced to the window. The cop was still in his squad car writing on a metal clipboard.

I desperately hit the floor in front of the safe. I swung back the book door and immediately began to twist the black, numbered dial, turning it so fast the intermittent clicks all ran together. Marbury, Thomas, and Sweetney, so quick it was like they were on a fast break. The door swung open.

Everything was exactly as I had last seen it. I opened my briefcase, which was on the ground to my right, and placed inside all the cash from the safe. I looked at the watches and Roddick ball, but didn't really pay either much attention. I went right for the rear wall and lowered it. When I did, it only took a few moments of searching to see I was still cold.

Before resealing the back compartment my eyes settled on Pop's watches. I thought about how much he loved them. How amazed he was by their tight, miniscule craftsmanship. Then I thought about how much I had learned to love watches.

And my stomach went sour.

He always told me you can tell a lot about a man from three things: his shoes, tie, and watch. I looked at my wrist. If only it was really that easy, I thought.

I stripped off my own piece and switched it with one of his, the Audemars given to him by my mother. I assumed she must have touched it at some point. I wanted her close. Especially since my father was slipping farther and farther away.

I headed back downstairs. As I passed through the main foyer, just before reaching the front door, the mid-nineteenth century Lomax of Blackburn grandfather clock in the living room sounded, signaling the turn of the hour. My feet stopped. I listened to the chimes, savored them. They had been ringing every hour since my youth though it seemed like years since I had heard them.

I moved to the parlor's doorway for one more look at the towering timepiece. When it finished singing my eyes began drifting. The couches, Persian rugs, end tables, piano, humidors, vases, flowers, coffee table.

My neck jerked.

Pop's antique cigar humidor collection.

"Don't go near the fucking piano," he'd growl. "I mean it. I find out you touched it, or any of the humidors on top, I'll break your fucking hand."

The same line came out of his mouth almost every time I entered the room. It became so commonplace that, like the clock's chimes, after a while I stopped hearing it. As I stood there looking at the mammoth instrument something occurred to me. When it did, my heart began racing.

Humidors lock.

I pulled out the key ring I'd found in the Ia file and started across the room. I had never once, from the time I was a baby until the day I left for college, expressed any sort of interest in playing the piano or any other instrument for that matter. Which meant I had never given him any reason to think I'd ever go near the Steinway. So why then, I asked myself as I crossed over one of the vintage carpets, was he so nuts about keeping me from the piano and humidors? Especially when he had never made mention of my staying away from anything else?

When I reached the piano I put my briefcase down and just stared, like I was twelve and taking the risk of a lifetime by disobeying my father. As I began to study the smooth ivory of the keys, it dawned on me while I felt I knew every inch of this house I had never really seen this up close. Having a new experience like this in the one place I considered most familiar was not only unexpected, it was eerie. From a distance the slick, black finish of the body had always seemed flawless. Up close it was dotted with nicks, marked with streaks. It had as much wear and tear as, I imagined, history.

I tapped two keys, one white, one black, and listened to each note hang in the room for a moment before dissolving. I walked around the side as my hand lightly grazed the casing. My eyes moved to the impressive antique cigar humidor collection, items that, like the piano, I had never examined up close. Spaced evenly across the dark landscape, maybe a dozen in total, the first thing I noticed was they were all very different from one another in both size and composition. A couple were simply large oak or mahogany boxes. Others had intricate inlaid patterns or hand-carved molding. One had corners adorned with pewter trim, another was accented with bronze. Another still was covered with leather.

I went to open one. It was locked. The fourth key I tried, one made of the same antique pewter as the box's trim, slid in comfortably and released the lid. I lifted it up. Aside from a musty, stale fist of air there was nothing.

Tick, tick —

I decided to go with the next humidor to my left, one of the large, basic, solid wood boxes. Key number two was the winner. This time, besides the antique air, there was far from nothing.

The silver oak humidor contained letters. Five of them. The edges of the once white envelopes became more yellow in descending order. I reached in and randomly plucked one out. It was addressed to my father in a woman's handwriting, the same handwriting that had dated the bottom right-hand corner August 20, 1985. I had seen this writing before. The numbers matched the 1974 from the drawing of young Andreu.

I crept over to the window and, still out of sight of the squad car, peered out the front window. The officer was still writing. He checked his watch, reminding me I needed to keep my ass moving. Then he looked up and answered his cell phone.

I raced back over to the piano, replaced the letter I had

removed and unlocked all the humidors. Nothing else, letters or otherwise, was in any of them. I pulled out the same letter I had originally removed. The thought of reading it naturally entered my mind. There was no time.

I heard another car coming. It was slowing down.

I darted again to the wall next to the window and peeked at the street. A huge, black SUV was stopping in front of the townhouse. Detective Morante was behind the wheel.

"Oh shit!" I exclaimed turning back toward the living room.

Easy access my ass.

Tick, tick —

React.

I raced to the piano, tucked the five letters into my briefcase, shut the humidors, and quickly returned to the window. Morante and the other officer talked as they headed for the house.

Still going full speed I bolted from the room. I pulled the door to the basement closed behind me, leaving it slightly ajar. I headed down the staircase and positioned myself under the ceiling-high window that, although mostly hidden by shrubbery on the outside, allowed me to look up at the front stoop. I could hear the two men approaching. As they stepped up to the home's entrance they were still talking. Though muted I could hear their conversation.

"You really think he has something to do with what happened?" asked the uniformed officer.

"Still not sure," said Morante. "He said he was home Friday night, but when we checked the building's cameras, he left at one point and didn't return for hours."

He knocked on the door and rang the bell. When he didn't get an answer he turned the knob, which I had left unlocked, and they entered. As quietly as I could, I moved back to the base of the staircase.

"Hello?" Morante called out. "Jonah, you here?"

The two cops, without hesitation, went straight to the stairs leading to the second floor. Since I mentioned coming by for work, I figured they were going for the study. As they neared the end of their ascent, I began my own, moving slowly and staying to the side on each step, where it didn't creak. Once at the top I stopped, pushed the door open a bit more, and listened again. Their inaudible voices were distant. Knowing it was only a matter of seconds before they picked up their pace, I made my move, escaping through the front door unnoticed. I strode to the corner and hailed a cab.

CHAPTER 43

I fell into the black, faux-leather seat of one of the new cabs with extra leg room, placed my briefcase on the seat next to me, and slammed the door. My eyes never left the street I had just come down. When I noticed we weren't moving, I looked forward to the rearview mirror. The cab driver didn't need to say a word. His expression told me he had questions.

I looked at his prominently placed, plastic-covered ID card on the glass partition.

"Let's go, Saul," I said.

Saul Cohen was a wrinkly, leathery little Jewish guy who looked like he'd been driving a cab since they were all hansoms. He was so small I couldn't help wondering if he could see over the dashboard. Aside from his eyes that I had seen in the reflective glass, all I could see from the backseat when he turned around was his weathered Mets cap.

"Where to?" he shot back, raspy.

I looked back out the window toward the townhouse. They'd be running out any second.

"Let's just get moving. I'll tell you in a minute."

"We staying uptown? Should I —"

I returned my eyes to Saul's doing my best to stay composed and keep any chance of his concerns from growing. His question, "where to?" was a more insightful inquiry than he knew. I could always tell Morante that when I slipped out of the townhouse the other officer was doing some work in his car and I didn't want to disturb him. But this, at best, was thin. Morante was quick. I was sure I had just considerably raised his suspicions about my being involved in my father's death. The fact I was hiding something completely different from what he thought wasn't the issue. The reality was that he'd probably come looking for me, which meant my apartment and office.

I had one criteria in order to read the letters, privacy, but no idea where to go. I decided to buy some time to get the taxi moving.

"Let's go through the Park."

No sooner than I could get the words out, Saul hit the gas. Before I could even exhale my cell phone let out a chime indicating I had a text message. I pulled the message up, figuring it was Morante. It wasn't.

The message read, "Decided to get a new phone. Same one as you. Didn't someone once say a picture is worth a thousand words?" There was a photograph attachment to the text message. Krissy had gone out and gotten herself the same camera phone I had. I was afraid to look.

As I readied myself for what I was about to see, the cab made a sharp right turn onto Sixty-sixth Street going west. Saul was trying to make the light. I grabbed for the seat to brace myself, my left hand bearing the brunt of my weight. Once both feet were on the floor again, I returned my eyes to the phone.

With the press of a button a bright, surprisingly high-resolution image filled the screen. The picture was clear. In disbelief I lifted it right to my eyes. It was a forearm. The shot was taken from up above as if snapped with the photographer's free hand. Freshly carved into it were the initials J.G., then a plus sign with the initials K.L. underneath. This was surrounded by a crude, bloody heart. I now assumed her last name started with an L. Krissy had sliced our initials into her arm like it was a tree trunk on the outskirts of some schoolyard. The initial blood that must have come from the wound had been cleared away, leaving just a few faint surrounding streaks.

I had dealt with crazy women in the past, but this was different.

This wasn't about me being some catch or some young, well-bred kid who could make people laugh at a party. This was someone's dangerous obsession. Krissy was out of control. It terrified me.

What Krissy L. didn't know was that I already had plans for her.

Within seconds of viewing the digital image, the cell rang, this time emitting a jingle associated with an incoming voice call. The caller ID, as usual, showed a blocked incoming number. I took a deep breath.

"Jonah Gray."

"You fuck! You lying fuck!"

"It isn't what you think —"

"You don't mean one fucking thing you say, do you?"

I actually found myself thinking about it.

"You just say what you need for me to buy your bullshit, and then —"

It was scary. She was genuinely angry with me. The strain in her voice, the pain, was unnerving.

"It's not like that," I cut her off.

Barreling through Central Park, old, cobblestone walls giving intermittent glimpses of the green pastures behind them, I could feel Saul's presence a little more than I wanted to. I looked at the rearview mirror. He pulled his curious eyes, and I assume ears, away in a hurry. I slid the Plexiglas divider door shut.

"Like what? What the hell does that mean? It's not like what?"

"I got caught up in —"

"Bullshit, Jonah. Complete bullshit. It's been like four days since we've spoken."

It was as if she had completely blocked out our last encounter.

"And I refuse to have you keep blowing me off so you can hide from the truth. Our truth."

"There was an accident," I responded, desperate.

A personal tragedy, I hoped, would bring her back to the trusting place I needed her.

"My father had an accident."

She fell silent. All I could hear on the other end were her deep, quickened breaths.

"Is he all right?" she pushed out.

"No," I said. "He's not."

"What happened?"

"It's a long story."

I paused for a second, horrified at the words about to pass through my lips.

"One I'd rather tell you in person."

I had come to understand how her mind worked. All she wanted was to see me. Give her that, I figured, and I could take anything from her I needed.

"I want to listen, Jonah. I want to be there for you."

"I know you do. So why don't we get together tonight. I'll meet you at One Little West Twelfth in the Meatpacking District at nine. I can bring you up to speed."

Just as my call ended we stopped at a light on Central Park West that meant the end of our crossing. Saul, aware I couldn't hear him, threw his blue sweatshirt-covered arms in the air. Looking outside I realized the best place to get lost in New York City was all around me. I reached forward and slid the partition open.

"Make a right, Saul. Drop me off at Eighty-first Street.

I entered the park, warm from the clear sky and strong sun working in concert, and briskly headed north toward one of my most trusted spots. I held my briefcase's handle in my right hand. It was Monday afternoon so the park was pretty empty. There were scattered runners and people talking and eating on patches of grass and the benches lining the pedestrian paths, but it was nothing more than a skeleton version of the weekends. Within two hundred yards of my entry, I came across one of the area's many playgrounds. Coming from it was more life it seemed than anywhere else in the park. Children were laughing, playing on swings, and sliding down slides. I thought of Perry. I thought of Max.

I cut across a gentle, rolling field, and couldn't resist the thought of a running Neo as I watched a guy play Frisbee with his two enthusiastic golden retrievers. I kept walking. At the equivalent of Eighty-third Street I came upon Summit Rock, the highest natural elevation in the whole park, both saddened and disheartened to see a couple of drug addicts passed out on benches. Their numb, glistening faces were red from crisping in the sun. Their clothes were soiled, ragged. One of them, a woman, had sores lining her legs and a black, charred crack pipe in her hand.

Seeing a pay phone, I looked at my wrist for the time. Afraid of talking on my cell, and realizing I had a schedule to stick to, I placed the briefcase down next to me, picked up the receiver, and wedged it between my shoulder and ear. I grabbed some change from my pocket, threw it in, and dialed as I surveyed the area.

"Luckman."

"It's me."

"Hold on."

I could hear L dismiss someone from his office. Then I heard the door close.

"You okay?"

"I think so. I wanted to see how you were doing on my request."

"I'm making it happen, Jonah. You just need to be patient. It hasn't even been twenty-four hours."

"You said it would happen quickly, L. You said I'd have them as fast as I needed them."

"I know, man, and you will. Remember, I'm putting a lot on the line here. I own the company across the street from this guy's boss. He's just some fucking illegal dock worker. I need to be really fucking careful. And you need to be patient."

"I don't have the time to be patient, L."

"I waved fifteen grand under his nose, Jonah. Believe me, he gets it that I'm looking to move fast. It won't be long."

"When? Give me a ballpark."

"Tomorrow morning. First thing."

I headed up the public walkway, a serpentine path of steps carved into the bedrock of the south slope, toward the apex of Summit Rock that sat about a hundred and forty feet in the air. As I climbed, my expensive dress shoes turning on me for treating them like sneakers, beads of sweat began showing on my arms and brow. My shirt began clinging to me. I took off my jacket and slung it over my shoulder. My tongue swiped the salty skin above my lip. Each upward step was accompanied by an image as my hard sole clashed with the harder rock. One was Pavel Derbyshev in the restroom in Baltimore. Another was my father on a gurney. Another was the view of Tommy's office from his doorway with all of us in it. One step brought a black-and-white photograph of my mother. Then there was Pangaea-Man putting a gun to my head, followed by Robie/Hart and Krissy and Archmont. Panic took over. I was near running, taking two, three steps at a time.

Just feet from the top I heard my cell ringing in my briefcase. I stopped and took it out. It was Lloyd Murdoch's office.

"Jonah Gray."

"How's everything going, Jonah?"

"What do you want?"

"It's a shame what happened to your father. I wanted to pass along my condolences."

"How thoughtful of you."

"He was a true businessman. Unlike some people he associated with."

"You may have fooled the cops, Lloyd, but not me."

"Jonah, please. Can't a man just —"

"There's only one man involved in this conversation. It's not you. You're the scumbag who should have watched where his ash fell."

Silence.

"That's right, you fuck. I'm on to you."

"I know this must be a difficult time."

I was seething. There were so many things I wanted to say. Instead I hung up.

I reached the top of Summit Rock and the beautiful amphitheater that sat on top. I was alone. Often I had longed for just a glimpse of the original view, a panoramic shot of not just New York City, but across the Hudson River to the New Jersey Palisades, but now I was thankful for the towering trees giving me privacy and shade. I walked across the grass that in a 1997 renovation replaced the cracked, broken pavement from the 1950s, and found a bench overlooking the wooded eastern slope.

I put my jacket down and sat next to it, placing the briefcase on the ground in front of me between my legs. I opened it and removed the letters. One by one I went through them. All were signed by Galina, confirming my suspicions and making me sick for my mother. Each letter accompanied one of the four Ia originals lining the townhouse staircase, and was an innocuous note offering birthday wishes, brief updates on life, and thank yous for little gifts from Pop like Writers Edition Mont Blanc pens. There was also an explanation of each artwork's centerpiece animal consisting of its background, location, things like that. The subjects, as the descriptions explained, were re-created exactly as seen in the Russian far eastern territory of Primorsky Krai, the location of Russia's most pristine forest. There wasn't much more, aside from all five concluding the same: "Look Close. Enjoy the gifts (so much in a name). Yours, Galina."

"Look close." The same words, or instructions, on the back of Andreu's baby picture. But what could "so much in a name" mean? Especially when each drawing's title was essentially the depicted animal?

The letters came a few years apart. Each date on the front of an envelope matched the year on one of the pictures lining the staircase. There was one inconsistency.

Four Ia original drawings.

Five letters.

CHAPTER 44

After stopping home for a shower, I walked past the entrance of the neighboring Hotel Ganesvoort and into ONE. Two beautiful hostesses greeted me. I told them my name and the taller of the two blonds then escorted me to my requested table, the only table on the premises that had no surveillance on it whatsoever. A friend of mine, Miles Rockwell, had designed the space. One night, while we were both plastered, he spilled it that this had been done at the request of one of the owners. The specific table was secluded in the rearmost corner of the champagne lounge, where my guest was already waiting.

As I was led through the seductive space, past the chic and wannabe chic, eyes moved toward me in the way I once enjoyed. Cocktails of all shades and sizes adorned the tables along with plates of ideal food for sharing, like Lobster and Goat Cheese Quesadillas and Chicken and Scallion Dumplings. I had my briefcase with me for no other reason than to hold my pistol. I knew there would most likely be an immediate hug from Krissy so I decided to keep my suit jacket's pockets free of anything but the essentials.

As I approached the table, Krissy stood up. The first thing I noticed was the gauze wrapped around her left forearm. To any male she wasn't psychotically stalking she looked incredibly hot.

Tight, black satin pants, a sexy black tank top, nicely spiked black, strappy Manolos, and smoky makeup. I was starting to have trouble seeing her as anything more than a pile of shit with eyes. As she greeted me, every guy from the surrounding tables, no matter who they were with, glanced in her direction.

"Enjoy your evening," the hostess said before turning away.

Krissy, an overdramatic look of sadness across her face, wrapped her arms around me.

"I wore black out of respect for your father," she whispered into my ear.

We broke apart. Unable to find the right words for such non-sense, I simply nodded. Then, startling me, a hand grabbed my right arm, the one holding my briefcase. Eyes squinted, intensely sharpened, my head swung around as if I was a lion ready to size up whatever offering had presented itself. I was ready to kill, run, maim, lie, do whatever I had to do. My instincts were in overdrive.

"I'm sorry," the hostess who hadn't yet left went on, eyes dilated. "I was just wondering if you wanted to leave your briefcase with the coat check."

I looked down at her hand, the one on my arm, then right back into her eyes.

"I'm fine," I said. "I think I'll keep it with me."

"Are you sure you want to be here?" Krissy asked as the hostess left us. "Would you rather we go somewhere more private?"

I knew ONE was a risky choice the night before my father's funeral, but my plan for Krissy required this specific table in this particular restaurant. Anyway, it was a nonholiday Monday night in the summer. Can you tell me of a night with a potentially lighter restaurant crowd during a calendar year in New York City? I didn't think so.

Krissy and I sat down. Our rear, corner table enabled me to have a clear view of the entire dining space, something that in the recent weeks had become protocol. As soon as we hit the cushions of our banquette, a waitress appeared and we ordered drinks. Then we were alone. Before I could turn in Krissy's direction, she had already taken my hand on top of the table.

"I need to start by apologizing, Jonah. I just hate myself for acting like such a pest."

I gently took my hand from her grasp and moved it lightly over
her skin, up her forearm toward the gauze.

"What does the L stand for?"

She paused. Then, accepting my faux trusting vibe, she smiled.

"Lockhart. Krissy Lockhart."

Relieved, as if a burden had been lifted, she let out a sigh.

"Can you ever forgive me for acting like such an ass?"

Demonstrate control. Get what you need.

"You don't need to apologize, Krissy."

"I do, Jonah. If I hadn't been so quick to feel discarded, I could
have been helping you through this all along. It makes me sick to
feel I'm responsible for this being so much harder for you."

"Go easy on yourself. I imagine if the situation had been
reversed, and I hadn't heard back from you considering how —
close we had become, I might have gone a bit overboard as well."

"That's sweet of you to say. But I'm going to do whatever I need
to in order to make it up to you, and you can't stop me! Don't you
see —"

Just like that, her starry-eyed gaze laced itself with a potent, yet
subtle, dose of fury.

"— that's why it has to be like this. That's why we always need
to be together."

The look in her eye was astonishing. She was speaking so
matter-of-factly, from the farthest corners of her disturbed core.
She really believed everything she was saying.

React.

"Actually, Krissy, I couldn't agree with you more."

I needed to play the game, so play the game I did. With each
phone call, with each psychotic instance, it was becoming more
and more clear that Krissy didn't seem to be part of the other million dramas that swirled around me. She was number one million
and one, and perhaps something more combustible than all the
others put together. Yet as far as I was concerned, she was, albeit
indirectly, a big part of everything that had happened. If it weren't

for her, chances are that time would have run out on Robie/Hart. He wouldn't have had the opportunity to plant *Danish Jubilee Egg* on me. I would have been free and clear, and Andreu Zhamovsky's scheme might have been thwarted. Because of her, my guard had been down. I took to her, got completely loaded then took to her even more. As a result, Robie/Hart saw his opening. Had she turned out to be the real thing, I probably would have been forgiving about her timing and felt different about including her in my plan. My revenge. Unfortunately for her, she turned out to be little more than an infection I couldn't shake or go to the cops with. So, as clouded as such judgment seems now, I was ready to cure myself of her. Like I said earlier, all she now truly needed, for reasons I imagine neither she nor I could accurately articulate, was to see me, be with me. My sole purpose, with regard to Krissy L., had become to feed off that.

For the next thirty minutes, over a second round and a couple of appetizers, I spoke a little about my ordeal while Krissy spoke a lot about our destiny as a couple. Then, the proper opening arose.

"Oh, by the way," I said.

I reached into my left, inside jacket pocket.

"I found this in one of my suits. I figured it was probably yours."

I placed in front of her a Spanish Fly MAC lipstick. I had finally found a use for all of the ridiculous cosmetic information I had picked up as a result of dating beautiful cosmopolitan women.

She picked it up.

"I do wear MAC."

She gave it a once over. She looked at the end of it for the color.

"Just not this color. But it's pretty. Spanish Fly," she went on. "I need to remember that. Nope."

She placed it back on the table in front of me, wearing an enigmatic grin.

"Must belong to one of your past flames."

I didn't touch the lipstick, I just stared at it for a second before responding.

"I'm surprised," I said, moving my eyes back in her direction. "I really figured it was yours."

"Oh yeah? And why's that?"

"Because you're who comes to mind when I think of sexy. The name Spanish Fly just oozes sexiness to me. I just figured it was yours."

I looked deeply into her eyes.

"You know —"

I looked away.

"No, forget it."

"What?"

"Forget it. Really. You'll just think I'm nuts."

"What, Jonah?"

Under the table, she placed her hand on my thigh.

"I want to be here. What?"

Again I stared into her eyes. I spoke in a half-whisper.

"I've been dying to be close to you, to your body. So much has happened in these past few days that my emotions have just been all over the place. There's been so much inner tension. I have all of these pent up feelings."

I felt her grip tighten.

"I just feel like I'm about to explode. And I would do anything to release this energy."

She slid her hand farther up my thigh and moved her lips to my ear so she could whisper.

"A chance to ease your pain and fuck you at the same time? You have no idea what you're doing to me."

She backed away.

"Why don't you ask for the check?" she said with a gentle lick of her lips.

"I don't think I can wait that long."

I reached into my pocket and pulled out a stack of cash.

"Tell you what —" I started.

I handed her two hundred dollar bills under the table.

"Why don't you go downstairs to the men's room and give this to the attendant. Then tell him to get lost for about fifteen minutes."

A smile crept across her face.

"I'll follow you by about sixty seconds."

Krissy took the cash from me under the table, grabbed her purse, then stood up. As she walked away she blew me a kiss. Once she was out of sight, I quickly pulled a small, plastic bag from one of my pants' pockets. Then, using the cocktail napkin I took from under my drink, I carefully placed the lipstick into the plastic bag and placed it back in my jacket pocket.

The plan was to leave once she was out of sight. Only once I got up, and started for the door, something occurred to me. To leave, to just walk out, would crush her. Once that happened, on top of how much I had already tried to blow her off, it was quite possible she would take "relentless" to a whole new level. I needed to satiate her. I needed us to part ways with her thinking we were cool, at least for now. It could buy me some time. I looked again toward the front of the restaurant. Then I looked at my watch.

I walked into the bathroom, briefcase in hand and my suit jacket slung over my arm. The lights were dim. The attendant was nowhere to be seen. Krissy, in just her black heels and forearm gauze, sauntered out of one of the stalls. I locked the door. For a few moments the two of us just stood there, drinking the other in.

We met like animals in the center of the room. Just before she reached me, I dropped my case and jacket on the floor. She jumped up and wrapped her legs around me as I carried her over to the sinks. She had no idea fifteen minutes later I'd be leaving her behind, fucked in more ways than one.

I had the cab drop me at a pay phone a few blocks from my building. I dialed L's apartment.

"Hello?"

"Do you have them yet?"

"I'm meeting him in front of the plant in an hour."

"Beautiful," I said. "Fucking beautiful."

"Jonah, when are we going to discuss all of this?"

"Your office, tomorrow morning. Ten "

L didn't respond.

"Did you hear me?"

"Jonah, we have your father's funeral at —"

"No we don't, L. I can't go."

"What do you mean you can't go?"

"It's complicated. Just trust me."

"Jesus Christ, Jonah. Don't do this."

I slammed the pay phone with my fist.

"Please, L. Just be at your office at 10 A.M. I promise to explain all of this."

His voice was a combination of concern and aggravation.

"Anything else?"

"Yeah. I need you to research a girl named Krissy Lockhart. She's around our age, and I think she's from the Hamptons. Start by Googling her, and go from there."

I entered my apartment, having just been told by doorman Parker a detective had come by looking for me, and locked the door. Neo came charging and we went through our greeting ritual. I fed him. My mind and body were exhausted.

I looked at my wrist: 10:58 P.M. I had a few hours until I'd be moving. I kept the lights off and fell back onto the couch, my gun and cell phone on the glass table in front of me. Neo, one of his favorite toys in tow, jumped up next to me. I grabbed hold of his toy with one hand for a game of tug-of-war, and I picked up the remote with the other. I switched on the plasma.

There I was. The news. Not just one story but what seemed to be the entire fucking broadcast, from one story to the next. First was the lead story, the fact that authorities were still stumped over the disappearance of *Danish Jubilee Egg*. The prime suspect, the former chief of security Lawrence Hart, was nowhere to be found, and neither was the prize. From here they went into an update on the real estate magnate murdered in front of his home, "old-world mobster-style" as they put it. Authorities were following a number of leads, the anchor said, but were yet to make any arrests. As they showed some video footage of the crime scene — Pop's townhouse — I straightened my posture. It was footage from Saturday when the property was still buzzing.

The next story, the "breaking news" piece, was the one that stopped me cold. It was footage of heavy activity along the banks of a body of water. In the top left-hand corner were the words RECORDED EARLIER.

"Earlier this evening," the anchor led in, "what was believed to be the body of Randall Davis was found in the East River, where authorities have been searching for over a week. Davis, a two-time-Emmy-nominated veteran actor who disappeared eight days ago in what is said to be a drug-related crime, is believed to have been dumped in this particular body of water —"

The camera then zoomed in to the nucleus of what was happening. A body was being retrieved from the water. Only it wasn't exactly a body. It was a duffel bag.

"You can imagine the recovery team's shock when they learned the discovered body was someone else —"

I rose to my feet. My hands went directly to my head. Fuck, I thought to myself. H-o-l-y-f-u-c-k. I had seen something about the actor in the news, but because of everything going on hadn't paid any attention.

"It appears the Caucasian male, believed to be one of NYPD's own, was the victim of a homicide. The city will not confirm nor deny his name until all relevant identity tests can be properly performed and completed. Little else in terms of information has been made available. As a call for further information linked to the crime, the police have released this sketch of the victim."

Mattheau apparently hadn't followed the actor story either. Two rivers, he drops the body in the wrong one. I turned to CNN. A drawing of Pangaea-Man filled the entire screen. Because we now live in the worldwide information age, and a murdered NYPD cop is a huge story, he had gone global in the blink of an eye. Just like that, larger than life, Pangaea-Man had sprung back into my world.

CHAPTER 45

Three a.m.

Jeans, Nike 'Shox', black T-shirt. I slid sideways between two fences separating the rear courtyards of homes backed up to the townhouse. A spiny wood plank faced me. A rusted wall of wire threatened from behind, its oxidized steel teeth finding my scalp twice. The city hummed quietly. I deftly sidestepped over the twigs and dry dirt beneath my feet, careful not to make noise. Up ahead, two feet beyond the vertical crawl space, but crossing it like the top of a "T," I could see the high, white cedar fence enclosing my father's property.

My feet landed flush on the patio's basketweave-pattern bricks. I looked up at my childhood home. It was pitch black. I looked at the backs of the houses to the left and right. Each showed strategic specks of nighttime illumination. A warm breeze rolled across the back of my neck. Ten-foot shrubs surrounding me, barely rustling, I was safe from eyes on any side but still vulnerable to those above.

I moved through the solid, wrought-iron-framed Kettler chairs and teak-topped table, past the white-cushioned Ralph Lauren loveseat, up close to the building. I tried the door leading into the kitchen. It was locked, as I figured it would be. Using my leather-gloved hands I slid open the 10" × 10" window situated only a couple feet to the door's left. On the inside it had a copper latch that had been broken my whole life. It had never been fixed for the same reason it was the only window in the house not connected to the alarm. It was too small, according to some genius, for anyone to get through. The same genius who didn't realize someone with long arms could reach in and flip the door's lock.

I closed the door behind me until it clicked, silencing the sounds of the night. Just inside I looked at the numeric keypad on the wall, expecting it to beep, only to remember the security system had been temporarily shut down once the police got involved. Crumbs of light helped outline the room as I acclimated. The omnipresent, syrupy smell filled my nose. In the center of the kitchen table, across the room, was a vase full of wilting lilies.

I walked toward the front of the townhouse. Before turning up the stairs I kept straight and stopped next to one of the windows. I peeked out. A black-and-white, front windows half-cracked, was in the usual spot. An officer was hard at work inside. I felt for the gun in my waist. I checked my left pocket for my cell phone then my right for my flashlight. Low, I headed upstairs.

I stepped in front of the first drawing. Just as I had mentally rehearsed, I lifted it off the wall and headed back in the direction I came from. The plan was simple. Get all four drawings into the kitchen for a side-by-side examination. The table was smaller than the one in the dining room but outside the officer's vision. One by one I brought them downstairs, grabbing the magnifying glass from the study before returning with the fourth.

I bent forward. I positioned the glass and switched on the flashlight. Each drawing was different from the next in size and frame. I started at the left. It was a tiger. He was captured in time lying in a field. There were mountains far in the distance. It was incredibly three-dimensional, not just the animal, but the entire scene. I could feel the clouds' movement.

I traced the tiger. Nothing, just as I figured.

Look closer.

I moved to the periphery. I started at the bottom, in the field. Careful to be thorough, I went slow. It was obvious to me quickly the ground wouldn't offer much. Too light, I thought. Nowhere to hide the letters.

I moved to the mountains, more particularly their edges, which were ripe for letters a touch bolder than their background or vice versa. The portion of the picture that filled the concave observation deck seemed to be protruding from the paper. I followed the peaks and valleys. It wasn't long until I found something. I moved in even closer. It was along the earth's crust going up toward the next peak. It looked like the word "We."

I moved the magnifying glass and kept the light on the paper. No letters or words whatsoever were noticeable to my naked eye. I returned the glass and let it take the lead. Along the fringe of the distant range, the same fluid writing a la the sterling silver rattle's "ours" spun into the shading, a message unfolded. "Miles apart. Answer lies in Omega. A could only be you."

I checked the rest of the painting. Nothing else. Three quick sentences. That was it.

I was confused as hell. I was blown away.

Why would someone go to such trouble?

I stood up. Shadows of the shimmying shrubs danced on the wall in front of me. An expanding floorboard or wall whined across the room interrupting the silence. I looked down and shined the light on the bottom right-hand corner. 1974.

"Answer lies in Omega," I repeated.

Omega. I racked my brain for any and everything I knew about or associated with the word. There was the obvious, the twenty-fourth and last letter of the Greek alphabet. There was the not so obvious, like the term or actual Greek letter being used to symbolize the phrase "the end" or the use of the word "omega" in the financial world as it relates to option pricing.

"The end," I whispered to myself. "The end of what?"

It didn't make sense. I stepped back from the table. I looked out the window. In the darkness I saw the light. In the light I saw the source of my trembling.

Omega.

As in Omega Seamaster, circa 1960.

Pop's untouchable watch.

Crouched, I entered the master bedroom, which was upstairs

but at the front of the house. I stopped at the foot of the bed. The morning Pop was shot he was going to play golf. This meant no Omega. My father, a six handicap, never wore a watch when he played; he said the uneven weight distribution threw him off. I looked at the rosewood nightstands. He never kept the watch in the safe. But it had to be close by.

I began with the nightstand to my left. I sat on the edge of the bed and scanned the top. Alarm clock, leather business card case, ceramic dish filled with change and collar stays, a letter opener, a pair of reading glasses, a pair of scissors, and a remote. I pulled out the one drawer. There were financial magazines, *Fortune* and *Forbes*. There were Clancy novels. Between the two small piles was a single, black calfskin watch box. I lifted it out and opened it. Inside was the Seamaster.

A couple of the room's windows faced the street so I stepped into the bathroom. I closed the door and turned on the flashlight. The watch, once removed from the box, was lighter than I expected. It was thin stainless steel from the bezel all the way down to the clasped bracelet. The hands looked like long, slim daggers. Ten of the hours were marked with a single stainless bar instead of a number. Hour twelve had two bars. Hour three was a window for the date.

I turned it over and looked at the back of the face. Just as I expected there was an engraving.

"Oceans apart. One soul together."

I leaned back against the wall. Under closed lids my eyes rolled back into my head. My theory about the watch had been right. What I was wrong about was the woman who gave it to him. I pinched the bridge of my nose, mashed my eyes, and sequestered some air. I held my breath for three seconds then exhaled loudly.

I recalled the message in the tiger drawing. "Miles apart." But the next line was "Answer lies in Omega," which, ultimately, just reiterated their connection. It didn't add up. Unless —

I took my hand from my face and opened my eyes. "Miles apart" was not about my father. It was about Alexander, her husband. The third line of the message told me so.

"A could only be you."

A. As in Andreu.

The year of this particular drawing was 1974. The year both Andreu and I were born.

She was validating the pregnancy. Which meant at some point, to her face or not I can't be sure, my father must have questioned it. Maybe even after receiving the initial drawing of newborn Andreu. I thought, why couldn't she just answer him? Better question, why could she only answer him like this?

I craved more time to process, but the circumstances wouldn't allow it. I still had work to do. Theories spinning; some compelling, some absurd, I replaced the watch, returned to the kitchen, and moved to the next drawing. 1977. It was a shot of a sprinting puma, all four legs off the ground mid-stride. The streamlined animal was consumed with purpose. Each blood-filled vein in his neck told me so.

The ground, like the previous picture, was light. A few birds scattered from the onslaught. My attention swung to the top of the paper. Some overhead trees edged the image on both sides.

The dense leaf clusters were the perfect camouflage for the rolled up message I found. "Union of necessity is my shame. Must stay true to my own. Darkness for A and J. Or ruin."

A and J. Andreu and Jonah.

The unfolding reality was a crushing one. My brain wanted to scramble, but I couldn't let it. Not yet. I moved to number three. 1998. It was a lion, facing forward, with a mane and expression daring you to taunt him. He stood on muddy ground. A few antelope scattered in the foreground. A marbled sky threatened from above.

I started straight away at the top. There it was, fused brilliantly within the heavy clouds. "Brutus 3. 2,1. Common goals no longer common. No matter — 4 of 6 confirmed your way."

My shoulders dropped. My right knee nearly buckled.

Brutus.

The conspiring villain from *Julius Caesar*.

What a soulless bastard. Same as the Omega. My whole life, no matter which of the two I asked about, my father made me think the connection was to my mother without ever saying her name. Subconsciously he must have thought this tactic made him a better man. Or, consciously, just less of a bad one.

My left hand balled in a fist, a tear welling in each eye, again I left the kitchen. Brutus 3. 2,1. The 2,1, in Shakespearean lingo, definitely meant act two, scene one. The 3 after Brutus, I deduced, meant Brutus's third time speaking in that particular scene. While I knew the play inside and out, I couldn't recall the exact passage. I had to refresh my memory.

As I turned into the living room, croucing, I could see the officer was still working. I went straight for Pop's Shakespeare collection and plucked *Julius Caesar*, written in 1599, from the middle of the row. Kneeling on one knee, I parked myself under one of the room's side, or east, windows. I opened the book. The parting of the browned pages emitted an aged scent. There was just enough nighttime light to read the text.

I traced down the page with the tip of my index finger. Brutus, Lucius, Brutus, Lucius, Brutus. "It must be by his death," the paragraph began. I read all twenty-five lines. It was Brutus explaining his desire to kill Julius Caesar. He felt the young militant's views were about to shift, the result of his ascension to greater power. He felt their common goals, once in sync, were about to change.

Four of six. The common goal that was no longer common.

Nineteen ninety-eight. The year Alexander Zhamovsky was murdered.

My hands started shaking. Deep down I knew why. As I hurried to replace the book in its central slot, I inadvertently set off what looked like two sets of dominos. Half the books fell left, the other half right. More than a few, along with the bronze bookends, went tumbling to the floor. The porcelain lamp went also, crashing in a heap.

Before I did anything, still ducking, I took a few steps toward the street. The cop was still in his car. Only he had stopped writing. He was looking at the house.

"Oh, fuck!"

As I placed the books, in no particular order, back on the chest and fastened the upright row with the bookends, a car door shut. I dashed to the room's exit, catching another look outside. The officer was walking toward the front door. I looked back at the pile of lamp.

No time.

Now in the foyer, adrenaline skyrocketing, I had two choices. I could turn right down the hall toward the kitchen with a good chance of being spotted. Or, even less desirable, I could jump behind the front door and wing it.

As close to the hinge as possible, I hugged the wall with my back like an escaping convict trying to avoid the tower spotlight. Careful not to let any air pass through my nose, I slightly parted my lips as I breathed. The satin-nickel, single-cylinder handle clicked. The door opened. Fusion of streetlights and the moon softly kindled the antechamber. Not two feet from me the officer stepped inside. A five-inch thick piece of mahogany was all that separated us.

The officer, soles snapping against the floor, turned right and walked toward the living room. He took five or six steps before stopping in the entryway. The more I calmed myself, the tighter my muscles wound. Neither of us offered a sound.

After a few more seconds, he flipped the switch to his left. A couple of the living room lights turned on. Faster than he'd previously walked, he headed, I figured, to the fallen lamp. Now was my chance.

Or was it?

I was confident I could slink around the door and disappear. On the other hand, what would happen if he checked the rest of the house? If he stumbled across the drawings laid out in the kitchen?

Fuck!

I couldn't leave. Unless, I thought, he was immediately pulled from the house once I did. Save myself now, clean up the mess later. I could put a rock through someone's window. Or set off a car alarm. I could dissolve into my old neighborhood. Then rehang the drawings later.

Fuck!

Bailing was the right decision. I knew this. Still, I couldn't move. Reminding myself freedom was my most vital ally, I ramped up my determination and got ready to go. Just as I did there were footsteps again. I returned to the wall.

I'd missed my chance.

He was coming back. Without stopping, midstride, he flipped the lights back off. Each step was louder than the previous as he approached. Quickly he reached the front door. Instead of leaving, he stopped.

Did he hear me? Could he see my shadow somewhere? A hint of my sneakers?

I was ready for him to peer around the door. I was ready because I had to be. The plan now was simple. Take him out with the door if even one hair on his head entered eyeshot. Then, using my knowledge of the layout, lose him by jetting out the exact way I came in. Head stationary, eyes anything but, I evaluated the door for what I could best determine as the sweet spot. I braced and prepared for impact.

The officer exited, closing the door behind him. I leaned my head back against the wall. I jump-started my breathing which in the previous seconds had stopped.

Knowing I was short on time, I scrambled back to the kitchen. I wanted to throw the drawings back on the wall and leave but couldn't. Not yet. One fact was as real as my near hypersonic heart rate. There would be no more returns to the townhouse.

I dove into the last drawing, the zebra. 1980. The writing was deep in the background where the brush met the sky. "DJE + ENE = 2. Return to Homeland? My proper thank you in Sardinia."

DJE. *Danish Jubilee Egg.*

ENE. *Empire Nephrite Egg*, found also in 1979.

I looked again at the date. 1980. The year *Danish Jubilee Egg*, currently in my possession, was anonymously purchased at auction by an American.

Purchased by my father.

Nothing registered from the phrase "Return to Homeland?" but Galina referring to her "union of necessity" now made sense. As did the phrase "4 of 6 confirmed your way."

Four of the six remaining missing eggs.

"Confirmed your way"; confirmed — in 1980 when the zebra was drawn — in the United States.

This explained why Pop had kept *Danish Jubilee Egg* on American Soil — most of the collection was already here and it didn't make sense to unnecessarily move individual pieces until the assemblage was complete. What could possibly serve as a better deterrent to potential pirates than a loan to the U.S. government so they'd watch it 24/7?

In a breath, again, my world changed. The implications were horrifying: from Galina and possibly my father involved in Alexander Zhamovsky's murder to Galina being the mutual acquaintance who led Andreu to Derbyshev. Arms at my side, a ray of light pointed at the floor, the moment filled me. I was tortured by all of the lies and utter betrayal by so many people on so many fronts. I remembered our family trips. Was my father so lonely, I thought, he'd fall for a woman like this? Was it the excitement? Why did Galina want these eggs so desperately, so recklessly, so heartlessly? What did she mean when she referred to "her own"?

All night, prior to reaching the townhouse, I kept coming back to the same thing. Five letters, four drawings. When Pop mentioned Ia signed her work with a date he mentioned something else. She didn't just draw.

A fifth letter. 2003. An Asiatic Black Bear on its hind legs, belly and fangs exposed. I turned off the flashlight. In the same order I took the drawings down, I returned them to the wall. I checked the window. The officer, still writing with one hand, sipped coffee with the other.

There had to be a fifth piece. I wasn't leaving until I found it. For time's sake I started with the closest rooms and stealthily, the officer back writing in his squad car, checked the dining room then the parlor. I checked the entire ground floor. I found nothing I hadn't seen.

Blending with the night I made my way upstairs. Something of interest appeared in the study. On one of the bookshelves was a small, ivory sculpture that in the dark could have been a bear as easily as a dog. The study faced the street so the flashlight was turned off. I moved in close. I didn't see any marks, dates or otherwise. I turned the animal over with my left hand. There was a year, 1989, followed by the signature of the famous Chinese sculptress Xie Jiang Ling.

A bathroom off the hallway produced a print that seemed to be new, but on first sight it was an abstract limited edition Barnett Newman. The guest bedrooms, my bedroom, and Pop's bedroom all proved fruitless. Pop's bathroom. Nothing. When I got to Pop's walk-in closet something grabbed my eye. I pulled the door closed behind me. I turned on the flashlight.

Hung high on a narrow stretch of wall between two suit racks was a small oil painting. It was a Black Bear on its hind legs, belly exposed and fangs poised. I approached for a closer look. I checked the bottom right-hand corner. 2003. It was at least six inches above my eye level, too high for a detailed scan. I removed it from the wall. I turned to place it on a dresser. When I did, I heard and felt something move. Something light. Something inside the painting. I turned it over. I gently shook the picture. Again, something inside shifted. In the brown papery backing, hugging the frame, was a five-inch slit. I angled the painting and slid the mystery item toward the opening. I gingerly inserted my pointer and index fingers. I pulled out a Russian stock certificate. It was exactly like the seven I found in the safe.

There was no English translation. Russian or not, I knew I was looking at shares for Prevkos subsidiary Alex Com II Exploration. It didn't take long for Galina's letters to reenter my mind. More precisely, how each ended.

"Enjoy the gifts (so much in a name)."

Gifts. A word, at first, I figured referred only to both the drawings and hidden messages.

"So much in a name." As in the names of Prevkos's subsidiaries, further illustrating her manipulation of Alexander, and not the titles of her artwork.

I turned the painting over. Like the drawings, the piece was done with uncanny precision and use of shading. The fine strokes meshed together as one everlasting image. Unlike the other pieces there were colors. The sky was a rich blue. The few soaring vultures were dark brown and black. The bear was predictably the focal point of the scene. He was face-forward, as described, standing on his hind legs in a grassy clearing. The surrounding green foliage faded evenly into the background, as did a distant military jeep that looked stolen from the show *Mash*.

I honed in on the jeep. It was heading in the opposite direction. I moved the magnifying glass closer still. On the side of the vehicle were two flags. One, dissected horizontally by a thick, diagonal white stripe, was red on the top and blue on the bottom. In the top left-hand corner was a small tiger. The other I had seen often growing up. It had a gold hammer and sickle, along with a five-point star, in a sea of red. It was the flag of the former USSR.

Like a brick to the head, the secrecy finally meant something. Communism. The Cold War. The classified seminar when my father met the Zhamovskys. Not too long ago the world was a different place. History spoke for itself. Galina Zhamovsky was the wife of a top-tier Soviet natural resource official. She was smart enough to understand to what extent she was being monitored.

As I scoured the painting, my mind kept going. Pop and Galina always found time to get together. Family trips, Pop's international business trips, maybe the words in the artworks were the answers to bigger questions, bigger discussions that went on when they met up. Maybe they were afterthoughts on things that happened as they parted.

What about the letter my father was writing to me? Was he apologizing? Was he trying to explain the situation? Did it matter anymore?

Of course it did. Sometimes, whether wrong or right, human nature is all about truth. Other times it's all about revenge.

For the first time, I found the correspondence at the bottom of a piece. It was systematically worked into the thick grass that got higher toward the sides. Four strung-together bullet points.

The most compelling message yet.

CHAPTER 46

It was eight thirty on Tuesday morning. I was standing at the side of my father's coffin in the funeral home. There was no one else around. It was just the two of us having our final one on one. The funeral wasn't to start for another two hours, but I didn't feel it was safe for me to be there. At this point I wasn't comfortable with anyone knowing where I was going to be at any certain time. There was too much going on, too many situations, too much I still didn't know or understand. The last thing I needed was to have to pretend to throngs of people that I was simply an innocent, mourning secondary victim to all of this while I constantly looked over my shoulder. From business associates to clients to Pop's friends to my partners to the egg to Detective Morante to Krissy Lockhart to God knows what else after what I had seen on the news the previous night, there were simply way too many chances for surprises, exposure. Besides, I was on a very tight schedule especially now that Pangaea-Man resurfaced.

"How the fuck could you do this? I was . . . there was . . ."

I was fumbling for the right words. I was talking to a dead man, but never had a conversation been more important to me.

"I know everything, Pop. Galina, Andreu, the artwork, the eggs, I know it all."

Pop was in the outfit I had picked out for him. Navy, wide pin-

striped Brioni suit with a white shirt and silver necktie. The colors
were a nice contrast to the burgundy velvet he was surrounded by. I
carefully scanned the topography of his face. I was amazed at the
job the funeral home had done putting his features back together.

"How could you betray us like this? All you've told me my
whole life is what an angel my mother was. So why? Why would
you willingly betray an angel?"

I sucked in a breath and shook my head. So many thoughts. So
many things I wanted to say.

"Justice is a funny thing. Seeing you lying on the ground, bullet
holes in your head, I went numb when I realized it was Murdoch. I
thought I had done this to you. Now it's painfully clear you did this
to yourself and fucked me pretty good in the process. I was actually
beating myself up about not being able to speak about you at the
funeral. Now I can't even be sure how well I knew you. I don't even
know what I would have said."

I dropped my eyes from my father's face to his necktie's perfect
knot. Then, for myself, for my mother, I shifted it ever so slightly off
center so he'd be annoyed for eternity.

"You always said it was a cruel world. I had no idea just how
cruel it could be."

An image of my half-brother ripped through my mind. Then I
saw Murdoch at The Four Seasons standing over me smoking a
Monte Cristo #2.

As I looked at my father for the last time I couldn't ignore the
irony. The lessons he taught me, the instincts he forced on me,
were now all I had to save myself.

Soon I was in a cab heading south on Fifth Avenue. I took my cell
phone from my pocket and dialed an international number that I
read from a document in my briefcase. I took a deep breath then hit
"send."

"*Privyet?*"

"Igor, Jonah Gray."

It was Andreu Zhamovsky's banker in Russia. Because Andreu

needed everything to be on the level, until his mission was complete, this meant his financial institutions had to be abreast of what was happening in New York. International wire transfers of escrow, due diligence contractor payments, etc., still needed to be handled without incident as Andreu had been doing thus far. Larionov, like everyone else who had been dragged into this sordid mess, was oblivious to the fact it was all horseshit.

"Good day, Jonah," Larionov said with a heavy Baltic accent. "What can I assist you with today?"

By this point, thankfully, Larionov and I had become comfortable with one another.

"Have you by any chance heard from Andreu about the transfer of some funds?"

"No sir, I have not."

Action.

"Fuck!" I said, pretending as if I had been trying to hold it in.

"What?"

"I'm sorry. It's just that Andreu has us all running around over here like chickens with our heads cut off to get this deal closed for him. We've absolutely dropped everything for him. And — and —"

"And what?"

"And all I asked him to do was take care of one fucking thing."

"Please Jonah, calm down. Perhaps there is some way I can be of assistance."

"I don't think you can. Andreu was supposed to make you aware of this a few days ago so you could prepare the proper funds. When they didn't come in this morning, I figured he had waited too long. I told him you'd need more time than just a few hours, but he wouldn't listen to me," I carried on, pretending as if I had shifted the conversation to me talking to myself. "Fuck it. He'll just have to live with the disappointment."

"What funds, Jonah? What disappointment? Please, perhaps I can help…"

I took a loud, deep breath into the phone.

"The short version goes like this. As you know, Andreu has us pitting three different deals against one another in order to weed out the most favorable one. In order to do this correctly, each of the three parties needs to believe they are, in fact, the buyer right up to the last second. The last second. You with me?"

"I am with you. Andreu informed me it is an aggressive tactic, hence all of the wire transfers over the last few weeks."

"That's right. The plan was to have all of them in position to come to the table this afternoon, at three different locations, to get the deals closed. Once it was determined who had stepped up to the plate the most seriously, the deal was to be completed with that party and that party only. The others were to fall away with only whatever reasons we gave them as to why their deals had fallen through. That's it."

Larionov was silent.

"Anyway, it doesn't matter now."

"Jonah, please excuse my confusion. I still do not understand."

"Because an all cash transaction has been proposed in each instance, Igor, sixty-five percent of the purchase price was to be in escrow at the time of closing with a note promising the delivery of the remaining thirty-five percent within forty-five days. This was part of the deal, in each case, since we were putting the sellers under such unheard of time constraints. Once the funds arrived via the account we've been using, the plan was to simply move the appropriate funds for each separate deal into three different dedicated escrow accounts that we have waiting. Because we needed to follow through with each deal as if it were the only deal, right through the end, we needed the funds in place for each separate deal."

Now the kicker.

"Once we were finished, the unneeded funds, roughly two-thirds of the cash transferred, was to be immediately wired back. But at this point, frankly, it's pointless to even discuss further."

"*Baw zhe moy,*" Larionov said, dumbfounded. "Perhaps we can find Andreu and—"

"Believe me, I've been trying for the last four hours. He's

absolutely nowhere to be found. Svetlana said he's most likely on his yacht."

Svetlana is Andreu's assistant.

"She said sometimes his itinerary changes so rapidly he forgets to leave word where he is. Especially in the summer. Anyway, there's no way we can get the funds together at this point. So I'll just have to stall everyone and hope for the best."

"More time would usually be required for a larger amount. The transfer of funds is not the problem. It is only machines. As long as the funds are available, the transfer of one dollar is the same as the transfer of one million dollars. The problem is making sure someone with the proper authority has signed off on the transfer."

Bingo.

Andreu Zhamovsky never imagined his plan failing, and in doing so made one very grave mistake. He willingly granted me power of attorney for the real estate deal in New York City. By limiting my access to his affairs to just this deal, and keeping me legally away from all of his other affairs, he figured he had protected himself. In readily granting me power-of-attorney when I said I needed the ability to maneuver freely as the deals called for it, he had given me the written authority to handle all aspects of any pending deals in New York City, including the handling of the finances. He figured all I would do was put each deal's earnest money into place, along with some due diligence cash, by the time he was ready to move the real money over so he could immediately screw Derbyshev and steal the eggs.

He was wrong.

"Wait a second," I responded, as if I was starting to get it. "So what you're telling me is that the funds aren't the issue as long as the transaction has been signed off on properly. Or, in other words, Andreu was not as wrong as I thought in waiting since he gave me power of attorney. He knew the funds could be transferred no problem."

"Well, yes, I guess so," he exclaimed.

"Yes!" I screamed into the phone. "Yes! Well then we better get those funds yesterday, Mister Larionov. If we don't, these deals will be gone by the end of the day. And I'd rather not think about where you and I will stand in the eyes of Andreu Zhamovsky and Prevkos if that happens. If you know what I mean."

"Of course, Mister Jonah. Of course. I need copies of the contracts. How fast can you get them to me?"

I had drafts of each proposed contract in my briefcase. They were being prepared simultaneously as the deals went along because of the obvious nature of the situation.

"I'll fax them to you. You'll have them in no more than thirty minutes. Remember, two-thirds of the currency will be back on your side of the ocean by the time you open your eyes tomorrow morning."

"Terrific. How much do we need to wire?"

I covered the phone and swallowed.

Never a shred of doubt. *Own the words.*

"In American currency, nine hundred and seventy-five million dollars."

CHAPTER 47

At ten fifteen A.M., I had L meet me on the sidewalk in front of his warehouse. The Meatpacking District was buzzing. People were scattered everywhere as refrigerated trucks wove in and out of the traffic through the old city streets. I jumped out of the cab with my briefcase.

"Let's go," I said following L inside. "Your office."

My phone would not stop ringing. Text messages were flooding in from my three partners. My father's funeral had started and I was nowhere to be found, which, for me, was exactly the point. I wouldn't have given it another thought until something dawned on me from a message from Perry. My unknown whereabouts was per-haps, for others, startling. "Where are you?" Perry wrote, "Should I be worried?" I wrote back, simply, "I'm fine. I promise. I'll explain later." Then, figuring she would pass this on to everyone else, I silenced my phone.

The building has been around for a hundred years. It's mostly warehouse with a few thousand square feet of office space upstairs. Luckman Meats was in full swing that morning. I followed L through his freezing-cold place of business toward the staircase. Conversations, spoken loud over machinery and the noise of in-coming and out-going trucks, were happening everywhere. Most were in broken English. Some were in completely other languages. A lot of the workers wore white, blood-streaked smocks as they scurried about carrying meat-related products or equipment. A few brushed my shoulders as we whisked by one another. The fresh, purposefully frigid air smelled fleshy, raw.

"Krissy Lockhart," I said following closely behind L. "Find anything?"

"East Hampton High School. Class of ninety-seven. There were a few articles that mentioned her name."

"Articles? About what?"

"Her mother. She died in some terrible car accident. The daughter was just mentioned."

"I need you to call the school today. I know it's summer, but I need you to try anyway."

"For what? What do you want me to ask?"

"Anything that gets me as much information about this girl as possible."

Once upstairs and in his office, L closed the door behind us. The place was a mess. There were file cabinets and stacks of papers everywhere. The office was an interesting study in contrasts. It looked the same as it probably did in the fifties except that all of the technological aspects of the space—computer, phone, fax—were up to the minute. The rear office wall, the one behind L's desk, was a window that overlooked part of the warehouse.

L sat down behind his desk. I sat in a chair in front of his desk facing him.

"We're missing your father's funeral, Jonah. What the fuck is going on?"

"Did you get them?"

I started to dig through my briefcase. L, unhappy I wasn't answering his questions, sighed angrily before opening his desk's top drawer. He pulled out a large manila envelope and threw it on top of his desk. He slammed the drawer shut.

I found and took the contracts from my briefcase and walked over to the fax.

"Face up or down?" I asked.

"Down."

I placed half of one of the three mini-stacks that was under my arm onto the machine and dialed Larionov's office. I hit "send." Then, with a thud, I dropped the remaining two and a half in front of L on his desk.

"I need you to send these after the first stack goes through."

Purchase agreements of the magnitude we were dealing with were each over an inch thick. Even L's high-speed fax would need some time for each.

I took a seat in one of the chairs facing my best friend's desk.

"And then I need you to burn them."

"You what?"

"You heard me. I can't take them with me. If, or more likely when, the authorities figure out that they were sent from here, you simply tell them I have a key. You tell them that I could have slipped in through the back while you were out. End of story."

"Jonah what the fuck are —"

I grabbed the manila envelope that was between us on the desk. I opened it, looked inside, and removed the identification card that had my picture on it. It was a driver's license.

"Alaska? This is the best he could do?"

Someone knocked on the door.

"Not now," L snapped.

They cracked it anyway.

"It's urgent," a woman responded.

"Make it quick, Hil."

The tall, forty-something brunette rushed to L's desk.

"The Lincoln and Holland tunnels are both closing in a matter of minutes. There's a suspicious abandoned truck just outside the Manhattan side of the Holland."

She handed him some papers. L rifled through them.

"Just thought you should know why at least seventy-five percent of our Jersey deliveries were going to be extremely late today."

"Thanks Hil."

She headed back toward the door.

"Hey, Jonah."

Hilary ran L's dispatch. Over the years I'd seen her from time to time.

"Hey, Hilary," I said back.

She left.

"What's the problem with Alaska?" L continued.

"Are you kidding me?"

"Jonah, they go with remote states on purpose. They do this because most people won't have a point of reference for comparison."

"What about my point of reference? Shouldn't it be somewhere I've been?"

"Juneau's fucking tiny. Just remember the governor's mansion on Calhoun Street and the Red Dog Saloon as landmarks. You'll be fine."

I looked in the envelope again.

"Did you remember to get me —"

"It's in there."

He was right. I pulled out a second Alaskan driver's license with my picture on it. The name on one was Stan Gray. The name on the first was Roy Gordon. Roy, a bartender at Bull & Bear, was my favorite barkeep in the city. I needed someone I would be able to remember, but who wasn't a traceable connection.

"There's one for each of your partners, just like you asked, along with matching passports."

"Huge," I exhaled. "Fucking huge."

Considering I had given him so little time, L had come up monstrous. The only sticking point we ran into when discussing it two nights earlier was the issue of passport pictures for all of the different documents. L had come up with the brilliant idea of scanning them from the PCBL marketing materials I always send him. L knows a ton of people. I always send him updated copies in case he runs into anyone who needs our services. They contain individual pictures of our team. All are nothing more than actual-size passport photos.

I threw them back into the envelope, which I placed in my briefcase, then sat up straight in my chair.

"Thank you," I said. "I mean that, L. That was some pretty under-the-gun shit."

"I'd kill for you, Jonah. You know that."

I nodded in agreement.

"Now all I'm asking for is the truth. You owe me that. Christ, we're missing your father's funeral. And we both know how pissed he'd be about that if he was alive —"

I stood and started to pace. L was right. I owed him the truth. Or at least as much of it as I had time for.

"I saw him this morning. I went by the funeral home and said good-bye to him."

"Why can't you be there?"

"It's too dangerous."

"Why?"

I drifted behind L's desk. I looked out over the warehouse then laughed nervously.

"I wouldn't even begin to know where to start. I know that sounds completely lame, but it's true."

"Start with why you've been acting so crazy. Not just since your father died, but since a week or more before that."

"You don't want to know that."

"Try me."

I dug in, lifted my chin in the air.

"I have the Fabergé egg that's been all over the news."

"You have to be kidding me."

"I didn't steal it. It was planted on me."

It sounded ridiculous even to me.

"Who planted it on you?"

Literally, all I could do was laugh. Across the huge building, standing down below, I saw Hilary talking on her cell. Even though far away, I could swear she was staring back in the direction of the office.

"Next question. No time. Not relevant right now."

"Do you still have it? The egg?"

"It doesn't matter."

"Can you get it back to the authorities?"

"It's not that simple. Too much has happened. There are a lot of bloody hands because of that fucking antique, including my own."

I continued to pace but didn't stray far from the window.

"Jonah, I'm sure they'd understand. All you have to —"

"Knowing who stole the thing is just the tip of the iceberg. Like I said, it's complicated. I want to give it back. But I can't until I know I can fully wash my hands of the fucking thing."

The fax machine beeped. Since I was up L handed me the second half of the first contract and I sent it through. I checked the window again. Hilary hadn't moved.

"This deal I've been working on? This project? It's all a set up. I don't even think I was supposed to know the egg had been planted on me. But not only did I realize it was, I figured out who put it there. Once that happened, I was screwed. Remember that Ryan Stern situation a couple years back? Remember how that federal agent said he'd be waiting for his chance to take me down?"

"The what situation?"

"The banker and the termination agreement and the cash that almost landed me in jail?"

L shook his head.

"Of course, right."

I moved to the glass again. Hilary continued to talk on the phone, only now she was looking around the warehouse between glances up at the office. Something felt wrong.

"How long has Hilary worked for you?" I changed directions.

"Almost ten years. Why?"

"She runs dispatch. Always knows where your trucks are, right?"

"Always."

Why was she staring up at me? Had she read about my father? Did she know from the paper I was missing his funeral? Fuck! Was I just being a paranoid lunatic?

"Why are you asking about Hilary?"

Suddenly her eyes settled on someone, or something, down below and she hung up the phone. She started walking. I looked in the direction she was headed. An officer in blues was navigating the bustling warehouse toward her.

"No," I whispered to myself. *How the fuck would she know?*

I heard L stand up. He moved next to me at the window. I pointed at the glass.

"How the fuck would —"

Hilary. Dispatch.

"Does Hilary use scanners to do her job? You know, listen to the cops and firemen to determine what activity may cause her trucks traffic?"

"Constantly."

Of course she did. That's how she knew the tunnels were about to close, unlike someone like me who wouldn't have known until after they had.

I looked at my watch. 10:23

"I'm not at the funeral. Morante must have bailed and put a look out for me over the frequency."

"Who must have bailed?"

"Hilary saw me in your office and called it in. Which means —"

The detective couldn't be far behind.

"Jonah, maybe you're jumping the gun here."

Hilary and the cop met in the center of the warehouse. In unison they looked up at the office.

We barreled down the stairs. I led. We hit the bottom and I headed toward the front door.

"Jonah!"

I stopped dead.

"He may have a friend waiting out front," L said.

"Don't we have to go past the cop to get out back?"

"This way."

Briefcase swinging I followed L down a narrow, dingy hall past some back offices I had never seen before. I could feel ghosts of big-haired secretaries and men in gray flannel suits. Dull brown and yellow vinyl tiling covered the floor. At the end we entered a storage room. I took the lead again.

"Just go straight," L advised.

We started bobbing and weaving through all kinds of boxes and equipment.

"Don't forget —" I started, "You need to send the last two documents."

"Then burn it all. I got it."

"I need you to play stupid to all of this, not just the contracts," I went on, my words as quick as my steps. "A million people are going to have questions, L, and they're going to come to you. You have to pretend that you're as confused as they are. Trust me, it won't be long until the thugs and cops trying to find me turn into the FBI and CIA. The less anyone knows the better. You understand what I'm saying here?"

"Got it. What about this cop? What do I say when he asks why you were here?"

"Tell him I was too distraught to go to the funeral. Tell him I asked you to meet me here, then you talked me into going, and I took off in a hurry to catch the end."

We continued through the metal and cardboard jungle.

"You see that red door at the end? Under the exit sign?" L pointed, "It's a fire door."

"I see it. Won't the alarm sound?"

"Uh-uh. Needs to be fixed."

As we got close, something dawned on me.

"This is probably the last time I'm ever going to see you, L," I blurted out. "I can't ever come back here. And I'm just basing that on the crimes I haven't even committied yet."

I didn't hear L's feet moving with mine anymore. I stopped and turned around.

"Don't say that, Jonah"

"I mean it, man. What do you think I need all of that crap for?" I asked, pointing to my briefcase.

L glanced back toward where we'd run from.

"I figured you just needed to lay low for a while. I mean does anyone even know if —"

"I hoped to have more time to tell you. I'm sorry."

"Jonah there has to be a way."

"Trust me, L. There isn't. My staying keeps anyone I care about in danger. Making sure you're all safe is part of making this all right."

I opened my arms, silently instructing L to give me a hug. He was pissed, devastated, and rightly so. What I was doing was completely unfair and I knew that. But I didn't have a choice.

He hesitated.

"Give me a fucking hug. I won't be able to leave if you don't."

We embraced like the brothers we had spent our whole lives becoming.

"Get the door alarm fixed," I said, hoping to hear his laugh one last time. "The fire marshall will write you up in a second for that shit."

"There must be some way."

We broke apart.

"It's past that, L. Someone tried to cut my balls off. Now they deserve everything they've got coming."

The door closed behind me. I had no sense of where I was. Puddles in the uneven cobblestone flipped hints of light down the dark alley. To my left, past the buildings, I saw cars flowing. Same to my right, only in this direction I saw something thirty feet above running parallel to the street. It was the rusted out foundation of the abandoned High Line, an elevated freight train last used in 1980. I raced toward it.

Within seconds I could see the weeds germinating from the structure. I knew I was on Washington, meaning I had correctly chosen the street behind L's warehouse. I turned right. I ran north.

CHAPTER 48

I walked into my apartment and locked the door behind me. I dropped my briefcase. Neo was next door playing at crazy animal lady's apartment. The space was quiet, different without him, always was. All I could hear were the faint sounds of the city outside. I rushed toward my study. The sound of my heels on the hardwood floor echoed loudly.

I sat down behind my desk. The room was dark, all the stained, wooden venetian blinds closed. I switched on the lamp next to my computer. I logged onto the Internet and clicked my way to the Salton Lynear Bank Web site. I typed in my username and password. Within seconds I was inside the account being used for the Prevkos deal. I looked to see if Larionov had successfully made the wire transfer. He hadn't.

I dropped my fist onto my desktop.

"Fuck."

The plan was to make sure the funds moved quickly and rested at the Federal Reserve, the middleman for all domestic and international transfers, for as little time as possible. Someone seeing this much money, unexpectedly, was sure to throw up a red flag. Because PCBL transfers big numbers electronically every day, the Fed has an understanding to keep our funds moving as expeditiously as possible, something I was counting on. I looked at a green, Tiffany four leaf clover paperweight on my desktop then back at the screen as if hoping the funds would have arrived while my head was down. They hadn't, which meant I had to anxiously sit and wait.

I looked up over the monitor at the opposite wall. Not just the wall, but the books lining it. It had been so long since I had noticed them, if I ever really had at all. I looked back at the screen. Still nothing. I looked again at the books. Slowly, without ever altering my stare, I rose to my feet and walked over to them.

I lightly ran my fingers across the spines that were facing out. They were all different widths, colors, textures. I was concentrating on them. Not the individual titles, just them, the books, as a whole. My eyes started to drift. I let my body follow.

I left the study. From room to room I made sure to notice all I had so often forgotten to recognize. I looked at everything, really looked. The artwork I had paid through the nose for. The framed photographs, some of friends, some of my father and me. Fresh flowers I had delivered each week but never really saw. I grazed them with my fingers, releasing their sweet perfume into the air.

I walked into the dining room I had never used. When I bought the place I used to tell myself how wonderful it would be to entertain. How nice it would be once I settled down for my girlfriend, wife, whoever, and I to enjoy elegant dinners with other couples. I used to close my eyes and see sleek flatware and china underneath simple, contemporary candelabras that fell perfectly in line with the apartment's décor. I would see earth-tone napkins, bottles of red and white wine, and trays of savory, tantalizing food. And I would see it all surrounded by beautiful, intelligent, interesting people all enraptured by my incredible, dark-haired girl's story as I just stared at her with the rest of them. It would never happen.

I reacquainted myself with the long, rectangular table's smooth, shiny wooden surface as I walked alongside of it. I laughed. I had paid almost twenty grand for it, including the surrounding chairs. Right then and there, standing in a room that signified possibilities, it dawned on me. Nothing I had worked so hard for all of these years means shit when the most important things in life are out of order.

My strides picked up as I passed through the living room on my

way back to the study. I sat back down at my desk and glanced at
the monitor. The funds had arrived. Nine hundred sixty-nine million, six hundred thirty-one thousand, eight hundred nineteen dollars and eleven cents had jumped the Arctic and Atlantic oceans in
a single bound. And it was right at my fingertips.

React.

My fingers began bouncing all over the keypad. As I had mentioned to Larionov, the plan was to move the funds into different,
dedicated escrow accounts. I intended on staying true to part of the
plan, moving the funds elsewhere. But that was as far as my honesty
went. The account where the funds would be traveling wasn't an
escrow account at all. That account wasn't even with the same
bank.

I set the funds up to be transferred. The account they would be
traveling to was #099-224581-7721 at SNPB, Swiss Nation Partners Bank. The name on the account was Stan Gray. He was dead
on earth, but at this point in time there was one place he was still
very much alive—within the confines of the global banking net-
work. Once all of the necessary codes, passwords, and information
had been entered into the appropriate fields, I sent the money on
its way.

I opened the browser again. I put the two windows side by side
with each taking half the screen. With the second one, the one on
the right, I clicked my way to the SNPB Web site and logged on as
my father. I entered his account and waited. Once the funds
showed up, without hesitation, I prepared the account to send the
money on its way once again. I typed in the desired account number and routing sequence, then confirmed the transaction.

I turned my attention back to the Salton Lynear Bank Web site
window on the left. I went up to the address line and typed in the
same SNPB address as in the window on the right, only with the
suffix ".it" as opposed to ".com." It was the Italian SNPB Web site.
I clicked on "client access." I typed in the appropriate information
and within seconds was looking at my father's private Italian
account, the first of two different accounts he kept overseas. Both
accounts were with the same bank. This was why he used a Swiss

bank in the States. Private Swiss bank accounts, which are actually within the borders of Switzerland, are the most secure bank accounts in the world. Because of this, they have unbelievably strict policies regarding their access. They will only accept wire transfers from subsidiaries of their own organization and absolutely no transfers with outside banks. I know, then why send it to Italy instead of Switzerland since it's coming from the same bank? This is where it gets tricky. Because some countries, such as America, are restricted with their use of encryption, banks in Switzerland will not allow Internet banking to be done for clients in those countries. They are simply concerned that the information being transferred isn't secure enough. But, banks in Italy don't have such tight policies. And they don't have heavy encryption restrictions of their own, therefore banks in Switzerland are fine to allow Internet banking for clients in Italy. Hence the chain: U.S. to Italy to Switzerland. That's why once the Internet took off, and my father didn't need to physically travel to Switzerland any more to access his account, he opened the account in Italy to serve as the middleman.

It wasn't long until the funds showed up in Europe. Once they did, I kept at it and immediately set the money up for the last leg of the day's journey. I entered in all of the appropriate destination information, confirmed the transaction, and once again sent it on its way.

I looked back to the screen on the right. I went to the address line and entered in the same SNPB information, only this time with the suffix ".ch," Switzerland. I logged on for the last time, only this time as "Leo 2235778." Another measure of security within the Swiss banking system is the ability to have a nameless, though coded and numbered account, better for anonymity. It was indeed my father's account. Leo was my mother's birth sign.

The money arrived.

It had traveled over 10,000 miles in only seventeen minutes.

CHAPTER 49

At two twenty-five P.M., after coming up through the Chrysler Center's service entrance, I stood at Carolyn's desk. I was dressed for success, polished as usual. She looked up.

"Jonah! Where have you been? What happened?"

Without answering her I placed the medium-sized TUMI bag I had with me under her desk, forcing her to move her legs.

"What is that?"

I turned to her and leaned in so as not to have to speak too loud.

"How'd everything go? We all set?"

"Yeah," she nodded, "we're all set."

"Good girl."

"Jonah, what is that?" she asked, nervously through her teeth.

She pointed to the TUMI bag with her eyes.

I carefully glanced around.

"I'll tell you, but only if you promise me you won't open it until you get home tonight."

She nodded.

I leaned down, over her, in order to whisper into her ear.

"Your numbers came in today."

One hundred and seventy thousand dollars. Cash. Carolyn was about to be out of a job, so the emergency stash from my safety deposit box, minus a little I'd need for myself, was the least I could do. I gave her a kiss on the cheek then stood up. She just stared at me.

Next, I headed for Perry's office.

"Jesus Christ, Jonah!"

Perry blasted out of her seat toward me. I put my briefcase down. We hugged. I closed my eyes. I could feel myself not wanting to let go.

"Listen to me, Per," I said, forcing myself to grab her arms and gently push her back. "I can't stay here."

"Why not? What's going on, Jonah? You miss your father's funeral, you totally disappear —"

"I know, it all seems crazy," I said, squeezing her arms tighter.

"We all love you, Jonah. We only want to help and you're not letting us. You're just shutting us out like —"

I started to say, "Because I'm scared for —" but caught myself. The last thing I wanted was for her to fear for her safety.

"What? What is it, Jonah? Let me in. You don't need to go through whatever it is you're dealing with alone."

"Per, all I can say right now is that you're right. Something is happening and it's fucked up. It's much more than just my father's death. But it's complicated. You have to just trust me when I say now is not the time and this is certainly not the place."

Her eyes saddened while at the same time becoming concerned.

"Should I be scared?"

I didn't know how to answer so I dismissed the question. I squared my jaw and spoke quietly, firm.

"I promise to tell you everything. I swear. Meet me tonight at eight o'clock in Tribeca at Acappella. It's on the corner of Hudson and Chambers. Don't tell anyone you're meeting me there. No one. Not Jake, not Tommy, no one."

I shot into Jake's office. He was talking to someone on speakerphone.

"Lionel, I'll have to call you back."

I closed the door.

"I can't move forward unless the numbers work Jake," the voice on the other end said.

"I know that. Work with me here—a few minutes."

"Fine. Just—"

Jake didn't wait for an answer and hung up.

"Fuck, Curtis—"

"Don't," I said.

My arm was up and I was closing in on him fast.

"Don't what?"

"Get up."

He stopped his ass midair. I sat down in one of the two chairs facing his desk.

"I don't have time," I went on.

He sat back down.

"Time? Jonah, man, what's happening here? Tell me how I can help."

"It's nothing like you think. I'm fine. I mean, with the grieving and everything, I'm fine."

"Then why weren't you—"

"Tribeca tonight. Eight o'clock. Acappella. Can you be there?"

Jake, caught off guard a bit by the danger in my words, my tone, looked back at me straight in the eye.

"Of course I can be."

"I'll tell you everything. Just promise me something. Not a word to anyone. Not to Tommy, not Perry, no one."

Tommy was next. Once I had played the same game with him, I left his office and started toward mine. Before I got there my phone rang. I looked at the caller ID. It was Andreu. I let it go to voice mail. Carolyn appeared behind me.

"Jonah, I—"

My phone rang again.

"Hold on, Carolyn," I said, continuing toward my destination without breaking stride.

It was Andreu again.

"Fuck," I said under my breath.

"Actually, I need to—"

Carolyn was still trying to get my attention. I didn't hear her. My mind was consumed with the different things my Russian comrade might want to discuss, the different games he might want to play.

I entered my office still looking at my phone, thinking.

"Now is that any way to treat a client?"

Surprised, I looked up. There he was, Andreu Zhamovsky, casually sitting in my office. He was dressed in Brioni and a reckless, devilish, hell-bent smirk, holding his own cell phone.

"Andreu! I, uh—"

I looked at Carolyn as I realized what she had been trying to tell me. I looked back at Andreu.

"Wow! What are you doing here?"

I put down my briefcase and moved toward him. He stood up. We hugged as we played each other's bluff.

"What? I'm not allowed to check up on you unannounced? See how you're holding up?"

I picked up my briefcase and headed behind my desk while Andreu retook his seat. Keep it business, I reminded myself. Stay even. Carolyn asked us if we wanted any coffee. We both passed. She left, closing the door behind her. For a moment there was silence.

"Have you stopped working long enough to grieve your father's passing?" he continued.

"My work *is* my grieving. Besides, two bullets to the brain hardly constitutes a passing."

"Can't argue with you there," he shrugged.

"When did you get in?" I asked.

I sat down slowly in my chair, reminding him whose office he was in.

"A couple of hours ago."

"I didn't know you were making the trip."

"Neither did I. Something unexpected came up."

"Really?"

My mind started throwing around possibilities like swelling kernels in a popcorn maker.

"Something that has to do with the deal? Anything I can help you with?"

"Nothing like that."

Andreu, confident, relaxed in his seat.

"Something personal," he continued.

"Personal?"

"That's right. I like to watch your CNN sometimes. It keeps me up to date on the happenings in the States. Anyway, one particular story caught my eye —"

Then just like that, in a move that made the hair on my arms stand up, he declared war on me. He took out the F. Scott Fitzgerald Mont Blanc Writers Edition pen — my father's personal favorite. Its shimmering white barrel caught my eye immediately. I could see the author's signature on the black resin cap. Andreu had taken aim. He tapped the end of the pen against one of his top front teeth.

It made perfect sense. The story on CNN was that of a cop who had been dumped in the river. I, consequently, was still yet to even be arrested. Andreu had no choice but to come to New York and assess the situation. He didn't like what he had found.

The gloves were off.

"Really? CNN. I'd take a guess, but I must admit that I've fallen behind a little bit with the news."

"Of course, you're a busy guy. I should know, on top of what you're going through, I'm the one who has you working like this."

I turned to my computer screen.

"What's this?" I said, pretending to be responding to something.

I looked at my watch.

"Fuck! I had no idea what time it was."

I hit the intercom on my phone.

"Yes, Jonah?"

"Carolyn, I'm late for a meeting with Merrill and I forgot to have you get me a car. Call downstairs and have Javier hail me a cab."

Javier was one of the building security guards. He did this for us, hailed cabs, when we were in a bind for time in exchange for a nice tip. So for Carolyn it was not at all curious.

"Of course, Jonah."

I jumped out of my chair, grabbed my briefcase and headed toward the door.

"Fuck, Andreu," I said looking at the time on my cell. "I have a meeting with the bank regarding your deal. If you had only told me you were going to be in town —"

"Of course, Jonah. Duty calls. I'll tell you what," Andreu said, "I have a car downstairs. Forget about the cab. Let me take you where you need to go. In fact, since I'm here, why don't I sit in with you on the meeting?"

The driver opened the door to the limo.

"Please." Andreu said, waving me in first.

I told the driver the address of my fictitious meeting. I took the far bench, the one sideways and up against the wall. Andreu followed me in, taking the rear. The car started moving. Once it did Andreu quickly started toward me. My back stiffened, my fists clenched. But all he was doing was going for the bar immediately to my right. He poured himself a straight Belvedere. He offered me one as well. I declined and he retook his seat. Without another word, he slugged down most of the drink in one gulp, then balanced the near-empty glass on the seat next to him.

"You're smart, Jonah. Tough. You always have been."

Andreu stopped as if he were waiting for a response. I didn't give him one so he continued.

"You know why I'm here, Jonah. Isn't that right?"

"Where did you get that pen?"

"I'm here," Andreu went on, ignoring me, "because of this."

He grabbed a *New York Post* from the seat and tossed it to me. The cover was Pangaea-Man's soft coffin being removed from the river.

"And the fact you're still working on a deal your partners should be completing without you."

There were so many words I wanted to spew at him. Instead of trying to sort them out, credit him, I turned away and looked out the window. I noticed we were going in the opposite direction of Merrill's office.

"That cop was supposed to sink you for this, Jonah."

I said nothing.

"There was someone waiting for the egg to be admitted into evidence so they could return it to me. Only it never made it into evidence, did it?"

Still I stayed silent.

"Look at you," Andreu talked down at me, "when did you become such a madman? I mean, killing police officers?"

The words were searing. I returned my eyes to Andreu's

"What's the matter? The six eggs from Baltimore weren't enough?"

His demeanor, expression did a 180-degree turn.

"What are you talking about?"

"I know everything, Andreu. I know about Derbyshev, you planting *Danish Jubilee Egg* on me, I know it all. I must say I was pretty confused for a while. Once I learned Hart was caught on camera less than a month before it was supposed to be moved to the Capital it all started coming together. The time frame of our little real estate deal, your gopher trying to get the egg back from me, all of it. The egg was going to be under much stronger lock and key once moved. Hart learned about the government cameras, but because of your plan to accumulate all of the eggs there wasn't time to abort, only improvise. That's why Hart immediately dumped it off on me and disappeared. I imagine on your very generous dime. There was only a small amount of time for him to handle the egg before the whole world was looking for him."

"You're out of your mind."

I leaned back in my seat.

"The only thing I couldn't figure out was if I was the intended mule or the best available option. Until, that is, I found the note in my father's handwriting on the cop who was accidentally killed, quite frankly, because of you. A note written on stationery with a Russian watermark."

Andreu tried to laugh it off.

"This is absurd," he chuckled.

"How'd she make you do it? How'd she convince you to throw both of our lives away for a bunch of antique eggs?"

"You don't know what you're talking about."

"Is that right? The same way I don't know she's the one who put you in touch with Derbyshev in the first place?"

Andreu threw the last remaining sip of his drink down his throat.

"She's a fucking black widow spider, Andreu. She's fooled everyone for thirty years. Alexander, Stan, you —"

Andreu fired his glass, narrowly missing my head. It exploded behind me.

"Don't say another word! Not another word! Your jealous, out-of-control father was the problem! He's always been the problem!"

"Is that what she told you?"

"What she told me is that my father was found facedown six years ago at Tealtralnaya Station, pumped full of over forty bullets, on your father's orders. Not the victim of a mugging like our foreign-investment-seeking government wanted to pretend."

"That's probably true. Only your mother left out one important fact."

"What's that?"

"The hit was her idea."

"Shut up, Jonah."

"I can't. You've left me no choice. The truth hurts me just as much as it hurts you. It doesn't change the fact it's the truth."

"My mother loved my father. She would never hurt him."

"She pretended to love him. Then she pretended to love her rich contingency plan, Stan Gray."

"Lies! All lies!"

"She's up to something, Andreu. She wants those eggs for herself, and she's wanted them for a long time."

"The missing Fabergé eggs were the dream of my father, not my mother."

"There's some interesting artwork hanging in my father's townhouse that says otherwise."

Andreu, confused, laughed.

"What do you mean, artwork?"

"Your mother's. Drawings and a painting. She used them to secretly correspond with my father. They had an affair since meeting when she and Alexander first came here."

"Wrong."

"Wrong?"

"Your father was an animal, Jonah. He tried to force himself on her. The reason she never said anything to my father was because she knew he'd kill Stan, and she felt he'd worked too hard to throw everything away. Your father spent every day after trying to keep her quiet."

He held up the F. Scott Fitzgerald Mont Blanc.

"One such example. Apparently Stan's favorite."

"So that's why you jumped on the opportunity to take me down," I humored him. "Hart's problem in your mind wasn't a problem at all. Plan B gave you the chance to give my father the ultimate payback. The public embarrassment of watching me swing and the shame of his own son thinking he'd set him up. The icing on the cake you undoubtedly had planned for him before someone saved you the trouble. You obtain the eggs and take us down all in three week's work."

Andreu said nothing.

"Pretty crafty job with the note," I went on. "For the life of me I couldn't figure out how you pulled that off, but now it's perfectly clear. With the gifts from my father must have come notes. Once you had these, or, should I say, once Mr. *Worldwide* had these in his possession, a near-authentic reproduction of the handwriting became easy. For someone who couldn't publicly point a finger at me, a note was the perfect solution. Clean. Simple. A sample of my father's handwriting, what would have been an obstacle, became a nonissue."

I paused. Andreu maintained his silence. I continued.

"Then you picked some cop at random to give the collar of a lifetime since all the egg had to do, as you said, was find its way into evidence."

Further denial was pointless. Andreu smiled wryly.

"Well I wouldn't say at random. Lawrence Hart knew him from living in the city. They lived in the same neighborhood. As for *Danish Jubilee Egg*, all these embassy workers know each other, Jonah. It's no different than bankers or lawyers. They stick to and mingle with their own. For obvious reasons I needed an insider. So an acquaintance of mine at the Russian consulate mentioned him to me as a hard worker, as a guy with a special fondness for earning money. Lucky for me, because he was running the security show over there, he was able to plan and carry out the theft on his own."

I hated that his explanation made such sense, seemed so plausible. Some of the greatest heists in history had happened because of their simplicity. In 1911, the *Mona Lisa* was stolen from the Louvre by a man named Vincenzo Peruggia. He waited in the exhibit room until he was alone with the painting then he quickly removed it from the wall and walked out with it under his smock. In 1990, two men wearing fake moustaches and police uniforms walked into the Isabella Stewart Gardner Museum in Boston during the early hours claiming they were responding to a disturbance. They left with over three hundred million dollars worth of paintings, including works by Vermeer, Rembrandt, and Manet. They are still missing.

"The only hitch was the set of hidden cameras. The way I see it any other pawn wouldn't have even known about them in the first place, and I would have been screwed. Anyway, once it became apparent he was the number-one candidate for the heist, I approached him, offered him a boatload of cash, and asylum in any paradise he desired. Voilà."

"So Hart recognized the sketch of the dead guy all over the news as his friend, the one he had the note delivered to," I said, mentally organizing all the facts aloud. "That's when you realized your plan had, again, hit a snag."

"I knew you were the right man to help me get into real estate."

"You've been had, Andreu. Everything your mother told you was a complete lie. The missing Fabergé eggs are all she's ever cared about. She's using you to get them."

"You're desperate, Jonah."

Andreu's vision of the truth was terminally veiled. Galina had made sure of it.

I reached into my suit jacket and pulled out a folded piece of paper. I started to open it.

"Two thousand three. The year Galina sent the fifth and final piece of art to Stan. I know because, as usual, she authenticated it in the bottom right-hand corner."

His smirk disappeared. I started to read.

"I must stay true to my own. Cement my legacy. At all costs."

I looked up.

"I'll use our A."

Andreu's eyes were ablaze. The corner of his lip was quivering.

"A is how she refers to you. For me, obviously, she uses—"

"It's bullshit. You're trying to fuck with me."

"A small oil painting in my father's closet says I'm not."

I tossed the piece of paper on the floor between us. He stared at it. Then he looked back at me.

"Galina pushed too hard, Andreu. She knew Derbyshev had the other six. Once she found out *Danish Jubilee Egg* was moving to the Capital she realized the complete collection she'd spent much of her life going after was about to escape her. She panicked. That's why my father had started writing me before he was killed. He may have been a prick, but he was a smart prick. He knew she was about to ruin all of us."

"Bullshit!"

"She was desperate, Andreu. She couldn't let the final piece to her puzzle be moved. She must have asked my father to return *Danish Jubilee Egg*, as she had, I imagine, many times in the past, to where it belongs —"

I thought about 1980's zebra drawing. *Return to Homeland?* She had tried getting the treasure into her possession from the first moment she could, which meant it was my father who was steadfast in his decision to keep it in the States.

"In Russia. My father said no. That's when she threatened she'd even use you."

"Your ... Stan? Impossible. That's impossible!"

"He was the anonymous buyer in 1979. He bid on it for Galina. First she used Alexander, then Stan, now you. She used you all to get the eggs she needs to stay true to 'her own.' Whatever that means."

Andreu shook his head.

"You're just trying to rattle me."

"I'm trying to get to the truth, Andreu. I'm trying to fit the pieces —"

"No!"

His eyes began to well up. His whole body began trembling. That was the moment I realized, whether Andreu knew it or not, he no longer believed I was fucking with him. He was hoping that I was fucking with him.

"Our A."

Our Andreu.

"Holy shit," I slowly pushed out. "You didn't know."

"This isn't working for you, Jonah. I'm way ahead of you and this was the best you could come up with."

"Stan was your father, Andreu. When Galina and Alexander —"

"Enough!"

Andreu pulled out a gun and pointed it at me.

"No more, Jonah!"

"I'm sorry to be the one to tell you, Andreu, but it doesn't have to be like this."

"I mean it, Jonah! Another word gets you killed!"

Andreu was coming undone. I could see the flying thoughts behind his fixed eyes and knew, all too well, an inadvertent squeeze of the trigger wasn't out of the question. I said nothing.

"I should end you for implying such a thing."

A tear fell from his eye. Gun still extended, Andreu dropped his head into his free hand.

Scared for my life I jumped forward. I grabbed the outstretched gun with both my hands and tried to pry it from him. He shook it loose and cracked me across the jaw with the gun's butt. Absorbing the blow I fell to my right, catching myself with my hands. Blood began rushing to, then through, the wound. I saw one of my teeth on the black rug of the car. My tongue was mostly numb but I used it anyway to search for the gap.

I got on my knees. Andreu's eyes were full of surprise, both at what he had done and how quickly I pushed myself through it. My mouth filled with blood again. I sprayed it in his face and jumped back in my seat.

He dragged his sleeve across his eyes. Baffled, infuriated, he lunged at me. I kicked him in the chest forcing him back on his ass. He propped himself on the edge of his seat and drew the gun again. His fingers shifted as he searched for the perfect grip.

"I knew it all along. Nothing but a desperate ploy. Where's the egg?"

"Put the gun away, Andreu. Don't make another mistake."

"Where's the egg?" he repeated.

"You kill me, you'll never know."

He pounced like a bengal. His knee in my chest, he pinned me to the seat. He stuck the gun dead-center in my forehead.

"I think you've forgotten who's running this deal."

I didn't respond, just swallowed.

"You keep playing with me, Jonah, I'll blow your head off. This is the last time I'll say it. I want that fucking egg."

He was desperate. So was I.

"Now!"

I slowly raised my right arm, parking it idly in midair.

"Keys—" I wheezed. "I can't get to them with you on top of me."

Andreu, using his knee and gun, drove me one last time into the cushion. Then he backed off, retaking his seat.

I sat back up. I pulled out my keys and held them up.

"It's in my father's townhouse," I lied.

Figuring the rotating cop out front would buy me some time I opened the key ring, pulled two silver keys off and chucked them at him, missing. He never moved. He let them hit the leather back of the seat and fall to the bench. I closed my key ring and put it back in my pocket.

Andreu barked orders to the driver. We changed course. Soon we turned onto my father's street.

No cop.

When the car pulled up to the townhouse, Andreu stepped out. My stomach went with him. I didn't exit right away. His face reappeared in the doorway to urge me.

There was a crack in the window of opportunity.

I jacked Andreu Zhamovsky in the face with my foot. He fell backward. I pulled the door shut, locked it, and pulled the gun from my briefcase. Andreu quickly regrouped. I could hear him tugging at the door handle. I pushed my upper torso through the divider and put my gun to the driver's temple.

"Move."

The driver froze.

"Now!"

A gunshot came screaming through the rear passenger window, shattering it. The driver put the pedal to the floor. Using my free hand, I braced myself grabbing the divider's frame. After a few seconds of keeping my head low I swung it around. Out the rear window I could see Andreu Zhamovsky standing alone.

CHAPTER 50

I walked briskly into my apartment building, never breaking stride as I went straight for the elevator.

"No one rings up for me, Damon."

Damon is doorman Parker's first name.

"No one! If anyone asks, I'm not in the building."

"Of course," he replied.

He grabbed some dry cleaning and came running up behind me.

"This was just delivered a few minutes ago. Let me bring it upstairs for you."

"Don't worry about it for now, Damon. I'm —"

"Please," he cut me off, stepping in the elevator behind me. "Not a problem."

The New York City doorman. I'd be lying if I said I didn't miss it. The service, the attention, the extra set of hands. It's one of those things you don't realize how much you'd miss until it's gone.

Once moving, Damon noticed the blood coming from my mouth.

"You all right?" he asked, concerned. "Anything I can do?"

"I got into it with some guy over a cab. Looks worse than it is."

"Only in this city. Only in this ridiculous city."

I wasn't in the mood for small talk. I looked at the elevator buttons. My mind was barreling ahead full throttle.

My cell rang. I looked at the caller ID. It was Detective

Morante. He had called earlier when I was at L's, but I had ignored it. To keep ducking him was not to my advantage. I also figured it couldn't hurt to get a jump start on why he was looking for me, as opposed to being surprised again.

Out of the corner of my eye I could see Damon looking at me. He was curious why I was just staring at the little screen while the phone continued to whine.

"Jonah Gray," I answered.

"Detective Morante. How are you today, Jonah?"

"I've been better, detective."

"I tried you earlier."

"I've been busy."

"I was surprised not to see you this morning."

"Detective, I'm in a hurry. What is it that I can do for you?"

"You're at the Chrysler Center. Right?"

"Actually I'm at my apartment building."

"Better, even closer."

"Closer to what?"

"I'm going to swing by for a few minutes. I just have a couple of questions."

"About?"

"Your father's basement. The tool chest, the weight set. I hate to bother you again with this nonsense, but I'm just looking to cross all the 'T's.' Standard procedure."

The missing items from the basement finally made sense. Mattheau must have used the tools for God knows what, and the weights, unsuccessfully, to hold the body below the water's surface. Fuck, I thought. He knew. There was no way he could know exactly what had gone on, but he knew. He knew — something. Because he was on the inside, dealing with an aggressive homicide, it was a no-brainer. He wanted the scoop on the body found in the river. When he got it, the tools, the weights of the same brand missing from my set, the connection became apparent.

"You know, I hate to do this to you detective, but —"

"It will only take a minute, Jonah. I promise."

"I'm on my way out."

"Just wait there for five minutes. You're breaking up, so I'm going to lose you —"

He was lying. He was as clear as when I had first picked up. Nonetheless, he was gone.

The elevator reached the penthouse and we got out. I opened my door and walked inside, heading for the kitchen. Neo was next door playing with his friends. Damon walked in behind me.

"I'm just going to put these over here."

As I placed my briefcase on the kitchen counter, I realized something. This was the part where I usually went back to the door, grabbed my steamed, pressed hanging clothes and handed Damon a tip. He had never before entered my apartment.

I heard a feathery crash. I turned around. My clothes were on the floor in a plastic covered ball. Damon, average, unassuming, was pointing a gun at me.

"Fuck," I exhaled. "Does everyone walk around with a fucking gun?"

"Sorry, Jonah. I just need you to sit tight."

"Damon, what the hell are you doing?"

"It's nothing personal. Some guy just —"

Damon paused then changed directions.

"I don't have the same choices as someone like you. It's a different city out there once I leave this nice building."

"It is for me too, Damon. It is for me too."

It was the perfect, profoundly empty line to soften his guard. His eyes even glazed over with shame as if I had slapped him across the face. Composed, seemingly trusting, I casually moved toward my briefcase.

"I have something I want to show you," I started. "It's something a good friend of mine once —"

I could feel the doorman's concentrating eyes on my briefcase. Before he had even a second to react, I was coming right back at him with a gun of my own. His expression was my answer. He knew I was far more prepared to use it than he was to use his.

"Let me guess. The 'some guy' you refer to was a six foot tall piece of well-dressed Russian shit. How much did he offer you?"

"Jonah, I — this whole —"

"You disappoint me, Damon. You, Clarence, Cal — you three are one area of my life that has never come with any bullshit. Everything between us has always been simple. It's been easy."

"I'm not exactly the guy you see downstairs everyday kissing your ass, collecting your shit. How could I be to do this job?"

"How did it happen?"

"The guy showed up here looking for you a couple hours ago. Told me the last thing he wanted was for you to get hurt, which was exactly what was going to happen if he didn't get to talk to you. Then he offered me cash to keep you here if you showed up. And this gun —"

"How much did he offer you?"

"He said I'd be helping you."

"How much?"

"More money than I could ever hope —"

I cut him off.

"You make me sad, Damon. Not only are you a greedy fuck, but you're an idiot. He doesn't want me here to talk. He wants me here so he can kill me."

He didn't answer me.

"You're involved in more than you bargained for. Just let it go before either of us gets hurt."

Gun still drawn, I grabbed my briefcase and started for the door. He took a step to his left, directly into my would-be path. His gun was still outstretched as well.

"I'm sorry. I can't."

I couldn't hold it in. Against my will I found myself starting to boil. Looking back now I understand why. It was at this moment my new reality had gotten to a point I had feared. The point where I wasn't even safe anymore in my own home.

"You ungrateful little bastard. How fucking generous have I been? How respectful of you, of what you do for a living everyday?"

"Jonah, if you just wait and talk —"

"And this is the thanks I get? You come into my own home and fuck with me? My own home?"

I looked him up and down in disgust.

"You pathetic fucking ingrate."

"Just listen to —"

"Listen? Damon, I don't think you get it! I have to leave. I'm not waiting for or listening to anyone. The only way you're going to keep me here is by killing me."

Damon, perplexed, was out of his depths. I wanted to pity him, but I couldn't. He had entered my home, my sanctuary, my safest haven. And blinded by greed he had threatened my life.

"I could just double your current offer in order to not hurt you." I thought out loud.

His face glimmered with hope. His mouth hung open. His gun started to droop. He realized he had made a terrible mistake. I was about to offer him a way out plus a bonus for being such an asshole.

Fuck that.

"But fuck that. You coming in here like this, with simply no regard for my life, my territory, it's unacceptable. In fact it's up there with the most anyone has ever disrespected me. Trust me — with what's happened in my life over the last couple of weeks that's saying a lot."

The lobby intercom/buzzer rang. Someone was calling upstairs. I was puzzled.

"If you're up here —" I said.

"Probably Gabriel," Damon replied.

Gabriel was one of the maintenance guys. He often covered the lobby if he noticed the doorman was away from his station, most likely assisting a tenant.

"Answer it," I said to Damon, waving him over to the intercom with my gun.

He did as I said. Then he hit a button and spoke.

Touching the intercom buttons activated a small, extremely high-resolution screen, which turned on. It was of the concierge desk area.

"Yes, Gabriel?"

"I have someone here to see Jonah."

I shuffled to my left in order to see the screen. Gabriel was standing with Andreu Zhamovsky.

"Is he in?"

Damon and I were in a stare down.

"Don't do it!" I whispered sharply.

Damon was hesitant.

"Damon? Is Jonah in?"

"I need to walk out of here," I continued, my voice low.

Damon thought for another second before pushing the button.

"He's in, Gabriel. Send his guest up."

Before he was finished I had grabbed my briefcase and headed out through the other side of the kitchen, into the dining room. I walked straight through the dining area and into the living room to my left. Having come around, almost in a circle, I could see Damon again. He had stepped out of the kitchen back into the foyer. He was guarding the door.

His gun was still drawn. I came through the living room and made a right turn down the hallway, walking away from him.

"You're killing me, Damon! You have no idea what you're doing to me!"

"I'm sorry to do this, Jonah," he called to me, his voice fading as I moved further away. "He just wants to talk to you —"

In a near run, I blew into my bedroom, into my closet, and grabbed a small, nimble Polo gym bag. I grabbed a couple of suits, ties, underwear, and socks and stuffed them in. I zipped it up, threw the strap over my shoulder, grabbed my briefcase, and headed back toward the front door.

"I'll ask one last time." I said as I came storming around the corner, gun drawn.

I wasn't kidding. Every second had become crucial. Andreu Zhamovsky was on his way upstairs. Detective Morante was probably around the corner.

"You going to let me walk out of my own home?"

Damon was startled by my return. He perked up, gun still out. I was coming at him, at the door, full speed.

"I...uh..."

I was done dicking around with my doorman. I had given him his chance and he blew it. I was simply out of time. I moved the point of the gun slightly left and fired, hitting the wall no more than six inches from his face. He jumped, gasped. He looked at the bullet hole then turned back to me. I was still coming, gun poised.

"The next one doesn't miss."

CHAPTER 51

Damon threw his gun down and stepped aside. My front door slammed behind me. I hadn't yet taken two steps before I could see an elevator opening. Just as I got a glimpse of Andreu, and he of me, I ducked into the stairwell. Briefcase in hand, gym bag slung over my shoulder, I bounded down the stairs—three, four, five at a time—like I was in a video game. I was listening for the stairwell door to open again, and was surprised when it didn't.

I kept going as if Andreu was right on my heels. I reached the basement and ran through the door leading to the garage. When I reached my car I dropped the briefcase and gym bag and peeled back the gray tarp. I wrestled the canvas sheet into the backseat and threw both bags into the passenger seat. Then I fired her up.

Once at street level, I inched up to the curb. The garage exited on the side street as opposed to Park, which was a good thing since the building's main entrance was on the avenue. The only problem was that the side street was a one way that flowed west, or back in the direction of the front of the building. I would have gone against the grain but there was a steady, single-file row of oncoming traffic. The light was green. I figured my best bet was to fly through the intersection and make a left on Park, heading downtown. I jumped into line. But just as I did, and was almost at the intersection, the light turned yellow then red. I was the second car back. To my right

I could see around the corner toward the area in front of my building. I could see Andreu out front looking for me, no more than a hundred feet away.

My eyes bounced back and forth between the traffic light and Andreu. For the fifth time I looked at the hanging red circle. Then I looked again at the slippery Russian, who was now looking at me dead-on. Our eyes locked. He started in the direction of the car. As he walked toward the Porsche, a greasy smile dripped onto his face. He pulled out his gun and kept coming. At about fifty feet he fired his first shot.

People walking on the sidewalks scattered immediately. Some hit the ground while others jumped into the first building they could. The light was still red, which by this point it seemed to have been for twenty minutes. Still slumped down I looked to my right over the top of the passenger door. Andreu was still coming. He was getting closer. As he did, realizing he needed me alive, he lowered his gun and fired for a second time. The bullet bored into the side of the car letting out a sharp ping. Andreu was aiming for my tires.

The light became irrelevant. I could swing around the Lincoln Town Car in front of me to either the right or left. I had two options. To go left meant squeezing between the boat with wheels and the BMW parallel parked next to it. To go right, even though there were no cars parked, left me exposed and kept him with a clear shot.

I slammed the car into gear. Tires spinning, screeching, I tore left. The amount of space was less than I thought. I scraped both cars as I blasted through, filling the street with the loud, piercing sound of metal sliding unwillingly against more metal. The Beamer's alarm went off. Once through, without hesitation, I barreled into the intersection with no safeguard other than my horn. Cars swerved, slammed on their brakes as I darted through. Still slouched, but driving aggressively, I went to make the left turn down Park. When I did I heard a third shot fired, then a fourth. Both hit the back of the car, neither finding the tires. About three blocks down I finally lifted myself up. With a final glance at the rearview mirror I took in a huge gulp of wind. As I did, I saw the unmarked SUV of one Detective Morante charging up the other side of Park Avenue. He never saw me.

"Tell me —"

It was a little after seven. I was on a pay phone downtown speaking with L.

"Fucked up girl, man. Her mother getting killed completely washed her out. Her grades went plummeting and she went wild with drugs and alcohol. She became a total burnout and basically disappeared for a while. Probably some kind of rehab or institution. Anyway, she came from the wrong side of the Hampton tracks. She was a local who didn't grow up with much. So once she resurfaced she was all about the high-rolling guys. Crashed a few parties, broke up a couple marriages, even got in trouble with the law…"

"How the fuck do you know all of this?"

"Played a little NYPD detective today, that's how."

"No, seriously."

"I am being serious," he responded, proud. "I called the East Hampton police station and pretended to be NYPD. Detective Robert Barone. I'll probably get in mad trouble for this shit."

"Detective —"

"Robert Barone." he repeated.

Ray's brother on *Everybody Loves Raymond*.

"I forgot to plan a name. It was the best I could come up with on short notice."

I smiled. Nothing like a real friend.

CHAPTER 52

I stepped off the Tribeca sidewalk and into Acappella at eight ten P.M. I nodded hello to the Mediterranean coat-check girl, wishing for a moment I could have responded to the twinkle in her eye, then walked past the bar that sat just beyond the entryway. Tony, one of the owner's sons, greeted me with the same enthusiasm he always did. As he spoke, I surveyed the dining room. My three partners were seated at a table for four at the far end.

As I made my way toward them I couldn't help noticing the alluring restaurant was buzzing just right. The crowd was eclectic. There were Wall Street suits and there were couples looking to have a romantic evening. The tables were full of people and dialogue. A small ocean of voices was rolling along not too loud for four colleagues to have a private conversation.

As I wove through the tables, robust scents of Northern Italian fare from the finest ingredients filled my nose. Aromas of different meats and sauces laced with flavorful spices danced in midair. As my feet continued to guide me toward my fate, I was surprised at myself for noticing such simple pleasures.

"Jonah, what's the deal?" Jake asked as I approached.

Finally, able to see my banged up face and unkempt hair, all three started to get out of their chairs.

"Christ, Jonah!" Perry quipped. "What happened? Who did this to you?"

I calmly motioned for them to sit back down.

"I'm fine."

"Tell me, Jonah," Jake said sternly. "I'm serious. I don't care who it is. I'll deal with them."

"Seriously, killer, I'm fine. It's just a split lip. Looks much worse than it feels."

A black-tied waiter pulled out my chair. I thanked him, put my briefcase down, unbuttoned my jacket, and took my seat. My partners sat back down with me. The same waiter then placed my napkin in my lap. He offered me a drink, which I declined, and left us.

"Why are we here?" continued Perry. "And why couldn't we know the others would be?"

"We're concerned, Jonah," Tommy said. "We appreciate that you're dealing with a lot of pain, but we can't function properly as a team—more important, we can't help you as your friends — if we're not all on the same page. Now we've given you respect and loyalty. We deserve the same in return."

I didn't know where to start. I remained silent.

"Well?" Perry went on, throwing her hands in the air.

I took a sip of ice water.

"I love you guys," I started, "I consider you family. You need to remember that above all that I'm about to tell you. No matter how this ends up —"

"All of what?" Perry asked.

I looked at my watch. All the time in the world wouldn't have been enough to tell them how sorry I was. As much as I wanted to unburden myself there simply wasn't time. I had to stick to the relevant facts. There was too much at stake for all of us.

"Fuck it," I exhaled. "The Prevkos deal. It's complete bullshit."

No one stirred.

"Excuse me?" Tommy said.

"It was a front."

"Come again?" he went on.

"Every aspect of the deal was a lie. As a company they may have had discussions about entering the world of commercial real estate. This deal, New York City, now, was a façade Andreu created for his own agenda. Everything about this specific deal was, is, complete nonsense."

The three tossed around predictable glances.

"Why?" asked Jake.

"You wouldn't believe me if I told you."

"Shouldn't we be allowed to determine that for ourselves?"

"Let's just say the deal was set up as a platform for moving cash, only not for buildings."

"Then for what?" asked Perry.

"It doesn't matter."

"It might matter to me," she shot back.

Part of me just wanted to tell them each detail step by step. I knew the less they knew about, well, all of it, the less lying they'd eventually have to do. I owed them that.

Suddenly I was famished. Not knowing when my next chance to eat might be, I popped a slice of hard salami, one of the delicious antipasti selections gracing the table, into my mouth.

"Andreu Zhamovsky has decided to use his shareholders' money to play a very dangerous game. One that includes my downfall. That's as much as I'm going to tell you. That's all you need to know."

They processed this for about three seconds.

"What do you mean your downfall?" Perry went on.

"It doesn't matter, Per."

"If it doesn't matter then —"

"I can't!" I snapped at her. "It serves no purpose. Knowing could get you guys fucking —"

My emotions were getting away from me. I couldn't even bring myself to say the word "killed," but from the looks on their faces I didn't need to.

I changed directions.

"I have something for you."

I reached down, opened my briefcase and took out the envelope I had gotten from L. Then I reached in, pulled out three smaller, sealed envelopes and passed them out according to the name written on each.

"What's this?" asked Jake.

"Don't open them. Just put them away and I'll tell you."

They did as I said. I continued.

"Each envelope contains an option. One that each of you needs to take a serious look at."

"What kind of option?"

"You each have a passport in there. And a driver's license, which is from Alaska but it was the best I could do."

"Jonah," Tommy started, "what are we missing here?"

I took a deep breath.

"I can't tell you, Tommy."

I was busting. Since the first day I had worked for Tommy Wingate he had been my mentor. I longed for his guidance. It was too late and I cared too much to seek it now.

"This isn't right, Jonah."

Perry sounded frightened.

"We're scared shitless for you right now."

Her eyes were smoldering. It was killing me.

"I'm telling you to trust me. The less you know the better. I couldn't live with myself if anything happened to you — any of you."

Point taken. I barreled forward.

"Andreu Zhamovsky gave us power of attorney over all affairs concerning his real estate dealings in New York City. Correct?"

"Correct." Jake confirmed out loud for all three.

"What he also gave us was power of attorney over Prevkos's finances as they related to, and only to, his deal in New York. The deal, in fact, he never planned on making. Andreu granted us this authority thinking the only money he had to worry about was the up-front costs to get the deal going: due diligence fees, good faith payments, stuff like that. What he didn't ever take into account was that I was in a prime position to work him over if I ever caught on to him. Which, as I just told you, I did."

"Jonah, what did you do?" Jake asked.

I remained silent.

"You didn't!" Perry whispered.

Still, I didn't answer.

"Jonah?" Tommy and Jake chimed in.

"I had no choice."

"How much?" Jake pushed out, all expression and color having fallen from his face.

I took a sip of my ice water. The next words needed to be unequivocal.

"Nine-hundred and seventy million."

Silence.

"And change."

Perry lifted her head.

"How could you do something like this?"

"It's like I said. I had no choice."

"That's the goddamn best you can do?" Perry scowled.

I dropped a restrained fist on the table. Perry jumped back.

"Andreu Zhamovsky tried to walk all over me. In three weeks he's turned my entire fucking life on its head for things I had nothing to do with."

I reeled in my voice.

"I didn't take the money because it is money. I took it because it is his."

"Did he kill your father?" Perry went on, concern returning to her voice.

"Yes. I mean, he didn't pull the trigger, but, yes."

"Meaning what?"

"I can't get into that."

"Why was he —"

"I don't have the time! I wanted to tell you guys what was happening, but I couldn't. Andreu finding out something was up with the deal would have endangered us all."

"Jonah, what are you saying?" asked Jake, taking his voice down to a whisper. "Is Andreu trying to kill you too?"

I didn't respond.

"My God, Jonah," Perry said as if in a trance, "what's happening to you?"

I looked into my glass of ice water.

"I'm leaving the country."

My eyes drifted to Perry's.

"I'm not coming back."

"This is completely ludicrous!" Tommy said.

"Trust me," I went back at him, "it's not."

Perry reached out and grabbed my hand.

"There has to be a way to fix this, Jonah. Let us help you fix all this."

"There's no quick fix, Per. Not this time."

"Why did you bring us the identification?" asked Tommy. "Because we're fucked too?"

"No. I mean — I hope not."

"Can't the cash be traced to you?"

"Theoretically, yes. But how hard that's pursued will ultimately be decided by what matters more to Andreu Zhamovsky. His past or his future. And let's just say I have a feeling I know which one he's going to choose."

"Then why? Why the identification?"

"Because I can't be one hundred percent sure you're not in danger. Besides, I wanted to give you guys something. I wanted to make it up to you."

"With fake federal documents?" quipped Perry, bemused. "Quite a gesture —"

"It's not fake anything," I said. "It's all United States Government authentic, and it's more than just paper. It's an option, a second chance should you need one. Or it's a door to a whole new life if you choose for it to be."

"Meaning?"

"Meaning I had Carolyn fill out Swiss Nation Partners Bank savings account applications that she overnighted from the post office, with no return address, to a long-time attorney friend of my father's and mine in Geneva. Secure savings accounts within the borders of Switzerland need to be opened by a well-respected attorney if the institution isn't familiar with the new client. It's almost like a vouching thing. Anyway, in no more than forty-eight hours each of you will have a Swiss account worth millions in the name of the person on the identification in your envelope."

"Christ Jonah!" Perry snapped in a whispery scream. "Stolen cash!"

"The cash isn't stolen," I calmly explained.

"Of course it is. You just said—"

"I know what I just said, Perry. I also had Carolyn open a Swiss savings account for Andreu Zhamovsky. I was able to supply my attorney over there with all of his vital information from the papers he gave to us. Don't worry, his firm's stolen cash, to the penny, will eventually be waiting patiently in the perfect embezzlement account with his name on it. Which should make for one interesting explanation."

"That doesn't make sense, Jonah. Then what—"

I put my hand up and cut her off.

"The cash is from me. A one hundred and fifty million dollar life insurance policy left by my father. I'm the sole beneficiary, and I'm sharing it equally with you guys. Thirty-seven and a half million each. This way, if you are forced to take off, you can do so quickly knowing money will never be an issue. You three have worked harder than anyone I've ever met for what you have. I threatened to fuck it all up. For that I'm so sorry."

A dish dropped in the kitchen. I was up before it settled.

"This is outrageous," sighed Jake.

I shook off a few questioning eyes and returned to my seat.

"The money's completely legit," I powered forward. "Swiss law prohibits the financial institution we, under false identities, will be banking with to divulge confidential client information without severe consequences. It's simply against the law over there. Besides, the money will have come from me, its rightful beneficiary."

I looked at the time. Sitting still like this, out in the open, was gut twisting.

"Jonah, you can't just do this. You can't just leave."

A nervous tear was forming in Perry's eye. I leaned over and took her hand.

"I have to go. I have to go right fucking now. I don't know if I'm saying to you leave tonight and run with your son forever or if I'm saying know this money is there for when you need it. Just be as strong as I know you can be. You owe that to yourself. To your son."

"Jonah, you know it doesn't just work like that."

"Maybe so, Per. Maybe so. But not because it can't."

My heart, which had been tearing all day, was finally about to break in two. I stood. The time had come. A quarter came sliding across the table toward me.

"You never know. One of these babies saved my ass." Jake said.

I smiled, snatched the tiny silver disk and tucked it away. Then I nodded in appreciation.

"Thanks for letting me into your family."

Outside, not ten feet from the restaurant, my past caught up with me as I turned up Hudson. Perry came running up behind me.

"Jonah!"

I turned around. Her feet stopped just before she reached me. She started to speak but couldn't. Finally she leaned forward and kissed me. Not like partners. In a way I had only previously dreamed of.

"I'm scared of never seeing you again."

"I'm scared too, Per. I'm so fucking scared."

She moved in close, putting her cheek against my chest.

"I'm sorry we never —"

She put her arms around me. I squeezed her back.

"I know, Per."

CHAPTER 53

At 5:50 A.M. the following morning, I was sitting on the twenty-eighth floor of a high-rent property on the East Side. I was alone and sitting on a couch. There were no lights on. It was somewhere between night and dawn. The sun had barely begun to supply enough light to help my eyes. The day hadn't yet changed from black-and-white to color.

I had only gotten a few shoddy hours of sleep in the cockpit of my tarp-covered roadster that was parked in a Tribeca garage. It didn't matter. My senses were geared-up, organized. The couch underneath me was soft Italian leather, the artwork was straight out of Chelsea's most important galleries, and the technology was state-of-the-art. As I sat there, thick, almost sticky smoke swirled all around, above me. The hard-hitting aroma in the room left a pleasant burn as it entered my nose. I could barely hear the city down below, though every couple of minutes I'd hear one of those large, metal sheets they use to temporarily fix streets go bouncing around from a truck.

At 5:55 A.M. Lloyd Murdoch entered his office through the doorway to my left. He never saw me. He went walking right past me toward his desk. For a few seconds I was just a fly on a shadowy wall, until he stopped and took a sniff of the spicy air. He slowly turned around and for a few seconds said nothing, then:

"What the fuck do you think you're doing?"

The fractures in my soul were slowly, surely, becoming complete breaks. I said nothing. On the ground, to the left of my feet, was my briefcase and gym bag. On the ground to my right was Neo who had arrived in Tribeca late the previous night via Crazy Animal Lady. He was sleeping in his bag, which was turned backward. I didn't want him traumatized by what was about to happen. I was dressed in a wrinkled Blue Canali suit, freshly unballed white herringbone shirt, and thick, gold, creased silk Brioni necktie that I made extra sure that morning had the perfect Windsor knot.

"You had to taunt me. Killing him wasn't enough."

"How did you get in here?"

"Did watching his head explode make you feel like a big man?"

Murdoch was old school. Hunting me would have been too simple, would have let me off too easy. That's why, like some gangster thug stuck in the fifties, he decided to come after me in a way that hurt more than any physical pain. By sending the ultimate message; by coming after my own.

Murdoch took a step toward me. I immediately rose to my feet, my arms hanging at my sides. In my left hand was the burning Monte Cristo #2. In my right hand was my gun. His eyes found it. He stopped no more than fifteen feet away.

I raised the cigar to my mouth and took a nice, long pull. I opened my mouth and let the smoke fester in its entryway before blowing it in a cloud. Then I waived him toward his desk with my gun.

"Why don't you have a seat."

"Jonah—"

My eyes focused. My arm straightened, stiffened as I pointed the gun dead between his eyes. He froze, unable to either speak or move. For a few seconds I simply lectured, berated him with my eyes. Then I dropped the gun and emptied a round into his thigh.

Following a delayed, primal scream he dropped in a heap. I walked over to him, stood over him then spit on him as he clasped his hands over his leg. Black liquid soaked through his pants and began to seep around his fingers. I kneeled down on one leg. I took a generous drag of the cigar and blew the smoke out evenly, watching as it thinned and eventually evaporated into the air.

"There's nothing like a Monte Cristo #2," I said.

I put it out on his cheek. His seared skin crackled, sizzled. The sound that poured from his lungs this time was still coming from the animal within, although this time it was different, more revealing. Now he wasn't just screaming from the pain. He was screaming because he feared for his life.

"Did you really think I'd let some washed-up old fool crap all over me and my family?"

I put the gun to his head as I placed the extinguished stogie in my pants' pocket, as not to leave behind any evidence of my presence. As if it even mattered anymore.

"Stand up," I said.

"Jonah, Please —"

I cracked his nose with the butt of the gun. His head bucked back. Blood streamed down as if a faucet had been turned on. It was running down, around, and into his mouth. I grabbed the back of his head with my left hand and pulled it back. Towering over him I put my eyes five inches from his. His breaths were creating tiny blood bubbles under his nostrils. I pointed the gun at, and pressed the tip against, his crotch.

"Stand up now and sit behind your desk or you get the most extreme of all makeovers."

Murdoch, whimpering and approaching hyperventilation, managed to begin standing. Soon, probably even surprising himself more than me, he had made it. I sat in one of the chairs in front of his desk, facing him. I started to play with the gun.

"Business is business, Lloyd," I started, "by the time I leave here in a few minutes you're going to be dead."

"Please, Jonah. It's not what you think —"

Murdoch was groaning, gasping between words.

"What I think?" I said, laughing. "I'll tell you what I think. I think the ash embedded in your face is the same as the fresh ash found in the street in front of my father's house the morning he was killed. That's what I think."

"Jonah — fuck! Look —"

"I have always respected the older generation of this business. You know why?"

He screamed as he grappled at his thigh.

"Because I thought you guys were always willing to fight like men, no matter if that meant winning or losing."

"Who the fuck do you think you are?" he fired back, digging deep and finding some fight left yet. "Those are my buildings, Jonah. My buildings. You arrogant prick! You don't just —"

"You know what a mortar and pestle is?" I asked.

"What?" he replied in disbelief.

"A mortar and pestle. You familiar?"

"Yes . . . ahhhhhh . . ."

"Imagine taking a mortar and pestle and putting big kernels of peppercorn inside. Big, fat kernels. Now imagine grinding that peppercorn and grinding that peppercorn, as it becomes finer and finer. Imagine the gritty, scraping sound as you grind that peppercorn. Can you do that?"

"Jonah, let's talk about all of this. I know you're angry. But you have —"

"I'm those kernels of peppercorn. What you did to me, how you disrespected me, that's just one knuckle on the hand grinding me. And do you know what's left? Do you know where that leaves me?"

"Jonah this is fucking crazy!" Murdoch said, freaked and torn between my words and his injuries.

"I'm powder, you fucking has-been," I growled, my voice strengthening. "I'm powder and I'm at the point of being poured out of that little clay cup because there's nothing left to grind."

Murdoch didn't talk. His frightened eyes were speaking for him.

"You see, once I let the cops know you ordered and witnessed the hit on my father, they put a needle in your arm. So I figured, why not keep that pleasure for myself. Either way you're six feet under. Justice. Wouldn't you say?"

Nothing.

I stood up and stormed around the back of his desk.

"I can't hear you," I snarled.

The adrenaline running through me was off the charts. I remember squeezing the gun so hard my fingers were going numb. My brain felt like it was literally pulsating, flexing within my skull.

"No Jonah," he pleaded as his hands went up. "Please — don't —"

I grabbed the back of his head with my left hand and jammed the barrel of the gun into his mouth with my right. The cold, solid steel blasting through his teeth created a crunch. His eyes lit up like headlights as a forceful, although primarily inaudible, scream reverberated internally through his body so hard he vibrated. Tears filled with both salt and terror began to well up in his eyes.

"For everyone you know, you're about to become nothing more than a frozen memory," I explained. "They will all remember the last time they saw you. They'll remember where you were, what you wore, maybe what you ate or said. They'll have a snapshot of that very last memory stamped on their brain."

The bottom half of Murdoch's face was a dark, oozing mess. He was crushed, submissive. His lips quivered as he begged silently.

"Most likely they'll think of you and see something pleasant. Me — my frozen memory of my father is him lying on a gurney with his head blown apart."

In the few minutes I had been there the sun had risen a bit. Colors were still muted but the office was slightly brighter. At that moment I saw a tear fall from his eye and run down a tiny stretch of skin before mixing with the blood.

"You better hope I don't end up in hell. If I do, I'm going to kill you all over again."

I took my left hand away from the back of his head.

"And when that happens you'll be thinking the exact same thing you are right now. Jonah Gray was the last person you should have ever fucked with."

I began to squeeze the trigger, only just as I did I smelled urine.

I looked down toward his groin. A dark stain, like that of the blood after I shot his leg, was growing down the inside of his undisturbed leg. I looked back at his face. My hand began to tremble.

Yes, this man deserved to die, I thought. And yes, I had killed once before myself. But that was different. That was accidental.

Wasn't it?

Or because Pangaea-Man and I both knew too much, like Murdoch did, would I have killed the bad lieutenant anyway?

Distinction between the real and the absurd was becoming increasingly difficult. I moved my eyes to the gun crammed into his mouth. Then, as I regripped the pistol, I focused my vision strictly on my hand, like I was trying to make sure the situation was really happening. Which, I accepted immediately, it was.

The room was silent. Time passed slowly now. I looked back at Murdoch.

He wasn't there.

My father was.

His silhouette. His presence.

I shivered.

I blinked.

There were Murdoch's eyes again. They were doing more than just quietly begging. With them he was telling me that it simply couldn't end like this. Not for me, anyway. To squeeze that trigger, here and now, meant in life's most basic terms that I had become the same kind of animal that he was.

Or my father was.

And at only half their age.

"Fuck!"

I wanted to shoot. But couldn't.

"Fuck!" I screamed, dropping my arms to my sides. Murdoch sat, broken.

I tore back around the desk. I tucked the pistol away, grabbed my bags, and bolted into the oncoming morning.

Twenty minutes later, underneath the barely risen sun, I jumped out of a cab down the street from the U.S. Mission to the United Nations. I told the driver to keep the meter running. Under my arm I held a FedEx box I had never touched, one with no account number on the air bill. Careful not to leave fingerprints it was sticking out from the middle of the neatly folded suit jacket.

"Want to make a couple bucks?" I asked a kid walking by in a collared, short-sleeved Starbucks shirt.

He looked around confused. I flashed him three fresh hundred-dollar bills.

"See the package under my arm?"

He nodded. I looked down the street.

"See the building down there? The one with the security guards out front?"

"Yeah."

I looked back at the kid.

"All you have to do is walk this package over to those security guards and tell them you found it on the sidewalk in front of the building. That's it."

He thought for a second.

"What's in the package?"

"Nothing dangerous and something they'll be very happy to see."

He looked at the cash in my hand then turned his attention back down the street.

"All I have to do is hand it to one of those guards?"

I watched from behind as he headed down the street. The unexpected sensation from dishing the package was a welcome one. It was exactly what I needed to start my new life. *Danish Jubilee Egg* embodied everything that had happened since even before she had been stolen. All of the hatred, the lies, the conspiracy, the murder, the hurt, the loss, and the history. But now she also encompassed something else.

Me.

I was, and am, still standing.

If anything could ever be a true, personal tribute to that, it was

Danish Jubilee Egg making her way back to her comfortable, rightful nest in the U.S. Mission. I had to ensure her safe return. I owed Andreu Zhamovsky that dagger-through-the-heart moment of seeing on the news that I had bested him in a way he wouldn't soon forget.

The kid approached the building. He caught the eye of one of the security guards. The two started conversing. I jumped back in the cab and took off.

CHAPTER 54

I got out of the cab in front of Newark Liberty International Airport, embarking on my new life. I held Neo's bag in my left hand. My briefcase, stripped of all incriminating documents and objects, was in my right. Because I had purchased my airline ticket the previous day in person at a travel agency, and paid in cash as Roy Gordon, in my mind I was already a ghost. By this point I was already doing as much to forget my real information as I was to remember the new. I even checked the gym bag with one of the skycaps.

My pace was controlled, deliberate as I moved through the terminal. Scattered cops, as usual, were walking about, keeping order with their mere presence. I made sure to avoid eye contact with any of them. Every chance I had, whether I walked by a Hudson News or caught a glimpse of CNN, I looked for anything in the media as it pertained to me. So far so good. The *Danish Jubilee Egg* situation was under control. Robie/Hart was still the prime suspect and he remained nowhere to be found. Pangaea-Man's grisly fate was still a mystery.

My nerves tightened as I hit each security checkpoint. I know, most of these employees are unquestionably more suited to be working at McDonald's than they are to be protecting national security, but this is still post-9/11 America. On that morning, I was by no means any ordinary traveler.

I went through all of the usual motions. I took my ThinkPad

out of my briefcase, placed it in its own gray plastic basket then put both on the conveyer belt. Next I did the same with the Audemars from my mother, my cell phone, and my shoes. I placed them together in one basket and sent them through.

As I watched my belongings start to move along the conveyer belt, my vision was suddenly drawn to one of the plasma screens hanging from the ceiling. A young, blond girl was reporting from the Upper East Side. The volume was sort of low and no one was really paying attention to it. All of the security officers were talking among themselves about their previous evenings and such. As for the passengers, they were all complaining about one of two things, either how slow the line was moving or how tired they were.

I was sure that I was familiar with the reporter. Something about her or maybe her backdrop, what was going on around her, was something I had seen before. It felt like I should know, but for some reason it wasn't coming together. Was it her eyes? Maybe her hair or shirt? Could it possibly be the street corner she was standing on?

Turns out it wasn't the reporter at all. It was the fact that she was standing in front of my apartment building. Just when the inevitable started to unfold, just as I began to silently pledge my firstborn to God if he spared me what could only be coming next, it happened. A picture of me filled the screen.

My thoughts turned right away to my gun. The one I had perfectly dumped off before walking into an airport with it. Silly me, I thought it had the potential to draw unwanted attention if I had gotten caught with it. The irony. Slowly I began to survey those around me. I didn't know what to be most ready for. All I knew for sure at this point was one thing. I had been through and risked too much. I was a warrior now, not because I wanted to be, but because it had been forced on me. I didn't know what scenario to expect. Frankly I didn't care. I was ready.

"Hey! Sir!"

I looked across the conveyer belt. A serious, older white woman in a security uniform was staring at me and moving closer. I squeezed my fist into a wrecking ball, ready to crack her jaw clear across the room. It felt as if it were the calm before the storm, like we were all just seconds from all hell breaking loose.

She started to move her lips again but when she did something unexplainable happened, something soothing. It was almost cathartic. I could literally feel the caution running downward, out of my body and settling in a puddle beneath me. It was almost as if at that exact moment I had finally accepted that I had to let go of who I had always been, and had to embrace who I now hoped to become.

React.

Demonstrate control.

Leave whatever mess necessary for later.

"Can you please move forward?" she asked.

"Excuse me?" I said, masking my uncertainty with bad hearing.

"I said move forward! People are waiting."

She motioned to the line behind me. I started to look at them as my aggression recoiled, but instead pretended to look at the conveyer belt as I really looked up again at the screen. My image was gone. Next story.

I stepped up, in socked feet, to the metal detector and prepared to walk through. Just as I did, I heard:

"Stop!"

"What's the problem?" I asked.

The armed security officer was a six foot-four African-American male with serious gym arms. He put his hand up, further telling me to stay still, and began to approach.

"What's the story?" I asked again.

The last thing I wanted to seem was excited, but every millionth of a second mattered and I knew it.

"I'll tell you what the story is, man," he said, reaching toward me.

I flinched backward. I could feel my brow lowering, my defense mechanisms uniformly shifting into motion.

"Your bag—" he continued.

He was pointing down at Neo's carrying case.

"— it needs to go through the X-ray."

Relieved, my balls dropped down from the back of my throat to their proper resting place.

"It's not just a bag," I said, lifting the carrying case higher. "My dog's in here."

The muscle head leaned in for a look. The two ends of the bag were made of mesh for ventilation so it was easy to see in. Neo was groggy, courtesy of two drops of Benadryl. He was curled up in a little ball leaning against his travel blanket, a cashmere Burberry scarf.

He leaned in closer.

"I'd go easy, man," I said. "He doesn't like being disturbed when he's sleeping. I mean he's little, but once he snaps into Alpha mode forget it."

I was saying this about a Chihuahua who once had to see me eat twenty blueberries before he'd bite into one.

"Proceed at your own risk."

He looked into my eyes, which were so desperate they must have become earnest. He nodded and stepped back. Then he told me to walk through.

At the first newsstand I saw, I stopped in and bought a New York Yankees hat and a *New York Post*. Then I took off my tie, stuffed it in my briefcase, opened my shirt's top button, and threw my suit jacket over my arm carrying Neo's case. The plan was to make one quick stop then head straight to my gate and sit there behind my paper until it was time to leave.

As my feet continued on down the exceptionally wide, retail-laden hallway, I hooked myself up to my cell phone's wireless earpiece and dialed a number.

"I was wondering when I'd hear from you."

Andreu's voice was well constructed but bitter.

"You mean you were wondering if you'd hear from me."

"Your face looks good on the big screen."

"That's the small screen, comrade."

"Where's the money, Jonah?"

I just smiled.

"Jonah, listen to me. When you —"

"It's you who needs to listen, Andreu. Not to your mother, to me."

The sun poured into the long hallway all around me through the floor-to-ceiling windows. Outside I could see shiny airplanes of all colors. An assortment of odd-shaped airport vehicles zipped about in every direction.

"Jonah—"

"I want to hate you, Andreu. I deserve to hate you. Sadly, you're just the pathetic messenger. You don't believe that, go have a look at my father's wall."

"None of that matters right now, Jonah! I need that egg! You holding my shareholders' money hostage won't keep me from coming after it."

"I'm not holding the money hostage, Andreu. You are."

Nothing.

"How are you going to explain that to your shareholders, Mr. Chairman?"

"You have no idea who you're fucking with, Jonah. I need that egg. And I'll do whatever I must to get it."

"Like what? You going to pump a few rounds into me, like the ones that shredded your real father's face?"

"My real father was Alexander Zhamovsky, not some American snake. Stan deserves what he got. Maybe if he hadn't—"

"Fucked some Russian whore?"

"Don't you dare disrespect her!"

"Because when I do, you have to question everything. Isn't that right?"

"I need that egg."

"Well, you can't have it."

Again, silence.

"Our father was *Danish Jubilee Egg's* rightful owner. I'm the sole beneficiary of his will which means even though she'll soon be back on display at the U.S. Mission to the UN, then the U.S. Capital, officially she's mine. Ironically, it also means I'm a pretty serious shareholder myself in Prevkos and all its subsidiaries. Didn't Mommy Dearest tell you any of that?"

"That's impossible."

"What that is, Andreu, is just the beginning. Stan bought *Danish Jubilee Egg* in 1979 after Galina had already got ahold of *Empire Nephrite Egg*. Let me guess — she also forgot to mention she already has that one."

"My mother would never lie to me like that, Jonah."

"The game's over, Andreu. I won. Don't be surprised when Derbyshev doesn't take your calls. We had an interesting talk. He wasn't too happy about the prospect of spending the rest of his days in prison while you ran off with his family's treasures."

I could hear him slam the phone against a hard surface. He put it back to his ear and took a deep breath.

"Jonah, listen to me. We can both come out whole here."

"You took everything from me, Andreu. Everything. I won't forget it."

"I'll find you."

"Sweet dreams to you and Galina. Like I said, the game's over. But my quest for the truth has just begun."

I closed my cell, pulled out the battery and threw the rest of the phone in the next trash can I passed. I spotted the, well, let's just say the equivalent of the Continental Presidents Club but for a different airline. I opened the door and stepped inside.

Two middle-aged women were sitting behind the counter.

"Good morning," said the one with an entire makeup counter on her face. "Are we flying this morning?"

"We are," I said. "But I'm on my way to the gate right now and I just needed to drop something off."

I opened my briefcase and pulled out a FedEx envelope. I handed it to the woman. She went to take it from me. Suddenly I wouldn't let go.

"Sir?"

"You know," I said, "I think I'll just use the restroom for a second."

I snatched the envelope back and started into the elite club.

"Uh, sir?"

I turned back to her.

"Your name and flight number?"

Fuck. I had no problem giving her my name, Roy Gordon, only chances were he probably wasn't a premier member of this airline's exclusive club.

"I'm only going to be a second. I really just need to —"

"I understand that, sir. But unfortunately I can't just let you into the club. If you'll just —"

One of the perks of being a rich man in America, one of the perks I always enjoyed, had just become my pain in the ass. All of the clubs.

"My flight number," I said to myself, pretending I was actually looking for it and not just buying time to grab my wallet. "My flight number —"

And who ever said membership doesn't have its privileges? I pulled out my American Express Centurion Card, covering my name of course, and flashed it. Like I said earlier, the Centurion Card makes the Platinum card look like Sears plastic. People simply don't fuck with it.

"Of course," she said after a quick look at the little black card. "Go right ahead."

The men's room I entered was one of three individual washrooms. I closed the wooden door behind me and locked the perfectly polished door lock. I placed Neo's case as well as my briefcase on the floor. Holding the FedEx envelope I positioned myself in front of the mirror, staring at myself. Then staring, in the reflection, at the envelope.

My eyes dropped. I focused them on the envelope not in the mirror but in my hand, my reality, my control. I pulled the zip tab of the envelope, opened it and looked inside. The sight of what I had originally placed inside inflated a lump in my throat. I could feel all of the right as well as all of the wrong of the last three weeks rushing through my veins from opposite ends, looking, hoping to collide with one another. Head on, like two rams locking horns, each looking to dole out a lesson.

The thin, white cardboard folder, the contents of which embodied so much of what I had become capable of, slid from my grasp onto the floor. I had finally accepted who I was. Now it was time to see if I could accept what I was.

Or if, more importantly, I could reject it and finally find my path.

I slammed my fists on the marble countertop. I shook my head. The energy became so strong it felt like it was about to blast through every nerve ending in my entire body. I lost it. I started to have an all-out brawl with the air. I started punching, looking to absolutely kill someone who wasn't even standing there. Conscious of the fact that I was in a somewhat public place, I knew I couldn't yell. But my mouth was wide opened nonetheless as I forced out this fierce, noiseless scream. I was cursing everyone and everything, only quietly. Little pieces of saliva along with reluctant tears were sprinkling the air all around me. I couldn't stop punching the air. I still don't know exactly who it was I was looking to knock down. Everyone who had dared step in my path, my father or the guy staring back at me in the reflection.

Eventually I stopped both punching and crying. I sat down on the toilet to catch my breath. I grabbed the FedEx envelope and stood back up. I removed the contents and placed the two items from inside on the countertop.

The first was a small, plastic bag containing the MAC lipstick with Krissy's fingerprints all over it. The second was a handwritten note to Detective Morante that read:

> I was dating a girl named Krissy Lockhart. Real nut-job. Her mother died in a car accident in the Hamptons a couple years ago and it scrambled her mind. I tried ending things, but she wouldn't accept it. She knew my father and I were close so she used to threaten that if I didn't give her a second chance she'd kill him. She said "Then I'd get to see what it is she has to go through everyday."
>
> I found this in front of the townhouse the morning my father was murdered and let's just say it's her brand. I know I should have told you right

away and maybe if you hadn't started to question me from the instant we met, I might have. I also know this probably doesn't look good in light of certain recent events that point to me. I promise you two things. Number one, I didn't give you this up front because I know how it looks and I didn't want to further implicate myself in something I had absolutely nothing to do with. Number two, nothing is truly as it seems.

Jonah.

I stood there more ashamed of myself than I had ever been. Yes, the girl was a complete psycho. Yes, I was at the point where I was willing to do whatever it took to get her off my back. But this? At a time when I wasn't ever going to have to worry about seeing her again? Something was wrong with this. It wasn't about Krissy anymore. It was about me. And it sickened me. God knows, the last shit I needed on top of my life over these weeks was the bullshit lunacy that came with Krissy Lockhart. But the truth of the matter is she was a sick girl. A girl who, like me, was willing to do whatever it took to get what she thought she needed. Not the kind of girl who deserved to be investigated for a murder she had no part in.

This was my low point. I was so afraid of having laid so much on the line, and walking away with nothing to show for any of it, that fucking with Angie, the pretty, bubbly girl from the Hamptons, almost became my back-up plan. She became my very own subconscious disgraceful excuse for a contingency plan that would have somehow given me an ounce, a single shred of satisfaction in my suddenly new satisfactionless world.

I ripped up the note and flushed it down the toilet. Then I rinsed the lipstick off under the water to remove all of the fingerprints and threw it, along with the FedEx envelope, in the trash can.

I grabbed Neo's carry-on bag and my briefcase, exited the washroom, and left the club. Hat pulled low, I headed for my gate. Until telling you this story it was the last time I thought of Krissy/Angie, again. At least, that is, while awake.

But I continue to see her in my dreams.

Angie's deceiving beauty.

Krissy's vacant eyes.

Time to board my flight. I handed the attendant my boarding pass. As I headed down the jetway I heard the jumbo jet's engines roar to life. I stepped onto the aircraft, and could literally see the fresh oxygen pouring out of the vents lining the cabin. I turned left toward first class. I was one of the first passengers on board.

"Can I bring you anything?" I heard as I settled in.

I turned to the dark-haired, forty-something woman in the face paint, as I thought, *Absolutely. Double Sapphire. No tonic, no olives.*

Then I gently looked around.

"Nothing for now. Thanks."

First class never filled up, so Neo's case was strapped into the window seat next to me, 2A. I took the aisle. I couldn't bear to watch New York City disappear beneath me.

Six hours after take-off, having fallen into a deep sleep, I woke up to dark, quiet surroundings. As my eyes adjusted and I remembered where I was, I focused on the calm humming of the aircraft. I reached past Neo and lifted the window's flimsy shade. Outside it was pitch black. I looked at my wrist. 4:38 P.M., eastern standard time.

I peeked inside my little partner's case. He was sleeping soundly. I peered back over my seat. Some people were out cold. Those up used the reading lights from above so they could see whatever it was they were tending to.

My eyes gravitated back to the black sky beyond the window. In an instant all that had happened, everyone I had left behind, came back to me. I relaxed back into my seat and closed my eyes. I clung to this peaceful moment, knowing it wouldn't last long.

CHAPTER 55

Like I said, I can't tell you where I am. The reasons are now obvious. They are the same reasons why I haven't told you what I look like. There is an enormous bounty on my head and charges that I didn't even know exist awaiting me should I return. This way, even if you find me you won't know because you won't have a clue who you're looking for. All you think of when you see me is a designer suit moving at a hundred miles per hour through the intense maze known as Midtown. I want to keep it this way. I can't afford not to.

I didn't ask for any of this. The chaos. The mayhem. I chose none of it. It chose me. Before I knew it, I couldn't tell whether I was coming or going as I went speeding down life's highway. All I knew was that I was speeding out of control.

I remember sitting in Jack Merrill's conference room not too long ago. It was just after we met, while we were talking shop, when he said to me:

"You've been taught well."

I absorbed his comment and arrogantly stuffed it away like someone who was bored of hearing it. I should have stopped and listened. I should have stopped and dissected the words.

Had I, in fact, been taught well?

Outside of real estate, had I really been taught anything of value at all?

I could never have imagined what I just laid out being the

sequence of events that would force me to judge myself. But it was. And for that I'm surprisingly grateful. I was programmed to go after, simply amass life, by a man who showed me it was important to crave extravagant, expensive watches when all I really ever wanted was to tell time. Just pile it up. Money, women, drugs, everything. Three weeks ago I hadn't yet had that one life-changing, mind-shaping experience to help make me finally ask what any of it was for. And to examine why I was letting it all clutter up the closet that is my mind. I have always been driven. I have always had the energy, desire to get what I want. That was the problem. Everything I have learned about my family, my faith, and my instincts has helped me see that. Without love, truth, and respect held above all, nothing will ever truly make sense.

It can't.

Many have said "life is funny." Life is far from funny. Life is flagrant, vicious, seductive, and cold. At other times it can be blatantly elevating, near perfect. Life chips at your soul yet toughens your skin. Life is our emotions, our abilities being pushed, tested at a constant clip. Life is obscene yet dazzling, dangerous yet divine.

Life is beyond tricky.

I now know this. I understand this.

Andreu, Detective Morante—no one will find me. At the end of the day, as I look out at the sheet of moonlight lying on top of the rippling water and I retrace all of my footsteps, my reality remains the same. The search party is already out. My body has traveled far away from what happened in New York. My mind has not. I feel guarded, but at the same time I feel exposed. Like the cop wearing the bullet-proof vest who gets shot in the face.

Perry is lying on the lounge chair to my right. She's wearing a purple bikini. Her bronze, oiled skin is glistening. Her body is as fine as I always imagined. It goes beautifully with her mind.

We both know running together doubles the danger. Perry, arms around me, had one question outside Acappella that night.

"Are you prepared to enter a life where even the fantasy of ending up together can never become a reality?"

I wasn't. So much, in fact, that the mere mention of it put so eloquently deflated my heart. The decision to go forward together, in life, was made right there. But, in order to do so, we both understood that getting out of the country separately was our best bet. It was at this point I uttered one last word to her. My destination. We didn't see each other again until she arrived.

Max is playing in the surf. I delivered his passport, crafted with his cut down wallet-sized class photo, in the same envelope with Perry's. Neo just jumped up on the lounge chair to my left. He's sitting upright, facing me, exposing his little pink belly. It's the only part of his body not covered with thick, white fur. The sun is bathing his face. Have you ever seen a Chihuahua squint in the sun? I'm holding a chunk of pineapple. He looks at it. His eyes return to mine and he licks his chops.

I throw Neo a taste of the sweet, yellow fruit. He eats it then jumps up on Perry. Max is running toward them from the water. I'm thankfully gazing at all three.

Like I already told you, I have gained and lost in a matter of weeks more than most people will in a lifetime. I have learned things about myself I never expected to learn. I now know one can both honor and disgrace their name with the same exact set of choices.

I will find Galina Zhamovsky. Tomorrow or ten years from now, I will find her. When I do, the truth won't be far behind. What that truth reveals or whether any of us can handle it is an entirely different story.

AUTHOR'S NOTE

Spoiler Alert: This author's note contains information that
will give away a key element of the plot of *The Deal*.

In *The Deal*, contemporary fiction collides with historical fact.

As one who makes his living, i.e., my day job, in the commercial real estate business, it has given me great pleasure to weave
day-to-day experience into this fictional drama. That the experi-
ences cited here might please and enrich others makes this journey
even more rewarding.

Yet while *The Deal* is contemporary, occurring in today's world
just as we know it, there is also a historical element that commem-
orates rare treasure. The fabled Fabergé imperial Easter eggs stand
among the world's most celebrated artistic achievements. If not for
others and their diligent research and writings, a bevy of which I
found online as well as in books and articles, it would have been
impossible for me to incorporate these mesmerizing antiques into
the story.

The eggs populating this novel are historically true-to-form in
everything from name to description. As described in the book,
fifty bejeweled Fabergé eggs were commissioned by the Russian
royal family between the years of 1885 and 1916, as gifts from the
czar to the czarina and other family members. It is also a fact that

after the Russian Revolution, only forty-two of these prized antiques ever resurfaced.

This is where fact ends and fiction begins. While in *The Deal* the errant eggs are discovered, in reality the eight missing since the early twentieth century are still unaccounted for. They were neither found underneath a home in eastern Russia, as the book suggests, nor anywhere else for that matter. Rather, everything surrounding the lost imperial eggs in *The Deal* and all the other events described were created purely for entertainment value. If any names, situations, or sequences of events that mirror true life have arisen as a result of my approach to telling this story, this is truly a circumstance born of coincidence.

If you enjoyed THE DEAL, you will also enjoy

THE DEAL: ABOUT FACE

Book Two of THE DEAL TRILOGY

BY

ADAM GITTLIN

An excerpt from
THE DEAL: ABOUT FACE
follows this page.

ISBN: 978-1-60809-107-2

Published in the United States by Oceanview Publishing,
Longboat Key, Florida
www.oceanviewpub.com

2 4 6 8 10 9 7 5 3 1

PRINTED IN THE UNITED STATES OF AMERICA

PROLOGUE

A hand from behind reaches over me and grabs my chin like a vice, pulling it back as far as it will go. I groan in agony. My eyes stare at the ceiling. A drop of filthy water hits me dead center on my forehead. Seconds later, my torturer's blue eyes meet mine from no more than two inches above.

"*Gereed om te spreken? Of jullie nog denken jullie wipen enigerlei handeling held?*"

What language is that, I think, his spittle spraying my skin. And why do I understand it? Given my restrained circumstances, my reflexes still function, and I attempt to shake my head. As I do, my assailant repeats himself. This time I hear it in English...

"You ready to speak? Or you still think you're some kind of action hero?"

...As I recall why I now process everything I hear in two languages.

He gently traces my face with his fingertips, like a blind man seeing something for the first time.

"My God, Jonah. Look at you..."

My thoughts are distorted, but I recognize the voice. Andreu Zhamovsky, my dear half-brother. My head slowly bobs back up. Then, in an instant, bright, beautiful colors flash across my mind. There are jewels—splendid green emeralds, luscious red rubies.

There is gold, silver. Subconsciously or consciously, I can't be sure, I squint from their sheer brilliance. I look forward. I could swear *Danish Jubilee Egg*, the one of the eight missing Fabergé Imperial Easter Eggs I had been saddled with years earlier in New York City, is suspended in mid-air. I think of how I had kept it—a true, rare treasure—out of harm's way. I smile.

"I have something you want, Jonah. And we both know what you have to give me first to get it."

My mouth fills with blood again. Instead of spitting it out, afraid of the ensuing pain from such force, I part my lips and gently push the deep red liquid down the front of me. Its warmth feels strangely comforting against my raw chin, my freezing chest.

"Why don't you uncuff me and face me like a man?" I ask.

In one swift motion a vodka-soaked rag is crammed into my mouth. The burning of my bleeding tongue and cheeks is off the charts. A clear plastic bag is pulled over my head. Trying to move is of no use. I simply can't. My heart is racing so fast I think it might explode. The unmistakable scratching sound of duct tape pulling away from its roll fills the room, though I can barely hear it. The plastic is thick. The noise seems distant. The tape is being wrapped around my neck, securing the bag to my skin. Moments later, breathing my own warm, recycled breath solely through my nose, the bag starts crumpling in and out. It won't be long until I'm dead.

He's bluffing.

He's got to be.

CHAPTER 1

Amsterdam, The Netherlands.
2013

It's dusk. Sleepy light sneaking in around the edges of my bedroom window blinds tells me so. My eyes, wide and alert, stare at the ceiling. Without adjusting my line of vision, I reach my right hand out for the other side of the bed. I'm feeling for Perry's arm. Once I feel her soft skin, I'll go straight for the crease on the inside of her elbow, one of her more sensitive spots. A handful of twelve-hundred thread count Egyptian sheets are all I get. My head rolls right. No Perry. She's gone.

Walking through the all-white master suite, past our walk-in closets and his-and-her changing areas, I head to the bathroom. I drag my index finger tip up a sensor on the wall where a switch undoubtedly used to be. The light zips from dim to blazing. As it bounces between the white marble walls, I can't fight the sense of surprise, even after all these years, of what I see when I catch myself in the mirror. I see a man I don't recognize. I don't mean figuratively, I mean a man who literally looks nothing like the man who fled the United States—more specifically, New York City, my home—nine years earlier. I still can't tell you what I used to look like. To do so would illustrate what I don't look like now. That alone tips the odds in your favor. What I can tell you is the eyes staring back at me belong to the Jonah Gray I remember. Everything else belongs to Ivan Janse. Like always, a PowerPoint presentation of my life plays out in fast-forward across my brain like it's rolling across a six-story IMAX screen. Within seconds I look at my hands, my fingertips, remembering I no longer even have fingerprints. More on all this later. We'll get to it soon enough.

Deciding I'm not yet ready for reality, I turn the lights back off and get in the shower. With the turn of a nozzle, water falls from the wide overhead fixture like the heavens are opening up. I savor the warmth as the water coats my body. And can't help but ask myself if it is me who has life by the throat, or if it's the other way around.

Like most days, even for a few minutes, I'm thinking about the summer of 2004. That's when a childhood friend from Moscow named Andreu Zhamovsky came calling in New York City. I was a commercial real estate power broker on one of the most dominant teams in Manhattan. Andreu was the son of one of my father's "friends in high places" scattered around the globe. What happened over the course of three weeks that summer became the impetus for every second I have lived since. Those events, and more important-ly the outcome of those events, are what consume me with every breath I take.

The bottom floor of my five-story canal house on Keizersgracht Straat—ultra-contemporary and white aside from the brushed steel fixtures and artwork, same as the four stories above—is strategical-ly lit for evening with a soft glow. Dressed in a solid navy Canali suit, white Armani button-down shirt open at the collar, and brown tie-up Ferragamos, I enter the kitchen. The room, like all rooms in our home, is state-of-the-art from the décor to the appli-ances, though I had no hand whatsoever in the design. In fact, I didn't even purchase the home. It was given to me, something else we'll get to. A second before I open the refrigerator, I hear a distant jingle. It's the bell on Neo's—long since renamed Aldo—collar. He's awoken from a nap on his favorite chaise in the living room. He realizes it's time for his dinner.

By the time he struts into the room, his short nails lightly click-ing on the white, polished marble underfoot, I've moved the plate of grilled chicken our housekeeper Laura prepared for him from the fridge to the counter and uncovered it. Neo looks at me without breaking stride. His mouth is open a bit. The spots where his lips meet on both sides of his face have receded giving him an appear-ance of smiling. Not as spry as he once was and unable to leap into my arms, my favorite white long-haired Chihuahua stops at my feet and extends a paw up to me asking for a lift. As always, I happily oblige. But before putting him on the counter, I hold him up so we're nose to nose. Excited, he licks my face. Even in the white fur of his adorable face I can see graying wisps. Again, as is the case multiple times a day, I'm reminded of the time that has passed, how my life has changed. I reciprocate his kisses with kisses of my own to his nose and face and place him next to his plate for his feast. I uncork a bottle of Brunello and spend a few relaxing moments with my precious friend as he eats.

I'm about to cross the threshold between my home and the Amsterdam evening. Before I do, I grab my keys. The simple ster-ling silver key ring has six keys on it: two for this house, one for my office, and two for another residence on Herengracht, which we'll get to later. The sixth key, I've just acquired.

And it's not for a home or an office.

My eyes catch a silver-framed photo on the side table just to the left of the front door. It's of Perry, Max, and me—not the Perry, Max, and me that ran from New York City, but the new version of us—three years ago on the beach in Mykonos. I touch my fingers to my lips, then to the photograph, and leave.

I head west on foot. It's a typical spring night in the Netherlands: drizzly, a bit windy, a touch chilly. Before arriving here, I'd never been to Amsterdam. All I'd heard about was the legal pot smoking and prostitution. I envisioned some tired, crumbling, dirty little European city with pubs and gas lamps lining the streets. Some bor-derline, irrelevant place stuck in an earlier century. Not the case.

This place is rich with history and wear, but it's also lively, forward thinking, and romantic, commerce driven, cosmopolitan, even a little spicy. I had no idea it was built on water much like Venice, only with streets as well as the four main half-moon canals that make up the heart of the city. Amsterdam is an inspiring, beautiful mixture of past and present.

I eventually turn on to PC Hooftstraat, the city's most upscale stretch of retail. Hermès, Zegna, Cartier, D&G—it's got them all. My destination is a watch store called Tourbillion. I look at the Audemars Piguet on my left wrist, a gift my mother gave my father and my only tie to my previous life. My mind drifts back to the summer of 2004, to Andreu Zhamovsky. Our fathers met in 1979 with Communism on the precipice of crumbling. Alexander Zhamovsky, Andreu's father, was in control of most of the Soviet Union's natural gas resources. He was attending New York City as part of a series of secret conferences with the purpose of strong American business minds teaching our Cold War counterparts about the finer points of Democratic capitalism, a win-win for both sides in the ultimate game of what all governments want most regardless of their actual political views: making money.

Andreu and I connected, clicked. We became fast friends. Though we lived on opposite ends of the globe, we remained tight. Our families traveled together. If my father and I were overseas—business or pleasure—we'd try to all meet up for a day or so. Andreu and I would write. We were like pen pals. As we got older, we drifted somewhat but only in terms of length between communications. If a week or a year passed it didn't matter, the next time we spoke it was like we had just done so five minutes ago. Like we were family.

In four days, I'll be making my long-anticipated return to the United States. The last thing I can allow to happen, after all these years being so careful and with much unfinished business, is for someone to put together who I am because of a hunch and an image of me caught on film at Newark Liberty International Airport the day I left with the Audemars on my wrist. Crazy paranoid? Maybe. But like I said, I've got unfinished business. And here's my reality.

When I'm driving, I stop farther than necessary behind the car in front of me at a light in case I need to make a break for it. When I walk into a restaurant—or any public place for that matter—I first scout all possible escape routes then survey every set of eyes in the room to see which might be the ones looking to arrest, or kill, me. When I sleep, I always do so with a gun within reach. When I fled America, I did so a wanted man. I was wanted by the law for inadvertently killing a crooked New York City cop and for taking the matter of my father's murder into my own hands. I was wanted by a very powerful Russian family for denying them the storied eight missing Fabergé Imperial Easter Eggs that are in fact not missing at all. Did I do some things I still, to this second, regret? Definitely. Were all of my actions, in my mind, justified? Absolutely.

I reach address number 72 and enter the store. The walls, like my home, are white, and the floor is darkly stained, wide, hardwood planks. There is a quaint sitting area comprised of four modern, cubelike brown leather chairs around a rectangular glass coffee table. In the center of the table is a vase with fresh white roses. The rest of the space is occupied by glass display cases filled with expensive timepieces. Realizing it feels like eons since I've shopped for a watch—or a trophy as I sometimes called them back in New York, since I usually bought one following the close of a deal—I can't shake the feeling of nostalgia that passes through me. I can't deny the sense of entitlement, wanted or unwanted, that hard-earned wealth brings.

I know, I know. Right now you're thinking, "Hasn't this guy learned his fucking lesson?"

The answer is yes.

I have.

I understand better than anyone that millions of dollars ensures only two things: a roof overhead, food in the mouth. Nothing else. Not love, not happiness, not faith, nothing. But I also know that in the big play of life, I've been cast in a new role. And this role, like my last part, calls for a certain level of wardrobe. At my core I'm fine with a Timex or Swatch. But all this would do is bring questions from those who surround me, successful professional types not very different from my old associates back in Manhattan. And questions, for me, bring one thing. Unwanted attention.

"*Dag*," the statuesque, brunette saleswoman says to me.

"*Dag*," I say back.

The true sign of a Netherlands native is the ability to speak either Dutch or English on a dime. Something I have been able to do for years now.

"*Bent u zoekt…*"

"*Perregaux?*" I cut her off.

"*Natuurlijk. Juist deze manier.*"

She leads me to the case holding the Girard-Perregaux watches. Like I said, the watch I'm buying is more prop than anything else. Therefore I don't need to spend much time browsing, especially since I have somewhere to be. The moment I learned I was going home, and that I needed to leave behind the watch that is the only connection to my mother who died when I was five, a Girard-Per-regaux World Time jumped into my head. It was next on my list of desired timepieces back when I was a commercial real estate power broker in New York who still cared about extravagant bullshit.

She hands me the watch. It is large and heavy. The rose-gold case is forty-three millimeters in diameter. The face is white with a cream inner bezel where the chronograph dials are located. It tells time in all twenty-four official time zones around the globe and has an exposed backing, allowing the handcrafted movement to be viewed as it works. I slide it on. The crystal backing glides silkily over the skin on my hand. The smell of the fresh leather strap fills my nose.

"*Hoeveel?*" I ask.

"*Zestien duizend, negan hindered negentig vijf Euro,*" she responds.

A little more than seventeen thousand Euro, or just under twenty-four thousand American dollars. To tell time.

I wear it out of the store.

CHAPTER 2

It's Saturday evening. The cool air feels refreshing. My destination is 23 Kerkstraat, which is just off Leidseplein—"Plein" meaning Square—one of three main Pleins in the city. Once I reach the Van Gogh Museum, it's only about another five minutes. I turn right on Kerkstraat, a quiet old cobblestone road. Old street lamps with energy-saving bulbs on top where a gas flame used to be supply the night light. I look at the two opposing rows of coach houses. When I arrived nine years ago, part of me was still so angry, so bitter, I saw these houses as nothing more than simple lines of four- or five-story buildings that seemingly ran in to one another, like the town-houses of Manhattan's Upper East Side can look at first glance.

Today I see these buildings for what they are: a twenty-four-foot-wide, five-story, red-brick coach house with red moldings and three tall ground-level windows; followed by a thirty-foot wide, four-story, brown-brick coach house with white moldings and what appears to be a single-windowed attic, or smaller level, on top; followed by a thirty-foot-wide, five-story—you get the idea. The houses, in actuality, are similar but far from the same. Even the pulley—each house has a pulley centrally located on top to hoist objects up since the internal stairways are so narrow—is different in quality and characteristics upon inspection from one to the next. Attention to detail in my constant battle to remain free of my past life, as if I'd shed that life like some spent reptilian skin, has been my greatest ally these past years. Just as it has been my greatest ally in becoming a professional success all over again from scratch.

I enter the restaurant. A happening bar and restaurant catering to Amsterdam's young elite throbs before me. Architecturally the space begins and ends with crisp lines. The colors—mostly browns and creams—are earthy yet rich. Although the space is packed, square mirrors running the entire shell of the rectangular bar give an odd illusion of a sea of legs. Slicing upward from the bar, beginning in the center of one of the rectangle's short sides to the second floor is a golden staircase.

Abeni, the striking, six-foot-tall African hostess with a shaved head, is mobbed. I wait for her eye. On sight of me, while mid-sentence with a patron, she smiles and motions me upstairs.

I reach the top, the main restaurant. A waiter points me in the right direction. Cocktail hour is well underway. In the far corner, enmeshed in conversation, is Cobus de Bont. Cobus is my boss. He is the founder of de Bont Beleggings—*Beleggings* means Investments in Dutch. De Bont Beleggings is one of the largest and most successful private investment firms—and the single largest private owner of commercial real estate—in the Netherlands. The dinner party is in honor of his wife, Annabelle's, fortieth birthday.

Cobus, chatting with local real estate player Martin Gemser, sees me. He waves me over. I pass through the crowd, shaking hands and kissing cheeks.

"*De heer Ivan. Hoe we vanavond gevoel?*"

Cobus, who also more readily chooses Dutch over English, just asked me how I'm feeling tonight. From this point on, to make things easier, I'll go with English in all cases.

"Feeling great, actually, I even managed to get in a nap this afternoon," I respond.

"You know I meant to ask," Cobus continues, "how was your

excursion to Hamburg last weekend? How was your visit with your friend from university?"

Was I in Hamburg?

Yes.

Was I with a friend from university?

Not quite.

"The weekend was great. It was a lot of fun catching up. Where's your beautiful wife?" I change directions. "Has she arrived yet?"

He points. Annabelle, a gorgeous, smart, blond fashion photographer, is across the room giggling with others at some guy's story. A waiter approaches, asking if we need cocktails. Before I can answer, Cobus tells him I need a Belvedere over rocks with a twist.

Yes—I even changed my drink of choice.

"Three buildings." Martin continues their previous conversation. "Forty-four Utrechtsestraat and Sixteen Muntplein definitely. Possibly also Eighteen Damrak. Utrechtsestraat and Muntplein alone could be stolen at a seven cap. Easily. We all know how Henrik Bosch markets property. These buildings should have occupancy levels much higher than seventy, seventy-two percent. Because Damrak—"

"How much?" Cobus interrupts.

"I—maybe—eighty-five; perhaps a bit—"

"Where are the rents today?" Cobus continues. "Where should they be?"

"For which property? I mean—if—"

"I need to cut you off, Martin. And I apologize in advance if I sound disrespectful. I know you think you're giving me information. But each time you do this—each time you present me with a potential property minus the meaningful numbers—all you're really doing is wasting both of our time."

"I'm not sure why you say that, Cobus. Even looking at the scenario in general terms—"

"I don't do general terms, Martin. You know why?"

Martin Gemser is a local real estate player with bigger dreams than bank accounts. He's in nowhere near Cobus's league and neither of us particularly like him. Unfortunately, Annabelle's sister is married to this guy. Martin stares back blankly.

"Because numbers don't lie. People do. Now, I'm not calling you a liar, Martin. What I'm saying is that, intentionally or unintentionally, people can paint the wrong picture when it comes to real estate. People's accounts can be—disputable. Not the numbers. The numbers do not—cannot—lie. The numbers, Martin, are indisputable. The numbers are irrefutable."

Martin takes a sip from the whiskey-filled lowball glass in his hand.

"You want to bring me a deal we can make?" Cobus goes on, "Here's the way I suggest you do it—"

Martin is too dim-witted to realize he's about to get a gift. Most individuals anywhere near the commercial real estate game in the Netherlands would kill to hear what Cobus de Bont needs to take a potential deal seriously.

"Numbers. Nail down every last number. Rents, occupancies, depreciation, commissions to be paid, operating expenses, capital improvements—I want every pertinent line item of the true financial run in front of me so I can see the financial landscape down to the last penny. Include conservative forecasts. Include aggressive forecasts. Include explanations of where the numbers might be improved and include explanations about which numbers may not be as appealing in the years to come. Don't worry about things like Bosch's ability to market a property or why a particular building may be a sleeper in terms of the retail space—I'm fine to evaluate all remaining tangible and intangible aspects on my own. All I want from you is one thing."

Cobus sips his glass of Chianti.

"Numbers," Martin says.

"Not after a deal is presented—before," Cobus goes on. "E-mail them to me. This way, to be frank, we'll both know if a discussion is even going to take place."

"Numbers first," Martin says again, gently nodding his head.

"Wrapped in a bow."

Cobus smiles. He takes another sip.

"Get me the numbers for the three buildings. If I like them, we'll talk."

This is one of the things—Cobus's respect for others—I respect most about Cobus. Real estate evaluation, from Amsterdam to New York City to anywhere else for that matter, is a multifaceted undertaking. But anyone with half a brain who plays in property understands clear as day that a deal begins and ends with the numbers. In this same situation another guy of Cobus's stature might have spoken down to Martin, in some way made him feel inferior. Not Cobus. In typical fashion he used the opportunity to enlighten Martin, to teach him. Knowing Cobus as well as I do, I clearly understand there are two reasons for this. Number one, he genuinely cares for, feels for, people. Number two, the buildings Martin speaks of may, in fact, work for him.

Martin walks away. Cobus leans over the table next to us. He grabs a toast point and scoops on some steak tartare.

"Eat something," he says before taking a bite.

I look at the table filled with appetizers. There's caprese with tomato, mozzarella, cucumber, mint, and feta. There's a rouille—rust sauce—based bouillabaisse, as well as the steak tartare. There are frog's legs sautéed in a fine fruit sauce paired with crisp, sliced potatoes to be dipped in a chili-pepper mayonnaise. After surveying my options, I, too, drag a toast point through the raw seasoned ground beef.

Cobus puts his arm around my shoulders. As I chew he takes a ip of his Chianti. Six-feet, two-inches tall with thick, dark hair nd dark skin to match his chestnut eyes, Cobus is dressed like vays. Black suit, black shirt, black tie. The clothes are perfectly t 'ored, every edge from hem to collar knifelike. Since the day I n him, I don't recall him wearing anything else. Summer, winter, m iing, evening—doesn't matter. He says he has a rare skin condi n called Solar urticaria. Exposure of his skin to sunlight results in   nful, burning lesions. Hence the ever-present, perfectly manicured five o'clock shadow completing his more Mediterranean than Nordic look. This may be the case, but part of me can't help feel Cobus doesn't mind his affliction. His approach to clothes means more time—even a few precious moments a day—to focus on the important matters at hand: Business.

"Tell me about Willem," he says to me. "He's been with us for eight years, Ivan. He's one of the best in this entire city."

Willem Krol. Chief building engineer of Astoria, one of the oldest office buildings in Amsterdam, located on the corner of the intersecting Keizersgracht and Leliegracht canals. Best known for its copper-plated roof, the six-story home to numerous companies is part of the de Bont Beleggings portfolio.

"It has recently come to my attention Willem Krol may be fabricating some overtime. I still need more facts. But it's not looking good."

Cobus sighs and drops his chin. The waiter arrives with my Belvedere. We clink glasses and each take a hearty sip of our drinks.

"How about—"

I answer Cobus's question before he's done asking. His tone alone tells me he's changing direction.

"Harkin Aeuronautic accepted the higher security deposit and signed the lease. I made it clear the option for another term at their discretion wasn't going to happen. Staying on the Vinoly Building—"

The official title is Mahler Four Office Tower, but because of its world-renowned architect—Rafael Vinoly—it is simply referred to as the Vinoly Building. It is one of the most prized office properties in Amsterdam's highest-end commercial market—the South Axis. It is here one can find modern skyscrapers like those found in New York City or London or Sydney, only on a much smaller scale.

Completed in 2005, the Vinoly Building is a twenty-four-story rectangular glass L. The bottom six stories make up the base, and the rest of the floors make up the high backstop. It is a sleek, refined structure that appears, oddly, to have a crack running down, around the edge of the tall backstop. Vinoly carved an external fire staircase into the building's shell. The goal was to incorporate Amsterdam's innovative spirit into his design. The result is a property that helps define architectural vision.

Cobus bought the building last spring for forty-four million euros. It is one of three he owns in the South Axis. Our offices are on the top floor.

"Jaap Jan de Geer let me know CCM Global will not be renewing. They'll be out in six months, which is more than enough time to market the space. I'm not sure if you recall but their build-out is really high-end. We're talking about—"

"Do you two ever tire of talking business?" a female voice asks from behind us.

We turn around. It's Annabelle. Wearing a tight, sleeveless, laurel-green embroidered dress with a black leather belt and high black heels, she's an image out of one of her own photo shoots.

"Sorry, boys. It's time for Cobus to toast his best girl."

Wasting no time, Annabelle grabs a random empty water glass and begins clinking it with a spoon.

"I appreciate the update," Cobus says to me, "but that's not what I was going to ask."

"What then?"

"If you still think New York City over Berlin is the right move?"

Ninety minutes later, as we're finishing dinner, I receive a text. The name pops up with the number. It is from Scott Green. After a few seconds I place the contact. He's in-house counsel—someone I've spoken with only a handful of times—for the Manhattan-based firm with whom we're about to make a deal.

CONFIDENTIAL, the text begins. IVAN—NED TO SEE YOU. IN TOWN HAMMERIG OUT DETAILS WITH YOR LAWYERS. MUST SEE YOU IMEDIATELY. TELL NO ONE.

I look around. Both confused and intrigued, I return my eyes to my iPhone and read it again. I can't help but be a bit thrown off by all the misspellings. I've seen numerous complicated, detailed legal documents drafted by this man. Scott Green doesn't strike me as such a careless texter.

I look at Cobus. He's whispering in Annabelle's ear, and she's grinning ear-to-ear absorbing the tender moment. Figuring it's most likely a fire I can squelch on my own, I decide not to bother him.

OF COURSE, I write back. AMSTEL HOTEL?

This, the finest hotel in the city, is where I recall members of the "Seller's" team stayed during their last trip to Amsterdam.

NO, he replies almost immediately. NIEUWE PRINSENGRACHT. HOUSEBOAT. NUMBER 030. CONFIDENTIAL. TEL NO ONE.